D0198589

# I WANT IT THAT WAY

*

**Coming soon from Ann Aguirre
and Harlequin HQN**

*As Long As You Love Me
The Shape of My Heart*

# I WANT IT THAT WAY

\*

## ANN AGUIRRE

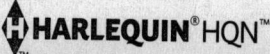

Recycling programs
for this product may
not exist in your area.

ISBN-13: 978-0-373-77983-3

I Want It That Way

This edition published by arrangement with Harlequin Books S.A.

For questions and comments about the quality of this book, please contact us at CustomerService@Harlequin.com.

**Printed in U.S.A.**

For Leigh Bardugo,
who speaks of love as if it's a question that must be answered.
And so I tried.

# AFTER

There's always a meet-cute, right?

The girl trips and the boy catches her, they're stuck together on an elevator, or she leaves her phone behind in a bar and he returns it to her. Later, when people ask the inevitable question, "How did you meet?" the story unspools with the woman telling part of it and the man finishing, or vice versa, while everyone admires them for staying together. I don't have a story like that, or at least, I have *a* story, but it's mine alone, and there's nobody finishing my sentences.

I want it that way.

*Right?*

# DURING

# CHAPTER ONE

The first time I saw Ty, I fell down the stairs and tore my pants.

A superstitious person might call that an omen. He had nothing to do with it, of course; that was just a quirk of timing. While Lauren and I struggled with the sofa, a guy I presumed to be a new neighbor came into the building. He had auburn hair, brown eyes and a strong jaw dusted with gold scruff. I'd always had a soft spot for gingers, probably a result of growing up on Harry Potter movies. He was also tall and lean with a sculpted, ascetic face, like an austere warrior who would be at home on the prow of a ship. Okay, it was possible I'd watched too many episodes of *Vikings* this week.

When he saw us wrangling such a heavy piece of furniture, he only sighed, stepped around the boxes cluttering the foyer and checked his mailbox. No greeting, no "welcome to the complex." I was halfway up the stairs to the landing, heaving my end of the sofa, when my hands slipped and the couch bounced away. I lunged for it, missed and came tum-

bling after. Lauren jumped aside like it was a sled on the sla-
lom track, so the brown plaid monstrosity thumped ahead of
me back down to the floor. The couch just missed slamming
into the wall; I wasn't so lucky. In honor of moving day, I had
on old comfy pants, and they'd been washed one too many
times, judging by the audible rip as I bounced off the wall and
landed at Lauren's feet.

She pulled me up, eyes wide. "You okay?"

"Just bruises to pride and pelvis," I mumbled.

She tilted her head at the workload awaiting us. "Maybe
we should wait for the guys to get back from their beer run?"

I surveyed the mess we'd created in front of the entrance
and just outside, conscious that we were inconveniencing our
neighbors. "We can't really leave things like this."

"I'll help you with the couch." As greetings went, it wasn't
the warmest. Grumpy Ginger strode toward us, rolling up
the sleeves on his dress shirt to reveal very nice forearms:
lightly tanned and dusted with auburn hair, lean but strong
with prominent wrist bones. His hands appealed to me just as
much, long-fingered and elegant, without being overly mani-
cured. You know, if you liked that sort of thing. I was bad at
estimating ages, but he was probably out of school, judging
by the business casual he had on.

Belatedly, I realized I'd been studying him for thirty seconds too long. "If you're sure."

"It's fine. I'll walk backward and guide it up."

"Thanks," Lauren put in. "We'd prefer not to commit so-
ficular homicide our first day in the building."

Since my back was to the wall, I escaped the ignominy of
the new neighbor seeing my panda underpants. He slid by
and hefted the sofa up a few stairs on his own. Lauren and I
worked together, and it was much easier with him doing the

heavy lifting up top. With a minimum of fuss, we maneuvered the couch up to the second floor, where GG paused.

"A or B?" he asked.

"B." I should win the prize for hilarious banter.

Nodding, he helped us carry it down the hall and into the apartment. We'd left the door open since we had so little in there. Most of it was still cluttering the lobby downstairs. Max and Angus had taken off as soon as we got everything unloaded: my car, Angus's and the rental truck. After that, they were gone like the wind with the excuse that moving in would be more fun with pizza, cold beer and a buzz on.

"You're right above me." He didn't look particularly happy about it, either.

I shot Lauren a *what's with this guy* look, and she shrugged.

"I'm Nadia," I said.

At first he didn't say anything, so she tried, "That makes me Lauren."

"Ty," he said finally, like this basic introduction was akin to signing a long-term cell contract.

Lauren started, "The guys will be back with drinks in a bit, if you want—"

"No, it's okay. I need to get home." If curt was a hat, he would be wearing it with jaunty disregard for our feelings.

*Awkward. And I still need to change my pants.*

"Well, thanks for helping us out. We can handle the rest of the boxes."

Ty took my comment as his cue to leave, so we followed him downstairs to work on the rest of our stuff. He looked tired as hell as he headed toward apartment 1B, the unit to the back of the building; it had a nice courtyard, unlike the front or upstairs. We had a balcony, but it wasn't big enough for a barbecue, unless you bought the kind people used for tailgating.

Lauren and I were moving in with a couple of friends, and since we'd lost the coin toss, we were sharing the master bedroom, while Angus and Max got their own rooms. The biggest perk was that we didn't have to use a grungy dude bathroom; we had an en-suite bath, along with a walk-in closet. Four people in a three-bedroom made the rent more manageable, and since I was often living on ramen by the end of the month, I couldn't complain. I grabbed one of my boxes, marked CLOTHING, and ran upstairs with it, wincing at the sore spot where I'd collided with the wall.

"Nice panda," Lauren said, deadpan.

"Shut up."

I ducked into our bathroom to put on sweats and then went back down, passing Lauren on the stairs. As I hefted a box, a gray-haired woman stepped out of 1B. She was distinctly pear-shaped, moving like her feet hurt, but she smiled as she came through the foyer, giving me a friendly wave.

"Normally, I'd say 'see you tomorrow' but this is my last day." With that cryptic remark, she left, and I hauled my carton upstairs.

As Lauren and I traipsed down to load up again, Max and Angus were just coming in. When I smelled the pizza, I decided they didn't suck as much as previously estimated. They each grabbed two boxes and let Lauren and me carry up the pizza and beer. With four of us on the job, pretty soon we had all of our stuff in the apartment. The place was a jumble, but at least we could close the door.

"Sorry we were gone so long." Angus was genuinely concerned. "Did the couch give you any trouble?"

I warned Lauren with a look not to mention my pratfall

or wardrobe malfunction. "Somewhat, but I gave it a stern talking-to, and it settled down. Promised to be less of a malcontent in the future."

Max dismissed the topic by frowning at the spot where we'd left the sofa. "It needs to face that way. That wall is better for movies and gaming."

*Typical.* Not that Max was a bad guy, but…

Since freshman year, he'd slept his way through half the women at Mount Albion. Since this was a midsize liberal arts college, that was both impressive and alarming. Lauren and I knew Max too well to be seduced. Oh, he'd tried early on, but we both shot him down. I had zero interest in troubled bad boys from broken homes. Someone else could love Max and fix him; I was just crossing my fingers that he'd do the dishes on schedule. Max *did* contribute a steady paycheck, and that weighed heavily into the roommate decision—I trusted him to pay his share of the rent on time. As for Angus, he came from a "good family," as my mother would say, so his dad had already prepaid his part of the rent with the leasing company. Lauren and I were on our own, but I had a part-time job, and so did she. *It should be fine.* I'd been telling myself that since I signed the lease last spring and put down the deposit, but this was a little scary, after living in the dorm as a freshman and sophomore.

"Fine," Lauren said, since nobody else seemed to care about couch placement, and helped Max move it.

He immediately conscripted her to help him set up the entertainment center while Angus and I situated the retro dining set I'd found at a rummage sale, complete with yellow vinyl chairs and cracked-ice Formica top, edged in chrome. It had plenty of character, and probably dated from the actual '50s, but I covered the scratches with place mats while

Angus organized the kitchen. I'd never lived in a house with a dishwasher before, though I wasn't about to admit that to the guys. Lauren knew, of course. My parents were covering my tuition with the help of an academic scholarship, but there had never been many luxuries. In fact, I was the first person in the family to go to college. Lauren and I had been friends since second grade. Her family used to have money, but her dad's investments didn't pan out, which left him bitter, and when she was eleven, he left the family entirely. Ten years later, we were in the same financial boat.

By the time Lauren and Max got the TV and peripherals set up, Angus had the kitchen done, and I'd set food and beer on the counter, along with plates I'd rinsed to get rid of packing dust and newspaper ink. I collapsed onto the sofa with a groan; more boxes could wait until later. Angus sat next to me, and Lauren settled on his other side, leaving Max the recliner. He promptly put on a noisy action movie from his collection, and I was too tired to argue.

"You've seen this twelve times," Angus said.

"Fourteen. What's your point?" Max flashed a grin that other people found charming.

I ate my pizza, staring blankly at a succession of car chases.

Afterward, I felt better, enough to start rummaging in the decor boxes. We didn't have a ton, but there were a few pictures, scented candles and a weird statue that Angus's mom made. Apparently, she was some kind of big-deal sculptor in Europe. I asked their opinions of where I should hang things at first, but it became obvious nobody cared, so I located hammer and nails and went to work.

Ten minutes later, someone knocked on the door. The other three looked at me.

"What?" Lauren said. "You're already up."

"Fine."

I answered, then my eyes widened when I saw Ty. If possible, he looked even wearier, damp and rumpled, too. He'd changed into a gray Converse T-shirt, and I had no idea what would create those splash patterns, but soft cotton clung to his upper body, revealing broad shoulders and a solid chest. His disheveled, touchable appeal made me smile until he opened his mouth.

"Do you mind turning down the TV and not banging on the walls so late?"

Surprised, I dug the phone out of my pocket. It read 8:42 p.m. For shit's sake, it wasn't even nine on a weeknight. I'd stayed up later than this in elementary school. "I think we disagree as to what constitutes late. But I'll tell Max about the TV." I pivoted to call, "Hey, he can hear your movie downstairs. Too loud, bro."

With a dirty look and a mumbled curse, Max pressed the volume on the remote. Holy crap, he had it all the way up to fifty. No wonder Couch Guy was cranky. It occurred to me that was why he'd sighed when he spotted Lauren and me moving in. College students were known to be pain-in-the-ass partiers, prone to aggravating their neighbors, barfing in strange places and occasionally leaving naked people where they didn't belong.

"Thanks." That was all he said before wheeling and heading off down the hall in a hurry.

"Great, we have a complete fun Nazi living downstairs," Max grumbled.

"We knew when we moved in this was a mixed community."

The all-college-student apartments we'd looked at cost more, both in monthly rent and damage deposits. This place rented to upperclassmen, and they didn't make us pay two months up front, either. It was a little farther from campus, but we had two cars between the four of us, and we'd worked out a good ride-share system. But we also couldn't be as wild as we might get away with elsewhere.

"I don't want our neighbors to hate me," Lauren said. "Especially hot ones who help us move furniture."

"You have terrible taste in guys," Max told her.

While they bickered, Angus snagged the remote and quietly turned the movie down another few notches. I put down the hammer and decorated more quietly, arranging knickknacks and candles; the picture-hanging could wait until the morning. For all I knew, Ty was a med student who hadn't slept in twenty-seven hours, so once I finished the living room, rather than agitate him on our first night, I dragged my boxes to my room and started hanging up clothes. Along the way, I found sheets and made up my bed. Elation burbled through me when I unearthed towels, too; at ten, I stopped organizing and took my first shower in our new place.

My mom called at half past, just as I was stepping onto the rug. It was surprising until I realized she must've forgotten the two-hour difference. Again. She was on Mountain time; I was on Eastern. This happened about once a month. She'd get an itch to talk to me and dial away.

I grabbed my cell and said, "Everything's fine, no hitches."

"You're sharing a room with Lauren, right? Not the broody, handsome boy?"

I grinned. Max would hate being described that way. "Not a chance."

"I don't mind the other one."

"Angus is gay, Mom."

"Are you sure? Sometimes they seem that way, but they're really metrosexual. You see it on the TV all the time."

"I've met his boyfriend."

"That's compelling evidence." She sounded disappointed. "Well, I just wanted to make sure you didn't have any problems with the apartment."

"Nope, it's great."

"When does school start?"

"In two days."

"Do you have everything you need? Things are tight, but—"

"Yes, I'm fine."

Whatever she was going to offer, I couldn't accept it. They had scrimped, saved and sacrificed enough for me. Two more years, and I'd graduate with a degree in special education; going forward, I was determined to stand on my own two feet. My parents didn't know this, but I had been keeping a tally of what they paid and I intended to reimburse them after I got my first teaching position. They'd never asked me to, but I knew how hard they'd worked. For a while my mom had two jobs to keep me in school, until she got promoted to management at the supermarket. Paying back that money would give them a nest egg for the future or maybe they could finally take a vacation. It made me smile to think about giving back.

"I'll send you a care package," she said, and I could *hear* the pride in her voice. "I can't wait to write your new address on the label."

"I thought you were supposed to be sad that your baby's grown up," I teased her.

"It makes me feel like I did my job to see you spread your wings and fly."

*Oh, Lord.* I had to get off the phone before my mom started in with the butterfly talk. I was an ugly duckling as a kid, slightly better in high school, and I'd more or less grown into my looks by college. I had dark, curly hair, a long nose, sharp chin and strong cheekbones. You could say my face had character. Mom claimed I had "good bones," which meant I'd age well, like Katharine Hepburn. Since I barely knew who that was now—and she was a really old woman who died when I was a kid—that wasn't much comfort at age nine.

"Love you, Mom. Kiss Dad and Rob for me." Rob being my older brother, who had gone into construction like my dad.

"Will do. I'm handing the phone to your father."

"Hey, bean." My brother used to call me string bean. Though I wasn't as skinny these days, my dad kept up the tradition.

"How are things?"

He hesitated. "Not bad. Not sure if your mother mentioned it, but Rob's looking at property. Might buy his own place soon."

"You approve?" I guessed.

"Yep. It's about time. Do you need anything?" Dad was taciturn at the best of times, prone to showing his affection in gestures more than words.

"Nah. Mom already asked. How's work?"

"I'm building a strip mall right now. Bit of an eyesore but it's a living."

His calm pragmatism reminded me of countless problems over the years. When the chain broke on my bike, he was there with the tools to fix it. "I miss you, Dad."

"Back at you. Talk soon." He hung up soon after.

When I went to the kitchen for some water, Lauren had nodded off on Angus's shoulder, and Max was gone. I didn't ask; Angus didn't tell me. With a silent wave, I got my drink and went out onto the balcony to look at the stars. Exhaling in a slow sigh, I listened to the crickets, eventually joined by the low murmur of a man's voice.

*The window must be open in the bedroom downstairs.*

It sounded like somebody—Ty?—was reading *Goodnight Moon,* in a tone that suggested he'd done it a hundred times before. A much lighter voice spoke in response and then there was silence. *That's definitely a kid.*

I didn't realize I'd leaned forward until a noise below froze me. Ty stepped out into his courtyard. In the moonlight, it was beautiful: solar lamps by the fence, a potted herb garden, hanging baskets of flowers and wicker furniture padded with striped cushions. My first thought was that a woman must live with him because a guy wouldn't take such good care of his patio. Then I chided myself for being judgmental; I hated when people made assumptions about me, based on my height and build.

*You must play basketball. No? Well, what's your favorite sport?*

As I thought that, he did the most peculiar thing. He walked to the edge of the wooden fence, rested his head on it, balled up a fist and pressed it to the back of his head. Not exactly what I'd do if I had a headache. More…exhaustion, despair or some emotion I couldn't name. This felt too personal for me to watch, and I hadn't *meant* to. But if I moved, he'd hear me.

Just then, like he sensed me watching, Ty turned and looked up. In the dark, I couldn't see his eyes, but I recalled them as golden-brown with all the sharpness of a hunting hawk. For some reason, I couldn't move; I didn't dare straighten. I didn't want him to think he'd driven me off my balcony, but I wasn't spying, either. We just stood there staring at each other, not stirring, not speaking. He didn't smile. Tension raveled between us in silvery skeins, pulled taut by his silence and my stillness.

Then he quietly went back inside, snapping our momentary connection with a certainty that stung on the recoil.

*

# CHAPTER TWO

The next day, I had to work.

My gig at the day-care center was better than most college jobs. This summer, they gave me more hours, as I covered shifts for teachers taking vacations. As of this week, I'd cut back to part-time, and they were great about scheduling around my classes. On Monday, Wednesday and Friday, I worked in the afternoons. Tuesday and Thursday, I had the morning shift. Occasionally, the director assigned me to assist in a particular classroom, but usually I floated, helping out wherever they needed me.

I owned one of the two cars; Angus drove the other. For obvious reasons, his was much nicer, but my Toyota had heart. It had a zillion miles when I bought it four years ago, and it was still puttering on. Max had a motorcycle that he had been restoring for as long as I'd known him, but between school and work, he didn't get to spend as much time on it as he'd like. Consequently, the thing ran only half the time, and at the moment, it was a big paperweight. But my ride started right up, no problem delivering me to work on time.

On arrival, they put me in with the two-year-olds, about as exciting as you'd expect. The lead teacher's name was Charlotte Reynolds, and she had an associate's degree in early childhood education. She was a sweet woman in her mid-thirties, usually patient, but she seemed a little frazzled this morning. Alongside her, I kept the kids from hurting each other, gave them things to color, supervised lunch and then nap time. In the afternoon, they played in the yard, more coloring, some educational activities, and at four-thirty, I sighed with relief that the day was almost over.

"They were stubborn today," Charlotte muttered.

"This is the last full shift for me," I reminded her.

"I'm aware. I hope your junior year's the best yet."

I nodded, tidying up the room as we talked. By six, all of the kids had gone, and we were free to head out. Tiredly I trudged out to the Toyota and drove home, though I made a wrong turn by reflex, heading toward the dorms instead of our new apartment. With a muttered curse, I swung a U-turn and corrected course, pulling into the parking lot behind a silver Ford Focus. I spotted Ty getting out of the car, but I didn't say anything. After last night on the balcony, I didn't want him to think I was the overinvolved neighbor from hell. I pulled my tote bag out of the backseat, imprinted with the day-care center's logo, some blocks and a rainbow—crafty, since the name was ABC Rainbow Academy. I locked up and headed past, trying to avoid tension and accusations.

But he acted like the night before never happened, his attention drawn by my bag. "Hey, do you work there?"

"Yeah, why?"

"Would you recommend it?"

*Goodnight Moon. Right. Wonder if there's a Mrs. Hot Ginger.* Guilt pinged through me for pondering his marital status; it was weird to be this curious, even if he was seriously appealing. *Wait, what did he ask me again?*

I stopped on the front step and nodded, launching into my spiel. "The teachers are well trained and the facility is clean. The curriculum is balanced. It's not a Montessori place, but it's solid pre-K education, combined with good socialization and excellent supervision. We haven't had a serious accident in the year I've been working there."

"That's a sound recommendation. Do you have a card?"

I did, actually, and went digging for it. My tote was a colorful mess of pictures the kids had made for me over the summer. Since I was shifting back to part-time, I'd brought some stuff home. Like most teachers, though I wasn't supposed to show bias, I had a few favorites at Rainbow Academy.

"Here you go. Ignore the note on the back."

He flipped the card over immediately. I got the sense that if you told Ty the paint was wet, he'd put a palm in it to test you. "'Erin, Lubriderm, three times a day.' Should I even ask?"

"A toddler came in with eczema last week. Her parents aren't big on organization."

His brows went up. "So that's their idea of care instructions?"

"Yep. Don't worry, she's better. I looked after her." I smiled at him; his look lightened in response, like toddler rashes were in any way amusing. "The director's name and phone number are on the front. You can make an appointment for a tour."

"Thanks."

Though I suspected the older woman I'd spoken to yesterday must have been his sitter, I didn't ask. I chose not to give him an excuse to tell me how badly he needed to get home.

So I just waved and went upstairs, leaving him with Erin's care instructions and the info about my employer. In the apartment, Max was watching a movie.

"Productive day?" I asked.

"Not really. Tomorrow's soon enough to start being ambitious."

I wasn't sure that word ever applied to Max, but his grades weren't as bad as you'd expect from someone who partied all the time. As for me, I'd already bought my textbooks online in digital form, so I could go straight to campus with my tablet and a note-taking app. *Leaving the dorm won't disrupt my routine. I hope.* This semester, I had four classes, along with a practicum, where I'd work in the classroom two days a week at the local junior high. Not student teaching; I wouldn't start that until my senior year.

"Where are the other two?" I asked.

"Lauren's at work, and Angus is shopping. He said he'll drive her home later." He paused, grinning at me. "If only there was some way you could keep in touch, other than passing messages through me."

"Whatever."

After rinsing off a day of sticky fingerprints, I fixed a bowl of cereal and sprawled on the couch. I was too late to make sense of Max's movie, but it didn't matter since I was just killing time until our roomies got home. If I wasn't comfortable ignoring Max, I never would've agreed to live with him. Eventually, I got bored and finished hanging the pictures, though I tried to do it quietly to avoid bothering the downstairs neighbor.

Weirdly, I was a little disappointed that Ty didn't come up to yell at us, even after Lauren and Angus got back at ten. But they were both too tired to hang out, so I ended up on the balcony again. I told myself I wasn't going out there to spy, just to enjoy some tea before bed. At some point, while the rest of us were gone, Max must've put a chair out there, a wooden Adirondack. It faced sideways and took up most of the space, but it was surprisingly nice. Peaceful.

This time, Ty wasn't by the fence. Relief shot through me. I didn't care to interrupt another private moment. I wasn't doing anything wrong, sitting on my balcony with a mug of Sleepytime tea, but it was a gray area since I could so easily invade his privacy. Tonight he was on the wicker love seat, and the empty spot beside him struck me as oddly poignant. I studied him as I sipped my drink. He had a backlit e-reader out there with him, head bent so the moon gilded lighter streaks in his coppery hair.

"You're quite a devoted stargazer," he said without looking up from his book. His voice was soft enough that I barely heard it…but he was speaking to me. Again.

I wondered why that was so thrilling. *Calm down, he might be married. Taken. Something. He's definitely in the market for day care, and—maybe I'm overthinking this.*

"I just like it out here," I answered, just as quietly.

Somehow this felt like a secret between the two of us. His spot and now mine—apparently, he didn't mind sharing the night with me. I didn't want to bother Angus or Max with our talk, and I'd rather Lauren didn't join the convo, either. No need for self-analysis, right?

"The best part about living here."

"What're you reading?"

His answer came slow, as if he was a little unsure whether he should encourage me. "Some chapters for class tomorrow."

"Oh, you're a student? I thought you must have an office job already."

"I do."

"Night school?" I guessed.

"Yeah."

"What are you studying?" I was conscious this was becoming more of an interrogation, so I resolved not to ask anything else unless he reciprocated. This was weirdly intimate, not being able to see his face, just the softness of our voices in the dark, warm air, perfumed with the flowers he'd planted below.

"Architecture."

"Sounds interesting," I said, and only just managed to keep from asking more questions in quick succession. *How many years do you have left? What's your day job? What kind of things do you want to build someday?*

Honestly, until Ty, I had never been the irrepressibly nosy type. Something about him just made me want to dig and find out all the secret, hidden things. The impulse was a little alarming. In silence, I sipped my tea, thinking he was done with small talk for the night.

Then he said, "What about you?"

It felt momentous, which was pretty absurd. "I'm in my third year studying special education." More than he'd asked, as that would give him a ballpark estimate of my age.

If he was interested.

But probably not.

In general, a certain type of guy went for me. They were usually sporty, extra tall, into outdoor activities, searching for a rugged girl to rock climb, go camping and be extreme with. That was definitely not my deal, even though I stood 5'11 in flats, and I put on muscle pretty easily. I worked out three times a week for my health, not because I was an athlete.

"That explains the day-care center," he said as he stood. "I'm going in now. Good night, Nadia."

A little shiver went through me, so stupid, because he remembered my name. My toes curled as he said it, and I hated that I was slightly breathless when I whispered, "'Night, Ty."

Somewhere in the back of my mind, a voice piped up, *He has a kid. This is crazy.* But the logical reminder didn't dispel his pull.

The next day, I found all my classes without problems, listened to first-class type of instructions and picked up course materials, and then I raced to work. It was a blur, and I didn't get out until nearly seven. The delinquent father showed up muttering about a traffic jam, but this was a town, not a city. Since his kid had been crying for an hour, afraid she'd been forgotten, again, I wasn't in the best mood when I left. Singing too loud to the radio burned off most of my annoyance, and I was okay by the time I got back to the apartment. But I sighed as I went up; our music was cranked enough that I could hear every note. I braced for another complaint, but it was hard to stay mad when I opened the door to find Max pretending to be a DJ while Angus and Lauren danced their asses off.

I smirked. "This is the saddest thing I've ever seen."

Max responded with his signature grin. "Come on, use your imagination. Think how great it'll be this weekend."

"I'm not ready for that jelly."

"Nobody is." Lauren drew me into the impromptu dance party, and I had never been able to resist her when she was in a good mood.

"Did something awesome happen?" I asked while shimmying.

Angus, it should be said, was the best bad dancer ever. Every dated move, he knew it—from lawnmower, running man, sprinkler to electric slide. I had a hard time watching him without laughing, but that was kind of the point. He was never happier than when he made his friends bust a gut.

"Yes." Lauren threw her arms in the air and twirled.

Angus kept dancing.

"No. Not the robot. I can't take it. I'm tired and hungry. Just tell me your news, LB." Her last name was Barrett.

"Okay, I don't want to hurt you."

Angus started singing "Do You Really Want to Hurt Me" while dancing in circles around us. That made Max laugh so hard he fell off the stool he'd set up, and he dropped the plates he was using as mock turntables. I could only imagine how noisy this was downstairs, but I hated to mention that while Lauren was so jacked up with excitement.

"Spill it already," I demanded, flopping onto the couch.

"I just worked my last shift at Teriyaki King. The career center finally came through and got me a decent campus job. I'll be working as an assistant in the fine arts building."

"Doing what?" Anything would likely be better than the food court, though.

"Answering phones, sending emails, filing, running errands. But only daytime hours, weekends off."

Max finally got off the floor. "See? That demands a party, a real one. I'll see what I can put together this weekend."

"Congrats, dude. Let me wash the kid goo off and then we'll figure out dinner."

"I brought home chicken," Lauren informed me. "Not from TK."

Blowing her a kiss over my shoulder, I said, "I knew there was a reason I love you better than all other Laurens."

"Just the Laurens?" she yelled after me. "I need to try harder."

During dinner, Angus turned off the music so we could actually hear each other talk. At least that was what he claimed, but I shot him a look that said *you're not fooling me; you're being superconsiderate right now.* He only smiled, even when Max gave him metric tons of shit about turning into an old man before his time.

So due to Angus, we didn't get an angry visit from our neighbor, and when I went out to the balcony with my tea, feeling like this could become a ritual, the patio below was empty. Disappointment swept over me in an embarrassing rush, and I was glad I hadn't said anything to Lauren about Ty. *Nothing's going on. You're so weird.* To prove it didn't bother me, I drank all my tea before heading inside. But long after I snuggled in, listening to Lauren wheeznore, which she claimed not to do, I rubbed my chest against an ache that shouldn't be there.

In the morning, I overslept, and I rushed out the door, straightening my work polo. No time for breakfast, which made me cranky. *Maybe if I'm lucky, Louisa will fix me a snack on the sly.* A portly woman on the wrong side of sixty, she was the cook at Rainbow Academy, and she was always trying to feed me. Usually, I didn't let her.

At my car, I stopped, puzzled, staring at the white square of folded paper tucked neatly under my windshield. *Probably a flyer.* I grabbed it and tossed it on the passenger seat; I didn't have time to check out what product or service someone was selling. As I drove, the air from the vents shifted the page, so I could read the single line written on it.

*Sorry I missed you last night. Ran late.*

My heart did that weird twisty-aching thing again, and I swallowed hard. Last night I figured I was alone in wanting to see him out there. To him, I must be the noisy, annoying upstairs neighbor who sounded like ten herds of goats tromping around.

*But then he left this. So maybe he likes talking to me.*

Such a small thing, but that flicker of excitement carried me through a morning of calming fussy babies and all my afternoon classes. Today marked the end of *getting to know you,* and the rest of the week, professors should get serious with assignments. Though I wasn't looking forward to that, I couldn't wait to meet the students I'd be working with at Calvin Coolidge Junior High, aka C-Cool. That nickname was supposed to make the school seem more badass and street, but since it was mostly attended by white kids, it didn't help much.

I got in early, just past four, and nobody else was in the apartment. I skimmed the lot for a silver Focus, but I didn't see Ty's car. He'd mentioned night classes, but I had no idea how often he took them. The more I learned about him, the hungrier I became to discover more.

But I put him out of my mind to do the required reading for my Oral Language Development class, quickly to be followed by the first chapter in my Literacy Instruction for Students with Mild Impairments textbook. By the time I finished—I was a slow reader—it was dark and still none of the roomies were back yet. I was hungry enough to rummage in the fridge. As I got up, I remembered I hadn't checked the mail, and my mom had mentioned a care package. Probably too soon, but she always sent Reese's Peanut Butter Cups.

Grabbing the key off the hook near the front door, I jogged downstairs to see if we had anything. As I unlocked the box, the foyer door opened, and Ty came in. He had a little boy with him, around four I guessed, with hair minted like a copper penny, and the sweetest smile I'd ever seen. It prompted one from me, which made the kid wave with his free hand. The other clutched a grubby, well-loved brown bear.

Ty, on the other hand, barely acknowledged me. I got a chin lift and then they breezed down the hall, like last night never happened, we weren't friends of any shade and he never wrote me a note.

The bewildered twinge in my chest went to eleven.

# CHAPTER THREE

Okay, whatever. I refused to play games.

So I retrieved the mail and went back upstairs to find some dinner. My roomies didn't come back until close to nine, and Lauren was full of talk about working in the fine arts department. She had the best gossip about one of the professors already. I listened as she gave the inside scoop. Max made mocking noises while Angus seemed more riveted than I was.

"Shut up, I thought he was married," he breathed.

"He *is*," Lauren said. "But that's not even the juiciest part."

Max feigned enthusiasm. "OMG, like, please tell us."

She cut him a dirty look, then faced Angus and me. "The TA they told me he's cheating with is a guy!"

"That *is* juicy," Angus said. "Before now, I haven't heard even a slight whisper that he's playing for my team."

Abruptly, Max pushed to his feet. "I'm going to my room."

I shrugged as Lauren asked with a look, *Something I said?* She and I had been able to stare-talk since junior high. Back then our conversations were a lot simpler, stuff like, *God, so cute, look,* and *I know, right?* It was something I'd only recently started trying to do with Angus, though I wasn't sure how much of my meaningful glances he could interpret. Sometimes I imagined his thoughts went like this: *Nadia sure stares at me a lot. She's a nut.*

For an hour or so, Angus and I played video games while Lauren paged through a magazine. Eventually the other two turned in, leaving me to decide if I was going out on the balcony. I put on the kettle, debating the issue with more ambivalence than the issue demanded. Impatient, I steeped the herbal tea, added natural sweetener and stepped outside.

It was a clear, beautiful evening, tons of stars twinkling overhead. The air was cool and fresh, and in two months or so, the weather wouldn't permit me to sit out here, anyway. I relaxed into my chair, making a mental note to tell Max how much I appreciated it. Closing my eyes, I listened to the rustle of squirrels in trees nearby and the symphony of insects singing to the night.

A bit later, I heard the unmistakable sound of Ty's patio door scraping open, so I took that as my cue to vacate. Even if he wanted to talk, I wasn't in the mood, after the cold shoulder earlier. So I slipped inside and took a quiet shower, tiptoeing so I didn't bother Lauren.

Between work, school and the new practicum, the week went fast, though I'd be lying if I said it hadn't lost a certain spark. Yet in getting ready, I still took great care; in honor of my first hands-on classroom experience, I wore a tailored navy skirt, white blouse and sensible shoes. *Does this look okay?* Nervous, I hurried out.

I loved C-Cool from the moment I pulled into the parking lot. The school was tan brick, built in the '60s. C-Cool was a sprawling, single-level structure that went around in a giant, rectangular loop. There were hallways branching off, but the main one ended up where it began, if you just kept following it and making right turns.

A glance into the classrooms said I might be overdressed. Mental note: nice pants and shirt would be fine for next time.

Eventually, I found my assigned room and teacher. My palms felt sweaty as I stepped in. A blonde woman turned, the dainty sort who made me feel like mooing as I stomped around, breaking china and generally trashing the place. But her bright smile diffused any awkwardness.

"You must be Nadia. I'm Madeline Parker." She was wearing jeans and a sweater, so I felt even more like a dork.

*Did you think this was a job interview? Sigh.*

Trying to be sly, I wiped my palm on my skirt then shook her hand. A glint of humor in her hazel eyes told me she was onto me, but she wasn't judging.

"Nice to meet you," I murmured.

"The pleasure is mine, believe me." She looked to be in her thirties, not so old as to be intimidating or perma-settled into cranky ways. "Some of my colleagues find this professional obligation annoying, but I can use your help. This is the tail end of my free period, so we can go over some things before wading in. You want to sit down?"

"Sure." I took a seat near her desk, ready to listen.

What she dropped on me was pretty stunning. "I work in the classroom as a co-teacher for social studies, English, science, math, though I teach the at-risk and special-ed students for math by myself, as I'm certified 4-8. Then I have a thirty-minute study hall where I help with homework as set up by the administration. This is a normal workload, though at the same time, I'm supposed to be teaching remedial English skills, study habits, behavior modification for discipline-issued students, as well as offer social instruction for those on the autism spectrum."

"Wow," I said.

"The most important thing for you to realize is that burn-out is high among special-ed teachers. I love my work, don't get me wrong, but don't forget to take care of yourself, okay?"

I thought of my Sleepytime tea ritual and nodded. "I won't. Thanks."

"Now that we've had our serious talk, I'll show you how rewarding this can be. Ready?"

A couple hours later, when I left the practicum, I was exhausted, and I understood what Ms. Parker meant. Though I didn't doubt my commitment to teaching, maybe I didn't have the tolerance or fortitude to work with special-needs students. There was such a diverse array of challenges, and I felt exhausted just trying to help my mentor address them. It seemed like every time I turned around, there was someone standing behind her, saying her name on repeat, having forgotten instructions or wanting an exception to the rule. Her patience was astonishing.

That night, I ate ramen for dinner and went to bed early. I didn't talk to my roomies or sit on the balcony. Thursday was a cipher of a day, but by evening, I shook off the bad mood and watched a movie with Angus and Lauren. Unsurprisingly, Max had a date, and it was two in the morning when he came in. I was still awake, though I didn't want to be. Apparently, Sleepytime tea at the kitchen table wasn't the same as drinking it by moonlight.

Max seemed surprised to see me when he shut the door. "Wild night, huh?"

"You know it. Nothing says party like an herbal-tea party."

"I'm worried about you, Conrad. You're out of control." His smirk prompted me to give him the finger.

"You wish." He sauntered past me, grabbed a bottle of water then said, "Don't stay up too late."

Since I was awake, anyway, I did some reading and started on a project that was due in two weeks. I got four hours of sleep, max, before I had to head to my first class. On Friday afternoon, I was surprised when the director pulled me off kitchen duty, where I was helping Louisa put together snack plates. Quickly, I washed my hands and followed her, confused, to the front of the center.

"I don't know how this happened," Mrs. Keller was saying, "but I double-booked myself. I'm meeting with a vendor about new equipment but I've also got a prospective parent wanting a tour. Can you handle it?"

"Sure, just introduce me."

But then I saw him. Ty stood near the front door in a pool of sunlight, holding a little boy's hand. The pair of them were just adorably ginger, and a smile beamed out of me before I could school my expression to something less *Wow, I'm so glad to see you,* more suited to a day-care center tour. Mrs. Keller was talking, making us known to each other. Though I could've said it was unnecessary, I didn't.

"So I'll leave you in Nadia's capable hands, all right? If you have questions she can't answer, I'll be available in half an hour or so."

"Understood. Thank you." His voice was always quiet and grave then, not just when dealing with random girls.

I had seen enough of Mrs. Keller's routine to know that I wasn't supposed to focus on the parents in this scenario, so I squatted down to eye level with mini-Ty and offered a warm smile. "We haven't met. I'm Nadia. I'll be showing you around today. Is that okay?"

He thought about it and then nodded without looking at his dad. That told me he was a confident kid. The bear was conspicuously absent, so he must be in big-boy mode.

"My name is Sam." He offered a small hand for a very grown-up shake, and it was all I could do not to hug him. Then he volunteered, "I have to go to school now. My auntie can't watch me anymore."

*That must be the gray-haired lady who said it was her last day.*

"I'm sorry to hear that" seemed like the safest response.

"But I get to play with other kids more." That sounded like he was quoting his dad's assessment of the bright side in this change to their routine.

"Very true. Once you've seen everything, I'll ask Mrs. Trent if you can play in her class for a little while."

Sam tipped his head back this time, asking permission with big brown eyes.

Ty nodded. "Sounds great."

While I gave the company pitch, I was conscious of unspoken things between us, unfinished business, and it didn't help having Ty right at my shoulder as we peered in the classroom windows while I talked about each teacher. Sam went to the door and stared through the glass. He didn't seem alarmed over the idea of switching from babysitter to day care, and it was probably time. Pre-K would help him get ready for kindergarten next year.

Eventually, we came to the end of the tour and I offered my hand to Sam. He took it without hesitation, and I glanced at his dad, who seemed more nervous about the whole thing. Taking his silence for assent, I tapped on Mrs. Trent's door. We had two pre-K teachers, but Mrs. T had spaces available.

"Sam is a prospective student. Would it be all right if he participated for a bit?"

"Absolutely. We're just about to have circle time. Sam, you can have this carpet square." She gave him blue shag to sit on, and I beckoned to Ty.

"It's best to leave while he's busy. We won't be gone long." I took him to the break room, which was near the kitchen. It had been only fifteen minutes, so Mrs. Keller wouldn't be done with her supply meeting yet. "Would you like coffee or tea?"

"Coffee would be great." As ever, he looked tired, though not rumpled. The weariness seemed to be a perpetual state with him.

"What questions do you have?" As part of the tour, I'd gone over hours, safety record and curriculum, but I hadn't covered the fees. I hated talking money with the parents. Some of them made me mad, acting like their kids weren't worth the cost of decent care.

While he thought about it, I poured the coffee into a white mug and offered him cream and sugar. "No thanks, black is fine." His golden-brown eyes held mine for a few seconds. "I guess the only question I have at this point is…where've you been all week?"

I could've made up an excuse. I could've lied.

"Avoiding you," I said honestly.

"Why?"

"I may not be the *best* neighbor, but I haven't done anything to deserve that snub, and I'm not interested in friends who only acknowledge me part of the time."

"Friends." He repeated the word in an odd tone, like it was a word from a foreign language that he'd heard once but couldn't place.

"What did you think we were?"

A confused laugh huffed out of him. "I don't know. I'm sorry."

I studied his face and he truly seemed apologetic. His hot-and-cold game was puzzling, but I didn't think he meant to be difficult. "Just...explain and we're cool."

"It was a knee-jerk reaction. Sam hadn't met you, and in the car, he was saying he had to go to the bathroom for ten minutes. I didn't want him to pee at your feet as a first impression."

From the tension in his shoulders, it was more complicated than that, but I didn't demand more. I'd worked at the day care long enough to know that public urination was the least of the problems that could crop up, dealing with a kid Sam's age. So he was most likely telling the truth about that, if not about why he'd acted like we didn't know each other at all.

"He's cute," I said, giving him a *get out of jail free* card.

"I think so." His smile became 50 percent more natural. He downed half his coffee in a single gulp, giving the sense it was his life support, necessary for survival.

"You must've been young when you had him." Okay, so now I was totally digging. It was possible that Sam was his little brother, but I didn't think so.

"Twenty when he was born."

*Yikes. Younger than me.* I couldn't imagine being a parent at my age. It was such a vast relief to leave Rainbow Academy once people reclaimed their offspring. When I went home, there was nobody relying on me for safety, comfort, wisdom, food or shelter. But for the past four years, Ty had been all of those things to Sam. Which meant he was twenty-four or so.

*So out of your league.* With a mental sigh, I added him to the list of delicious guys who were out of my reach, mostly celebrities. *Damn.* No prospective parent had ever tempted me during a tour. Usually, the fact that the guy had a kid was enough to put me off, but something about Ty... My gaze dropped to his artistic hands curled around his coffee mug. For a few seconds, I watched his fingertips play around the rim. My lips tingled.

*Stop that.*

"You've done a great job with Sam," I managed to say.

"Thanks."

"Will your partner want a tour before you decide if Rainbow Academy's the right fit?" Somehow the question came out casual and professional when I was dying to know about Sam's mom, mostly as pertained to Ty's relationship status.

"No, I'm making the decision on my own."

*Single dad, check. I bet that's a story.* I wondered if Sam's mom was out of the picture entirely, and if so, why? *Did she leave or...die? Sad, either way.* I quelled my curiosity.

"Will our hours work for you? We're only open until six."

"Not a problem. My parents look after him during my night classes."

*He works during the day, takes classes in the evenings. When exactly does he sleep?* Well, that explained the constant exhaustion.

Ty must've seen something in my face that he took for disapproval because he snapped, "I always spend Sundays with Sam. Always."

I raised a brow. "I heard you reading *Goodnight Moon*. And I saw the way that kid looks at you. I have no doubt you're an amazing dad."

A muscle flexed in his jaw and he closed his eyes for a few seconds, as if I'd stroked him in an unspeakably intimate place. My fingers curled against the urge to touch him, brush the bright hair away from his brow or test the gold bristles on his jaw. A rush of longing hammered at my composure, a visceral attraction unlike any I'd ever known. He rubbed his palm over his mouth, and I could've sworn he whispered something like, *Make it stop, I don't have time for this right now*, but it was more of a breath or a sigh, and it could've been my imagination.

To cover my confusion, I checked my watch. "Why don't you touch base with Mrs. Keller? She should be ready. I'll get Sam, wash him off if necessary and bring him to the front."

"Okay. Thanks, Nadia."

God, I had no idea what it was about him, but every time he said my name, it went through me like gasping, shivering sex. And the *thanks* hit me just about as hard because I had the feeling he didn't say it often.

Blushing, I whirled to do as I'd suggested. Circle time was wrapping up when I got to Mrs. Trent's class. Sam was clapping along with the other kids, then he followed instructions politely, piling his rug on top of the others. He spotted me and lit up, as if we were old friends. His openness spoke volumes about his sunny nature. I imagined he was a lively kid, full of energy and boundless curiosity.

"Do I have to go?" he asked, his chin drooping when I opened the door.

"I'm sorry, yeah. Your dad's waiting for you. But once he fills out the papers, you can come to school with the other kids."

"Like Daddy goes to work."

"Exactly like that. And your job will be learning."

He nodded at me firmly. "It's a deal."

My heart quivered at how seriously he was taking this. He put his hand in mine, trustingly, and I led him to the front office, where Ty was already filling out forms. Rather than bother them, I sat down with Sam and we built an awesome block tower in the play area nearby. By the time we finished, they were wrapping up, and Ty came out with his paperwork. From experience, I knew we needed certain medical records and proof of vaccinations, but he could email that stuff later.

"Congratulations," Mrs. Keller told Sam. "You're our newest student."

He grinned at her. "My job is learning."

"I like your style." She offered Sam a low five, and he nailed it.

I was itchy, unsure if I should walk them out or go back to the kitchen, and Mrs. K didn't help by dashing off to answer her cell phone, buzz-ringing away on her desk. For a few seconds, I fidgeted. Pushed out a nervous breath. And that was stupid because *I* was the one who said we were friends. Friends didn't make me feel like *this,* but I couldn't admit that to Ty.

"He starts on Monday in Mrs. Trent's class. I'm going to call the parents she gave me for reference, but I don't expect any problems." He shifted, eyes on mine.

Heat shimmered up my spine. *So completely inappropriate.*

"Awesome."

Then Ty gave me a smile that surpassed his son's in both sweetness and intensity as he turned for the door. "So...see you tonight."

# * CHAPTER FOUR

*That could've meant nothing,* I told myself. *It could've meant anything, just a casual comment, like people say "see ya later" when they don't expect to run into you again for years.*

But that didn't keep me from being excited as I skimmed the fridge message board. Angus had written, *Out with Josh, don't wait up,* in red marker. Lauren's scrawl read, *Fine arts department dude is fine, let's hope he's interesting, too. Back late!* Since we'd both worked full-time over the summer, it seemed like forever since we'd talked.

*She's not avoiding me, right? Nah. That's silly.*

Max studied me as he stood in front of the fridge, devouring a leftover sub. The girls he dated would doubtless find him less charming if they knew he left his underwear in the bathroom and Angus had to yell at him about it, and that he was prone to drinking from the milk carton, then putting it back. But he had a fantastic bod and a brooding, dark-horse stare. In their eyes, that might make up for the rest.

"So what're you doing?" I asked.

Friday night, I should probably have something social going on, but the first week of school, job and practicum wiped me out.

"Eating."

"Smart-ass. You know what I mean."

"I'll get my bike running if it's the last thing I do. I won't have a chance to work on it for a while. Don't make any plans tomorrow, by the way. The party is most definitely on."

"Cool. Who's coming?"

He listed a bunch of mutual friends, people we hung out with in the dorm and then some names I didn't recognize. Bottom line, at least thirty people would be here. I had mixed feelings about it. At the best of times, I wasn't a party animal, though I had barfed in the bushes a few times my freshman year. Ironically, on one of those occasions, I hadn't been drinking at all; instead I'd sucked down too many energy drinks and caffeine pills cramming for midterms. Now I didn't let myself get more than a buzz on, mostly because I hated hangovers so much. Recovery could kill the whole day.

Max was looking expectant. "Aren't you gonna tell me how awesome I am?"

I stretched lazily. "Nope. There's no point. You say it as part of your daily morning affirmation, anyway."

"Can't argue with my own mirror." He smirked.

"Good luck with your bike."

"Thanks." He tousled my hair and headed out.

A glance at the clock told it wasn't remotely late enough to sit on the balcony and expect company, so I worked on coursework for an hour and a half. After that, I lost interest in being virtuous and rummaged through my mom's care package. She'd maximized value from flat-rate, priority shipping, as I'd also received homemade gingersnaps, a handmade scarf and a poster she thought would look nice on the living room wall.

On a whim, I dug a small basket out of my closet. I'd gotten a bath set in this, and it was light enough to serve. Next I located a ball of yarn, left over from my failed attempts to learn to knit. My mother was so good at it, and she'd tried so hard to teach me, but I never made anything that didn't look like a cat had killed it. I threaded the string through the straw on four sides, and then let it out, guessing how long it needed to be for Ty to reach it. Finally, I tied the strands off on top, creating a messy sort of handle.

By this time, it was after eight, nearly dark. I cracked the balcony doors for a breeze; it wasn't hot enough to run the air conditioner, and it would only get cooler from here. Through the sliding glass doors, the last of the sunlight glimmered over the treetops, like a farewell, and I watched until the shadows lengthened completely. As soon as they did, I made a cup of tea, but I was a wild woman and chose orange Ceylon spice instead of the usual infusion. I also took a pack of peanut butter cups from the Mom stash. With the doors open and ears straining, I heard when Ty stepped out.

Smiling, I lined the basket with a paper napkin, then set a tea bag atop it, along with a gingersnap and a peanut butter cup. Maybe I should've acted like I wasn't waiting for him so obviously, but I had never been good at pretending I didn't want things when I did. So I stepped out onto the balcony, maneuvered around the lounge chair and carefully lowered the basket toward him. He was just staring, as if willing me to appear. Sparks crackled to life inside me.

"What's this?" he asked, steadying the gift drop as it came to him.

"My mom sent treats. I'm sharing them, so we'll both have delicious things."

To my surprise, he didn't argue, and his smile flashed, visible in the shadows. Part of me wondered why he didn't ask me downstairs to talk, but his reticence must relate to Sam somehow. The basket lightened when he took his share of the goodies.

Then he said, "Let me heat some water. I could use a cup of tea."

"Sure."

I settled into the Adirondack, waiting for him to return. Peace stole over me, along with gladness that we hadn't gone with a place closer to campus, all full-time college students. *I would never have met Ty.* Because it seemed polite, I didn't eat any sweets and only sipped at my tea, cooling on the arm of my chair. He must've used the microwave because it didn't take long enough for a kettle to boil.

"Back." The wicker love seat creaked as he settled onto it.

"Cookie first."

In silent harmony, we devoured them. I loved the combination of sweetness and the spicy bite on the tongue afterward. I could taste the molasses, remember the scent of the kitchen while Mom was baking. A pleasant homesickness swept over me. This summer, I was so busy, saving up for lean times through the fall and winter, I hadn't gone home at all since it was a sixteen-hour drive. *I'll make sure to see them at Thanksgiving.* With any luck, the Toyota had a few more road trips in her.

"Phenomenal," he said.

"Gingersnaps are my favorite, though at Christmas she does a peppermint-and-white-chocolate cookie that's a serious contender."

"Sounds like you miss your family."

"Yeah."

"Where are you from?"

*Ah, an actual question. That means I can ask one back.*

"Nebraska, toward the South Dakota and Wyoming side, if that helps."

"I've never met anyone from there."

Michigan *was* a long way from home. "I usually get 'not in Nebraska anymore' jokes, and then I have to decide if I'm going to remind them that's Kansas or play along."

"What do you usually do?"

"Play along."

"You don't like conflict, huh?" He sounded normal tonight, as if talking to me wasn't an unpleasant chore anymore.

That was a relief since I'd come to look forward to these moments with him so much. More, maybe, than I'd like to admit. *Right. Friends.* I distracted myself by considering his question. "Not if it can be avoided. I'm not what you'd call pugnacious, no. But I like to think I don't back off important issues. What about you?"

"No." His voice was bleak and quiet. "I don't. Even when I should."

*Wow, that took a dark turn.*

If I could've jumped onto his patio without breaking an ankle or waking Sam, I'd have been down there like a shot. The distance between us seemed intolerable, and from the knot in my throat, I didn't see how I could live another second without touching him, finding out if his hair was as soft as it looked or what he smelled like. I *wanted* him in a way I never had before.

In high school, I had a boyfriend who played basketball, and we broke up when I left the state. It was a rational decision, and I didn't miss him that much once I was gone. My freshman year, I went out with a lot of different guys, one date here, two dates there, but I never clicked with anyone enough to focus on them. Sometimes there were hookups with no strings, no expectations. Classes, friends and work seemed a lot more important. The intensity of this attraction was foreign and frightening, if exhilarating. I might already be backing off if I had the faintest sense that Ty was jerking me around on purpose.

*Wish he didn't make me feel this way. It'd be so much simpler if I could friend-zone him.*

I realized I still hadn't touched his verbal grenade. "We all have things we'd do differently in hindsight."

"What is it about you?" he asked in a wondering tone.

"Huh?"

"You make me...better. Calmer."

"Like a sedative?" I snickered. It was the *least* sexy thing a guy had ever said to me, including a junior high squeeze who said my face wasn't actually that bad.

He laughed, too, a sheepish sound. "I didn't mean it like that. Just...I'm worried pretty much all the time that I'm dropping the ball somewhere, about to face-plant, but when I come out here and hear your voice, everything backs off, like, ten steps. I can breathe again."

*God.* I swallowed hard, unable to speak for a few seconds.

"I'm glad you look forward to this as much as I do." The darkness made me brave enough to add, "I wasn't trying to intrude that first night."

"I know. But the unit had been vacant for a while. So I guess I forgot I wasn't alone anymore." The way he said it summoned a rush of heat, though he couldn't *mean* it like that.

We'd only just met then, and I doubted I'd made a great

first impression, dropping couches, falling down stairs. It was a wonder he didn't think I was a danger to myself and others. On the other hand, this was the longest we'd spent together without him retreating, so maybe I was accruing more hash marks in the *make Ty want to stick around* column.

"Nope," I said. "You're stuck with me now." It occurred to me that I ought to warn him. "By the way, we're having a party tomorrow night, at least thirty people, and the way word gets around, it may be more like fifty. I hope it won't be too loud for Sam to sleep."

There was a long silence. Finally, he said, "Thanks for the heads-up."

"Are you mad?"

"No, I'm problem-solving. I'll put him to bed with headphones on. Don't worry, you're not the only people with social lives around here, and most of them don't check in with me." Rueful tone, as if he was aware he had no right to expect it.

"I'd invite you to come, but—"

"Another time," he cut in, surprising me. "My folks watch him the last weekend of the month. They tell me to get out, have fun, but I usually just sleep as much as I can."

"And that's the *only* time," I muttered.

"I heard that." Incredible as it seemed, I could actually sense the smile in his voice, and I sat forward, peering over the railing to confirm.

My heart skipped when he leaned into the light, a golden glow from his living room, and our eyes met, more of that hungry-looking. I felt the skim of his gaze over my bare shoulders, on the curve of my cheek and the line of my neck. I'd swear to my grave it was the night air, but my nipples actually tightened, just from that look. I licked my lips. He watched me.

"I wasn't trying to slip it past you."

"That doesn't seem like your style," he agreed.

"I only meant that you *look* tired. Not that you aren't also—" I bit my tongue to stanch the flood of potentially humiliating words.

"What?"

"Nothing."

"Finish that sentence. Please, Nadia?"

A little shiver went through me. If he ever figured out how much power he wielded over me with those three syllables, I was doomed. He might not even be aware of it, but his voice deepened, softened, just a touch, when he spoke my name. Enough to make me think he might be into me a little bit.

*Appealing as all hell. So incredibly hot. Get-in-my-bed sexy.* Since I had a single, that wasn't even a fantasy I could indulge without adding a bunch of details like a hotel room or whatever. I wondered what kind of bed Ty slept in. *God, stop thinking about him that way. This can't happen.*

But my mouth wasn't taking orders from my brain. "On one condition."

"What's that?"

"Answer one question for me."

His voice went flat. "That depends on what it is."

In that moment, I imagined shutters coming down, gates being drawn across windows for the night. I suspected he thought I was going to ask about Sam's mom. And I hoped I would surprise him, always, in good ways. It was clear to me he didn't want to discuss that sort of thing with me. At least not yet. We were baby-new, just starting, whatever we were.

*Friends.*

So I said, "Tell me what you dream of designing, once you're a big-deal architect."

"Oh." Relief and perplexity colored his tone, warmed it.

He was smiling again—I couldn't resist peeking at him. Ty ate the peanut butter cup as he thought. "It's good to hear you say it so implicitly, like my success is assured. The road feels really long sometimes."

"I can imagine."

"I've been in school since I was eighteen, but after Sam was born, I cut down to part-time. Anyway, you didn't ask to hear me whine." He paused, tapping at the arm of his chair with a shy look. "Damn. I don't know if I can answer this after all. I've never told anyone."

That startled me, making the question seem more meaningful than I'd realized. "It's okay, but…in that case, I won't be completing my sentence."

He cursed, the first time I'd heard him swear. My smile felt like it might crack my cheeks. The ache in my chest was back, but it was all things irresistibly sweet and good. I set my fingers on the railing like I could touch him from here, and in tiny, incremental gestures, I traced the almost-distinguishable shape of his features. Someday I wanted to trace his nose like this and kiss his ears and— *God. No more.* I trembled a little, not from cold, but from *want*. How crazy, this was the best first date I ever had.

And it wasn't one. Was it?

*Definitely not.*

"You drive a hard bargain. Okay. I want to design churches." He shifted, creaking the love seat, and then went on, "I doubt I'll be able to right away. I'll probably end up doing offices or condos to start, but eventually? I would desperately love to design a church someday, see it built from each individual stone to stained glass panels so I can stand inside it and marvel."

"Why?" I didn't think it was an odd question. Up until

this moment, Ty hadn't struck me as particularly religious; he didn't have the Jesus fish on his car.

He exhaled in a soft, trembling sigh. "So I can thank God personally for Sam."

The need to make such a grand gesture spoke of such a deep, abiding love that tears actually welled up in my eyes. Despite my best efforts, they spilled over, trickling down my cheeks. I covered it by cramming a peanut butter cup into my mouth and washing it down with tepid tea, but it didn't taste quite right. My voice would probably give me away.

But when I didn't speak, he said, "That probably sounds dumb. Or pretentious. I can't believe I—"

"No." I couldn't let him think that, and I leaned forward in my chair for emphasis. "Not at all. It's the most amazing thing I've ever heard. Sam is *so* lucky to have you, Ty."

"I'm the lucky one. I just wish I could remember it for more than five minutes at a time." He paused, cocking his head, and I drew back, not wanting him to *see* but it was too late. "Are you crying?"

"Maybe a little. Shut up. It's just…so very sweet." My voice broke slightly, and I swiped at my eyes, embarrassed at how easily he got to me.

*He could reach right into my chest and pluck out my heart.*

"I'm glad I told you," he said softly.

"Me, too."

"But we had a deal, remember? No backing out."

"I wouldn't." Finding the right words felt like a lightning-fast fencing match in my brain. Deliberately I repeated what I'd babbled only in my head before, measured this time, conscious of what I was putting out there between us. It didn't matter if this was a bad idea. I'd promised.

"Not that you aren't also…hot as hell, completely irresistible in every conceivable way."

A sharp intake of breath from Ty.

Once I said it, I didn't have the guts to wait for his reply. Quickly, I grabbed my stuff and carried it inside, closing the glass doors firmly behind me. Shaking like a leaf, I padded to my room and shut *that* door, as well, like he might be chasing me. The wood was all that held me upright. God only knew what I'd say to Lauren if she came home right now, because I wasn't ready to dish.

*Not by a long shot.*

Even then, I suspected what was to come between us. His silent, secret yearning to build a church for his son marked the beginning of my complete and utter fascination with the man downstairs. Yoga breathing steadied my nerves, but not the flutters deep in my belly. I'd lobbed the ball pretty firmly into his court.

Now I just had to wait and see if he'd pass or play.

*

# CHAPTER FIVE

Music throbbed from the speakers, vibrating the floor. Saturday night our apartment was crammed with people, standing room only. Max seemed pleased, and Angus was mellow, making out with his boyfriend, Josh, up against the kitchen counter. Josh was a tall, lean guy of Puerto Rican descent with black hair and melting brown eyes. He caught me looking and smirked over Angus's shoulder.

"Perv," he mouthed.

Lauren nudged me with a grin, pointing out one of Max's friends. She smelled like she'd been drinking for a while, but her balance was fine. "What do you think?"

"He's all right. You didn't invite fine arts guy?"

"Hell, no. He was mad boring." She took a deep breath. "Okay, I'm going in."

Really, it was amazing how much she'd changed. In junior high and early high school, she was a complete computer geek with a paralyzing crush on my older brother. But after our sophomore year, she gave herself a complete makeover, personality and everything. Looking at her, nobody would ever guess that she used to be shy. She navigated the crowd wearing a bright smile and tapped her target on the shoulder. The guy's name was Gabe or Garth, something beginning with G, and by the way he leaned in for a kiss ten minutes later, he was into her. Watching him squeeze my best friend's ass was oddly hypnotic. Shaking my head, I turned away to grab a beer from the metal ice bucket in the corner.

Four hours ago, we weren't remotely ready to host anything, but then Max roared up—on his working bike—along with five friends, and things came together fast. Between coolers, buckets, booze and multiple bags of ice, it started to look like a party. Girls wandered in later, each bearing chips or dip or a snack plate. It was amazing how Max got women he'd slept with to do this kind of thing. But whatever the magic, he had the apartment ready to rock by eight.

I, on the other hand, would be lucky to manage a side-to-side sway. To feign party spirit, I downed half my beer and joined a game of Kings Cup. The others were already pretty hammered, so it was easy to avoid losing by answering the questions right, and when the "all girls drink" came around, I sipped my beer. There was no way I was getting sloppy smashed.

"You look superserious," Josh said in my ear.

I glanced over my shoulder and found Angus on my other side. I smiled up at them, pitching my voice to be heard over the music. "If I get distracted, I could be forced to drink that." With a grimace, I pointed at the unholy cocktail in the center of the table.

Angus shook his head. "Then this would be forever known as the night Nadia got her stomach pumped."

"You're a wise man, Angus Starr."

"Come on. This is disgusting." Josh pulled me away from the game.

"Where are we going?"

"It's better in your bedroom," Angus said.

I smirked. "If I had a dollar for every time I've heard that."

"You'd have a dollar." Josh was sharper than Angus, more prone to incisive comments that could cut you to the bone; he laughingly called this tactic the queen's razor.

"True."

Dipping my head in mock-chagrin, I followed them down the hall and found ten people sitting on my floor in a circle. Nobody was humping on my bed yet, but the night was young, give it time. I shot Angus a curious look, but Josh was already asking them to make room for us. If this was another drinking game, I might hide in my closet for the rest of the night. Or...I could go to the library.

"Courtney is bending spoons with her mind," a girl named Emily said.

"Sure she is."

A big-eyed blonde spoke up. "No, seriously, watch. It will blow your mind."

Belatedly I sniffed the air. No wonder. It reeked of weed in here, so Courtney could be cheating like crazy and these people were so baked they'd never notice.

I whispered to Josh, "Is it that time of night already?"

"Mess with the stoned people? You know it."

"Are you ready?" Courtney asked. "I'm only doing this one more time."

She threw me a wink; I stifled a laugh. With a dramatic flourish, she pressed a metal spoon to her forehead and slowly the bottom began to twist outward. The way she was holding it, you'd have to be sober and paying attention to catch how she was pressing with one finger. The tokers let out a collective gasp.

"See, what'd I tell you." Emily tried to nudge me and almost fell over.

"That was truly amazing."

Courtney stood, took a bow then said, "Now pony up. Twenty bucks, you dipshits."

*Wonder what the bet was.* Crumpled singles made their way to her, and she counted them before throwing up both arms to make a rock-star exit. She shoved a path down the crowded hall to pounce Max with a deep, sexy kiss. Apparently, conning high people made her horny.

"Our turn!" Josh said.

I had no idea what was about to happen, but this was definitely better than Kings Cup. While Josh could be puckish, he was never cruel. He went on to explain the rules of the game, which he was calling Suckface Trivia. I could tell by their hazy expressions that he'd already lost them, but most of them were grinning like they didn't care about being let in on the joke.

"I'll simplify," Angus put in. "If you answer the question correctly, you get to kiss whoever you want that's playing the game. If you get it wrong, you kiss the person immediately to your left."

*Simple enough.*

Though it might be slightly heartless, I couldn't wait to hear the questions. *This should be hilarious.* Josh kicked the game off by pointing at the big-eyed, blonde girl. "At what temperature does water boil?"

"Um. Celsius or Fahrenheit?"

"Either," Angus said. "In the spirit of being fair to our neighbors to the north."

She thought for a few seconds, then said, "I dunno."

It didn't seem to bother her that she was sitting next to a girl, the one named Emily. In fact, they kissed for a good, long minute, sort of lazy and sensual. *Huh. If they keep this up, there will totally be an orgy on my bedroom floor.*

"You see how it's done," Josh said.

"Uh-huh." Half the guys in the room now looked even more glazed.

I whispered to Angus, "I don't think it's gonna pan out the way Josh expected. Unless he's trying to start a sex pile?"

Two easy questions followed—and each got it wrong—so there was more random kissing. In fact, two straight guys got so into it that the first pushed the other down onto the floor. I watched them together, hands digging into shoulders, breathing hard. My skin prickled, but I'd be lying if I claimed I wasn't squirming a bit. This felt slightly indecent, but nobody was *making* these people play the game.

Angus smiled faintly. "Trust me, this is *exactly* what he had in mind. He's devilish."

"Next question." Josh turned to me. "Your turn."

I doubted he could stump me since I hadn't smoked anything, and it was tough to cloud your brain with a single beer. "Go for it."

"What's the capital of Illinois?"

*Springfield.*

Now I had to decide if I wanted to play it safe—and give the wrong answer—which meant kissing Angus. If I answered right, I could get in on the real action. As I glanced around the circle, I noticed a couple of the guys were cute, if burning at low brain wattage. I could pick someone up for the night. There was no question I was in the mood, but...

*There's nobody here I want.*

"Cairo," I said deliberately.

Josh narrowed his eyes. "You cow. You just want to kiss my boyfriend."

"Who doesn't? Have you seen him?" I grinned teasingly. "But hey, it's your game, J-Rod. I didn't make the rules."

Angus turned his head, offering his mouth, but I pecked beside it, instead. Smiling, he slung an arm around my shoulders and squeezed me briefly then let go. The guys from two turns back were getting hot and heavy, probably more than even Josh could've predicted. I got up and wandered out before I ended up watching somebody get lucky in my room before I did.

Outside, the rest of the apartment was just wall-to-wall people. I didn't realize I'd made the decision to bail until I grabbed my purse and keys. No plan, I just couldn't stand the noise for another second. I much preferred attending parties to hosting them. In that scenario, if I got sick of the bullshit, I could always come home. Navigating through the crush, I got out the front door and down the steps before I heard someone come after me.

*Crap. I thought that was a clean getaway.*

"Where're you going?" Lauren asked.

"Out. But don't let me ruin your night."

"You sure you're okay?" She surveyed me with a concerned look.

"Positive. Look out for the sex show Josh is running in our bedroom, by the way." As expected, that drove her back inside without another word.

The music had my head aching. Really, I just wanted to find a quiet place and…what? I had no idea. Before I could make up my mind where to go, Ty's door opened, and he stepped into the hall. After last night when I all but offered myself naked on a platter, I half suspected he'd shut it again when he spotted me, but instead he gave me a half smile, ducking his head with a bashful air. Tentatively, I smiled back.

"You want to come in? When Sam has his SleepPhones on, he rarely wakes, unless I forget to set the music to loop. Tonight I remembered."

This was so momentous, and I couldn't stop smiling. This had to be my karmic reward for not making out with a random stoned guy. "That would be great. I was about to flee."

Ty gestured at his place. "You can hide out with me until things settle down."

"Thanks." I brushed by. From the clean smell of him and his damp hair, I guessed he'd just gotten out of the shower.

Inside, his apartment looked *much* nicer than ours, decorated with a quirky charm that immediately made me feel at home. The basic floor plan was the same with a galley-style kitchen visible on entry, the front door opening into a combination living and dining room, where there was also a breakfast bar. He had three rustic, leather-topped stools set up plus a small wooden bistro table. The space had very little glass, probably because of Sam, and I loved the padded red L-shaped sectional. A geometric-patterned area rug covered the worn beige carpet, and he had an antique steamer trunk in the middle instead of a coffee table, very cool; it was wood, covered in leather and bound in bronze. The walls were adorned with an interesting combination of pen-and-ink cityscapes and some really colorful abstract art. On closer examination, I was pretty sure Ty had framed both his own work and Sam's. Overall it was impressively tidy, and I said so.

"The auntie Sam mentioned is my mom's older sister, and she's always cleaning when she's here," he said sheepishly. "But she needs knee surgery, and she won't be up to chasing after him for a long while, if ever."

"So that's why you asked about day care."

"Yeah. Do you want something to drink?" He spoke softly, though he'd said Sam wasn't likely to wake up.

And if he did, it wasn't a huge deal, right? Surely Ty had friends over occasionally.

"Tea?" I suggested.

"I don't have orange Ceylon spice, but I can offer chai or honey lemon."

"Honey lemon sounds good. My nerves could use some soothing. If we had stairs, they'd definitely be diving down them."

"Let's hope they don't take the party into the hall and follow in your footsteps." The teasing glance as he put two mugs of water in the microwave sent heat straight to my cheeks.

"Yeah, yeah, I fought the steps and the steps won."

"Make yourself at home. I'll be right there."

"Sure." After I sat down, I couldn't resist the cream chenille throw draped over the back of the couch. I snuggled up in it, listening to the music booming from my apartment and the constant thumping overhead. "Sounds like they're coming through the ceiling, huh?"

"It's about what I expected when I saw college students were moving in."

"Spoken as if you aren't one," I said, slightly defensive.

Ty leveled a long look at me as the microwave beeped. "Are you really planning to argue that my circumstances are the same as yours?"

"I guess not." I felt young and stupid now, the first time he'd made me feel that way.

The silence thickened until I almost got up to leave. Then

he said, "Sorry. I'm a little...sensitive. People are always telling me to get out, live while I'm young. Like it's that easy."

I took the mug he handed me and played sink the tea bag with the spoon for a few seconds. "It's okay. How about a deal? I won't bother you about having more fun, if you don't bug me to try out for women's basketball."

"I'm enjoying myself now," he said. "And pestering people really isn't my thing."

He sank down on the other end of the couch. It was too noisy for us to watch anything, and we didn't need more music. That left talking, and I was totally okay with that.

"Me, too. So you said something about SleepPhones before. Is that different from normal headphones?"

"Yeah, it's a headband with speakers in it. Much more comfortable to sleep in."

"That sounds cool, actually. Maybe I need that. What music does Sam fall asleep listening to?" I asked.

"You'll laugh."

"Maybe. Tell me, anyway."

"He might be the world's smallest One Direction fan."

It took all of my self-control, but I didn't let out a peep, though my eyes watered. "You know that's insanely cute, right?"

"*I* think so."

"What about you? Your favorite bands?" I congratulated myself on acting normal, like I hadn't basically told Ty last night that he was everything I wanted for Christmas. The fact that he hadn't made use of that opening told me everything I needed to know about his intentions.

*Friends it is.*

"Right now I'm into Grouplove, Tove Lo, Passenger, The National and Speedy Ortiz."

"Would you think I'm superlame if I admit I've only heard of one of those?"

"Passenger," he guessed.

I nodded. "He toured with Ed Sheeran. I have a friend who saw their show. She said it was amazing."

He sipped his tea, seeming pensive. "That's one thing I miss."

"What?"

"Concerts. And going to clubs in the city to check out a new indie group." At my expression, which was probably something like *well, you can still go,* he added, "I know what you're thinking. When my parents have Sam, I could still see a concert or hit up a club."

I pretended to peer at him suspiciously. "You didn't tell me you were psychic."

"It's complicated," he muttered.

"Enlighten me. The party's still going strong, so I have nothing but time."

"The people I started college with have graduated, gotten jobs and moved away. The guys at work are all a lot older, and they're not interested in hanging out after hours."

"Make new friends," I suggested.

"Most people aren't interested in getting to know someone who can't be spontaneous, who's on a completely fixed schedule and may be a grumpy asshole on any given day."

"Yet here I am."

"Yeah, well. You're…unique."

*Is that a compliment? It could go either way.* I decided it didn't matter; I'd already settled on friendship. *Still, I can't believe I'm suggesting this.*

"We could see a concert sometime—on your off weekend.

If you plan for it, you could nap on Saturday afternoon and be primed for revelry that night."

"Maybe," he said.

To cover my disappointment, I lowered my head and stared into my mug. The tea was a lovely shade of amber; if it steeped any longer it would be too strong, so I fished the bag out with my spoon, wrapped the string around the handle and set it on the steamer trunk. For the life of me, I couldn't think of a thing to say. Tonight wasn't working out like I'd hoped, and the first achy burn of tears stung at the back of my throat.

"God. This face, you show me everything. I hope you don't play poker. They'd rob you blind." His voice was disturbingly gentle, tender even, and closer than I expected.

While I was looking everywhere but at him, Ty slid closer, his hand hovering in the air between us. From this distance I could feel the overwhelming warmth of him, and I wanted his touch more than my next breath. So I held it, fighting ridiculous, uncharacteristic tears, until his palm settled on my cheek.

"What—" I started to say, but I had no idea where I was going with that sentence.

"I'm going to be straight with you…because this dance is killing me. Don't imagine for a second that I don't want you. Your legs keep me up at night, and those eyes… You know when I first saw you, I thought you were probably a model?"

I laughed shakily. "Really?"

*Finally, we're getting somewhere.*

"If you were wondering, the answer is yes. I want to fuck you so bad it hurts."

The breath whooshed right out of me, and all the tingles centered low. "I like where this is going."

"It's a problem," he said frankly. "Because I really like you. And I don't date. I don't bring girls home to Sam."

"But…he's already met me," I said foolishly.

"That's why I can't sleep with you. We're friends. We have to be. Because you live in my building, because you're smart, funny, and I like you, and you work at Rainbow Academy. If we hook up and it doesn't work out, it'll change how we are together, and that would hurt Sam. Is any of this making sense?"

To be honest, I was still fixed on him saying he wanted to fuck me so much it hurt. I let that longing wash over me for a moment, then I nodded, his palm sliding with a seductive rasp against my cheek. "I understand, that all makes sense. But it doesn't explain why you've been staring at my mouth for the last five minutes."

Deep in his throat, Ty made a sound that curled my toes, and then, as if he couldn't help it, he brought his other hand up to frame my face.

# CHAPTER SIX

As Ty gazed at me, his nostrils flared and his breath came faster. His brown eyes had a sleepy, hooded look. I knew he wanted to kiss me, despite all the sound reasons he'd just listed why it could never happen.

"There are no rules against it," he said huskily.

*What? Looking.*

It was really hard to think with his face so close, but I couldn't make myself pull back. So I did the only reasonable thing; I put my arms around him. When I leaned into him, he let go of my face and cradled me against his chest. His heat and solid strength sent a delicious shock through me, and he didn't help matters by rubbing his cheek against my head.

*It's a hug. Friends hug.*

There was no way I could resist touching his hair, now that I finally had him so close, and it slipped through my fingers like coppery satin. He let out a little groan and leaned into my hands. Encouraged, I stroked in gentle little swoops, until he was practically purring.

"You're a ginger tabby," I teased as he turned, so I could reach the other side.

"Please," he mumbled. "I'm totally a battle-scarred tom."

He nuzzled his face against my neck, making my pulse jump. This was a misty gray area because he was definitely turning me on with the rasp of his scruff against the tender skin of my throat. But his heartbeat was slowing. Getting comfortable, I kicked off my shoes, and Ty, who wasn't wearing any, ended up sprawled in my lap, and he closed his eyes as I brushed the hair from his brow in rhythmic strokes.

"Whatever." I couldn't believe I was in his apartment, cuddling him.

It wasn't what I wanted but it was better than nothing. It would have to be enough. "This okay?" I asked, just to be sure.

"Better than. Don't stop."

Featherlight, I traced the slight arch of his nose, the plane of his cheekbone down to his jaw, around his mouth and over the bristled jut of his chin, which he lifted to give me better access. Eyes closed, he was smiling with an expression that registered as pure bliss. I'd swear he was starved for physical contact, let alone sex.

"Can I ask a personal question?"

"This is probably the best time." Dreamy tone.

"How long's it been?"

His gold-tipped lashes fluttered, revealing brown eyes that focused intently on my face. "Since I got laid?"

"Yeah."

"Couple of months."

That wasn't as long as I expected, the way he was reacting. "Huh."

"Did you think I've been celibate for years or something?"

"Maybe."

"Disappointed?"

"Why would I be?" I smiled down at him.

"Sometimes girls romanticize the situation. 'Poor Ty, if only he had a woman giving it to him regular and helping with Sam, his life wouldn't be such a black hole of suck.'" He lifted one shoulder in a lazy half shrug and demanded, "Ears."

I was only half-sure what he wanted, so I rubbed up and down the shell, gently, with thumb and forefinger. "Like that?"

He hissed out a breath when I scraped my fingernails behind them. "Exactly."

It might be wrong, but I secretly hoped this was turning him on a fraction as much as me. Even the weight of his head in my lap felt like foreplay, but I didn't roll my hips. *Ears are sensitive. Wonder what lips, teeth and tongue would do to him.* I swallowed hard and went back to running my fingers through his hair. It seemed safer. The party was still going strong, and it was only eleven. I might have several good hours of Ty-petting left.

"I hope you don't think I see you that way," I said.

"Hmm?"

"The 'black hole of suck' thing."

"Nah. You don't give off the *fix Ty* vibe. If you did, I'd be avoiding you like the plague, not hanging out on a Saturday night." He sounded relaxed, sleepy even. "Though I have no idea what's in it for you."

"I like you," I said softly.

*You have no idea how much.*

"You're crazy. Didn't you hear the grumpy asshole part earlier?"

"Maybe you save that for other people." I decided to get creative and scooped my hands beneath his head, like I'd seen masseuses do on TV. Since I had no training, I couldn't be sure what I was supposed to be doing, but I flexed my palms and rubbed the heels of my hands against the base of his skull. Ty arched his neck, lifting his chin until I heard a faint pop.

He groaned. "God. You're so good, I'd pay you."

"First I'm a barbiturate and now—"

"You really should've hit me by now." Ty flung an arm across his face, cheeks flushed.

"I'll snuggle you into submission."

"It's working."

"What else do you miss? Besides the music scene."

He turned his head side to side, increasing the pressure until I was worried about hurting him, and it reminded me of how he'd dug his knuckles into the back of his head. This had to be my unconscious responding to that moment, wanting to make him feel better. From the way he was smiling, it seemed to be doing the trick.

"How honest am I supposed to be?"

"Completely. I won't tell."

"You want me to bare my soul, huh?"

*I want you to take off your pants. But I'll settle for deep, meaningful conversation.* I was only half kidding, even in my head, but Ty's friendship felt rare and precious, a leap of faith that he didn't offer many people. I might not be special, but he made me feel that way.

"Yep," I said aloud.

"I miss sleeping in. I miss waking up with someone else and having time for slow, lazy morning sex."

*Oh, hello. Yes. Please.* The mental images his words conjured were so very tantalizing. I pictured a sleepy, horny Ty, wrapped around me, his lips on my neck, nibbling down to my shoulder while he took me from behind, his cock working in and out with infinite patience. His hands would be all over me, stroking, caressing in counterpoint to his thrusts. We'd take hours making each other come, maybe not even getting out of bed until well into the afternoon.

I stifled a whimper.

Oblivious to what a firestarter he was, he went on, "I miss showering after and fixing breakfast while mock-arguing about whether we should go grocery shopping or back to bed." There was a tight, drawn cast to his mouth, as if those were memories of the girl who left him.

*Damn.* Intuition whispered that he'd be a different sort of sad if she was dead, haunted instead of laced with regret. He radiated self-recrimination in the angle of his shoulders and the way his gaze turned inward when he spoke of her.

I tried to distract him by offering an emotional snapshot of my own. "I've never had that. Not in high school for obvious reasons, and until this year, I lived in the dorm. Most people bitch about the lack of privacy, but..." My voice dropped to a shy whisper. "I liked it."

"What?" His eyes snapped open, and he stared up at me, fascinated, fully in the moment.

I'd never told anyone this, not even Lauren. "Sometimes, when my roommate was drunk, she'd bring a guy back to our room. I always pretended like I was asleep, but I loved listening, watching the shadows under the covers, seeing them twist and move."

Telling him that sometimes I got off was probably too much information. So I shut up, studying his expression. At least he didn't look sad anymore.

"And I'm *right* back to wanting to fuck your brains out," he said hoarsely. "Is this party ever going to end?"

In his sweats, it was obvious that he was telling the truth.

Tipping my head back, I implored the universe for moral fortitude. "I can go."

"I can take it," he said softly. "I'm a pro at not getting what I want."

Like a bite of poisoned apple, I swallowed the argument that the old frustration didn't have to apply to me. "Back to things you miss?"

"Yeah. This will sound really specific, but…"

"What?"

"Little things. Like…I had a girlfriend in high school. We'd study on her bed, me lying down, her propped against the headboard reading. She had the habit of pulling my shirt up and running her nails lightly up and down my back. Drove me crazy, but I loved it."

"It turned you on?" Maybe I shouldn't ask, but I couldn't resist.

He laughed. "Well, yeah. Goose bumps over my entire body. But I was sixteen. Walking to the bathroom got me hot."

"Fair point." I desperately needed a change of topic, or I'd have to ask him to take a cold shower. "Is Ty short for Tyler?"

"Yeah. But it's my last name."

"What's your first?"

"Daniel. Your last?"

"Conrad."

Glancing down, I caught him shaping the syllables with his mouth, and I was tempted to tell him that my middle name was Rose, just to see him do it again. But I had to save some secrets for next time, or he might get bored. From there, I diverted the conversation to music because I couldn't take more sex talk; I was on the verge of vibrating, and if the sparks popped any brighter between us, we'd burn his apartment down. Small comfort, but at least I knew *why* it wasn't happening.

An hour later, he fell asleep in my lap, and fifteen minutes after, I dozed off, too. Later, the silence roused me, the absence of vibrations and cessation of music. Somehow we were tangled together, him on his back and me on his chest, though I didn't remember shifting. He smelled incredible, so much that I surreptitiously rubbed my cheek against him, breathing in honey and shea butter along with the clean, cottony scent of his shirt.

My heart ached as I mustered the resolve to move. One breath, another, listening to his heartbeat, then inch by inch, I slid out of his arms, trying my damnedest not to rouse him. He stirred once, his hand tangling in my hair. I froze. It would kill me if he woke up and saw me leaving when I wanted so badly to stay.

*But I can't. I never* can. *When Sam wakes up, I can't be here. Ty's sacrificed so much for him. He'll never change his mind about us.* And I should probably be grateful for his common sense. Yet half-strangled yearning swept over me like a tidal wave, and I shivered with the force of it while Ty let his hand drop. Swallowing those feelings, I pressed a ghost of a kiss over his heart, and I rolled away, grabbed my shoes and purse and tiptoed to the door. I was a mouse creeping out of his apartment, though I did silently test the doorknob to make sure it locked behind me. No way to turn the dead bolt from this side, so that would have to do.

I let myself in upstairs and found the apartment completely trashed. To get to my room, I stepped around four people, two of whom weren't wearing any pants. There was nobody in my bed, at least, and it looked as if Lauren had defended it before passing out in the closet. She was drinking more these days, but I didn't know if I should mention it. Maybe she'd just tell me I was no fun. The last time I brought it up, she said, *All you do is work, Nadia. Some of us want to live a little.* Sighing, I went to the bathroom, brushed my teeth and then stumbled to bed, wrecked by the intensity of the night.

Yet despite gritty-eyed exhaustion, I couldn't sleep. For half an hour, until the glowing numbers on my alarm clock read 4:30 a.m., I shifted and rolled, until I gave in to temptation. Feature by feature, I built Ty's face in my mind's eye, complete down to the tiniest detail like the faint cleft in his lower lip and the tiny, nearly imperceptible scar that bisected his left eyebrow. Once he was there with me, I dipped two fingers into my panties. One stroke, two, three, God, it was good, and I was still so slick. As the clock ticked over, I came in silence.

My whole body went limp, and I passed out a few seconds later.

The next morning, I woke in a panic, thinking I was late for class or work, then I fell back with a muffled groan. A glance at my phone told me it was just past eleven. Lauren propped herself on an elbow, looking as miserable as I'd ever seen. At some point, she must've crawled from the closet into bed.

"I can feel my heartbeat in my lips," she whimpered.

"That can't be good." I knew to whisper.

Since I wasn't hungover, I headed into the bathroom to wash my hands, and then I got her a cup of water and some ibuprofen. "You want toast?"

"Just let me die. You'll have the room to yourself then."

"We can't afford the place without you," I teased. "Plus...I love you too much. So what'll it be, toast or crackers?"

"Crackers."

I padded to the kitchen and was pleased to find Max cleaning. He'd also shooed out the floor surfers. "You weren't kidding when you said you'd be ambitious once school started."

"I noticed that you bugged out early last night. You okay?"

"Liar. You were banging Courtney up against your door when I left."

He grinned. "Okay, so maybe I didn't exactly *notice*. Lauren told me."

"Yep, I'm good." I opened the cupboard and grabbed a pack of saltines. "Have you seen Angus yet today?"

"Think he's still in bed."

As I nodded, I carried the breakfast of champions to Lauren. "Here, these should make you feel better."

"You realize they're made of flour and salt, not magic?" she asked.

"Don't make that face, drunkie. You're just mad because I'm not sharing your misery."

A reluctant smile formed as she nibbled the cracker. "You may have a point. A tiny one."

"Microscopic," I said.

"Do you ever wish we were still in Sharon?" It was such a non sequitur that I turned on my way to the door, brows raised.

"Not really. But I miss my family." That wasn't the same thing.

Lauren's expression shifted. "What do you think Rob's doing night now?"

My brother didn't rank high on my list of things to ponder on Sunday morning. But if he ran true to form… "Probably having brunch with our folks. Why?"

"Idle curiosity. I've been thinking about home lately, wondering what people are up to. Krista texted me the other day. We were talking about the old days."

After a moment's thought, I remembered her as a mutual friend who'd moved away before graduation, though I was bad at keeping in touch. "How's she doing?"

"I dunno, we talked more about high school. Remember the party where Rob punched Kent Walker?"

"Not really," I admitted. "Rest, I'm going to help Max with the fumigation."

"Wait, he's cleaning up his own mess?" She sat forward, then clutched her head. "I think hell has actually frozen."

"He couldn't be a pain in the ass forever."

Lauren was still mumbling in wonder, saltines in hand, when I left the room. It took us three full hours to make the apartment look even remotely close to how it did when we moved in. Which wasn't that long ago.

Angus got up just as we finished, and Max scowled at him. "Don't even pretend you weren't awake before now."

I didn't feel like refereeing, weird as it was for Max to complain about someone else slacking. So I said, "Nothing valuable broken, no stolen furniture and no vomit in my shoes. This went pretty well, huh?"

Max nodded. "But I think I'm done hosting for the semester. This shit is exhausting. Someone else can deal with the mess next time."

"No argument from me," I said.

By this point, I desperately needed a shower, so I took one quietly, as Lauren was still asleep. My hair went up in a ponytail, then I put on sweats and went in search of lunch. As if to apologize for shirking, Angus was making a beef stir-fry while Max waited on the other side of the breakfast bar.

"That smells fantastic." My stomach made a weird noise.

Max teased, "You ate a T. rex, didn't you? That sound *can't* have come from a girl."

Plunking down beside Max, I watched Angus cook through the open space over the counter. Our stools were cheap plastic, though, nowhere as nice as the ones at Ty's place. And once his name crept in, I couldn't banish it. That was a gateway thought, leading me to wonder where he was, if he'd taken Sam to the park, a movie or the zoo. I'd give a lot to be with them right now, but he'd made it superclear where the boundaries lay.

In under half an hour, Angus had the food on the table. I ate like it had been days. He didn't strut his culinary prowess often, but he'd apparently learned to cook from their housekeeper. Likely he could've afforded this place on his own, but he didn't want to live by himself, and he wasn't ready to move in with Josh yet.

"It was delish, thanks." I scraped my fork across my plate twice, saddened that there was no more food.

Max agreed, "Yep, awesome grub. I'm not even holding a grudge anymore."

"That was the plan." Angus grinned.

I killed the rest of the afternoon on assigned reading and coursework. By evening, Lauren was ambulatory—without barfing up her guts—so that was a good sign. I heated up a plate for her and then put on my shoes.

Max let his gaze drift over me in the insolent, up-and-down elevator look that made me want to punch him. "Hot date?"

Since I was in sweats and an old T-shirt that read The Penguin Ate My Homework, he was obviously being a tool. "With the elliptical machine. I haven't been to the fitness center here since we moved in."

Lauren said, "It's nowhere near as nice as the one on campus."

"And it smells," Angus added.

I tilted my face heavenward. "Why are they trying so hard to crush my motivation?"

"Because secretly you'd rather sit on the couch and watch TV with us, instead." Max patted the cushion next to him invitingly.

Shaking my head, I had to laugh. "That's *not* a secret."

"Where did you go last night, anyway?" Lauren wore a curious, quizzical look.

"Now that's a secret." Smirking, I swept out of the apartment amid vocal protests. Someone even threw a shoe after me for being such a tease; it thunked hard against the door as I jogged away and down the stairs.

I kept up the pace until I reached the clubhouse, though that was a big name for such an unimpressive building. There was someone on the elliptical, so I went for the treadmill, instead. I put in twenty minutes until the guy finished, and then I shifted. Forty minutes later, I was ready to call it a night. Swiping away the sweat, I headed back.

In the streaky purple twilight, Ty was helping Sam from his car seat. After last night, I wasn't sure how to act, so I waved and kept walking. They responded with raised hands, a bright smile from the kid and a hungry stare from Ty that made my panties glow in the dark.

*I won't survive this, will I? But the fireworks will be spectacular.*

*

# CHAPTER SEVEN

Monday started strong.

When the professor called on me in my first class, I knew the answer and avoided his caustic wit. If you weren't on point, Lynch was known for saying things like, "So you want to teach yet you can't be bothered to prepare for my class. In five years, I hope you're blessed with students exactly like you." The rest of the day went just as well.

I grabbed a sandwich at a convenience store on the way to Rainbow Academy and ate it in the car. Guilt flared when I remembered what Ms. Parker had said about taking care of myself. So far, I was doing a top-notch job.

At the day-care center, I parked in my usual spot and ran in. The director waved. "I need you in Mrs. Trent's room. Her assistant called in sick."

"Got it."

"Nadia…I was wondering if you'd be interested in a permanent classroom assignment? This is the fourth time Elaine has called off in two weeks. I don't think she's going to work out."

"You'd put me in Mrs. Trent's room?"

Mrs. Keller nodded. "It's a good placement. Four-year-olds aren't as trying as the twos."

"Could I still work a flexible schedule?" I hesitated, wondering how Ty would feel about me spending that much time with Sam.

"Sure. Instead of hiring a full-time assistant to replace Elaine, I'll advertise for a floater to cover the hours when you aren't around."

And two part-timers meant she didn't have to pay benefits. But I couldn't blame her for cutting costs where she could. Times were tough.

"Okay, sign me up."

"Excellent. I'll have a couple of things for you to sign when you finish up today."

Because certain ratios had to be observed—for four-year-olds, it was 12:1, children to adult—they had the assistant director, Jan Greenly, in the classroom with Mrs. Trent. The kids were doing free play, a short period after lunch, which I'd just missed, and Mrs. Trent was tidying up the room. Miss Greenly looked relieved when I showed up, and she hurried to her office without looking back.

Mrs. Trent laughed. "That woman much prefers paperwork to dealing with kids. So I hear you're joining us, going forward?"

"Wow, Keller was sure of me, huh?"

"To be honest, I asked for you."

I was flattered, but... "How come?"

"You're patient, good with kids, and you haven't missed a day in the last year."

"Thanks. What can I do to help?" Sometimes I wished I was more like Lauren, less known by traits like steady and dependable. But I'd worked hard for my reputation, living up to parental expectations, and mostly I didn't have *time* for emotional turmoil. Which was why Ty constituted such a dangerous side road in my neatly mapped life.

"Wipe down the tables. Once we're done, start setting up the cots for nap time."

"In the closet, right?"

"Yep. Thanks a lot."

"Not a problem."

I got the spray bottle and washcloth, then scrubbed away all signs of lunch. While I was working, Sam ran up to me. "Nadia! You're my new teacher?"

"Mrs. Trent's in charge. I'm her helper."

"Can you help me, too?" Gazing up at me, he looked so much like Ty that I couldn't stand it. I resisted the impulse to ruffle his hair.

"Sure, if you need something. Do you?"

"Not right now. I was just checking." Cute overload.

He chattered while I sanitized tables and did a quick head count, not easy with the kids running around. Nineteen. That meant it would be like Tetris, getting all of the cots on the floor without placing them so close that the kids could poke each other, and I also had to leave some kind of path to the door. Crazy as it seemed, as long as there were two of us in here, Mrs. Trent could take five more students. I just didn't know where the cots would go.

While I prepared, Mrs. Trent said, "Okay, time to clean up." They put away toys with the usual giggling and pushing, nothing serious. She had the routine down.

"I have to potty," a little girl said.

"Yep, it's that time," I answered with a glance at Mrs. T. "Should I get that started?"

"Please."

It was a lot easier than in the twos, where there might be diaper changes. In here, the kids went by themselves, but would occasionally come out with pants around their ankles, and I set them to rights then helped them wash their hands at the tiny sink. Getting nineteen pre-K kids to pee and clean up took twenty minutes, minimum.

"All right, everyone, get your nap-time bags from your cubbies and get on your cots. I'll read one story, then it's lights out." Mrs. Trent motioned toward the cupboards.

Nobody complained, though Sam looked worried. *Maybe he's scared of the dark?* I felt like telling him that it wouldn't be pitch-black in here, even with the blinds partly closed. The goal was to relax the kids, not freak them out through sensory deprivation. But he went obediently to his cubby and pulled down a tiny Hulk backpack, then he carried it to a cot near the windows. The kids didn't seem to have assigned spots, and there was only a little bickering before they got out pint-size pillows and blankets. A few had stuffed animals, and I stifled a smile when Sam dragged out his dog-eared bear. As they got comfortable, Mrs. Trent produced a copy of *Crazy Town Upside Down.*

She was a fantastic reader, exciting and expressive. I noted some things I'd like to incorporate in my own teaching style. Though I'd be working with older students, some might have a similar mental age. Once she closed the book, I went around doing tuck-ins as she turned on a soothing CD. Next she pulled the blinds three-quarters closed and I hit the lights. The room was pleasantly dim, but I could still see all of the little faces. Some of them closed their eyes right away; others were obviously wrigglers who would be begging to get up in fifteen minutes.

Mrs. Trent and I moved off to a corner, where we sat on a pile of rugs. From this vantage point, we could spot potential trouble before it got out of hand. I started to whisper a question, but she held up a hand and gave me a notebook, instead. *Good thinking.* Our talk would only encourage the kids to chatter instead of sleep.

So I wrote, *What do we do with those who refuse to nap?*

She replied, *Wait half an hour, then give them a book. Per regs, they have to rest quietly for two hours. We can't make them sleep.*

*Gotcha.*

She added, *Usually, I go to lunch now, but I'll stay for the first hour, until most of them fall asleep.*

*Okay, thanks.*

*If a kid gives you problems after I leave, rub his back. That sometimes works. If it escalates to tantrum territory, call me.* Then she scrawled her number. *I'll come in to regulate.*

The kids were fine, though. Fifteen of them dropped off in the first twenty minutes, and another succumbed as Mrs. Trent slipped out to take a well-deserved break. As if that was his cue, Sam popped up on his cot. *Oooh, you little faker.*

He peered around the room. "Nadia?"

I navigated through sleeping children, afraid he'd wake them up, and it would be a huge, chaotic mess when Mrs. Trent got back. Kneeling down beside him, I whispered, "What is it?"

"I can't sleep. There's too much breathing."

"Do you want to look at a book?" If I'd known he was still awake, I'd have offered him one earlier.

"Okay."

He was close enough to the window that I wasn't worried about his eyesight. I got him the book Mrs. Trent had read earlier, thinking it might help if he was familiar with it, since

I didn't have a clear sense of Sam's reading aptitude. Some four-year-olds could sound out words like first graders—others were still struggling to remember what sound each letter made.

"Can you sit next to me?"

Without answering, I slid down, wedged between Sam and the wall. I could still see all the other kids, though. He turned onto his stomach and opened the book. At this point, I wasn't sure it was even worth trying, but I followed Mrs. Trent's advice and rubbed his back in little circles. Honest to God, I was surprised when he shoved the book to the side and flopped on his pillow. Sam gave me a sleepy smile and then closed his eyes. His breath evened out, joining the rest of the class. It was silly how happy it made me, as if I'd scaled Everest or invented a lifesaving vaccine.

On tiptoe, I went back to the carpet pile, and when Mrs. Trent flipped the lights on, the kids were bright-eyed, ready to put their stuff away. She got them settled for snack while I wiped down and put away the cots. Afterward, another potty break, and then they lined up so they could take their turn playing outside. In a month or so, this ritual would include jackets, then hats and scarves, and eventually, they'd lose outdoor playtime to frosty weather. Usually, I'd have been pulled away by now, so it was interesting to see how routine made things easier.

Mrs. Trent led them out the side door and onto the playground. I came last to make sure nobody was left behind. Sam immediately ran for the slide while some kids raced for the swings, and others jumped on wobbly bees and dragonflies. I circulated, giving a push here, admiring a rock there, until the break was over. When we took them inside, it was almost four, and time for more face- and hand-washing.

While I set out crayons and pictures to color, Mrs. Trent

sat down to write up her daily reports, detailing any problems or milestones. I got the kids settled and sat with them while they created masterpieces for their parents, who started arriving half an hour later. I shook a lot of hands, confirmed that I would be replacing Elaine part-time and made people happy by confessing that I was a college junior, studying education. By 5:15 p.m. we were down to thirteen students, and Sam was one of them.

"One more pickup, and you can head out, Nadia."

"That would be great." As a floater, I often ended up closing the facility down, and I had homework waiting, not to mention more reading, and a sample lesson plan project with only a week until it was due.

Ty was the next person to walk in. Sam jumped up from the table and ran to him, waving his picture excitedly. He had about a thousand things to say, all at once, and his dad beamed, like *this* was the best part of his day, and it made everything else worth it. Quite often, at pickup, the dads were impatient or irritated; Ty's interaction with his son only made him seem hotter.

*I've got to get over this.*

"...and I slept for, like, twelve hours!" Sam finished.

He glanced at me, brow raised, so I clarified, "It was more like forty-five minutes."

"But he did nap? Impressive. He stopped sleeping during the day with my aunt when he was three."

"Everyone else was napping," Sam said. "It was really quiet."

I hung back while Mrs. Trent chatted over first-day impressions, then she gave Ty the report. Left to my own devices, I probably would've lingered to avoid potential awkwardness, but Mrs. T turned and made a shooing motion. "I'm down to twelve. Get out of here."

So I signed out, grabbed my purse and left with Ty and Sam, who was swinging hard on his dad's arm. Ty carried his backpack, glancing over at me now and then with an inscrutable look. But Mrs. Keller flagged me at the front door.

"Forms, remember? It won't take long."

I waved as Ty led Sam out. Five minutes later, I followed. It was dumb to be disappointed that the silver Focus was gone. I climbed into my Toyota and drove home. Our timing was off because Ty's car was parked but they were already inside. I had no excuse to see him again, and I didn't know if he wanted to go back to the balcony chats, after Saturday night. Maybe some distance would be good? Tired, I trudged up to our apartment and found everyone at home. At this hour, that was so surprising that I pretended to stare at them suspiciously.

"Is this an intervention?"

Lauren narrowed her eyes. "Have you been up to something that calls for it?"

"Probably," I said, smirking.

She demanded that I spill, but I couldn't. The whole Ty thing was complicated; I felt like I'd be violating his privacy if I dished like he was just any other guy, and there was Sam to consider. So I just shrugged and fell into the recliner, since Lauren was cuddling with Angus while making Max rub her feet. *One of these days, I have to learn that trick.* With natural blond hair and blue eyes, Lauren was pretty, though she was constantly saying she needed to lose twenty pounds. More to the point, she was sweet and had been at age seven, when she became my best friend by hitting Billy Derwent in the head with a glue bottle; he was trying to steal my lunch at the time.

"Your secrecy is starting to trouble me," she said in an ominous tone.

"I'll talk only when there's something to say."

"Said no woman ever." Angus groaned when Lauren elbowed him.

"Fascinating as this is," Max cut in, "I was wondering if you guys want to go to the dollar house tonight."

There were two cinemas in Mount Albion, a regular-priced new cineplex, and a grubby, cut-rate one that had four screens and you paid between two and four dollars for a ticket, depending on the type of movie. Old blockbusters were usually four; the weird shit Max liked to watch was generally two.

"I still haven't forgiven you for *Thankskilling,*" Lauren said. "But if I get to a good stopping point on my history paper, I could be persuaded to go sit in the dark and eat nachos."

Angus shook his head. "Pass for me. Josh is cooking dinner."

"Fancy," I said.

"Oh, it'll be revolting. But I didn't have the heart to say no. He's so cute when he tries." Angus shoved Lauren off him and got up. "Speaking of which, I need to get moving."

"What about you, Conrad? If you *don't* go, Lauren might get overexcited over riding on the back of my bike. She might even think this is a date. It'll be anarchy."

"Cats living with dogs," I said seriously.

I thought for a few seconds, listening to Angus bang around his room, presumably looking for something. He ran out a few seconds later. If I stayed home, I would have complete privacy for a balcony chat. On the other hand, I'd been neglecting my roomies lately, and I couldn't let my fascination with Ty bloom into a full obsession, especially when he had been crystal clear about his intentions.

"I'm in, as long as we go to the late show. I have work to do first."

"All work and no play, something something, make me a sandwich?" Max tried.

I smacked him on the way to the kitchen for some ramen, then I took the cup to my room and cracked open a virtual textbook while I ate. The reading went fast—well, for *me;* my lesson plan project less so, but I typed up some ideas and compiled a folder full of samples to give me more direction. Later, Lauren came in and got on her laptop, tapping away on her paper.

By nine, Max was wandering around our room, bored and touching things. When he opened my underwear drawer, I kicked him. "Fine, I get it. You're ready to leave."

I went in the bathroom, tried to tame my curls and brushed my teeth. Then I dodged into the closet and changed my shirt. The jeans were fine. I added a swipe of gloss, a beanie when I realized my hair was horrible, and emerged, scowling.

"It's about time." Lauren grinned to show she was kidding.

"I take it I'm driving."

"If only I had a sidecar," Max said.

Though I grumbled, I didn't mind playing chauffeur. Max climbed in the back, letting Lauren have shotgun. I turned the music up really loud—to the point that it was impossible to do anything but scream along. Turned out it was a horror-movie parody Max wanted to see, so it was two bucks, as predicted. I ate nachos and chocolate for dinner, plus I laughed a lot.

*Not bad.*

It was late when we got home because Max talked us into swinging by the diner for midnight pancakes. They were delicious, but now I had to add a gym visit to my to-do list tomorrow. While Lauren and Max went straight to bed, I made a cup of tea and drank it alone on the balcony. *Ty must be in bed by now.* His patio was dark apart from the fading twinkle of his solar lights, and his living room lamp was off, too.

I drained the mug in a hurry and didn't look up at the stars, not remotely ready to see if they'd shine as bright without him. It couldn't happen, and I planned to fight this feeling, no surrender, until I could treat Ty with the same affection I gave my roomies.

"We could've been so good together," I whispered to the night.

Leaving *if only* behind, I squared my shoulders and went silently inside.

*

# CHAPTER EIGHT

The rest of September, I was strong.

I went to school and hung out with friends, did coursework, turned in my project on time and continued to doubt myself as I struggled in the practicum. Pretty much the only time I saw Ty was when he picked Sam up from school. Since he didn't ask why I'd backed off, I figured he knew. If he minded, he'd say something, right? This wasn't the typical dating move—run to see if he'll chase you. It was far more basic and for the sake of self-preservation. I'd skated right up to the edge of falling for him, and had fallen hard, but since he was honest with me about his situation, I regrouped.

After that first time, Ty never acted like he didn't know me. When our paths crossed outside the building or at the fitness center, we made casual conversation. He was friendly. Sometimes we talked about how Sam was doing at day care. If it stung a bit for things to be like this when we had so much damned potential, well, it was better than huge heartbreak later.

*I'm being sensible. It makes no sense to fixate on a guy I can't have.*

Things were on a pretty even keel, and I wasn't horrified by my test scores, mostly As and Bs. I had almost forgotten—okay, not at all—the rush of excitement I'd felt waiting for Ty on the balcony, so I was surprised to find him waiting one night after work. He'd picked Sam up and they left the building before me, but as I stepped outside, I saw them in the parking lot.

"Do you have a minute?" he asked.

"Sure." I was too startled to say anything else.

"Let me get Sam squared away. Walk us to the car?"

"Please, Nadia?" The small Tyler gazed up at me imploringly, and I probably wouldn't say no if he asked for a kidney.

"No problem, bud."

He looked at me mock-reproachfully. "My name is Sam." Then he laughed, because he never tired of that game.

While I'd spent less time with his dad lately, I spent twenty-odd hours a week with Sam. He was smart, adorable, funny, all-around awesome. Late at night, after doing my homework, I got on joke sites because he was obsessed with dinosaurs. So now, whenever I first saw him, I had to come up with a new one every time as a greeting. Today it was: *What do you get when dinosaurs crash their cars? Tyrannosaurus wrecks!* Then I wrote out the words, so he could really appreciate the joke. The day before, I hit him with, *What do you call it when a dinosaur makes a goal with a soccer ball? A dino-score!* His giggle was seriously the light of my life.

Tonight he melted my heart by hugging me tight around the neck and giving me a wet kiss on the cheek. "See you Monday!"

Then Ty buckled him into his car seat and shut the door, giving us a moment of privacy. I hadn't let myself think about him or miss him, but right then, those repressed feelings swamped me. I was probably doing the hungry staring at the moment but I couldn't help it.

"It feels like I haven't talked to you in forever," he said quietly.

"Been a few weeks."

"But you're never out of mind. Sam's favorite sentence these days starts with 'Nadia says…' He's always chattering about you."

Trying for a friendly smile, I answered, "I'm glad he likes it here. I wouldn't have recommended it if I didn't honestly think it's a great environment."

"Yeah. That's not what I wanted to talk to you about, though."

"What's up?" My faux-chipper expression wouldn't give anything away, right?

Ty put a hand on my shoulder. "Stop that. Stop."

"Huh?"

"Be real. Be *you*."

It shook me that he knew me well enough already to understand that three weeks away from him hadn't cured my feelings or even lessened them. *Damn. I was so totally fooling myself.* The warmth of his palm nearly melted my spine. Somehow I managed not to lean into him.

"Okay." My smile dropped, and I gave him what he wanted. *This face, you show me everything.* "I missed you. But it seemed like a good idea to back off. We got in deep that night."

"True, it was a little fast, and I'm not known for insta-bonding. So I appreciate the thinking time. And…I'd like to take you up on that offer, if it still stands."

My heart skittered. "Which one?"

"Broken Arrow is playing this weekend, and I've been

curious about their live shows. I'm dropping Sam off with my parents tonight. Would you go with me tomorrow?"

For a few seconds, I considered playing it cool. This was short notice, but if Lauren was asking, I wouldn't blink over last-minute plans. "Absolutely. I'm going to a party tonight, but I haven't made plans for Saturday yet."

"I'd say I'll pick you up, but it makes more sense for you to come downstairs when you're ready."

"Agreed. What kind of place is it?" I was wondering how I should dress.

"Underground whiskey bar, styled after a speakeasy. Do you know what that is?"

"Are you serious? Roaring '20s. Prohibition. I *did* take U.S. History."

He smiled down at me and the humor went clear through to his eyes, lighting them from within. "You're cute when you're defensive. Don't take it personally. Most people in our age bracket would blank stare in response to the word *speakeasy*."

"God, the way you talk."

"I'm not a silver-tongued devil, I take it?"

I smirked. "Closer with the grumpy asshole warning."

"You're breaking my heart. Anyway, jeans will be fine, unless you just can't resist dressing like a flapper. I respect the need for cosplay."

The minute he said that, I mentally ransacked my closet, trying to remember if I had anything sparkly that could fit the bill. "You'll just have to wait and see."

"I refuse. I'll invent a time machine as soon as I get home."

"I highly suspect that will take longer than twenty-four hours."

"Always, the ladies underestimate me," he said mournfully.

*If only you knew how colossally untrue that is.*

But I kept it light. "The true burden of greatness is being so painfully misunderstood in your own time."

"You *do* get me. I have Sam's bag in the car, and I'm having dinner with my parents, so I won't be home until later." My expression must've given away my confusion, because he added, "In case you change your mind or something. Maybe I should give you my number, just in case."

Getting out my phone, I said, "Go for it."

There was no way I'd decide not to go tomorrow, but he didn't know that, and even if I did, I could knock on his door and tell him. But I *wanted* his cell info, and I texted Test right away, so he'd have mine.

The message popped up with a ping, and Ty smiled, so pleased that I wanted to capture that expression for posterity. "So that's you, huh?"

"Yep. Gotcha." With a smirk, I snapped a picture of him.

"I think you just invaded my privacy." But he didn't ask me to see it or to delete the pic. Instead, with a measured sort of consideration, he took one of me. "And that's payback."

I flushed, beyond pleased that he'd reciprocated. *Stop it, you can't get all crazy over this.* "We're good to go?"

"Yeah. See you."

Tapping on the glass made Sam glance up from his picture book. I waved to them both as Ty got in the car, and then I jogged to the Toyota. Before I left the parking lot, I created a contact for him, adding all the information I possessed, including the picture I'd just taken. The sun was behind him, adding gold lights to his auburn hair. Crinkles beside his eyes made him even more adorable, and his lips were slightly parted. *This face. I could love this face. And everything about the guy that goes along with it.*

In hindsight, it would've been much wiser to explain that

I liked him too much to make a go of the friendship thing, so sorry, but there were limits to my capacity for self-denial. Hanging out with Ty, even if it was tempting, frustrating even, would likely be the best part of my weekend. I drove home, practically bouncing with excitement.

I might've exaggerated when I said there was a party tonight. Angus had invited us to Josh's to catch up on *Project Runway*. Max wasn't going, but Lauren and I were, along with a couple of other friends, Courtney and Darius, who wasn't gay. He was just into fashion.

Lauren was pacing when I came in. "Do you know how many times Josh has texted me?"

"Twenty-seven?"

"Eight." She sounded disgruntled that by overguessing I'd made the situation seem less dire. "I told him to calm his tits and start without us if necessary."

"Just let me change out of beige and navy, then we'll leave, I swear."

True to my word, I took the world's quickest shower, dressed in jeans and a hoodie, and then raced to the living room. "Let's go."

Josh had a fantastic apartment, nicer than ours, and closer to campus, too. He didn't have roommates, so there was nobody to bitch at him for hogging the TV with four hours of *Project Runway*. We joked around, ordered pizza, mocked the designers and generally sucked the juice out of the lime called life. There was beer, but I had only one since I was driving.

"Tim Gunn is a god," Angus said.

"Pretty sure I saw a movie where he was actually playing God," Courtney informed us.

Josh got his iPad and searched until he found it. "Not God,

but some kind of heavenly associate. I approve. Another night, you will be mine, *Teen Spirit*."

Shortly thereafter, the *party* broke up. Lauren and I headed out together while Angus stayed at Josh's. She looked pensive as I drove.

"Something wrong?"

"Just your standard existential life crisis."

"Lay it on me."

"I'm just questioning if I can actually make a difference. PoliSci seems like so much crap, and I wonder if they're grooming me to become a slick-shit politician."

"Do you want to change your major?" People did it all the time, but she likely wouldn't graduate with us if she did.

"Maybe. I don't know. That's part of the problem." Her tone sounded strange enough that I glanced over.

"What is?"

She sighed. "Never mind. It's possible that I'm freaking out because they'll expect us to get real jobs soon. This year, next, and then you'll be gone, teaching somewhere. Who knows what I'll be doing? Probably asking people if they want fries with that." She forced a laugh, but I could tell she was seriously stressed.

I couldn't let her think she was alone in questioning… everything. "This practicum is kicking my ass, dude. It's, like, 100 percent harder than I expected, and the kids break my heart in a hundred different ways. Sometimes I can tell they want to learn something so bad, but the pathways just won't connect. That's when they explode or throw stuff—there's this one girl who rocks and moans. And I want so bad to fix it, but I can't, and that's the reality I'll be facing for the next thirty years. I can *help* but I can't—"

"Wow," Lauren breathed. "Sounds like you have your own existential crisis."

"I don't know if I'm strong enough for special needs. I *want* to be. Not sure if I am."

"Helps to know I'm not the only one worried about The Future and Real Life."

I thought about that as I pulled into our complex. "That's part of the problem, LB, labeling this, right now, as *not life*. I mean, we work, we're paying rent. We play around sometimes, but it's real. Every moment is. And I know there will come a time when I am sad as hell to wake up in the middle of the night and not find you there."

She stared at me for a few seconds, and then I got a ferocious scowl as she swiped at her eyes. "I could kill you for making me cry tonight, seriously."

"Liar." I hugged her and then got out of the car. "If you want, I'll whip up some no-bake cookies and we can talk about how crappy our prospects are, instead of our feelings."

"Can we watch TV instead?"

"Totally."

I went in the kitchen and made a batch from memory. Since I'd been cooking these since I was twelve, they came out perfect. When I came back to the living room, Lauren was watching some action flick; she curled her lip at rom-coms, which you wouldn't guess by looking. On the surface, she seemed like a girlie-girl, but past precedent suggested that she preferred first-person shooter games and movies with lots of car chases and explosions. In high school, she spent more time online, coding or playing MMOs, but these days, she was a party beast.

Ten minutes later, I got up. "I stuck them in the freezer so they'd set faster. Should be done now."

"Then bring me my cookies, woman." She waved an imperious hand.

Refusing to feel guilty, I plunked eight on a plate, then delivered with a flourish. Lauren inhaled deeply, then aimed a mock-accusing look upward. "You're trying to fatten me up so you can eat me during the lean times. Aren't you?"

"Please stop writing *Hunger Games* fan fiction. Seriously. I'm begging. Also, half of these are for me, and I will totally bite you if you try to nom them."

We watched half the movie and ate all eight cookies before Lauren fell asleep. I pulled the throw over her and turned to head down the hall when my phone pinged. Picking it up, the screen said 2:37 a.m., 1 message. I tapped it. The picture of Ty popped up.

I hear you walking around. Do you KNOW what time it is?

Grinning, I sent back, Adventure time?

Don't tempt me. I'm completely unsupervised.

Shouldn't you be asleep? I thought you had epic plans tomorrow night.

Maybe that's why I can't sleep. Come outside?

As we were closer to October, the nights held a chill instead of the balmy warmth left over from a summer day. So I took a blanket with me, along with my gift drop basket. Luckily, the TV was still on, or I'd probably have woken Lauren going outside. I had four chocolate no-bakes neatly lined up, and as soon as I spotted Ty, I lowered the basket to him.

"Bribing your neighbor to stop complaining about your

night-stomping with baked goods? That's shady. Felony territory." But he emptied the basket before sending it up.

"Not at all. These are stove-top hush cookies, a misdemeanor at best."

I was about to settle into my chair when Ty said, "Come down."

My heart thumped like crazy. "My roommate's asleep on the couch. I might wake her."

"Then climb over. I'll catch you."

"Are you *crazy?*"

"Probably. Get your keys and then come down."

The safe thing to do would be to say no. But I failed at self-preservation by sneaking in to grab my house keys, and then I came back out, quietly closing the balcony door behind me. Lauren stirred but she didn't wake. Good thing, because she'd scream bloody murder if she saw me clambering over the edge of the balcony like this. I lowered myself slowly down the bars until I was hanging from the bottom of the ledge. Ty's hands wrapped around my ankles.

"I've got you, don't worry."

"I'm trusting you." It was a crazy, reckless leap, but he caught me. For a few perfect seconds, he just held me against him, but all too soon he set me on my feet. His hands slipped down my arms, and it seemed as if he lingered a beat too long, another. Silent, forbidden touching that argued that no matter how we tried, we'd never only be friends.

"You're cold," he said. "Let me get a blanket."

In a flash, he came back with the chenille throw from the couch. It took all my self-control not to point out that his bed was probably even warmer. Ty led me over to the wicker love seat, and it gave me such a happy jolt to settle beside him. His patio was prettier close-up, and I admired it until he distracted me by dropping an arm around my shoulders. It could've passed as companionable, but we both knew the truth. Or *I* did, at least. Yet it didn't stop me from snuggling into him, soaking in every shade of this experience.

"You know something?" he said quietly.

"Many somethings. But probably not the one you're referring to."

"The night of the party, I woke up before you did. Your head was back against the couch and I could've said something like, *It's time for you to leave.* Instead, I made us more comfortable. You didn't stir once."

"Why?" I asked.

"I just…didn't want you to go. I was simultaneously relieved and disappointed when Sam got me up later and you were gone."

"Did he wonder why you weren't in bed?"

"Nah. I've crashed out on the couch before while watching TV."

"That's good at least." Pulling my legs to the side let me lean on Ty a little more, and by the way his arm tightened, he didn't mind.

"You really got in my head that night."

"What do you mean?"

"What you told me. About watching? Now it's my favorite thing to think about."

A surge of heat went through me. "Me, watching you?"

"Yeah." He was looking at my mouth again. "If I'm not fantasizing about kissing you, then it's that, and it never was before. You're driving me crazy."

"I'm not doing anything," I protested.

Ty ran his fingers through my hair, conflict etched in the play of shadow on his face. "That's part of the problem."

*

# CHAPTER NINE

"If I thought this is what you really want…" I hesitated long enough for him to say, *Yes, let's go for it. There's nothing stopping us.* The night was quiet apart from the wind whispering through the leaves. Deliberately, I pulled back, though I hated it when his hands dropped away.

"See you later?" His expression was unreadable; I couldn't tell if he was pleased or disappointed that I respected his boundaries.

But if he'd changed his mind about us, he needed to say so. Otherwise, I couldn't move forward without worrying that he'd regret it. I slipped out of the blanket and let myself out of the garden by the external gate, then I circled around to the front doors. Every muscle was tense as I slipped into the apartment, fearing I'd wake Lauren, and then have to answer questions about where I'd gone.

Max and I froze at the same time, eyes on each other, silently assessing. His face was naked and frightened when he realized I'd caught him being sweet. Lauren was sound asleep in his arms, and I guessed he was on the verge of carrying her to bed. So I made a *go ahead* gesture, but I didn't speak. I was waiting with arms folded, one foot tapping silently, when he came back from tucking her in.

"How long has this been going on?" I whispered.

In the half-light from the flickering TV, his expression was an odd mixture of embarrassment and defiance. "What?"

"You're into her."

I was waiting for him to deny it, but he flopped onto the couch with a deep sigh. "So? It's not happening."

"This is why you wanted me to come to the movies the other night. You didn't want to be alone with her."

"I *do*," he said quietly. "She just doesn't want it back."

"Am I actually hearing this? I could be persuaded to help, if you can convince me you don't just want to hump and dump her."

"If I got with Lauren, I wouldn't be doing the leaving."

"But Courtney, at the party—"

"We kissed, yeah. Afterward, we were bouncing a basketball off my door, genius. Neither one of us was particularly in a festive mood."

"But it was your idea." Then I realized the truth. "Because *Lauren* wanted to celebrate her new job. Damn, Max. I had no idea."

I thought back, and for the past six months, more even, any little thing Lauren hinted at, Max made it happen. Not in a way that anyone would notice, of course; he was subtler than that. My heart ached a bit for him, but he and I had never been that close, more *joke around* friends than *heartfelt moment* ones.

"Nobody does," he said with a shrug.

"You were kind of weird when she was gossiping with Angus before. I wondered what was up then."

"I was jealous. He's funny, he's interesting, and she's always snuggled up with him."

"You remember he's gay?"

"He's still got more with her than I'll ever have. I didn't say it was reasonable."

"Is there anything I can do?"

"Sure." He turned a laser-sharp stare my way. "Explain why you were coming in past 3:00 a.m. with no shoes."

I could've lied, but I doubted anything I came up with on the fly would fool Max, and since I knew one of his secrets, it seemed right that I should answer honestly. "I've been hanging out with our downstairs neighbor off and on."

He didn't react like I expected, a frown building. "Did he hit you up for a booty call?"

"God, I *wish*. But no, we're just friends."

"So we're in the same predicament." Max's expression lightened, and he reached over to tousle my hair. "But don't let some asshole use you for sex, Conrad. You're better than that."

"Hello, double standard. What if I want to use him for sex?"

Max cocked his head. "It'd be a lot less complicated if I asked *you* out."

"Please. You have your pick of partners who're just looking for some fun." Standing up, I kissed the top of his head. "G'night."

Lauren was snuggled in bed, oblivious as to how she got there, when I completed my bedtime ritual and climbed under the covers. Since it was almost four in the morning, I slept in the next day, until nearly noon. The rest of my no-bakes were gone, which pissed me off, since I'd planned to eat them for breakfast. *Oats and peanut butter is healthy, dammit.* Instead, I had to make do with generic cereal.

I had a text waiting from Ty.

Forgot to tell you what time. Show starts at eight. It's an hour drive. So by seven if you can.

I replied, See you then.

All my roomies were sprawled in the living room, and Angus looked like shit. Normally, he was the best put-together of us all, even for apartment lounging, but today he was wearing sweats, and his hair had no product at all. A plate sat nearby that showed signs he was responsible for my missing cookies. I sat down beside him. Both Lauren and Max mouthed something, trying to warn me.

"What happened?" I asked.

Max groaned. "Crap, we just got his mind off it."

"Josh cheated on me," Angus said flatly.

I frowned at Max. "Look at that face. You didn't distract him at all. Do you want to talk about it?" I said to Angus.

He acted like he didn't hear me. "The insane thing is, it happened last summer. I had *no* idea. He claims it was one time, while I was in Europe for three weeks."

"Why the hell did he tell you now?" Lauren wondered.

"He said he needed to clear his conscience, otherwise he'd feel too guilty for us to build a future together."

"That makes sense," Max said. "Sounds like he's serious and wants a clean slate going forward. If he feels bad every time he looks at you, it'll poison your relationship."

Neither of the other two noticed how thoughtful and serious a response that was, how *unlike* the Max we'd known since freshman year. Before, he was all about the quick comeback, refusing to get deep, refusing to admit he had emotions at all. He was the life of the party, and as far as anyone could tell, that was all there was to him. I knew better now.

"But he doesn't get a free pass at Angus's expense," Lauren argued. "He's the one who acted like a dick, and now he's doing it again by hurting him with this sudden confession."

"True," Max said. "But sometimes you just have to tell the truth, even when it's tough."

I nodded. "Yeah. Any future they built together would be founded on bullshit. It sucks, but Angus has to decide if he can forgive Josh before they'll have anything real."

"Lauren, I appreciate the unconditional love." Angus hugged her.

She was always fiercely, ferociously on the side of people she cared about—didn't matter if they were even in the right. Lauren always had your back, and that was what I loved most about her. No matter how much she'd changed, that part stayed the same. Her face over Angus's shoulder looked so sad, like she was the one with the cheating boyfriend, or a problem too heavy to solve alone, but she blinked away the tears with a determined lift of her chin.

"You know it," she murmured.

Angus went on, "It's awful, and I feel like puking, but Josh telling me? It was the right call. At this point, I don't know if I can move past this, but I'm…glad he told me."

"You feel like barfing because you inhaled all my cookies, feeling-eater." I smiled, rubbing Angus's back.

He narrowed his eyes. "In retrospect…they were fucking delicious and I'd do it again."

"I can hang out today, but I have plans tonight. Will you be okay?"

"I'm taking him shopping," Lauren put in.

Angus sighed. "I don't want to go."

Max pretended to fall out of his chair. "Call the paramedics."

I was hoping Angus's situation would divert attention from my plans, but Lauren was too sharp. "Where are *you* going that Angus can't come in his hour of need?"

Time to tell them…something, though Max already knew. I kept my tone casual. "Ty, the guy who lives in 1B, asked me to go to a club in the city. We're seeing Broken Arrow."

"Oh, my God. You're dating Hot Ginger?" Lauren said that so loud, I wouldn't be surprised if Ty heard it. I pondered crawling under my bed and never coming out.

"We're going as friends," I said firmly.

Angus put in, "That sucks. He's delicious." When I raised my brows, he added, "What? Looking is *not* cheating."

I could only say softly, "He is pretty delicious."

"Maybe he'll get drunk and grope you," Lauren offered.

Max wore a horrified yet fascinated look. "That's not something a girl wants. Is it?"

"If she's into the guy, she does, especially if he's not making the move sober." Lauren seemed ready to argue with him, and I left them to it.

A long, long shower restored some of my equilibrium, and then I exfoliated, treating this like a date even though I had assured them it wasn't. When I waxed my legs, I told myself it was because I might wear a dress, not because Ty might be touching them. Afterward, I moisturized and used a light bronzer, so they wouldn't look pasty.

"Wow," Lauren said, coming into our room. "You're really into this guy."

I could've denied it, but that would've been pointless. "It's not going anywhere. He has a four-year-old, he works full-time, takes college night classes, and he doesn't date."

"Ouch. Your odds of a happily-ever-after don't seem high.

But let me do your toes, anyway." She smiled and got out her kit, chock-full of sparkling colors. "Ruby-red?"

"I think so."

To show her support, Lauren gave me a full mani-pedi. Since her self-makeover, her whole outlook had changed. At this point, she knew way more about beauty than me. Once she finished, I lounged around for an hour to make sure I didn't ruin the polish. By now, it was almost five, and I was hungry but too nervous to eat. *It's not a date,* I kept telling myself, but I couldn't seem to internalize that fact.

"Want me to do your hair and face?"

This was part of why I loved her. Though she was worried about Angus, she'd also noticed that tonight was a big deal. No prying questions, she accepted what I offered in front of everyone else, and she was doing her best to back me up, even if she didn't 100 percent get what was going on. Hell, neither did I.

"That would be great."

"What are you wearing? That will determine how I make you up."

Standing up, I duck-stepped to the closet, still being careful of my toes. I had exactly four dresses, one of which I'd worn in my cousin's wedding, and never wanted to put on again. The other three were wrong, too, just in different ways. Lauren came to join me, then she dug into her side of the walk-in.

"I stopped being able to borrow your clothes in junior high, LB."

"This one might work. It never hung right on me. I think it'll be a mini on you, but try it. See how it looks."

It was a white, diaphanous wisp of a dress, all chiffon and flutters, not the sort of thing I'd usually wear, but it was enough of a nod at flapper-style that I was willing to try.

Shrugging out of my clothes, I pulled it over my head. Lauren had more chest and butt, less leg, so it was slightly loose, and it hit three inches above my knees.

"How is it?"

"It looks really cute. You'll need a jacket, though."

"The red one?" I tried it on.

"I think you look fantastic." She swung the closet door closed, so I could look in the full-length mirror on the back of it. "Shoes?"

Since I wore a ten, and she wore a seven and a half, she couldn't help me there. I settled on a pair of silver wedge sandals. Lauren agreed they looked fine, even if they wouldn't be her first choice, but my other options were boots, more boots and Converse.

"Okay, I'll finish your hair and makeup." She draped a towel around my shoulders to keep the dress clean, then she went to work.

When she finished, I was honestly stunned. Part of me had been a bit afraid it would come out beauty-pageant overdone, and that Ty would think I was trying too hard, but she'd gone for sun-kissed subtle with slightly heavier hits on lips and eyes; mine had never looked so blue. I had rarely looked so striking, and my hair was fantastic. She'd loosened the curls and tamed them, so they cascaded down my back instead of sticking out every which way.

"You're hired."

"Glad you like it. If 1B can resist you tonight, then I'm afraid you're destined for his friend-zone forever."

When I walked into the living room, Max dropped the remote. "I don't think I can let you go out looking like that."

I grinned. "Your compliment is noted."

"Look at those legs," Angus said. "If you had more of a boy

bum, I could be persuaded to get drunk and do bad things with you."

Obviously, he was joking, though our freshman year before he came out, Angus had a girlfriend, and nobody knew how far that had gone. It wasn't the kind of thing you could ask politely. From what I recalled, she had been thin to the point of boyishness. He didn't talk about Chelsea, and after their breakup, she didn't stay in our friend circle. The grapevine suggested she was pretty wrecked, though, and she had all kinds of self-doubt, like she should've noticed before he surprised her with the confession.

"You can't make Josh jealous with me," I pointed out.

He acknowledged that with a sigh. "Turn, show me the rest."

I pivoted, showing off the arch of my calves. *Hmm. How tall is Ty?* The sandals put me over six feet, and some guys got testy if you loomed; I'd dated a depressing number of them. In fact, my high school boyfriend's height had more to do with the duration of our relationship than chemistry or personality. Then I reminded myself that it didn't matter how tall Ty was.

*This isn't a date.*

"Fabulous. Should I be hurt that you two managed without me?"

That was a joke since Angus had never frolicked into our closets to do spontaneous consultations. Sometimes he told me my shoes were terrible, but that was the limit of our personal fashion bonding. Since I loved my Chucks, I didn't usually care what he thought of them. But it was a good sign that he felt well enough to tease me.

"Definitely not. Lauren would've been sad if you had stolen her glory."

"Maybe I should become a celebrity stylist if I drop PoliSci," she said, thoughtful.

That started a whole different conversation, one that lasted fifteen minutes. I sat down to watch TV while Max tried to get inside Lauren's head. Like everyone else, she rebuffed him with witty banter. I'd never seen her connect with a guy, though she used to spy on my brother with hardcore dedication. That was years ago, though. Most of us had an embarrassing crush we'd rather not discuss—for me, it was Matt Pomerico, the dude I stalked through junior high.

"What time is your chariot leaving?" Max glanced over at me, raising a dark brow.

"Seven."

Angus observed, "You're half an hour early. That says you're anxious."

"Thanks for that," I mumbled. "What happened to shopping?"

"We're waiting for you to leave," Lauren informed me. "How else can I judge his reaction to my kick-ass cosmetology?"

I sighed, tempted to make a break for it, but in these shoes, they'd catch me. There was no help for it but to endure. At ten to seven, I stood up, brushed my teeth and came back to the living room with my purse. All three of them were waiting by the door.

"Please tell me you're not walking me to his apartment."

Max laughed. "She's screwing with you. We're going to dinner."

"Thank God."

Though we all left together, they went straight out the front while I continued to Ty's apartment. Maybe some of Lauren's teasing had taken root, though, because I fantasized about him taking one look at me then shoving me against the wall. I needed that kiss, to dig my fingers into his shoulders and wrap my legs around his hips. The reasonable me would never press him, never ask for more than he was willing to give, but I wanted him so bad it hurt. His words. My pulse thundered in my ears.

At my knock, Ty threw the door open and literally froze. His eyes locked on mine, then they swept lower, skimming my breasts, the flare of my hips, and the line of my legs. Usually, I hated when guys did that instead of maintaining eye contact, but with him, I craved it. His gaze lingered on my thighs, and his hands curled into fists at his sides. A shuddering breath escaped him, a more visceral response than I'd dared expect.

"Wow." He sighed, shaking his head. "From this I can only extrapolate that you hate and want to kill me."

Not exactly the reaction I was expecting. "Excuse me?"

"I told you how I feel about your legs. Now you're showing them off, fully aware I'll be thinking about them all night."

Put that way, it did sound diabolical. I struggled not to reveal how much he turned me on, just with words. The fact that he was so honest about what he wanted and why he couldn't have it—Ty was perfect. How good would it be if we ever touched, if he ever lost control? Heat worked through me as I considered it even as I battled my longing, because if we fucked and he regretted it—not worth considering. In that scenario, our friendship went down in flames and didn't rise from the ashes like a phoenix. Afterward, there would be only awkward silence and endless remorse.

"My outfit was not, in fact, selected from homicidal design. Don't I look like a flapper?"

"You look like heaven. Let me get my keys."

# CHAPTER TEN

We walked out of the building in silence.

Ty opened the passenger door for me, a gesture that shot holes in my platonic pretense. I slid into the Focus and then looked for the lever to slide the seat back a few inches. He shook his head at me, grinning.

"Must everything you do be orchestrated to remind me?"

I cut him a look, smiling with my eyes. "Is it my fault you only give rides to hobbits?"

"My mother resembles that remark."

That surprised a laugh out of me. "Don't you mean *resents?*"

He winked. "You haven't seen her feet."

"If I ever meet her, I'm telling her you said that."

"She'll laugh," he predicted. "Plus, you were the one who mentioned hobbits. You can't implicate me without revealing your own complicity."

"Crap. Foiled again by logic."

"Feel free to mess with the radio or you can connect my iPod, if you want."

"That could be interesting." Taking that as an invitation, I opened the storage arm between us and plugged in his music player, then I set it on shuffle. "Let's see what your musical taste says about you."

"You already know more than most anyone."

*Not everything. Not about Sam or his mom, why she left or where you work.* The National came on first, but he'd already told me he liked them. *No secrets there.* I set the volume so we could talk.

"Really?"

"Yeah. It's never been this easy with anyone else."

The way my heart crimped, it actually hurt. "I know what you mean."

Before he could answer, his cell phone rang. Ty glanced at the screen and shook his head. "Nope. This is my only weekend off. Sam is the best kid ever, but he's not restful."

"Work?" I guessed.

"Yeah. Whenever a project hits a snag, the foreman calls me to sort it out. I didn't even know we had any crews working tonight." He sighed faintly. "I'll hear about ignoring the call on Monday. 'I took a chance on you, Tyler, but you have to pull your weight.'"

"Took a chance? Weren't you qualified?"

"Not really. My dad's buddy runs a construction company, and he needed an office manager. I didn't have any experience, and only general studies classes behind me, but my dad convinced him I was smart enough to learn on the job. So Bill hired me on the cheap with the understanding he'd only keep me if I made good on Dad's claims."

"How did that go?"

"The first year, I was exhausted and screwed up *all* the time. I had to learn so much shit, it's a wonder Bill didn't fire me. So I took some online management classes while going quietly insane. I've got a handle on things now, but…it was a long haul."

"Do you get calls on the weekends a lot? What about Sam?"

"It's usually some bullshit about paperwork, permits, did I file this or that, what did the inspector say again, that kind of thing. I don't take extra shifts, so Sam's fine."

He sounded so disgruntled that I had to ask, "Is there any part of the job you do like?"

"The benefits are good. And it's not bad to learn this side of building, considering that I want to work in design later on. And yeah, I know that architecture's a pretty depressed field right now, but it's supposed to rebound in five years or so. At the rate I'm going it'll take me that long to complete my undergrad work, let alone a master's."

"You don't need to justify your dreams to me, Ty."

"If that's true, you'd be the first," he muttered. "Anyway, sorry for letting work put me in a bad mood. Monday is soon enough to deal with whatever that was."

"You already warned me that you're a grumpy asshole," I pointed out.

"True." But he was utterly charming for the remainder of the drive.

He told me the history behind the whiskey bar we were going to. Apparently, it really was a speakeasy back in the twenties, and it was situated below another bar. I'd never been anywhere like that, so I was excited on that note alone, but going with Ty, that was the frosting on the cake. Downtown Ann Arbor was hopping, so we parked a few blocks away. He came around to open my door, and when I climbed out, I realized we were exactly at eye level.

"You're 6'1," I said.

He grinned. "Tonight, so are you."

"You don't mind?"

"I don't mind anything about you, Nadia."

Briefly, I entertained the idea of pushing him against the car, but I wrapped a choke chain around the impulse.

"Which way?" I murmured.

Ty set a hand in the small of my back to guide me, below the red jacket, so there was only the thin chiffon between his palm and my skin. He kept close as we walked, his hand on me like a claim. By the time we got to the venue, his palm felt like a searing brand. Though it had been a while, Ty had obviously been here before. He led me to the side steps and down into the cellar.

Inside, the ceilings were low and resembled chalkboards. Buckets of chalk sitting around indicated we were supposed to scrawl our own messages if we felt like it. The place was half-full, casual seating throughout. A few people were milling around; others had claimed conversation pits while still more preferred regular tables and chairs. The small stage gave the space a sense of intimacy; if the acoustics were good, this should be awesome.

Ty homed in on a pair of chairs toward the corner of the room, fairly close to the entertainment. With a glance, he confirmed it was fine with me, and I followed him over. Once I was seated, he said, "Get you a drink?"

"Sure. See what interesting beers they have. Something local, if possible."

"Your wish is my command."

I really wished he wouldn't say things like that. If *this* was how Ty treated a friend, then I'd eat Lauren's damned dress. Hungrily, I watched him walk away, admiring the fit of his jeans. Since he was wearing a blue-striped button-up and a navy corduroy jacket, I didn't think that was how he'd dress to hang out with a pal, either. *Talk about mixed messages.* But maybe he didn't realize how it was coming across, how much this seemed like a date.

"All set?" I asked, as he sat down next to me.

"I ordered the five-beer sampler. They brew all their beers on-site, apparently. And I got us a basket of thyme and cheddar biscuits."

"That sounds incredible." Until he said that, I didn't realize how hungry I was.

"They're my favorite thing here, though the pulled pork nachos are awesome, too."

I glanced down at my lap and grinned. "Thank you for thinking of my dignity."

"In that dress, I promise your dignity is not remotely on my mind."

*Okay, enough.* "Ty, you have to stop flirting with me. I can't take it."

"Sorry. It's just that when I look at you, I forget about being smart and reasonable and I just—" For once he seemed to be at a loss for words.

"I get it," I said softly. "You have the same pull for me. But you're the one who said you don't date."

"I'm sorry. We probably shouldn't even be here."

I stared at him. "Why?"

"Because no matter how I try, I can't think of you as my buddy Nadia, Sam's teacher Nadia, my cool neighbor Nadia. You're just Nadia, who I desperately want to see naked."

"You're not the only one struggling with that," I murmured.

"Why?" He paused for a single, mischievous beat. "You see yourself naked all the time."

I laughed, teasing him. "And it's *amazing*. Sometimes I don't leave the house for days."

The band came on then, forestalling whatever he might've said, but the glint in his eyes promised delightful retribution. The fact that we could joke around gave me hope for salvaging our friendship. If sex would ruin things, we could work around it. Right?

Five minutes later, the server brought beer and biscuits, so we had grub when the music started. Both were delicious; I sampled all five of the brews, though I didn't finish any. Ty devoured the rest. Broken Arrow's set lasted for two hours, give or take, and had more of a bluesy tone than I expected, given Ty's other musical inclinations, but the group was talented, full of energy and fun to watch. They engaged the audience, got us clapping and singing along. Since I didn't know the words, I mostly hummed. Then they played a fifteen-minute encore, at which point, Ty glanced toward the door.

"Should we head out?"

Just before eleven, the place was pretty packed. It was getting harder to hear him for people talking, and since we'd come to see the show—and now we had—the night was done. Disappointment flicked through me, yet I pushed to my feet.

"Sure. We have the drive back—"

"Are you in a hurry to get home?" he asked, visibly downcast.

"No, I thought you were."

"Then as long as we're in Ann Arbor, we can't go without dinner at the Fleetwood. They have the best meaty hash."

"I only understood half of those words."

"Can you walk in those shoes? From here, it's, like, three blocks, maybe five minutes at the most. It would probably take longer to move the car."

"Sure, I'm fine." As soon as I said that, turning to follow him, I stumbled on a crack in the sidewalk.

Ty grabbed my hand to steady me and he didn't let go. As our fingers laced together, I half closed my eyes, savoring the rasp of his calluses and the heat of his skin. Crazy that palm-on-palm contact could make me feel like this. Maybe it was because we'd agreed it would never happen, but the little things had never gotten to me so much before.

"This way, come on."

As promised, it wasn't far at all. The Fleetwood Diner was the consummate dive, housed in an Airstream trailer. Inside there were so few tables that it seemed like more than fifteen people couldn't fit, and it was chilly enough that sitting outside was out of the question. Luckily, a table for two was open and Ty grabbed it.

The servers were weird, rude almost, but Ty claimed that was part of the charm. Since I wanted to talk to him anyway and not the waitress, I was cool with that. On his advice, I got the meaty hash, and it was insanely good. While we ate, he talked a little more about his job, and from there, he moved on to his family.

I took the opening to ask, "Do you have any brothers or sisters?"

"Two sisters, both older. But they don't live in Michigan. Sarah's in California and Valerie went to Florida."

"Whoa. They both went a long way chasing the sun."

"You'll laugh but I swear that was exactly why they moved. No more Michigan winters. My mom and dad have talked about joining Val in a few years." He hesitated, scraping the food around on his plate with his fork. "I kinda suspect they're only still here because of me."

"In case you need help with Sam?"

"Yeah. I try not to make them feel like they're obligated, but—"

"They're your parents, and they love you. They love Sam, too. It's their choice, Ty. You have to learn how to accept help. Saying, *hey, I need a hand here* doesn't mean you're failing, only that you're human."

He scowled at me. "Have you been talking to my mom?"

"Yeah, we get together to gossip about you over coffee."

With a mock-shiver, he rubbed his arms. "That wouldn't surprise me. Mom is crafty."

By this time, the servers were giving us the stink eye, making me think this was a place where they encouraged you to eat and get out. Not surprising, considering the dining room size. Ty paid the bill over my protests and then we walked back to the car. When he took my hand, I didn't say anything, though I was steady on my feet.

*I love you,* I thought.

It wasn't rockets or fireworks or any of the Hollywood effects I'd been led to expect. Instead, it was crisp air lightly touched by the scent of burning wood, spiced with insatiable longing. A bonfire was burning nearby, and love was Ty's hand around mine, warm and fast, binding us together. Other people walked down the sidewalk, but they weren't part of *us.* They had their own lives, heading to clubs whose music pounded out of open doorways. This was a perfect moment, one I'd remember forever. *Because I've never been in love before.* It didn't matter that he didn't feel the same way, or that he wouldn't let himself.

*Not all love stories end happily. Sometimes they just end.*

And I could see the blind curve looming in the distance while I raced with him down this slope. At this point, the crash seemed inevitable, but I couldn't make myself leap out of the car. So I walked with him, noticing everything, like the way he matched his strides to mine without realizing, the way he turned to look at me when we passed beneath a lamppost, as if he didn't want to miss a single glimpse. His thumb slid back and forth over the heel of my hand, and he played with my fingers, shaping them, until longing spiraled inside me like a typhoon. My chest wasn't big enough to hold this feeling, for the sweet intensity of it.

For me, sex had always been about interlocking parts. Sometimes it felt *really* good, but I'd never fucked anyone and then had the urge to whisper, *You complete me.* I never cried afterward or felt much of anything, other than physical satisfaction. With Ty, I suspected it would be completely different. Not that I'd ever know.

*It'll be fine. You're tough.*

"You're quiet," he said as we reached the car.

"Just thinking."

"About…how I'm an ass and you can't wait to get away?"

"Not even close."

"Hmm, challenge accepted. Let me see if I can figure this out." As he helped me into the car, he seemed determined to make a game of guessing what was on my mind.

First he started the engine and drove us out of town, heading back toward Mount Albion. "You looked really serious. Is it about school?"

"Cold."

"Some guy you like?" Was he seriously asking that? But maybe he didn't realize how much of my mental attention he occupied.

"Warmer."

His half smile faded, as if I'd slapped him. "Do you have a boyfriend?"

"Not at the moment." There was no way I'd ever admit that I was pondering how awesome sex between us would be.

"Okay, I give. I don't want to talk about some guy you like." He shrugged. "Sorry, but I'm not there mentally. Give me a few months, maybe I can give advice then."

I rallied, teasing him. "Please, you don't even date, so what help would you be?"

"You have a point. And even when I did, it wasn't great."

*He's talking about Sam's mom.*

"Do you want to tell me?"

"No. Maybe." He gripped the wheel tightly, knuckles whitening. "It might change how you see me. I don't know if—"

"I'm willing to listen if you'd like to talk. We have an hour."

He exhaled in a slow rush, as if bracing to lift a heavy weight. In a way, maybe he was, but I hoped in sharing this with me, he'd also feel like he'd cast one off, too.

"Diana and I met freshman year. We got together right away, and I...I loved her *so* much." His voice cracked.

It hurt, hearing that. Ty, before, wasn't afraid of dating. Before Diana—now I knew her name—he must've been fearless. He believed in happy endings.

"She was clever. Ambitious. She was studying genetics and had her sights set on running her own lab by the time she was thirty."

*Wow.*

"Early in our sophomore year, she got bronchitis. She was on the pill, and they gave her antibiotics at the med center. Nobody said it could mess with the effectiveness of birth control."

"Which was how she got pregnant," I guessed.

He nodded, carefully not looking at me. "As soon as she

realized, she wanted to get an abortion and move on. She didn't want kids."

"Obviously, that didn't happen."

"Because of me. I begged her to keep Sam. I said there was no reason we couldn't make it work. Other people do."

I was shaking, because he *radiated* pain, and there was nothing I could do. "But...?"

"Diana hated pregnancy. By the time she gave birth, she hated me for making her go through it. We broke up the day Sam was born. I kept my promises, took care of things the way we'd planned, but two days after she came home from the hospital, she moved out. Then we shared custody, but she hated being a mom. And I couldn't understand, couldn't see her side...because the minute I heard about Sam, when he was a tiny peanut, I just loved him so much."

"Some women aren't cut out to be mothers," I said quietly.

"I know. And that's understandable. I should've respected her choice. Pressuring her like that is the worst thing I've ever done, and yet how can I be sorry? Because she gave me Sam."

"And you put her through so much pain." It wasn't a judgment, just a summary.

"Exactly. The scales can never be balanced. Five weeks after Sam was born, Diana dropped him off and I never heard from her again."

"She left town?"

"Yeah. I made her so miserable, she ran from her whole life. Her parents don't even know where she is. They've tried to find her."

"Damn." For me, it was tough to fathom the misery and sorrow that would drive a woman to burn all bridges behind her.

He made a soft, agonized sound. "And you wonder why I don't date."

"Not anymore," I said as my heart snapped quietly in two.

*

# CHAPTER ELEVEN

After the concert, I saw Ty a fair amount, often when he picked Sam up from day care, and a few nights a week, I sat with him on the balcony. Well, me up above and him down below. It was no longer a private thing, though, because my roomies were home more. The first time it happened when Lauren was around, she'd stared at me in puzzlement when I came in.

"Why don't you just go downstairs to talk to him?"

"It's complicated," I said.

Since we went to Ann Arbor, there was distance between us. His story didn't change the way I felt about him, but it affected his sense of how we were together. Before I knew the truth, I was a safe haven. Now I was somebody who might be judging him. That night, I'd tried to make him understand that I didn't blame him. It was shitty how he'd pushed Diana, no question, but having met Sam, how could I be sorry he was born? Some questions had no right answers, only shades of wrong, and people couldn't live in black-and-white. Sometimes there were pops of glorious color, and on other occasions, gray was the only visible hue. Mostly, I hoped Diana had made peace with her decision to start fresh and that she was happy, wherever she might be.

So now, halfway through October, I took a much-needed breather. Lauren was watching *Storage Wars* that afternoon when I sat down on the couch. The guys were out, something to do with Max's bike; Angus had gone along because he still hadn't forgiven Josh. At this point, I suspected a permanent breakup was inevitable.

"No homework?" she asked.

"I'm cramming for midterms. Taking a break."

"I should do the same. Can't muster the drive."

Lazily, I reached over and snagged her drink. I spluttered when I realized she was sipping rum and Diet Coke, strong stuff for watching TV. "Are you...okay?"

"Do I get a lecture now on the deleterious effects of day drinking on productivity?"

"It just seems like something's bothering you." At the moment, she didn't seem drunk, but maybe she'd gotten to the point where her tolerance was so high, I wouldn't realize if she had a serious problem. And that scared me.

Instead of answering, she tipped her head back with a soft, wistful sigh. "You remember in ninth grade, we were so worried about homecoming?"

I nodded. Unlike the last thing she'd asked about, I recalled this angst all too clearly. "If nobody asked us, should we go together, should we make the first move but what if he says no and if he says yes, how are we getting to the mall to buy a dress—"

"I miss that simplicity," she said quietly. "Back then, our

problems seemed so huge and insurmountable. But we obsessed and we got through."

"That's because we had each other. And we still do, LB. Whatever's going on, I'm here when you want to talk."

She smiled and handed me the rest of her drink. "Thanks. Can we just watch TV today?"

"Sure." We vegged for half an hour in silence before I remembered to ask, "Want to go home for Thanksgiving? If I go alone it'll take two days, and that'll hardly be worth it."

"My mom would love it," she said thoughtfully. "And it'd be cool to see your family, along with some of our old crew."

"Most of them are gone but they might be back for the holiday. Rob's there, though. Want to catch up with *him?*"

She surprised me by blushing, which she covered by smacking me with a pillow. "Shut up. I don't need to remind you of Matt Pomerico, do I?"

I laughed. "God, remember how I logged his movements? *9:15 a.m. Matt asks for bathroom pass.* I was *such* a weirdo."

"What do you mean, *was?*" She dodged my return swat, seeming more cheerful than she had in days. "And sure, definitely. Let's go home this year."

"I was thinking we could take turns driving, swap every two hours. It'll be a long-ass day, eight hours each, but if we leave at 6:00 a.m. on Wednesday, we should be there by ten—"

"Which is eight, Mountain Time. Not bad. Can you skip your practicum on Wednesday?"

"It's canceled, along with the rest of my classes. I think my professors wanted to get on the road early."

Lauren laughed. "Maybe they're driving to Nebraska, too. I have class at eight, but I'll ditch. The TA will probably just show a movie, anyway."

"It's a plan. What else do you have going on today?"

"Not much. I should call my mom and tell her, though. Otherwise, I might show up, say 'Surprise!' and the next day, we'll be eating TV dinners."

"It's a lot of trouble to cook the whole spread for two people. Why don't you both come to my house?"

"Your parents won't mind?"

I figured I should touch base before extending hospitality somewhere that I didn't live anymore. "Let me call home first. I'll check, and then you can tell your mom."

My phone was charging in my room, so I went to get it. We didn't have a landline in the apartment since everyone had a cell, and this way, there were no mystery charges to argue about. My mom probably wouldn't be working at the grocery store on a Saturday, at least not since her promotion. Sure enough, she picked up on the third ring.

"Hey," I said.

"Nadia! I got your email. Are you wearing the scarf I sent you?"

I grinned. "Not at the moment."

"Smart-ass. I meant when you go outside."

"Then yes. How are you?"

"Good. Trying to keep your father from cutting down that pine tree in the backyard. He thinks it's got some kind of bark disease. I think it's fine."

My dad yelled, "The tree is a menace! Next big storm and it'll be on the neighbor's roof."

I laughed while they argued. When my mom gave me her full attention again, I asked, "And Rob?"

"He's still working with your father. Oh, he's dating one of your friends now. You used to run around with her when you were little."

"Who?" For the life of me, I couldn't imagine.

"Avery Jacobs."

"Mom, we haven't been friends since sixth grade."

That didn't faze her at all. Being wrong rarely did. My mom was delightfully, disturbingly cheerful. "Well, she used to be over here all the time, and now she is again."

"Good for them, I guess." Avery turned into kind of a bitch in junior high. For Rob's sake, I hoped she'd gotten over that. "Anyway, that's not why I called."

"What's up?"

"Lauren and I are planning to come home for Thanksgiving. I hope that's all right?"

"That's wonderful! I can't wait to see you and to tell *everyone*. Your aunts and uncles will want to come and your cousins. Rob and Avery will be here—"

"Sounds like a full house. Would it be okay if Lauren and her mom came, too?"

"Of course! Ask her to bring a salad. With so many people, I usually do potluck. We supply the bird and trimmings, guests bring salads, sides and desserts."

"Yum. I can bring wine."

"If you want. But I don't expect you and Lauren to do anything after such a long drive."

"Okay. I'll tell her Thanksgiving at Casa Conrad is a go, and I'll see you next month."

"I'm so excited! Love you."

"Love you, too."

Mom had already hung up by the time I put the phone down. I went back to the living room to give Lauren the good news.

She wriggled happily. "You know what this means, right?"

I nodded. "Road trip!"

We hadn't gone anywhere for a while since gas was so

expensive. There was no question of buying plane tickets. But with some tightening, we could trim enough from our budgets to afford the trip there and back.

"This means no booze money for the next month," Lauren said.

"Yep." That was where I planned to cut corners, too. In some matters, she and I were always in sync without even trying. It relieved me that she didn't seem too panicked at the idea of drying out for a while.

Then she said, "We could go to a few campus parties. There's always free beer."

"The cheap, shitty kind," I muttered. The last guy I dated said I was a beer snob. He wasn't wrong.

Lauren poked me as I settled onto the couch and picked the perfect pillow to cuddle. "Do you want to be a hipster or do you want to get drunk?"

"Neither." I hoped she didn't, either.

Lucky for my peace of mind, she accepted the veto with good grace. "So what *do* you want to do tonight?"

I shrugged. "I'm open, as long as it doesn't cost a lot."

"There go most of our options."

In a town the size of Mount Albion, there were college parties of variable quality, two cinemas, numerous bars and one dance club, which was usually a waste of time. But there was no cover. So I said, "We could hit up the Majestic."

"Eh." From her expression, she wasn't enthused but couldn't think of anything better.

The problem was, the Majestic had been a theater back in its glory days, then new owners bought and gutted the place. They kept the baroque charm on the outside and turned the inside into an industrial mess—all exposed pipes and dummy wires—their idea of where "college kids" would party down.

The dance floor was decent, the booze was watered down, music tolerable, but since it was an 18+ club, there were a lot of high school seniors. Management made it easy to spot them by the neon-blue wristbands. People with proper ID got a hand stamp.

"I don't feel like sitting around tonight. Let's check it out. If the DJ blows, we can leave early, come home and watch more *Storage Wars*." Though I didn't love the show, Lauren did, so this was a good offer. Left to my own devices, I'd binge on *Vikings*.

"You've convinced me. I could stand to dance." I sang "I Hope You Dance," until she attempted to smother me with a pillow.

"Don't quit your day job," she advised.

"Wouldn't dream of it. Without teaching, I'll be forced to rely on the hope that some rich businessman will decide to keep me as a pet."

"You should never be allowed to watch *Pretty Woman*."

"It's a terrible movie," I agreed.

"I hates it, my precious."

For lunch, I made grilled cheese and salad. Lauren and I watched TV while pretending to study until it was time to get ready to go out. Later, Angus and Max came in, but we were already in the bedroom.

A knock sounded, then some scratching. "Nadia? Lauren? We miss you. It's *so lonely* out here." That was Max. He thumped against the door for a few seconds, then we heard him shuffling away with noisy, exaggerated grief.

Lauren laughed. "Is it me or is he better this year?"

"It's not you. Maybe give him a shot?" I'd told Max I supported his Lauren-crush, and it seemed unlikely I'd get a better segue to put in a good word.

"Are you serious? He's such a man-whore."

"Hey, we'd get pissed if someone slut-shamed one of our female friends. We'd argue that it's totally okay for a woman to hook up for fun. But since Max is a dude, it's fine to judge?"

"What—"

Talking over her attempted interjection, I concluded, "I don't think Max lies to get girls in bed. They wouldn't stay friends afterward if he did. Remember how they showed up with food for the party?"

*The one he threw for you.* But I couldn't say that.

Lauren frowned, looking utterly bewildered. "Do you *like* Max?"

"As a friend. I just think we're both hard on him. Granted, he was a tool our freshman year, but he's settled down since then."

"Maybe you're right. He's been a better roomie than I expected."

At that point, I dropped the subject because if I listed all his good points, Lauren would know something was up. Beyond this convo, I couldn't help him anymore.

After my shower, I dressed in old jeans, knee boots and a red wrap top. My battered leather jacket completed the outfit, much more my style than the white dress I'd worn out with Ty. Lauren went with a flirty miniskirt, paired with a sparkly T-shirt and open-crochet shrug. She also put on a pair of leggings because otherwise, the way she danced, she'd probably end up flashing a high school kid before the night ended. I did a quick nod at makeup with lipstick and eyeliner, put my hair up in a tousled twist and called it a day. It took her a bit longer, so I ambled to the living room to wait.

Angus was cooking some kind of rice dish. He turned as I went by. "Going out?"

"Yeah, we'll see if the Majestic is any less lame tonight."

"Oooh, dancing. If you give me half an hour, I'll come." Since he'd been pretty bummed from the whole Josh thing, it was the least we could do.

And Lauren would probably take that long on her hair, anyway.

"No problem. I'm driving, though." I'd promised we could leave early if it sucked, but if Angus was having a blast, he might not want to take off.

"Am I invited?" Max asked.

"Do you seriously want to hit up the Majestic?" I raised a brow.

The answer shone in his dark eyes: *Duh. Lauren will be there.* It was weird that I was the only one who saw it. His answer came across indifferent. "Better than sitting home."

We ate Angus's mushroom pilaf, then he got ready, which involved a quick shower, cologne, a new outfit and some major wailing about his hair. It was more like an hour, but nobody was complaining. Finally, we piled into my car and I drove us to the club. The parking lot didn't promise much excitement, but maybe it was better inside.

When I stepped in, I saw it hadn't changed much, the same flashing lights and iron pipes overhead, black dance floor, sparsely populated at the moment. However, the DJ was playing Beyoncé, a good start. Max went to get a drink while Lauren, Angus and I hit the floor. None of us could resist doing a slightly campy version of "Single Ladies." When that song ended, the DJ went straight to KE$HA; though I didn't like her music that much, I couldn't argue that it was catchy and danceable.

In addition to being the best bad dancer ever, Angus could move well when he was being serious—to the point that people loved watching him. Generally speaking, somebody always was. I hadn't been kidding at the party when Josh accused me of wanting to kiss him and I answered, *Who doesn't? Have you seen him?* Angus had dramatic good looks that made folks turn their heads: shining blond hair, vivid green eyes, tanned skin, fit body. His sweetness only made him a bigger catch once you got to know him.

For once, the Majestic was on point, musically. By now, usually they'd be playing hair metal or some old, outdated power ballads that drove everyone under forty off the floor. It was beyond me how people danced to that, though my mom said you didn't; you just flung your hair around a lot and screamed. I didn't like picturing my mom in the club scene, but there was no denying she'd spoken with a certain authority.

I danced through five songs, until I was actually sweaty. If I kept this up, I could sleep through my Sunday workout. I left Lauren rocking out with Angus and went to beg the bartender for some water. Since he was young and cute, a little flirting had him slipping me a bottle, on the house. Even better, since I'd only wanted ice water from the tap.

Max was propped up against the bar, watching Lauren. I sighed at him.

"You're not even trying. Get out there."

"Easy for you to say. You're a great dancer."

"You're not?"

"Hardly. I can do the white-boy shuffle. And just *look* at Angus."

It was impressive, no joke. Since he was so tall and slim, the sorts of things he could do with hips and arms and legs should not work, should not be so amazingly graceful. Just then, he was spinning, completely throwing himself into the song. I'd seen a clip of Tom Hiddleston dancing once, and while he was impressive, Angus was better.

"You realize he's not your rival, right?"

"I know."

"First slow dance, you get out there and ask her. Promise?"

Max knocked back his shot. "Fine. I can probably manage that."

I chugged my water as another good song came on. So I grabbed his hand. "Don't be self-conscious. I'm going to teach you some moves. Nothing fancy."

He watched me for a few seconds then shook his head. "My pelvis only moves that way under one circumstance. This isn't it."

"Okay, maybe that's not for you. How about this?" I showed him a one-two back-and-forth step that was a little better than the *can't dance* shuffle he'd mentioned.

Wearing a martyred expression, he tried until he could execute it, but it was obvious he'd never love dancing like Angus, Lauren and I did.

A few minutes later, Lauren danced up, studying his moves. "Excuse me, but who's the better dancer? Shouldn't I be teaching him?"

I decided to tease. "Technically, Angus is the best."

Max didn't seem to mind the idea of private lessons. "He's too busy."

Suppressing the urge to hug him, I said, "You're definitely above my pay grade, LB. Feel free to take over."

At that, Max shot me a look that was a strange mix of terror and delight, but I didn't save him. By this point, Angus was dancing with a cute guy. He looked young, but I didn't spot the blue wristband. *So he's probably in college, at least*. It might be just what he needed, to hook up with someone else. Maybe if he evened the score, he'd feel like forgiving Josh. Or maybe he'd realize it was time to fish or cut line. Either way, Angus needed some movement in his life.

*So do I.*

With my roomies paired off, it was hard not to think of Ty, hard not to imagine him sitting on the red couch, probably wrapped up in the chenille throw. Sam would be in bed by now, after five or six stories. Most days, I kept my feelings boxed up, and I didn't let an impossible love ruin the rest of my life. Right then, it was tough.

The ache tightened my throat as a guy circled toward me on the dance floor. He was tall, and he danced pretty well. He jerked his head toward the bar, the silent equivalent to *Buy you a drink?* Shaking my head, I kept dancing, and he turned away.

Since I loved Ty, I refused to use someone else as a substitute. Once I accepted it was impossible and put him behind me, things would be different. I just needed some time. Right?

# CHAPTER TWELVE

$A$ week and a half later, my cell phone rang. I was almost home and I started to leave it until I parked, but when I noticed Ty's picture, I picked up. "Hey, how are you?"

"Not great. I have to go back to work."

"But you just picked Sam up."

"I know. But if I don't fix this mess, I could lose my job. If they don't break ground tomorrow on-site, as scheduled, Bill will have my ass. My parents are busy tonight, and I wouldn't ask if it wasn't an emergency, but can you—"

"Sure, I'll watch Sam. I'm pulling in now. I'll be at your door in two minutes." I parked in my usual spot, grabbed my backpack from the floor beside me and raced to his apartment. Ty had the door open by the time I knocked, so obviously freaked that I fought the urge to hug him.

"I appreciate this so much. He hasn't had dinner and—"

"Relax, Ty. We've got this, right, buddy?"

"My name is Sam!" Then he low-fived me. "It's okay, Dad."

Ty paused at the door, studying the two of us, as I took my

jacket off and hung it on the coatrack in the corner. Then a half smile stole across his face as I knelt to hug Sam and whisper a fresh dinosaur joke in his ear. He giggled and waved as his dad slipped out.

"So what's your favorite thing to eat?" I asked, peering in the cupboard.

"Chicken nuggets, mac and cheese, pizza, hot dogs and orange Jell-O."

"I'm not making all of that. We'd get sick."

"Mac and cheese with hot dogs in it," he tried.

Folding my arms, I offered my best *let's negotiate* look. Possibly, I was overestimating Sam's ability to read subtext. "I could be persuaded, if you eat some vegetables."

A tiny frown pinched his brows together, so cute. "But they taste like evil."

"And how would you know what evil tastes like?" It was all I could do not to laugh, which would ruin the serious tone of our discussion.

"Because I ate vegetables before." That was such a reasonable and ironclad argument that I couldn't shake it.

Still, I'd be a terrible babysitter if I agreed he could live on mac and cheese with hot dog pieces. "Well, that's the deal, take it or leave it."

"Will you put extra cheese in the macaroni?" Sam was being cagey.

I grinned at him. "Obviously. Two slices of American, extra gooey when it melts."

"Okay." He shook hands with me to seal the agreement.

Poking through the cabinets didn't reveal many vegetables. I found a can of corn, peas and carrots, some frozen mixed veggies and half a pack of broccoli. So I lined it all up and showed Sam his choices.

"Which one of these do you like best?"

"Broccoli," he said with the saddest face ever.

I gathered from his look that all veggies were some level of evil, and broccoli was just the least demonic in the gospel according to Sam. "That's a very mature choice."

He nodded like he totally knew what *mature* meant. Maybe he did. From what I'd seen, Ty didn't skimp on vocabulary in their conversations.

"Dad puts cheese on it."

I was hearing an awful lot about pasteurized dairy products. "So basically you'd eat a stick if someone put cheese on it."

"Dunno. Maybe."

*So cute.*

As Sam watched, I put away the losing veggies and got out a pot big enough to make Kraft blue box. I filled the pot with water, salted it and set it on the stove then located the hot dogs and sliced them up. His eyes widened when I put them in a skillet.

"What're you doing?"

"Sautéing them."

"Dad puts them in the microwave."

"That doesn't get your dogs crispy, my friend. It only makes them bloated."

"What's that?"

I puffed out my cheeks to show him. "This is."

"Oh. Auntie Gloria gets that in her knees."

"Ouch. That's probably why she needs surgery." I remembered Ty mentioning that as the reason she couldn't watch Sam anymore.

At some point, I expected Sam would get bored watching me cook, but he followed me around the kitchen asking things like, why did I wait until the water was boiling so hard before adding the macaroni, why did I put the butter and milk in before the cheese powder, how come I was still cooking it when it looked done, why were the hot dogs so brown when I stirred them in. Since I was used to kids, it didn't bother me, but he hardly seemed to breathe for the questions. As the final step, I thawed the broccoli and chopped it superfine, then stirred it into the casserole. That counted as a vegetable.

It was around seven by then, so I figured he must be starving. I definitely was. "Should we see how it turned out?"

"Yes!"

I served up two plates and poured us both cups of milk, then we sat down. All things considered, it wasn't bad, though tailored to a kid's palate. Head down, he ate with adorable gusto, like his dinner might disappear. For dessert, I gave him a cup of orange Jell-O, prepackaged and in the fridge. For an hour afterward, we played with trucks because as it turned out, the steamer trunk that doubled as a coffee table was also a toy box.

When he asked to watch TV, I gave him a suspicious look. "I don't think so. If I called your dad, he'd say it was bath time, am I right?"

Sam angled the most angelic look imaginable up at me. "I dunno. I'm only four. I can't tell time yet."

"Nice try. *I* know what time small humans go to bed. To the bath with you!"

That was an insane, shambolic affair. By the time I got him washed, rinsed and dried, I was a sopping mess, and since I'd worked at day care *and* had my practicum today as well, every muscle in my body hurt. But I kept my smile bright for Sam. Pretending to be a monster, I chased him down the hall. He had the master bedroom, like the one Lauren and I shared upstairs. Down here, half the space contained a twin bed and kid's furniture while the rest provided a play area. Since it was a three-bedroom, Ty was using one as his own room and the other seemed to be a studio, complete with computer desk and drafting table.

"Okay, jammies on, teeth brushed. Now let's find *Goodnight Moon—*"

"Where's Mr. O'Beary?" He tugged on the bottom of my shirt.

"Hmm?" I shoved damp hair away from my face as I turned back his covers. His dark blue sheets were spangled with silver crescent moons and five-point stars trailing golden dust.

"He's my friend. I can't sleep without him."

"Give me a minute here." I'd definitely seen him hauling the plushie around, so I'd recognize it when I spotted it.

As I dug through crates of toys, Sam transformed from adorable kid to shrieking demon. I couldn't understand more than one word in ten due to both volume and sobbing, but if he kept it up, his head might explode. The tantrum started with wailing, then escalated to Sam flinging himself on his face and pounding with hands and feet. When he banged his head on the floor, I picked him up, but that only made it worse. He fought me, weeping so hard that his nose ran and he smeared snot all over my already wet shirt. With him yelling in my ear, I could hardly think where to look. My head throbbed in cadence with each shrill cry, scraping raw over my nerves. He clung to my side while I stumbled around the apartment, turning everything inside out. It took me forty-five minutes to find that damned bear, still in his backpack from nap time at school, left beside the door. *If only I'd thought of that sooner.* Still sniffling, he climbed into bed, strangling Mr. O'Beary with his love.

*Finally, sweet, blessed silence.* I'd dealt with difficult kids before but never one who switched so fast from pure sunshine to a monsoon of misery. Gathering the tatters of my composure, I wiped his face with a damp cloth. My hands shook in reaction when I pulled up his covers, and a steel band tightened around my skull, a souvenir of the fit. I also had a fierce kink between my shoulders from hauling him around for an hour. This felt almost like a hangover, though it was emotional, not physical.

He spoke in a tiny, chastened voice. "Are you mad, Nadia?"

"No. Just tired."

Then I leaned down and hugged him, so he'd know I meant it. By this point, he was exhausted, but he clung to my hand as I read *Goodnight Moon*. Before I finished the story, he passed out, eyes still red and swollen. For a few seconds, I stayed on the side of his bed, afraid to move, afraid I'd jar him awake and start the noise again.

Eventually, I stole out of the room, swallowing a huge sigh. My clothes were still wet, and I was shivering. Hoping Ty wouldn't mind, I went to his room and opened the closet door. *Better to ask forgiveness than permission, right?* No snooping, I grabbed the first shirt I found and changed into it. White dress shirt, good quality. It didn't cover as much of me as it would have a smaller woman. Even my socks were wet, so I hung my clothes to dry in the bathroom. Not for the first time, I wished these units had a built-in washer and dryer.

Afterward, I arched my back and stretched. *Sounds like my spine's made of bubble wrap.* I assessed the apartment, wincing. *So trashed.* I'd dumped just about everything Sam owned onto the floor. My body shouted at me to collapse, but I couldn't. *Not yet.* Mustering the last of my reserves, I set the bathroom to rights, tidied up the kitchen and put Sam's toys away.

*There, that's fine.*

When Ty's key rattled in the door at ten-fifteen, I was barely awake, snuggled on the couch beneath the chenille throw. He stepped inside, shoulders slumped in exhaustion. Man, I knew exactly how he felt. The scruff on his jaw said he hadn't shaved in two or three days, and his hair was rumpled. A crooked tie spoke of frustration.

"Did you solve the problem?" I managed a smile.

"Yeah. I found the permits, thank God. I *knew* we had them. Everything go okay here?" he asked, glancing around the room warily.

That was exactly why I had to clean up. "More or less. Sam ate dinner, took a bath and brushed his teeth. I read him a story. Now he's asleep."

"This sounds too good to be true."

Momentarily sidestepping the implicit question, I scooted out of my warm nest, went to the kitchen, pressed a few buttons and came back. "There's a plate of casserole in the microwave. I'm nuking it for you."

He was still standing, frozen, beside the couch. "Is that... my shirt?"

*Oh, my God. How could I forget? Shit.* My cheeks filled with enough heat to power the whole town. "My stuff got soaked during Sam's bath. It's drip-drying. I'm sorry, I didn't—"

"No, it's fine. I was just...surprised. I don't expect you to sit around in wet clothes."

The microwave beeped, saving me. "Sit down. I'll get it."

To my relief, he did as I suggested. Maybe he was just so tired, walking another step sounded like too much effort. So I delivered the gourmet—according to Sam—meal, along with a bottle of beer. Embarrassed, I sat and pulled the throw over my legs.

*Lord, he must think this is the lamest seduction ever.*

Ty stared at his plate. "This is...pretty much his favorite

dinner, though I don't usually put the broccoli in it. Sneaky, I like it. So how was Sam, really?"

"One minor snafu." That was a hell of an understatement, but complaining wouldn't diminish his stress or mine. "Took me forty-five minutes to find Mr. O'Beary."

"You…" He stared at me, spoon arrested partway to his mouth.

"What?"

Ty shook his head as if in disbelief. "I know what Sam's like when we can't find that stupid bear. How come you're not rocking and weeping?"

I smiled at him in reassurance. "There are a few difficult students in my practicum, so this wasn't my first time. Yeah, Sam was upset, but he settled down as soon as I realized where to look. He's a sweet kid."

"I quit," he said softly.

"Huh?"

He rubbed his chest, like it was aching. "You made his favorite dinner, and you found his bear. I come home, and you're *wearing* my shirt. I can't fight this anymore, Nadia."

"I'm sorry—" I started.

His expression silenced me. Never in my life had I seen that exact combination of need and longing.

"Unless you don't want me to, I might literally die if I don't kiss you."

"I want," I whispered.

In an instant, Ty closed the distance between us and cupped my face in his hands. His palms, oh, we'd been here before, but never like this. I licked my lips as his gaze skated over my face, kindled like a jar of honey in the sunlight. He made the hungriest sound I'd ever heard as he leaned in. But his lips were whisper-soft when they brushed mine, moonbeams and starlight. Shocking heat surged through me from that slight contact. He backed off just for a few seconds, gazing at me with a sort of startled adoration. Then he went back in for a deeper taste. I hadn't fantasized beyond this moment—I hadn't dared—but dreams couldn't have done it justice. He kissed like all the best kinds of sin, slow and steamy, echoed by nips and bites, soft sounds and nuzzling. I gave back, more, more, mouths, tongues, his hands in my hair, mine on his shoulders.

It went on for ages, until he was practically on top of me.

"Too much?" he panted.

*Not enough.*

Somewhere in my head, there was a brain, but it was sizzling in pleasure and pheromones, drowning in the sweet, slick rush of endorphins, because he felt and tasted perfect. *Hot skin, bristly jaw, soft lips, a touch chapped, and I'm licking them—mmm, that chin*—Ty wrapped his arms around me and drew me onto his lap. Ty was hot and hard underneath me, throbbing. In his shirt, my legs were bare as I straddled him, still kissing. He trailed his lips away from my mouth, over my jaw and down my throat, counterpoint of teeth and tongue to make me moan. He took each sound, each gasp, with a quick lunge back to my lips. He stroked a path down my back, pausing at my hips then sliding lower. A shudder went through both of us when he grazed my bare thighs.

"Nadia," he whispered against my neck.

"Mmm."

"I wanted you the first time I saw you."

I shifted, bit him gently on the ear. "It was mutual."

"Christ."

"Take your shirt off." All my big words were gone. I was beyond thinking or caring about consequences. Obstacles between us faded to flutters in the back of my head.

He leaned back so I could unbutton him. Ty had a lean build, long and wiry, with broad shoulders tapering to a taut stomach. The auburn hair that arrowed toward his belt only made him sexier, so I yielded to the impulse to rub my hands against his chest. He sucked in a sharp breath in response to that touch, cause and effect. His heart hammered away beneath my palms.

"That's so good," he whispered.

"Yeah." I was hardly paying attention to what he said anymore, only the tone, lost in the magic of making him react. At long last, I had permission to touch.

Teasing, I brushed my thumbs against his nipples, admiring the ruddy stripe on his cheekbones as they tightened. Now he was quiet, too. He couldn't stop moving under me, a shift here, push there. My weight promised all kinds of things, and Ty pulled me in for a long, hungry kiss, his hand firm on the back of my neck. As we kissed, I raked my nails over his shoulders, and he groaned.

"Can't tonight," he growled. "I'm not... I don't—"

"It's okay." The bleary comprehension that he didn't have any condoms didn't stop me from circling my hips, grinding.

"Want to. Think you..." Muffled moan, as he rubbed my thighs, up and down, working us together. "Know how much."

"No more mixed feelings?" It was all I could do to ask the question.

"W-we can... We have to..." He lost the thread as I kissed my way down his neck and bit softly into his shoulder. *"Fuck."*

A whimper escaped me. "I agree."

"Not what I— Oh, God." He held my hips hard, just moving me on him, and I watched his face, watched the pleasure build. "Can't think. I just... I need—"

He went rigid, jaw flexing. Ty's legs jerked underneath me as he held on to my thighs, stroking them compulsively. "Nadia, fuck, *Nadia*."

*"Yes."* The word hissed out of me when he parted the tails of his shirt. It was sexier with that intent look, his fingers skating down my belly toward my damp panties. He dipped past the elastic and down, until he could stroke me. I lifted up on my knees, desperate to come. Four strokes, and I was gone, lost in his arms. I melted over him, draping my head on his shoulder.

"Your turn," I whispered.

Ty's head fell back and he squeezed his eyes shut with a choky laugh. "About that…"

My eyes widened. "Wow. Really?"

"I haven't done that since— Shit, I *never* did that." He opened his arms, freeing me to snuggle beside him, and I did.

Part of me was relieved that he wasn't feeling a cocktail of horrible things right now, including regret. But I had questions now that I could think again. "So…what is this?"

"Afterglow?" He looked positively beatific.

I kissed him. "You know what I mean."

He brushed his lips against my temple in turn. "Give me a minute. I'm seeing stars here. It was a long day before we went to wonderland."

"Okay." Utterly relaxed, I closed my eyes.

It was a good five minutes before he spoke again. "I don't know what the hell we're doing. Objectively, it's still a bad idea, and if you don't want a repeat once you understand what I can offer, I understand. No hard feelings."

I already wanted a repeat and didn't much care about the terms. "I'm listening."

"I was afraid this would complicate things, and it still might. But I'd like to find a balance, if we can."

"To what?"

"Being friends with benefits. If you meet someone else or it starts feeling wrong, we go back to being friends."

"The same goes for you," I said.

The twist of his mouth said hell would freeze first. "Obviously, we have to be careful. More than we were tonight. I won't do anything to hurt Sam."

"I know."

"If he'd had a nightmare or woken up with a stomachache…" A shaky sigh escaped him. "I'm aware that you care for him, too. So you understand why we have to keep this…separate. Private." Ty's expression went butter-soft and twice as sweet as he kissed me. "If this works out as I hope, you'll be around for him long after you lose interest in me."

*That's never going to happen.*

But I didn't say it out loud. Too many promises had been broken for him to believe something like that from a woman who just came all over his hand. To his mind, I'd probably say anything to get those clever fingers in my panties again.

"I think you might entertain me for a while," I said, trying for a flirty look.

The relief in his gaze told me I'd struck the right note. *Yeah, your good friend Nadia just wants to objectify you sexually. No scary emotions here.* If he knew how I *really* felt, he'd probably break the world speed record running away.

"Likewise."

"I hate to make you feel used, but I should probably get home. It's late."

He hugged me hard before helping me to my feet. "It's a

tough life, but I'll think of you while I'm shame-weeping. Where are your clothes?"

"Bathroom."

Ty fetched them quietly, and I shivered as I wriggled into still-damp jeans. He made it really hard to finish getting dressed because he kept trying to peek inside the shirt I was wearing, his shirt, and it was both frustrating and sexy as hell. By the time I got my jacket and boots on, I was ready to fool around some more. So I rose up on tiptoes, gave him a scorching kiss and let myself out of his apartment to the gratifying sound of Ty cursing.

I probably radiated the *just fucked* vibe, so thank God Max was the only person home, and he barely glanced at me. Angus and Lauren would've given me the third degree, and I'd bet Max would've paid more attention, had Lauren come home looking the same way. In the bedroom, I confirmed it. *Yep, sex hair, swollen lips, wow, he marked my neck behind my ear.*

A little shiver went through me.

I took a shower, imagining how it would be with Ty, all wet, steamy nakedness, and then sex afterward in a warm bed. For us, those moments were likely to be few and far between. As I stepped out of the tub, I realized they'd be confined to the end of the month. Otherwise, any time we snatched would feel sneaky and furtive. And maybe that would be hot under some conditions, but trying not to get caught by a four-year-old was not one of those scenarios. Plus, my turn-on was watching, not getting caught in the act.

I wrapped a towel around me and opened the bathroom door in time to hear my phone buzzing away. Digging it out of my purse, I already had a message from Ty. *A pic, too.* My breath caught as I opened it. He wasn't pervy enough to send me a close-up of his junk, but I got one of his soapy chest, droplets of water on the phone when he took it. *Hot as hell. He must've taken this in the shower.*

The text read, Wish you were here.

*

# CHAPTER THIRTEEN

The next morning, Angus woke me just past six by collapsing at the foot of my bed with a sigh. Normally, I'd be up on my own since I had to be at work by eight. *Shit, I must've turned off my alarm.* But he didn't seem to realize he'd done me a favor.

"You okay?"

"I broke up with Josh for good."

I'd suspected that was coming. If he'd been able to move past it, he probably wouldn't have spent so long mentally debating the issue. "I'm sorry. Give me a sec."

After a quick hug, I wriggled my feet out from under him and raced to the bathroom. Once I took care of business, I washed my hands and brushed my teeth before opening the door. We'd chatted many times while I got ready, so this was nothing new. By this point, Angus had stolen the warm spot in my bed. He had no early classes on Thursday, lucky bastard.

"Can we talk now?"

"Go for it." I rummaged in my closet, trying to find a clean day-care shirt and tan pants.

"If he can't control himself for three weeks, what will it be like down the line? I don't want to be tied to a serial cheater, constantly accepting the apologies and lies."

Since I'd liked Josh, but I didn't think he was the best guy ever, I supported this move. "I get it. You made the smart choice dumping J-Rod."

"But I miss him," he whispered.

I'd never broken up with anyone I truly cared about, so my advice would be worthless. "Did you meet anyone good at the Majestic?"

"I had some fun with the guy I was dancing with, but he was of the *shh, don't speak* school of handsome."

"Yikes. So not relationship material."

"Not remotely." He rolled over and snuggled onto his side. "Can I sleep in your bed while you're gone?"

"Somebody should enjoy it." Some people might find this weird, I supposed, but Angus had crashed in my room before.

When I unearthed a pair of wrinkled khakis, I punched the air in triumph and got dressed. There was no time for anything but a ponytail and I shoved my feet into a pair of dark blue Converse. Because he needed TLC, I crossed to the bed and kissed Angus on the forehead.

"Thanks."

"We'll hang out tonight if you want."

"Not *Project Runway*," he muttered.

"I'll take you out drinking, and I can be your designated driver." That should be the perfect distraction from his personal problems.

He pushed up on an elbow. "I haven't done the stupid drunk break-up phase yet."

"It's followed by sitting in the recliner in sweatpants, eating Cheetos, right?"

Angus shuddered. "I'll skip to the hangover cure and a good workout."

"I'll see you tonight." With one last pat, I ran to the kitchen, where I fried an egg and made toast.

Ten minutes later, as I got in the car, I realized I should be grateful to Angus. Focusing on his issues prevented me from waking up in a cold sweat, wondering if Ty would boomerang into iceberg territory, no contact between us for weeks, like that one time. Of course, now that the possibility had occurred to me, anxiety squatted in my mind, swelling like a tick.

But something else distracted me. This morning, under normal circumstances, Lauren would've been part of that discussion. She should've woken up and bitched at us for bothering her and then offered to come to the bar tonight. I sorted through a jumble of impressions and I noted that her bed had still been made at six-thirty in the morning.

*She didn't come home last night.*

As I parked, I got out my phone to text her.

You okay?

Fine, why?

Because you weren't around when I left. Get lucky?

Woke up superearly. Went to the library to study for midterms.

I stared at my phone, unsure how to handle this. Usually, when Lauren didn't want to talk about something, she said so. Never in my experience had she lied to me. But in a town the size of Mount Albion, the buses didn't run at all hours, so how did she get to campus that early? It was theoretically possible that she'd walked; it was three miles. But that didn't ring true.

Good luck, I finally sent back. If she wanted me to know what was going on with her, she'd tell me. No poking around on my end; I had enough shit on my plate.

My hand was on the door handle when my phone buzzed again, but this time, it was Ty. The message just read, No regrets.

Smiling, I answered, None here. Encore?

Soon.

Sam was already in the classroom when I arrived. He smiled at me, completely recovered from the night's drama. Mrs. Trent put me to work, and the morning went fast. I actually liked it better than afternoons because keeping nineteen four-year-olds on their cots during nap time wasn't the easiest job. Mornings were quick-paced with a dynamic mix of activities, lessons, snack and circle time. When noon rolled around, the new floater came in to relieve me.

I hesitated outside Mrs. Keller's office, troubled, but something had to give. If I kept up at this rate, I'd burn out like my mentor at C-Cool had warned me. Mustering my nerve, I tapped on the door frame and she looked up.

"Come in!"

"I have a couple of things to talk to you about," I said.

"You're not quitting, are you?" Her look of alarm was flattering. "Then close the door, sit down, and let's hear it."

"The first request is, can I have the Friday after Thanksgiving off? I'm going home for the first time since last Christmas. It's a sixteen-hour drive," I added so she'd understand how big a deal it was, not like visiting Ann Arbor.

She nodded, making a note. "Thanks for the advance notice. I can work around it. We're closed on Thanksgiving."

"Yeah, that's why I was hoping it wouldn't be too big a deal."

"It shouldn't be. We run a skeleton crew on Black Friday because so many companies offer two days' holiday, anyway. It's mostly parents who have retail jobs that need us open."

"Okay, thank you."

"That was easy enough. You looked so serious when you came in, you scared me."

"Sorry," I said sheepishly. "I hate asking for favors. This might be harder to handle but…I need to shave a couple hours off my schedule on Wednesdays and Fridays."

In a rush, I told her how the practicum was killing me—class at eight and then I had to race straight to C-Cool, where I was helping in the classroom for two hours. Afterward, there was another sprint to the day-care center to get me here by noon and if I was lucky, I might get a convenience-store sandwich along the way.

I concluded, "I just can't keep going like that."

"No, obviously not. Would it help if we shifted your hours to late afternoon? I could schedule you from two to six and you'd only lose an hour of paid time, but it should give you more of a lunch break, and I only have one hour to cover daily. I'm sure the new floater wouldn't mind adding two hours." Mrs. Keller got out her calendar and started looking at the shifts. "Right now you're working twenty-three hours a week and she's got seventeen. With this new division, it would be twenty-one and nineteen."

"Yeah, that would be better." Already the tension in my neck and shoulders eased. I could afford to pare down by twenty bucks a week, less with taxes.

She wrote up the sample schedule: Monday, 12–5. Tuesday, 8–12. Wednesday, 2–6. Thursday, 8–12. Friday, 2–6. I looked it over, checked the math. Yep, twenty-one hours a week, but those two trimmed hours would make my life a lot easier. With a grateful smile, I stood up.

"Thank you."

"Not a problem. I wish more employees would talk to me instead of calling in until I have no choice but to let them go."

"They probably don't like working here as much as I do," I said. "When will the change kick in?"

"I have to talk to Claire first, but I hope next week." Claire must be the floater who had my old job.

"Thanks again." I waved as I let myself out of her office, relief practically swamping me.

Time wasn't so tight on Tuesdays and Thursdays, so I had the leisure to go home and make lunch, eat and change clothes, before heading to campus for afternoon classes. On the downside, I had them back-to-back until six. Which sounded like a lot of classes, but the Tues-Thurs ones ran longer to make up for meeting only twice a week.

It was half past six when I got home, and I had zero desire to go drinking, but I'd promised Angus. He was waiting on the couch, ready to party. I summoned a smile.

"Do you mind if I eat first?" The prospect of peanuts and microwaved chicken wings for dinner didn't sound enticing.

He raised a brow at me. "Oh, Nadia of little faith. Take the lid off the pot on the stove."

Curious, I did as he suggested and found homemade chicken noodle soup. I was already spooning some into a bowl as I said, "You're too good to me, seriously."

Angus grinned. "I know. I'm spoiling you for all other men."

That was not even remotely true, but it boosted his ego, so I played along. Plus, when his food tasted this delicious, he deserved the praise. With a happy sigh, I plonked onto the couch and savored the goodness.

"You know this is why we asked you to room with us, right?" I teased.

"Why must you be so cruel? Am I only a sassy apron to you?"

"Of course not. You're also a sassy wok and wooden spoon." Angus hit me with a pillow, nearly tipping my bowl over. I glared in mock-outrage. "You *dare*. Do what you will with me but the soup deserves better."

To my delight, he burst out laughing. *Bodes well for tonight.* I hadn't seen his eyes shadow free and shining since Josh cleared his conscience. Angus had a tendency to internalize things and to obsess, so he must've been wondering if it was something he did before he went to Europe or something he didn't do. I wanted him to stop with all of that and just cut loose tonight. My reluctance to go out faded.

Before we left, I ate two bowls of soup, then I let Angus fiddle with my hair. He hated the sheer laziness of the band keeping my hair out of my face. The funny part was, he wasn't the genius of a stylist that pop culture implied all gay men should be. In my opinion, Lauren was much better. *What's up with her, anyway?* But tonight was about Angus, so I let him give me bad sex-vixen hair, then we went down to the parking lot.

"Let's take the Audi," he suggested.

I'd driven his car before, but not often. A vehicle that expensive made me nervous. "Are you sure?"

"Positive. I'll hand over my keys when we get there."

Angus drove us to 42 North, a bar cunningly named after

its own address. It was the closest thing Mount Albion had to a hipster bar, where students and townies could mingle. Typically, the blue-collar types drank across town, however, at the place off the interstate. So at the tail end of happy hour, we had some men in business suits, a few people I recognized from campus and some older folks. Interesting mix, not too exciting, but it was Thursday. Tonight, they had a piano player, plinking out old favorites from my mom's day.

"Well, this is…mellow," Angus said with a lip curl. "I suppose they'll play 'Piano Man,' and everyone will weep into their beers."

"Don't be snide. You came here to get drunk, not bitch about ambiance."

"Can't I do both? I'm an excellent multitasker. Watch. Excuse me! Vodka and cranberry for me, ginger ale for the lady." While we waited for our drinks, he whispered in my ear all of the things that were wrong with this bar *and* its patrons.

In a bitchy mood, Angus could be beyond mordant, but he was also hilarious. I snickered as the bartender delivered the first round. "Paying cash or should I start a tab?"

"A tab, definitely." He handed over a platinum AmEx, courtesy of his dad. I usually didn't notice the difference in our circumstances, but it was weird to realize how little money meant to him. He'd probably never scrimped or saved a day in his life.

The bartender brightened when he saw the card and service became brisk. I nursed two ginger ales while Angus polished off what I reckoned to be nearly a fifth of vodka by himself. As I'd promised that morning, he was drunk off his ass when I helped him to the car. Once he was buckled in, I ran around to the driver's seat, somewhat excited about taking the wheel. The inside was posh leather and fine engineering.

On the way home, Angus sang the Spice Girls at the top of his lungs. Rather than fight it, I found "Wannabe" on his hard drive and blasted it. His good humor lasted until we pulled into the parking lot, then he turned with a horrified face. I guessed where this was going.

"Open the door, honey. Fast."

Clumsily, he did, and he barfed all over the pavement. *Better than the car.* Wincing, I waited until he was done heaving, then I went around to help him out. Managing that without either of us falling down in the vomit was a feat worthy of the circus. My shoes took a hit, but friends before Converse, or something like that.

"I want to die," Angus was moaning as we staggered into the foyer. "You're the only one who loves me."

That was untrue, but he'd clearly reached the sad-drunk stage. So I murmured encouraging noises as I practically herniated myself getting him up the stairs. Down the hall toward Ty's place, I heard a noise, like the door clicking shut quietly, but I couldn't investigate until I dealt with Angus. And that might take a while.

Ten minutes later, I got him up the stairs and into the apartment. I convinced him to strip and get in the shower, but I couldn't stop him from wandering around naked afterward. Max came out of his room, surveyed the situation and then shook his head.

"Nope." He retreated.

Thankfully, Lauren was home, and she helped me get him dressed and into bed. We flopped him on his stomach and left his trash can beside his bed in case he got sick. By the time Lauren shut Angus's door, I felt like I had the night before, after listening to Sam scream for almost an hour. The comparison amused me.

"What the *hell?*" she demanded.

"He split with Josh for keeps."

"Ohhh. Then it could've been worse. Why didn't you tell me?" Her tone was…something. I didn't know what. Accusing, maybe, like this was a conspiracy to make her feel left out. "I would've come with you."

After dealing with drunk Angus, taking care of him and keeping him safe, I was tired, cranky, and the implication raised my hackles. "I thought you might be at the *library*."

Yeah, that made it pretty clear I knew she was shitting me earlier. I held her eyes for a couple beats until her gaze slid away. For the first time, like, ever, I didn't want to sleep in the same room with her. We were best friends, and she was lying to me; it hurt her, too, I could tell, but not enough for her to stop. She let me push past and out the door.

I had no idea where I was going until my feet carried me to Ty's place. *It's too late. He's probably in bed.* So I wheeled without knocking, but his door opened as I moved away.

Tired eyes, running pants, black T-shirt. He opened his arms. I kissed him.

"Rough night?" he asked when we broke apart.

"Yeah. I'm sorry to bother you."

"You can come in if you need to talk."

Probably I shouldn't, but dumping your problems was definitely a friend thing to do, and I could use the opinion of someone who didn't live with us. So I sat down while he brewed some tea—in an actual kettle, I noticed—and I told him about the drama with Lauren and Angus.

When I ran out of words, he had me snuggled close, a hot mug in my hands. I was so upset I didn't even notice it happening.

"Okay, Angus, you did fine, he needed to cut loose. Lauren obviously has something going on. Sometimes people just aren't ready to talk. Whatever it is, it's making her feel…" He paused, trying to think of the right word. "Lonely. But it's not your fault. And you can't help unless she lets you. I get why you're upset, though. Try not to hold it against her."

I cupped his cheek and kissed him softly. "You're good at this."

"I'm out of practice," he admitted. "It's been a while since anyone but Sam dumped their problems in my lap and expected me to make sense of them."

"Sorry to bother you so late."

"I couldn't sleep." At the curious tilt of my head, he added, "Started to worry when you didn't answer my texts, nothing since I said, *Soon*. In my head, I went immediately to, I'll never talk to her again and never find out why."

*Courtesy of Diana.*

It was stunning to hear Ty admit to overthinking things, just like I did. "I turned my phone off for class and forgot to turn it back on. I promise, if I ever decide this isn't working, I won't vanish, and we'll talk before it ends. Okay?"

"Thanks," he said softly.

I wished I could lead him to the bedroom and lose myself in him. Sex would be *amazing,* the perfect remedy for a shitty day. A wistful thorn pricked my palm, the yearning for more than he could give. When I came in, I was a mess, but now there was only love, welling up with the irresistible force of laughter or tears.

A love I couldn't acknowledge if I wanted him to stay.

# CHAPTER FOURTEEN

Friday morning, Angus was so hungover he couldn't move without moaning.

I couldn't stay home to coddle him, though; maybe Lauren or Max would take over. Before I left, I put water, crackers and ibuprofen on his bedside table. He fumbled through the remedies then pulled the covers over his head.

"You'll be okay," I told him.

"Thanks, Nadia." The words came out muffled.

Exhausted, I ate breakfast, rushed out to class and then drove to C-Cool. Talking and texting, students eddied around me. A few kids were already in Ms. Parker's room; one of them liked to follow me around, which freaked me out at the beginning of the year. Now I chatted with her while putting away my things. All things considered, the practicum went well. Instead of getting in my mentor's way, I anticipated her requests a couple of times.

She tapped my shoulder as I was leaving. "I know it's tough, and you're having doubts, but the kids respond to you, and the patience you possess naturally, it's a gift, Nadia. I've known people to bail, even at this stage."

"I appreciate hearing it. I'm hanging in." It would get better once the schedule change started at Rainbow Academy.

But for now, I had to run. Because I'd chatted with Ms. Parker, there was no convenience-store sandwich, but Louisa was waiting for me at the classroom with a plate she'd saved from lunch. I suspected Mrs. Keller had asked her to mother me, after our talk the other day.

"Careful, if the kids see it, they'll ask for seconds."

In five minutes, I scarfed the corn dog, carrots and celery, and the apple slices. It wasn't enough to fill me up, but I'd be nicer to a class full of four-year-olds if my stomach wasn't growling the whole time. With thirty seconds to spare, I darted into Mrs. Trent's room, feeling like I'd won the Boston Marathon.

"You're all sweaty," Sam said, running over to hug me.

I patted him on the head. Sometimes it was hard not to show favoritism. "Why did the dinosaur cross the road?"

"To get to the other side?"

"Good guess, but no. Because the chicken hadn't been invented yet!"

He giggled. "That was stupid."

"Hey, you're the one who loves these." Hopefully, the internet wouldn't run out of dinosaur material before he grew out of this stage.

I survived Friday and spent the weekend studying, as this was my last chance; next week I'd be taking midterms. Lauren and I didn't talk much, but Angus was doing better, so Thursday night was worth the drama. Max was around less both Saturday and Sunday. If he was prepping for his exams or working more, I had no idea.

Sunday night, I got a text from Ty.

I'm free the weekend of the 25th. Are you?

That was next weekend. I might be wiped from midterms, work and the practicum, but I had no plans.

What did you have in mind? I sent back.

You. Me. All weekend.

Suddenly I had more energy than I knew what to do with. My hands actually trembled when I asked,

Are you asking me to spend the weekend with you?

At my place, he clarified, like I really thought we were going on vacation together.

Can't wait.

That was a massive understatement.

During the next week, the promise of the twenty-fifth acted on me like a lure, spurring me on. I didn't sleep at all Sunday night, and on Monday, I was bleary-eyed but jacked up on energy drinks. I raced through the tests like the information was liquid that might trickle out my ears and onto my desk. My brain actually felt like that might be true.

At work, I was so sluggish, Sam noticed. I was sitting in one of the tiny chairs, watching the kids color, when he turned to me. "You look sad, Nadia."

"Just tired."

"You were tired before," he noted. "Dad is, too. It makes him grumpy."

Hearing Sam's impression of Ty put a smile on my face. "Being a grown-up is hard. I'm not very good at it yet, I suspect."

"Then stop," he advised.

It was a compelling suggestion, but I didn't think my parents or my academic adviser would be amused to find me hiding in a ball pit while screaming the Toys R Us theme song. But it seemed like a good idea to warn Mrs. Trent that I might be less than stellar this week.

"Midterms," she guessed.

"Yeah. So if I seem like I've taken up recreational drugs, I promise it's just exhaustion, so don't make me pee in a cup."

"Noted."

She went easy on me the rest of the day, and on Tuesday morning, she found jobs that required me to sit and watch the kids a lot. Not that I was complaining. I resolved to work extra hard for her once I got over this hurdle. Instead of going to Chuck E. Cheese's, I took my Tuesday exams and then fell asleep hugging my tablet, trying to cram even more for Wednesday morning. The final was tough enough that it made my practicum feel like a welcome break; at least there was no test.

At work, I responded to Ty's texts, though they were sporadic and low-key, stuff like, *Thinking of you* and *Is it Friday yet?* That night when I got home, Lauren had dinner ready, plus her famous oatmeal cookies. I took the gesture as an apology.

"Are we good?" she asked.

"Yeah. I think this is the longest we've ever *not* been. Is your mom sick?" It was the only thing I could think of.

She shook her head. "No, it's... I just did a stupid thing, that's all."

"What?"

"Max."

For a minute, I wasn't sure I heard right. "Huh?"

"I wasn't in our room that night because I was in Max's." But from her expression, that wasn't good.

"Don't tell me he's terrible."

"No, the sex was fine."

Suddenly, I thought I understood the problem. "And *now* you've hooked up with someone we live with, and it's kind of weird."

"Yep. I can't look at him now, and he leaves the room pretty much as soon as I walk in. I don't know what we were thinking."

*Oh, Lauren. He was thinking,* finally. *This must be killing Max.*

On some level, I'd registered that he wasn't around much anymore, but I had so much stuff going on that I couldn't keep tabs on all of them. Sometimes I had to get my own house in order before I could do any freelance cleaning, so to speak. Unfortunately, there was no way to clue her in without breaking his confidence.

"What are you going to do?" I decided on a noncommittal response.

"Right now, I'm mostly surprised you're not making fun of me. Max, of all people." She shook her head, sighing.

Restraining a wince on his behalf, I answered, "Like I would."

It was clear she saw the whole thing as good sex, bad idea, which meant she had no inkling how he felt. Punching him in the head might be my next move. Lauren thought she was no more important than anyone else he'd slept with. *Good luck changing her mind,* I thought.

"Try to act normal. So you're friends with benefits." The irony of me saying that didn't escape me. "It's not that big a deal, right?"

"I don't think we'll be benefiting each other again," she said.

"Why not?"

"It was…" She paused, as if trying to organize her thoughts. "It happened for the wrong reason, that's all."

"Were you drunk?" I tried not to sound judgmental.

"It's complicated." Her expression darkened.

Somehow I didn't think Max had done anything to warrant that look. If I had to guess, I'd say she was thinking of her father. The guy hadn't called or written since he left ten years ago. It wasn't an exaggeration to figure she had daddy issues, and there was a reason why she preferred no-strings sex to getting deep. Relationships required trust, and she didn't have much to spare.

Since she'd opened up, I should do the same, as much as I could. "Speaking of beneficial arrangements, I'm kinda seeing the guy downstairs."

"Hot Ginger?"

"Stop calling him that. His name is Ty."

"And you're dating? How long has this been going on?"

"Let's say we're conducting field research to find out if the friends with benefits thing can ever really work out."

"So you're fuck buddies."

"Not yet," I muttered. "But I have high hopes for this weekend."

"I'd tell you to be careful, but given my own situation, I feel like that'd just be inviting some pot-kettle commentary."

"Whatever. Let's watch TV before I go back to studying. How are midterms going?"

*There, now she knows about Ty. He's not my secret anymore.*

She shrugged. "I'm not off to an awesome start this semester, so…about as well as I expected. I hope to do better on finals."

Angus came home while we were watching a cooking show. He dismissed the contestants with a wave of a hand. "Amateurs. How are my two favorite ladies?"

"Sleepy," I said. "But determined to reread the last of the material before tomorrow. I'll catch you guys later."

Taking my tablet, I got into bed, which probably wasn't the best move. I read half a chapter before passing out, and when my alarm went off in the morning, I fell out of bed trying to turn it off. If I was rich, I could break clocks on a daily basis, just for the satisfaction of shutting them up permanently. Of course, being independently wealthy would also likely mean I could sleep as long as I wanted.

With a sigh, I crawled into the shower. My whole body ached with weariness. I had been skipping out on sleep, trying to make it up in caffeine, and I was about to hit my tipping point. I felt so shitty, I didn't even care about the weekend with Ty. By the time Friday arrived, I'd be in no shape to enjoy it. I washed that bitter thought down with some coffee and granola, then I headed to work.

*Thursday. Thursday sucks.*

When I pulled into the Rainbow Academy parking lot, I was in no mood to deal with children. This foul mood seemed etched in stone until Ty came out of the building. He usually dropped Sam off earlier; must be running late. My first instinct was to let him go, but as if he sensed me watching him, like that first night on his balcony, he spun until he found me looking.

"Nadia." I swore I heard him say my name from all the way over here, his expression brightening like I was all the good things in the world. Then he was jogging toward me.

I'd rarely seen him all put-together for work. Usually, I saw the aftermath of a long day, wrinkled pants, ink-stained tie. But this Ty was crisp and gorgeous: navy trousers and jacket, white shirt, red-and-blue-striped tie. More conservative than I'd have pictured, but he looked amazingly sharp for a guy who had wrangled a four-year-old before work.

By comparison, I felt like a crumpled dollar bill.

"Best morning ever," he said.

Before I could ask what he meant, he pushed me up against the car and kissed me. In the side lot, it was doubtful anyone could see us, certainly not Sam, and I wanted this too much to push him away. His mouth was magical, chock-full of endorphins and sweetness. He was syrup and pancakes for the soul.

"Wow," I said, breathless.

"Yep." Such a lazy, delicious smile. Why had I never noticed how devilish he could be? "I might start leaving ten minutes later, if this is the payoff. Hate to kiss and run. I just needed a top-up to last until tomorrow night."

When I realized I was that close to finishing midterms, I nearly burst into tears. "What time should I be there?"

Ty was already rushing toward his car, long legs putting distance between us. I'd never seen him run before, and I was transfixed by the sheer, animal grace of him. He called over his shoulder, "Should be home by nine. I'll text as soon as I pull up."

*Like I won't be watching.*

The memory of that kiss carried me through my morning shift and through afternoon exams. Somehow I lived through Friday, as well, and then I drove home, unable to believe I'd come out on the other side with my sanity intact. Stumbling into the apartment, I didn't see anyone at first, but as I closed the door, I spotted Max just standing in the kitchen, leaning on the fridge; I hadn't seen him since I'd talked to Lauren on Wednesday.

"It works better if you open it," I said.

When he turned, I sucked in a sharp breath. Scratches and bruises marred his face, and one of his eyes was nearly swollen shut. I dropped my backpack and raced to his bedroom door, anticipating his next move, and I was barely fast enough to stop him from pushing past me.

"I don't want to talk," he said.

"Okay." Though I originally planned to hop in the shower and get ready for tonight, I had time. Grabbing his arm, I tugged him into his bedroom and shut the door behind us.

"Don't take this the wrong way, Conrad, but I'm not remotely in the mood."

Smirking, I ignored the lame joke aimed at saving face and picked up a game controller. "Let's shoot some things."

He sighed. "You won't go away?"

"In an hour, I will."

"Fine." Max plopped down on his bed and put in a noisy, violent game. For a good half hour, neither of us said a word, just tag-teaming on zombies. This wasn't my favorite type of game, and I was usually too busy to play them, but it was worth it when he stopped looking quite so fucking alone.

Eventually, he paused the game and flopped backward on his bed. "You're not asking."

"Do you want me to?"

"Not really."

"There you go, then." Gently I put a hand on his head.

To my surprise, Max sat up and hugged me. Not really

understanding, I wrapped my arms around him and rubbed his back. His breath came in ragged gulps, and he wasn't crying, but it felt the same, just endless waves of shudders mixed with painful gasps. I just held him and said nothing because I knew Lauren had to be mixed up in it somehow. She hadn't mentioned a fight the other day, but maybe this was a new development.

In time, he pulled away, still battered, still bruised, but there was a hint of a shy smile in his eyes. I'd call that progress.

"You're not so bad," he said.

"This is your home, okay? Don't roam the streets looking for trouble. There are people here who love you."

"Do *you* love me?" He pretended to leer.

"I'd call you the annoying brother I never had, but I have one already. So you can be my irritating cousin." I stood up, stretched and caught sight of the clock.

*Shit.* It was past eight, and I'd left my phone in my backpack. *If Ty got home early, he must be wondering where the hell I am. I'm not standing you up, I promise.*

"You can clock out. I'm fine." Max smiled, the motion pulling at his split lip.

After stepping out of his room, I immediately checked my messages. Relief surged through me when I realized Ty must still be with his parents. I emptied my backpack of notebooks and tablet, then added my phone and charger, two pairs of underwear, a couple of T-shirts, my toothbrush. I'd never spent the weekend with a guy before, at home or otherwise. I had no idea what to bring. Though I suspected I didn't need it, I put in my cosmetic bag.

*Maybe I should've cooked something? Is it weird to assume we'll be naked the whole time? Should I pack more pants? Pajamas?* With a shrug, I decided I could run upstairs for anything I needed, though I was trying to avoid the teasing and inquisition from my roomies. Bizarre enough that this sex-a-thon would take place in our building. The usual presex rituals calmed me a little. I showered, waxed, moisturized and then put on yoga pants and a T-shirt for easy off/on. Maybe I should dress to impress, instead, but I had the feeling anything I wore would end up on his floor. *Hope so, anyway.*

At fifteen after nine, my phone beeped. Ty:

I'm home in 5 4 3 2...you ready?

You have no idea.

I ran down the stairs to meet him.

# CHAPTER FIFTEEN

Ty was stepping inside when I reached the foyer. At the front doors, he squeezed me close, kissed my forehead and then left his arm around my shoulders as he moved us toward his place. "You have no idea how much I've been looking forward to this weekend."

"It got me through midterms," I confessed.

That prompted a smile as he unlocked the door and flipped on the lights. This was the messiest I'd ever seen his place, likely because he had to feed Sam, pack for day care, plus the weekend bag, and get his son out of the house early. This was probably the first time he'd been back all day. It didn't bother me, but Ty went around collecting stray toys, like he didn't want any reminders. He stuffed them in the trunk and then turned to me.

"Let me take a quick shower, okay?" I was a little surprised that he didn't suggest taking one together, and he must've read that in my face, because he added with a small grin, "Shower sex can be complicated. We need to work up to it. Plus, I want to take my time in bed, not worrying about how much hot water we have left."

"I like the way you think."

He disappeared into the bathroom, and I turned on the TV. Now that we were finally on the cusp of changing everything, butterflies flapped like pterodactyls in my stomach. There had been so much buildup, so much tension. What if reality couldn't live up to expectations? I was frowning at an infomercial when Ty came into the living room, toweling his hair dry.

"You don't believe that nonstick cookware traps the flavor inside and requires no oil?"

The flutter inside me turned into a different feeling when I realized he was naked, apart from the blue towel knotted around his waist. My gaze slipped to his feet, second toes longer than the first, traveled up to well-muscled calves and lean thighs. Skipping upward, I admired the beads of water clinging to his chest. His stomach was slightly ridged, not a six-pack—he didn't have time for that—but cut enough to tempt me to trace the lines. Broad shoulders, strong arms, he was the total package, and even more when you considered how smart and funny he was, what an amazing person.

When I shifted my gaze upward, he was flushed, either with excitement or embarrassment. "Damn. That look felt like foreplay. I was going to offer you a drink, but—"

"I'm not thirsty."

"Then turn that off. Too much TV is bad for you."

Smiling, I stood up and he took my hand. We walked down the hall toward his room, and I noticed that Sam's door was closed. Symbolic, most likely—representing Ty's commitment to keeping these two parts of his life separate. He had a full-size bed with a black wrought-iron headboard, and it was already turned back, revealing brown sheets beneath the blue-and-brown circle-patterned comforter.

He turned and put his palm to my cheek. "I don't know what I'm doing. I've never had a woman in this bed."

Perversely, I was glad to hear that. Even if we never had a regular relationship, this part of him was mine. "I thought you said it had only been—"

"I go out occasionally, pick someone up, either at a bar or a party. Then we go to her place. I don't stay the night."

Put that way, it sounded depressing, not the right mood for our first time. But I couldn't help asking, "How is that better than beating off?"

A wry smile. "I'm not alone. Let's not talk about this, okay?"

"I just need to ask one more thing."

"Feel free."

"Will you still be doing that while we're doing this?" I tried not to sound bothered because we didn't have a commitment.

"Of course not. But you can…do what you want." To my vast pleasure, he gritted that last part out, as if he hated saying the words.

I laughed softly. "I wouldn't have the time or energy. This is enough. *You* are."

"If that's true, you're wearing too many clothes." He grasped the bottom of my T-shirt and pulled it over my head in a smooth movement.

I didn't think he expected me to be topless so fast because he stilled, eyes on my breasts. I'd had guys touch me and not turn me on as much as that look. I watched his face as I worked my yoga pants down and stepped out of them. Now I had on my panties, and he was still sporting the towel. My hand trembled as I flicked it away from his hips. I had never been prone to comparing male packages, but his made my mouth water. In a glance, it was deliciously obvious how much he wanted me.

"You are so beautiful," he whispered.

It didn't matter if I was; only that he thought so. "Come to bed."

Teasingly, I scrambled across the mattress, making him come to me. He was gentle when he did, and I squirmed down onto my side, eyes locked on his face. Ty wore an expression of incredulity and longing, like he just couldn't believe I was actually here. He kissed me at last, lips delicate as a flower petal when I wanted so much more. That lightness didn't last long. With a hungry growl, he deepened the kiss, and I tasted mint on his tongue.

Against my mouth, he whispered, "I've imagined you here so often."

"Yeah?" I loved knowing he'd fantasized about me.

"In my favorite scene, you slip in through the patio door. I'm sound asleep in bed and you wake me."

"How do I do that?"

A shudder worked through him as he touched a fingertip to my lower lip. "With your mouth."

Teasing him, I whispered, "That's dirty. I'm not sure how I feel about taking advantage of a helpless, sleeping man."

He shivered. "Just so we're clear, consent is granted ahead of time."

More kissing. I initiated it, using Ty's favorite move. I loved the rasp of his scruff against my palms. As I nibbled his lower lip, he brought me closer, until my breasts fit against his chest. He made a sound in his throat and I wrapped a thigh around his hip, trying to get closer. The shift rubbed us together deliciously, only my panties between us.

Considering how wild, how desperate, he had been the first

time we touched, his patience seemed unusual. Suddenly, I suspected I knew why. "You cheated, didn't you?"

"Hmm?" He was kissing a tender path down my throat, nibbling, licking and evoking *all* the tingles.

"I know what you did in the shower." Turning his head to the side, I bit his shoulder. *That drove him nuts last time.* He rewarded me with a hiss of pleasure. "And I can't believe you didn't let me watch."

Ty throbbed against me; the push and surge made me moan. "You deserve more than seven minutes in heaven, so to speak."

"But I missed out on you. In the shower. All soapy and wet. I promise it would've been good for me. I'd be even more turned on than I am right now."

Ty fell onto his back when I gave a little push and by the jump in his breathing, he was into the idea of me watching him. "Next time," he promised. "Although why I'd be doing that again when you're here—"

"It was your idea," I whispered. "And it's rude to invite someone over and then keep all the fun for yourself."

"I'll make it up to you." When I nuzzled down his chest toward his belly, he fisted his hands in the sheets. "If it's any... consolation, it's not helping as much as I h-hoped."

*Good.* I didn't say it out loud, but I wanted him in bed like he had been that night on the couch. Incoherent, shaking, completely on fire. I kissed and licked a path around his navel, then reversed directions, bit his nipple on the way up to his ears. I set a palm on his inner thigh, a whisper away, but I didn't move it upward. Instead, I leaned in and nibbled his ear, remembering how he'd begged me to touch them.

"Shit," he breathed, closing his eyes.

He turned his head, giving me better access. I nibbled and licked, bit gently, until he was shivering. Such an odd, specific hot zone, but clearly it drove him nuts. Then I went for his other ear and he moaned. Now he was closer to where I wanted him, wild and demanding, not tender and civilized. There might come a point when I'd enjoy the latter but not tonight.

He shoved me onto my back, no finesse, and lowered his head. His mouth on my breasts was pretty close to the best thing I'd ever felt. Ty played the game my way, never touching me below the waist, no matter how much I wanted it. I squirmed and writhed while he worked his mouth over me, sipping at my nipples until I clutched his head, demanding more. Then he gave me teases of teeth, still not enough. I rolled my hips, desperate for pressure. He ripped off my panties with a guttural protest that I should still be wearing them.

"If I don't get inside you," he whispered, "I'm going to hump the mattress and come."

"Condom," I managed to answer.

"God, yes."

My hands were shaking too much to help him, and he was clumsy. It took two tries to get him covered, and then he pulled me upright and sat back at an angle against the pillows. I came down on top of him slowly, wrapping my legs around his hips. Perfect fit, he throbbed inside me, so hot, so hard. I tightened, and he trembled, lips parted. With the moonlight streaming in, his face was the sexiest thing I'd ever seen.

"Like this?" I moved.

"*Yes*. I have to see you, hold you, taste you." His eyes were on mine as he cupped my ass, working us together, slow first and then faster. "Show me it feels good."

I caught the rhythm quickly, loving the friction, the hot rub of his sweaty skin on mine, his chest against my breasts. If I tilted forward a little, it was even better. Sharp sparks of pleasure rocked through me with each push and glide. He bit the side of my neck, a tender pain, and I whispered his name.

"Jesus." He swelled inside me, reacting, so I said it again, until there was only his name, and our bodies, grinding together, faster, harder, harder. His fingers might be bruising my hips, and I didn't mind.

"*Nadia.*"

Heated breath misted my lips, so I leaned in those two inches and took his mouth. *Almost there.* I thought it, didn't say it, but his mouth said it back, as we pushed home. He jerked and shuddered, and the spiked pleasure rolled through me in waves, tightening my thighs, again, again, until we were panting into each other's shoulders. My whole body felt loose and warm, the perfect culmination of so many weeks of wanting what I thought I'd never have.

It didn't happen as I'd expected, but it was amazing sex. Ty kissed my sweaty temple and lifted me off him. He was gone two minutes according to his bedside clock. When he returned, I was a melted puddle of girl on one side of the bed, too spent to crawl under the covers. He shifted them over me and then slipped in beside me. I wouldn't have been surprised if he had rolled over, but instead he drew me against him, finding the perfect spot for my head on his shoulder. We fit together like jigsaw pieces, and happiness sparkled through me like a kaleidoscope, all the scintillating colors wheeling through the spectrum in my head.

"Two days isn't enough," Ty said. "So I have to ask you to come back in November."

It thrilled me that he seemed so sure. But then I realized, "That's Thanksgiving. Won't you be with your parents? And even if you aren't, I'm going to Nebraska with Lauren."

"Fucking holidays."

I smirked. "Not for me. I'll be too far away."

His arms tightened around me. "Don't say that."

"I'm coming back, Ty."

"I know. But I'll miss you."

"Me, too. But if you have video chat, we can watch each other do dirty things."

He turned his head toward me and I caught the faint smile. "You have my attention."

"It's not like being here, but—" He already knew that it got me hot to watch, so no need to elaborate.

"I wouldn't even consider doing it for anyone but you," he admitted.

"Clearly, I'm special."

"You have no idea." Ty kissed the top of my head, my cheeks, my chin and finally my mouth. This kissing was slow and lazy, exploratory and tender, because we were both tapped out, no chance it could lead to sex without us sleeping a few hours first.

But I recalled what he'd said about the little things. I didn't have long nails, so maybe it wouldn't be as good, but I drew my fingers lightly down his back. Goose bumps immediately sprang up in the wake of my touch. He practically purred.

"Don't stop," he demanded.

"Definitely not. This is one of the benefits of sleeping together."

"Mmm. God, Nadia. This is too good. You are."

That alone kept me stroking for ten minutes. But eventually a yawn burst out of me. "I know it's only ten-thirty, but would you hate me if I went to sleep?"

"Now I know you were made for me. I was just thinking the same thing."

Never in my life had I slept with a guy, but with Ty, it was perfect. Easy. I just rolled over on my left side, he tucked himself behind me, and we both winked out. Four hours later, according to the clock, I woke up needing to pee. He was still holding me, so it took some doing to get out from under his arm without waking him.

Tiptoeing back from the bathroom, I remembered his confession, and a devilish impulse took over. Instead of settling quietly on my side of the bed, I burrowed under the covers and found him half-hard already. A few gentle strokes and he grew out of my palm.

He shifted, spreading his thighs to make room, and for a few tense seconds, I thought he was awake. But his breathing remained steady, and I hoped like hell that he was dreaming what I suspected he might be. Imagining the moment when he came in the dream and woke up coming, well, it was all I could do not to put my hand between my legs right then.

I didn't tease. Gently I licked up and down until he was well lubricated, then I sucked him into my mouth. He tasted clean and I savored the contrast of hardness and silky skin rubbing over my tongue. Keeping my teeth well away, I gradually increased the pressure of the suction, until he started to move, taking my mouth in slow, dreamy thrusts.

"Harder. Suck harder." By the mumbling quality of his tone, he had to be mostly still asleep, but lost in the pleasure, lost in me.

I had to shift, get the covers between my legs, so I had something to rub against. For long, delicious moments, I made love to him with my mouth while circling my hips and squeezing my thighs against the comforter. Not ideal, but I needed two hands to caress and make it good for him. *Mmm. Getting close.* I was slick and moving faster, sucking harder. A minute later, dream and reality merged when he arched and groaned out my name. Ty spurted into my mouth as I came, and then he was up on an elbow, such a delicious mix of rosy sex and confusion. His eyes were half-open, and he pulled back the covers to rest his hands on my head while I gently eased him through the aftershocks. For a few seconds, his throat worked, but no sound emerged.

Then he dragged me up on top of him, kissing me so fiercely that I went light-headed. He had to taste himself on my tongue, but it didn't seem to bother him. His cock was slick and sticky between us, softening against me, but he didn't ease up on the fervor of his hold or the ferocious gratitude of his mouth.

When he finally pulled back, he couldn't seem to stop tasting me. Lips, eyelids, cheeks, chin, temples. Everywhere, everything, he wanted all of me.

"Nobody's ever made my dreams come true before," he finally whispered.

"Then you were due."

"I'm afraid if I blink, you'll be gone. I didn't think anyone would put up with the rules and limitations that go along with me."

"You're worth it." My tone must've convinced him I meant it because his expression softened, and he shifted so he could hold me properly; a relief because it wasn't comfortable to rest directly on top of him. I was too tall, too worried that I might be crushing him.

"I swear, you moving into this building is the best thing that ever happened to me."

With a grin, I answered, "If I'd known the complex came with such perks, I'd have signed the lease sooner. You're *way* better than the weight room."

"Am I?" Teasingly, he dipped his fingers between my

thighs, and then breathed out a soft curse. "*Fuck.* Sucking me made you come."

"Yep." *Well, the blanket helped.* But it was better for his ego not to hear that, and he could use the self-confidence. Fixed on old mistakes, Ty didn't seem to have a clue how incredible he was.

I intended to spend the weekend showing him.

# CHAPTER SIXTEEN

Around eleven the next morning, Ty stirred beside me. I had been awake for fifteen minutes, but it was such a luxury to cuddle with him that I didn't move. His hand stirred on my back in lazy sweeps, long before he opened his eyes. The smile started there, when his gaze met mine. It wasn't awkward or strange, and I could tell he was happy to see me, not just in the euphemistic sense.

He stretched lazily. "I feel fantastic."

"Me, too. Should we get up?"

"Probably."

I rolled out of bed and used the bathroom first, then he took a turn, and afterward, we shared a splashy, playful shower. He dried me off with slow, teasing sweeps of the towel, and if I wasn't so damn hungry, I would've hauled him back to bed. While I dug through my backpack, looking for my cosmetic case, he kissed my shoulder.

"Lose something?"

"I found it."

"Cucumber lotion?" He didn't even look at the label.

Curious, I opened the bottle and warmed some in my palms. "It's cucumber and green tea. But how did you know?"

"I notice everything about you," he said simply. "You don't wear perfume often, but when you do, it smells like cucumbers and melon. You don't wear much makeup. You prefer boots to any other footwear. Converse are a close second. Should I go on?"

My heart rate trebled, and to hide the shocked pleasure of my reaction, I challenged him with a raised brow. "What's my favorite color? Food? Song? Movie?"

"Those aren't things I can learn from observation. You have to tell me."

His smile was so gentle; I'd never had *anyone* look at me that way. He smoothed his palms against mine, taking the lotion onto his skin, then he applied it smoothly, rubbing up and down my arms. Turning, I offered my back and he covered every inch, instead of my usual after-shower slapdash efforts.

As I did my legs, I managed to flirt. "Are you asking?"

"Yeah. But before you drop that knowledge, do you want to make food or go out?"

"Hmm. It's supposed to be our weekend off, but I can't decide which is lazier."

"Would it impact your decision to know I didn't do any shopping this week?"

I laughed. "Yeah, and my skills don't extend too far past hot dog casserole."

"Hey, that was amazing. Just ask Sam."

Still thinking, I padded to the bedroom and put on clean underwear, yoga pants, T-shirt. "I didn't bring much with me but—"

"You want to order pizza?"

"I'd rather have breakfast," I confessed. "Let's see what's in the kitchen."

I found enough eggs to fry some and make French toast. "I can work with what's here."

"Are you sure?" he asked. "I can do it."

"You'll get a turn tomorrow. I'm warning you, I have high expectations."

Ty sat on a kitchen stool and watched me crack the eggs, whisk in the milk and vanilla, like it was totally astounding. "You said you can't cook."

First I tested my pan, making sure it was hot enough. Then I dipped the bread in the mixture and set it in the skillet. "When I was in high school, I worked at a diner helping out in the kitchen. Dishes mostly, but the fry cook showed me enough to cover his breaks."

"So…burgers, fries, sandwiches, French toast, eggs, what else?"

Okay, so maybe I was showing off a little when I flipped the toast without a spatula. "Pancakes from a mix. I can also boil pasta and fry things."

"Sounds good to me."

Pretty soon I had six pieces of toast done, and I put them in his oven, set on low, to keep warm while I fried the eggs. It didn't occur to me to ask permission before rummaging in his fridge and cupboards; maybe that was rude, but Ty didn't complain. After setting out butter and syrup, I located the coffee and got some brewing. He had a simple machine, which was a relief because I hated the kind with tons of buttons and attachments. I'd never make it as a barista.

"How do you want your eggs?"

"Over easy."

I made those briskly, then plated our breakfast. Ty caught

the dish I slid toward him: two fried eggs, three pieces of French toast. Smiling, I poured two coffees and rounded the counter to sit beside him. I'd eaten breakfast with a few boyfriends now and then, but never one I cooked. This was a weekend for all kinds of firsts.

"Okay, now I get to test you," I teased.

"Abraham Lincoln."

"Good guess, but no. Based on your impressive observations, what do you think my favorite color is?"

"Green?"

I tilted my head, surprised. "How did you know?"

"You wear it a lot."

Mentally, I sorted through my closet and realized I had three green hoodies, different shades, and four green sweaters, though to be fair, one of those could pass as turquoise in the right light. And it was amazing that he paid attention. That deserved a victory kiss, so I leaned over, planning to press my lips to his cheek, but Ty turned his head and took it on the mouth. He tasted like syrup, butter and coffee, absolute morning perfection. I licked my lips.

"I like this game," he murmured. "I think I'm winning."

"I won't ask you to guess my favorite food. Since we haven't eaten together much, it wouldn't be fair."

"So tell me."

"My grandma was from Russia, and when I was a kid, every winter when the first snow fell, she'd make a big pot of mushroom, beef and barley soup." It was odd to talk about her; she died when I was sixteen. "And since she's been gone, I've never had any that tasted as good, not even my mom's. Which is weird—it's the same recipe. She made the most delicious black bread to go with it. To me, those two things, that's what winter tastes like."

---

and gravy. Spring is grilled salmon, seasoned with lime. What the hell is squash casserole?"

Laughing, I got my phone and looked up a recipe for him.

"See? Sounds gross, but it's really good, I swear."

"I'll take your word for it. Are you done?"

"Yep. Thanks."

He took my plate and set the dishes to soak in the sink while we went to snuggle on the couch. It wasn't cold enough to turn on the heat yet, but it was chilly enough that it felt good to tuck up beside him and cover us with the chenille throw. His [ar]m around my shoulders felt perfect, and as I leaned against [hi]m, it was hard to imagine that this was just a time-out, so [a]nd that real life would resume soon—with none

us.

...efits.

he prompted, resting a hand on the back

tilted my head, and soon, he was idly
twining curls around his fingers. A
into ...ugh me.
whet...ne, because the music I
thing ... only pick o
"At the
National."

"Dark cho
I felt him st
"We're up to
"Yeah."

I glanced at him, embarrassed about turning my favorite food into such a personal story, but Ty was just watching me. I lifted my chin, daring him to make a joke.

His response was surprisingly serious. "For me, winter is my mom's shepherd's pie. We have relatives in Ireland—on her side—who taught her the recipe. Yeah," he added, sheepish. "That's where the hair comes from."

"I like it," I said softly.

"You can imagine how it was in grade school."

"I got tall jokes. Started growing when I was twelve and didn't stop until I was eighteen."

"You're stunning."

There went my heart again. I forgot about breakfast on my plate and focused on his face like there would be a test. In response to my look, he leaned over and kissed me, tracing a fingertip down my cheek to rest it lightly on my chin. My eyes closed, but he didn't take it further, and I opened them, faintly disappointed.

"Not now, you have a headache?"

"We're talking. If you cut it short, I'll feel cheap and dirty."

I grinned. "You say that like it's a bad thing."

"Dirty's not, but I seriously do want to get to know you better. I feel like before now, our time has been stolen, rushed, whatever."

"That's fair. Okay, so where were we?"

"We talked about winter food. I'm _____ _____ for the other three seasons."

"That's easy. Su_____ _____ _____
That required _____ _____ _____
breakfast. "Squa_____ _____ _____
strawberry short_____ _____

"Summer is an _____ _____

"Don't laugh. This is an old one. But I never get tired of Groundhog Day. It's deeper than the premise seems like, almost existential." I'd had this conversation with other people, most of whom thought I was crazy, especially when I started sending links to internet essays about the symbolism and interviews with the producers.

"You're so cute." Ty wrapped his other arm around me and shifted so I was cuddled between his legs, braced against his chest. "Never watched it, but maybe we should check it out this weekend. It's probably on Netflix." He pointed at his TV, and I noticed he had a laptop hooked up. "Cheaper than cable."

"Good idea. Maybe we can do that upstairs. So what's your pick?"

"Old JGL movie, indie. It's called Brick."

"Never heard of it." He was lucky I knew who JGL wa_____

"It's cool, this noir story set in a high school about _____

"Never mind. Let's watch both," I suggested. "_____

"I'm intrigued. _____ figure out who killed his girlfriend."

we think of each other's pick."

"We can go out for dinner later, if you're up f_____

That sounded so much like a date that at first_____

what to say. But honestly, how did you see this_____

Nothing but sex interspersed with Ty ignoring yo_____

Aloud I said. "Can we do the double fe_____

"It can be arranged."

"So tell me what you were like in h_____

wondered what he'd say, but I was a_____

before. Before Diana, before Sam, _____

"I played basketball. Not well _____

doing crazy shit; I'd seen him on_____

coach pestered the shit out of _____

"So you grew up in Mou_____

"Yep, born and raised. I didn't intend to graduate from here, though. I was planning to earn some credits and then transfer to a college with a better architecture program."

*But Sam came along, and your plans changed.*

"My friend Lauren and I applied to the same schools, and this was the only one where they offered both of us a scholarship."

"I'm glad you're here." He kissed the top of my head.

"Tell me more about high school Ty."

"Daniel," he corrected quietly.

"Huh?"

"Nobody called me Ty back then. I've never been Dan… because that's my dad, and Danny—with this hair? I'd never survive."

"So what changed?" I didn't realize it was a sensitive topic until his hand knotted in my hair, not hurting me, but sending an unmistakable message about his tension.

His voice was quiet when he answered. "Diana. When we met, I was Daniel, and… Are you sure you want to hear this story? It's kind of stupid."

"I'm interested, unless it bothers you."

"Okay, so she read an article about how couples with alliterative names are more likely to stay together—I think I told you she was a scientist. So we met in freshman biology, and she goes, 'Hello, Daniel. I'm Diana,' like it was hugely significant. Her approach was really…awkward, and I thought she was shitting me until she explained the premise, and then I said *what the hell* and went out for coffee."

"You must've had a good time." *If you fell in love with her.*

"Yeah. Once I got past all the scientific terminology, she was so funny. Beautiful." He sighed quietly, unknotting his fingers from my hair. "We had so many plans. I wish…I wish I could apologize. By the end, it got so ugly between us."

Pain crimped my chest, listening to him talk, but I couldn't blame Ty. I'd asked. Moments like this, my experience felt inadequate since nobody I knew had deep, dark relationships broken behind them. None of my friends had kids. Sometimes I wondered if he saw me as immature, but I didn't really want to learn the answer. I made some kind of encouraging noise, as if I didn't wish he'd stop talking about Diana.

He was practically whispering, like the words weren't even for me, more of a message to the universe, to be carried to the girl who went away. "I hope she's happy, you know? It feels like I took everything away from her."

"She probably needed to start over," I said weakly.

"Anyway, after she left, I couldn't be Daniel. And a few of the guys from the b-ball team used to call me Ty, and it felt better, a clean slate for me, too."

*Jesus. How can I compete with that?* He loved her so much that when she left, he had to change his name. And now, Ty was so messed up that he didn't let anyone close. I had no sense of how much he cared about me—if we really were just friends with surprising sexual chemistry. But I'd agreed to this setup, and I couldn't let doubts spoil our weekend.

*I'm here. She's not. The end.*

"If it matters, I can't picture you as Daniel. Maybe it's because of Daniel Radcliffe, but for me, that's a very serious, bespectacled name. Ty suits you. It's tough and terse, but there's another syllable hiding, if you care enough to look."

His arms tightened on me, and he growled in my ear, "When you say ridiculous, adorable things like that, it makes me want to take you to bed."

"What's stopping you? We've rested for an hour after eating. We won't get cramps."

"I think that applies to swimming, not sex. But I'll take you." And then he did.

Ty swooped me into his arms and carried me to his room. He made a fair job of acting like I wasn't heavy or ungainly, either, which I appreciated. As he lowered me gently to the bed, his eyes were soft, and the sunlight framed him, so he was all the warmth in the world, shades of amber, copper and gold. Beneath the anticipation thrummed a bittersweet yearning; I wanted so much more than this. But I craved the heat of his hands and the blind need of his lips, too.

"Every time I kiss you," he whispered, "it's a little better. Why is that?"

"I'm constantly upgrading the system, just to keep you on your toes." His hair was somewhere between short and shaggy, perfect for tangling my fingers in.

"You seem to be wearing clothes. Didn't I decree this was naked Saturday?"

"Nope." I kissed the tip of his nose.

"Damn. I should have."

With palpable impatience, Ty stripped away my clothes, and I sprawled nude on his navy comforter. Though I wasn't used to posing like a calendar girl, I tried, stretching out my legs because he liked them. "I could get on board with that. Would this be a monthly event?"

"It could be. I think it needs to be."

"Yeah?"

"Yeah." His gaze blazed down my body as he shucked his running shorts. "I planned on taking my time, you know that? I had it all planned out. Multi-orgasms for you, massive self-control for me."

"How's that working out for you?"

"It's not. You said that sweet stuff about my name, and now you're all gorgeous thighs, breasts and sex hair. Which *I* gave you. My ideals have seriously outpaced my willpower."

Stroking a hand down his cheek, I whispered, "I don't really want you to be a fuck machine. It gets me hot when you can't help it, when you cut loose—"

His mouth took mine. His hands were everywhere, like he couldn't touch me fast enough, and the kisses blurred into a hot sparkle of pleasure: lips and teeth on my jaw, throat, shoulders and nipples, lower, the curve of my hips and my inner thighs. Need slammed through me until I ached, so slick and hot, but Ty was merciless. I'd given him permission to lose control, and apparently, he wanted to drive me insane. I moaned as he nuzzled deeper, teeth sinking into the tender flesh of my inner thighs.

Tugging on his hair, I begged, "Make me come."

To show him how serious I was, I teased my palm down my stomach and touched two fingers to my clit. *So close.* He didn't answer verbally, but his hands shook as he rolled on the condom. Ty was rough when he grabbed my legs and yanked me to the edge of the bed. His voice was a gravelly dip when he said, "Lift your hips."

I'd never done it like this, but I was too turned on to refuse anything he wanted. Ty slid a pillow under my ass, then took me in a sharp, sudden thrust. *Oh. Yeah.* He was so hard, throbbing inside me, and the tension jacked higher when I wrapped my legs around his hips and moved with him, grinding into each thrust. With him looming over me, watching everything, the heat quadrupled: each jerk of my body, each bounce of my breasts, if my mouth opened, if my lashes drifted shut, he saw it. *God, yes.* He held my hips, jerking me onto him faster each time, and I wanted it just as much: hard, dirty, rough.

"No, don't close your eyes." He locked his gaze on me, watching, savoring the helpless way I arched.

*Almost.*

Awash in need, I hardly knew what I was doing when my hands went to my breasts. But his ragged breathing said he liked it, and soon, the motions were for both of us. I twisted and writhed. The angle wasn't quite right, but Ty's avid expression said he knew—and that he wanted me screaming, every bit as much as I wanted him to lose control. And Christ, I was so close to—

With a growl, I grabbed his shoulders and pulled as hard as I could. He tumbled down on top of me, and while he was regrouping, I rolled us so I was on top. He slipped out, and we both snarled, but I swung my leg over his hips and sank down with a shivering moan. Tilting forward, I fucked him as hard as I could, no more than six strokes, and I came so hard that I took him with me; a surprise by the shocked, agonized bliss of his expression. His hands hurt on my thighs where he gripped me, but it felt so good when he held me still, so I felt each pulse, each throb.

"I think I might be in danger of dying of dehydration," he mumbled.

I collapsed and rolled onto my side, letting him deal with the condom. He wasn't gone long, and he wrapped his arms around me with adorable greed.

More kisses. I hoarded them like a squirrel chasing nuts around the yard. "Let me shower. Again. Then we can get a drink. Some food might also be nice."

"Agreed."

Once we cleaned up, he took me to a dive close to campus, where I could wear my yoga pants and hoodie without attracting a second look. I devoured a huge burger dripping with cheese and bacon without any regrets. He had steak and a basket of chili-cheese fries. As we stepped out of the restaurant, he wrapped an arm around my shoulders, and I slid mine around his waist. Our steps matched naturally, easily, on the way to the car.

The air was crisp, cold enough that I could see my breath, and the stars shone like chips of ice overhead. Ty opened my door then jogged around to his side. *I love you,* I thought silently. *You are* so *fucking wonderful.* I watched his profile as he drove, wishing that we could have more of this. But hey, one weekend a month was better than nothing, right? And the rest of the time I'd concentrate on work and classes.

*This is actually better than a relationship that would suck up my time.*

As promised, we watched the double feature of *Brick* and *Groundhog Day.* I loved his choice, and he seemed to like mine. By eleven, he was kissing my neck and hinting that he'd like to go to bed. I didn't require much persuasion. Upstairs, I could hear my roommates tromping around as I got naked and crawled into Ty's bed.

On a whim, I asked, "Can you tell us apart?"

He raised a brow. "Excuse me?"

"When we're moving around upstairs."

Ty didn't seem to want to answer, so I tickled him until he admitted, "No idea about the others, but I *always* know when it's you."

"How?"

"A guy has a right to his secrets." He kissed me as if to make up for refusing to answer, but there was no way I'd accept defeat so easily.

"Come on, tell me. I once pestered my mother for four hours. Believe me, I can go all night, and that's not how you want me to direct my stamina."

"You won't believe me. Or you'll think it's cheesy."

"Try me." I kissed his ear like a dirty cheater.

His breath caught. "Fine. I just feel you, that's all. If you're anywhere nearby, I know it. I can always tell when you're looking at me, too."

From past experience, I could verify that, and it took some of the sting out of the name thing from earlier. Quietly glowing, I said, "I hope you're not *too* tired."

Ty gave me the most devilish smile and pushed me back. "Not remotely. I have some catching up to do."

Then he put his face between my thighs.

# CHAPTER SEVENTEEN

His hair slipped against my legs like silk in contrast to his stubbled jaw.

I'd seen bad porn where the guys got down there and motorboated, but Ty was *really* good with his tongue. I arched and squirmed, hands tangled in his hair, while he licked and nuzzled and teased my inner thighs. Guys before had lost interest if I didn't come in five minutes, but it wasn't easy to relax with someone's head down there. But he eased his way north until I lost all sense of time. My world narrowed to his lips and tongue, the hands pressing my thighs apart and the escalating urgency quaking through me with each stroke, each lick. He was tender and patient, relentlessly wicked with his mouth. In the end, I screamed and came so hard, my legs cramped.

Once I recovered, I tried to give him a turn, but he didn't let me.

"Come here," he said.

He snuggled me close and held me for a good ten minutes. Then we took a final bedtime shower and managed tricky shower sex. He'd been right not to start with it, because it took some doing, and once he almost fell over. Afterward, we got into bed while I tried not to think how few hours were left. He was quiet, too. It could be that we'd done so much talking earlier, neither of us had much to say. But I didn't think so.

"This weekend went so fast," he whispered.

"I know."

And in November, there would be no time for us. But what about December? Counting in my head, I figured that the end of the month wouldn't be a holiday, as both Christmas and New Year's fell midweek this year. I had to ask.

"So…do you have any plans for December 28?" I hoped he didn't think the question sounded desperate, but at the idea that we had to wait two months to be together again, I nearly broke into tears.

"That weekend's yours," he said softly.

*Thank God.*

"We'll text." That sounded stupid, considering he lived downstairs, not in Australia.

"Soon it'll be too cold for us to talk outside. I'll miss it. I looked forward to it, wondering if I'd see you."

I wished I had the nerve to suggest I knock on his door to give up a good-morning kiss before we went our separate ways, but that pretty solidly contradicted the terms of the friends-with-benefits thing. So I said nothing and curled into his arms when he wrapped them around me. The last thing I did was try to memorize how he felt, so close and warm, because I'd want to picture it through sixty nights alone. I fought sleep as long as I could.

I lost.

In the morning, Ty was subtly different. Not that he was cold or showed signs of regrets, but I could see him changing, putting away the person he'd permitted himself to be and shifting back to dad mode. As promised, he made us a couple of omelets for breakfast, and they were delicious. But after we ate, it was past ten, and I could tell he was ready to go pick Sam up. I recalled what he'd told me about spending Sundays with his son, and I didn't imagine it was different, even on his off weekend.

To make it easier, I said, "I hope you don't mind, but I need to get going. I finished midterms last week, but I already have assigned reading and some projects to work on."

That was an exaggeration. I had one chapter and an actual lesson plan to prepare, but it wasn't due until December. Ms. Parker had told me weeks ago that I'd be expected to work up a lesson that fit with her curriculum and teach a class before I left the practicum. I hadn't spent much time on it yet, so that wasn't a huge lie. Just a white one that relaxed him and made him feel like he wasn't kicking me out to get back to his life.

"No, I get it. I have some work for tonight, too, after Sam goes to bed."

So I hugged him, and Ty kissed me until my toes curled. Which I thought was a fictional physiological response, until he made it happen. When I broke away, my fingers were fisted in his shirt, and I had to make myself let go. *Symbolic, huh?* Then I scooped my belongings into my backpack and went upstairs. It shouldn't have hurt, but it did. Leaving probably always would.

Nobody was awake when I crept in. Though I had my tablet in my lap, pretending to read, I heard when Ty left. But on a deeper level, I felt it, too, just like he'd said. It sounded poetic and slightly improbable, but the whole building felt emptier, an echo where there had been warmth. Shaking my head, I actually did read the chapter for my mild-impairment class, and I was dozing on the couch when Lauren got up just past noon.

She showed no mercy in poking me awake. "So how was it?"

"Phenomenal."

"One word? That's all I get?"

Before I could respond, Angus came tromping out of his room, disheveled and adorable. "About what? Did something delicious happen?"

"From Nadia's expression, yeah. Repeatedly. But she's refusing to tell me more."

"It's rude to kiss and tell, especially when we can gawk at the sex monster who lives downstairs. We totally heard you screaming through the floor." His back was to me as he made coffee, using the fancy machine I hated, and for a few seconds, I just stared in mute horror, remembering how I cried out while Ty was going down on me.

Lauren took pity. "He's kidding. We heard nothing."

"Thank God."

"But apparently, it was scream-worthy," Angus said, dropping onto the couch next to me. "Now that *is* interesting."

"If you two don't shut up, I'm hiding in Max's room."

Lauren's expression flickered, some strange combination of sadness and remorse. "That would be fine. He's not in it."

"Oooh, sour." Angus didn't know they'd slept together, I suspected, or he wouldn't poke at her. "I didn't get any play this weekend, either, so try not to be grumpy that our roomies did."

"Who's up for going out later?" A change in topic seemed to be in order.

She seemed grateful. "Count me in. I haven't left the apartment since Friday."

"You could've borrowed my car. I left the keys on the hook by the door."

"I know. There were some parties I could've gone to. I was just feeling lazy." The way her eyes cut away from mine told me she was lying. Indolence had nothing to do with it.

Before I could call her on it, Angus put in, "I know a guy who's throwing a Halloween bash tonight. We could check it out."

"Costumes?" Lauren wondered aloud.

He made a face. "Hell, no."

Since I had no plan when I made the suggestion, this sounded fine. "I don't feel like dressing up, but I'm down for a party. What time?"

"Starts at eight, which means it should be good by nine," Angus answered.

Lauren hesitated, glancing between us like she had mixed feelings. "I don't know. When you mentioned going out, I thought it would be the mall or a movie."

"You don't have to," I said. "If you're not up to it."

She appeared to square away some inner conflict. "No, it's fine. I'm in."

"Leave by eight-thirty?" Angus asked.

I confirmed with a nod, then I escaped to my room on the pretext of working on my lesson plan for the practicum. Instead, I took a nap. It was late afternoon when I rolled out of bed. Hunger drove me to the kitchen, where I showed off my mad culinary skills by making cup ramen. I didn't see Lauren or Angus, so maybe they went to lunch. Max was parked on the couch, still bruised, but the marks were fading.

"Good weekend?" I asked.

"It was shit," he muttered.

"What happened?"

"I spent it at the garage. The owner doesn't mind if I crash on the couch in his office."

It seemed like our talk on Friday hadn't helped. "Maybe you should consider subletting. I don't *want* you to go, but you shouldn't pay rent if you can't stand to sleep here."

"I know," he said tiredly. "I just need to get over it. She doesn't care what I do."

"You should tell her how you feel, dude. Lauren can't read your mind."

In all honesty, I wasn't sure it would make a difference. I didn't get the sense that she was haunted by their night together. Something else seemed to be eating at her, but she'd stopped confiding in me, and I didn't know what to do about it. With a pang, I remembered how we used to make a pillow fort in my room, hide inside and whisper our secrets. Back then, there was *nothing* I didn't know about Lauren Barrett. I couldn't pinpoint the precise moment that changed.

He swallowed hard. "I'd rather get punched in the face again."

"Are you ever going to tell me what happened?" My gaze skimmed over his battered features, worried about both him *and* Lauren.

"I promised not to talk about it. With anyone."

That shot holes in my theory that he was out fighting because he was pissed off. "Promised who? Lauren?"

"Stop digging. This is her story, not mine. If she wanted you to know—"

"Okay, I get it." But it stung realizing how completely she'd iced me out. Other than reiterating that I was willing to listen, I didn't know how else to help.

"Stop looking at me that way. She didn't invite me into her business. I was just there."

I understood Max well enough to be sure he wouldn't spill Lauren's secrets, even to me. Accepting that, I changed the subject. "So we're going to a party tonight, some guy Angus knows. You in?"

Max thought about it. "I guess."

That settled, I sucked down my ramen and went to get ready. Despite the tension between Max and Lauren, it had been a while since the four of us went out together, and excitement percolated through me, enough to dispel the residual gloom over leaving Ty's place. Focusing on fun—not my normal mandate—I put aside the subtext. The closer we got to departure, the more pumped I got, so by the time I put on my boots and jacket, I was ready to cut loose.

"I'll be the DD tonight," Angus said. "I definitely owe you, Nadia, and I've got that awful hangover memory to keep me straight."

"Really?" Lauren smirked at him.

Angus flipped his hand at her in a *whatever* gesture. "You can be so literal."

Max and I snickered as we followed them to the car. Lauren got in front with Angus, so I crawled into the back of the Audi. The drive took fifteen minutes, as the party was being held off campus, hosted by somebody who lived with his parents. I'd met Scott a couple of times, but we'd never hung out. Angus was in Biology, preparing for med school, and they had classes together.

Mount Albion didn't have posh neighborhoods or houses worth millions, but this much land would definitely cost a lot. Scott lived in a farmhouse on at least twenty acres, judging by the length of the private-access road. It was an old place, but from what I could tell in the dark, beautifully restored, and the wooded privacy of the area meant nobody would call the cops. Part of me was also glad that we wouldn't be bothering Sam and Ty. The sheer number of cars in the gravel parking area was insane. Later, they'd probably be lined up all the way down the drive.

"Who else is glad we don't have to clean up?" I said as Angus parked.

"Cosigned," Max answered.

The farmhouse was lit up from all angles, and Scott hadn't skimped on the decor. Most of it was cheesy, holiday-store stuff, like the motion-activated skull that said "Happy Halloween" when you walked by. There were also paper witches and glowing, plastic jack-o'-lanterns. Already, the music was loud as hell, and we were still fifty yards from the house.

"Looks like Scott posted the invite somewhere. We'll end up with bikers and truck drivers," Angus predicted.

I shrugged. It wasn't *my* house.

Max led the way inside, and I followed. The kitchen was bright yellow and jam-packed with people. Some of them were grabbing at chip bags while others were prowling through the alcoholic options. Scott was down the hall, but he recognized Angus and yelled something at him, then gave a thumbs-up. Following Max, I grabbed a beer as he forged a path into the living room, which was big enough to dance with the furniture shoved back against the walls. The floors were hardwood, easier to move; I could never spin quite the same on carpet. As I bent to take off my boots, my mood picked up even more. I shouldn't feel responsible for Lauren or obsess over my relationship with Ty.

*See, it's fine. The weekend was fantastic, and now it's over. Life goes on.*

I worked my way into the cluster of thrashing drunk people and found a guy who seemed more sober than most. He moved well—not like Angus—but decent for a farmhouse party in Michigan. Not that the guys in Nebraska were the best dancers ever, either. Like Max, most of the dudes I went to high school with had just barely mastered the white-boy shuffle. Arms over my head, I threw myself into the music and danced for almost an hour. The guy signaled that he was getting a drink, and I just waved and kept going. Angus joined me after that, which was good. It kept other guys at bay, and he was a great partner, challenging me to vary my moves and try to execute some I'd normally be too self-conscious to attempt.

Finally, around midnight, I went looking for food and drink. Most of the chip bags were empty, and I was lucky to score a beer. I didn't see Scott anywhere, and people were starting to pair off. Lauren was talking to a blond guy, a skater wannabe who never went without a beanie and couldn't actually do any tricks on his board. Typical poser.

It didn't take long to spot Max, watching intently. He had one hand balled up in a fist. Carrying my beer, I navigated through the crowd toward him. "Hey, dial it down. They're just talking, and you look like you're trying to make his head explode with your mind."

"Would that be so wrong?" he muttered.

"Have you said anything to her?"

"Not about that."

"God, you're such weaksauce at telling someone how you feel." Maybe that was too tough a stance since I'd just counseled him to talk to her earlier today.

But before I could apologize, he snapped, "Is this your idea of a pep talk, Conrad? You might need to up your game or risk turning all your little impaired kids into cutters."

"Wow." That was much harsher than Max usually came across. Shocked, I stared at him for a few seconds, and then I wheeled and started to walk away, but he put a hand on my arm.

"I'm sorry, okay? Sorry."

Shrugging him off, I turned with a glare. "I've been nothing but supportive, you asshole, even when I have plenty of
my own shit going on. But do you ever ask how *I'm* doing?
Fuck, no. I'm tired of you slouching around acting like nobody ever had a problem besides you."

"Are you guys fighting?" Lauren must've broken away from
skater boy when she registered the tension; by nature, she was
a fixer and a people-pleaser.

"No," Max answered, as I said, "Kinda."

"Well, which is it?" She aimed a hard look at us.

"Nadia doesn't agree with how I'm handling a personal
problem, so she's pushing me to make a move, and I snapped
back. Then I apologized. *Before* you walked up, Lauren. It's
handled. We're good. Right, Nadia?" His eyes begged me
not to say anything, like he was scared to death she'd take his
heart and stomp on it.

I sighed. "Yeah. That's exactly what happened. And we're
fine. To prove how fine, Max just asked me to dance."

He bit out a curse that Lauren couldn't hear because just
then, a slow song came on. Max wanted to slow dance with
me as much as I wanted to do the Macarena. I took one step
toward the couples getting cozy and pretended to wince. I
bent to rub my toes, as if I had a blister.

"Do you mind?" I asked Lauren. "Max loves this song."

Behind me, he was mouthing, *what the hell,* but when she
shrugged and took his hand, I grinned like a crazy person. I
gave him a *this is your chance* look, but he shook his head. He
was a good six inches taller than Lauren, if not more, so she
couldn't see the expression on his face as she settled into his
arms. He touched his cheek briefly to the top of her head, and
it was one of the sweetest things I'd ever seen.

Angus came up beside me, eyes wide in horror. "Dear God. How did I miss this?"

"You had Josh problems."

"Come on, let's talk and dance." He led me out and added, "So do we support this?"

Since he knew something was up, there was no point in hiding it. "Top secret, you swear?"

"Cross my heart, all appropriate solemnities."

"Max digs her. She doesn't know and probably wouldn't believe it if she did. I've been trying to get him to be brave, but so far, he prefers silent anguish. Otherwise, I'm not interfering." I didn't mention the fact that they'd hooked up once or that Max's fading bruises had something to do with Lauren.

"Right. And your sore toes have miraculously improved," he said with a head shake.

"It's you. Have you considered becoming a faith healer?"

"I might enjoy the laying on of hands. But no. These hands will heal as God intended, via modern medicine with a high premium attached."

"I don't think plastic surgery technically counts as healing, Angus." Last I knew, that was his intended area of concentration once he finished med school.

"It is for burn victims."

"And you'll be doing mostly restorative procedures?"

"Shut up and dance," he muttered.

Just past one, the party got really loud and crazy. As predicted, some noncollege people showed up, and they looked like a rough crew. We decided en masse to roll out then, not least of all because I had an early morning. Angus was sober, a relief, because I'd had enough beer to buzz me pretty good. In the back with Max, I was feeling mellow, so when a sharp curve threw me against him, I stayed.

"You're heavy," he complained.

"You're an asshole. Don't ever say that to a girl."

"Even when it's true?"

"Especially then."

With a faint sigh, he put his arm around me, and I couldn't help but compare Max to Ty. He felt wrong, smelled wrong, even held me wrong. But he was warm at least.

"Fine, you're made of moonlight and gossamer. Better?"

"Immeasurably."

We sat together companionably until Angus parked in his spot outside the building. "This will probably be my last fiesta for a while. I have to get serious before finals."

That was no joke since Angus's program was mad competitive. But I was in the same boat. Depending on how I did on midterms, I might need to focus even more to make sure my GPA stayed high enough for me to keep my scholarship. Other people skipped class more than I did, partied harder and longer, but they didn't have parents who were mortgaging their future, gambling everything on one kid making good.

"We'll party again after exams," Lauren said.

Everyone nodded, even Max. Then we headed up to the apartment. After checking my alarm, I brushed my teeth and got ready for bed. *Have to be up in five hours.* Wincing at that, I plugged in my phone for the first time all day. Deliberately I hadn't looked at it since I left Ty's. *I don't want to be that girl, living for text messages.*

But I had one waiting from him, sent four hours ago.

I miss you already.

Smiling, I sent back, Me, too.

*

# CHAPTER EIGHTEEN

November went by in a flurry of work, classes and practicum. In my off hours, I studied hard and worked on the lesson I'd be teaching before winter break. Ty messaged me regularly, and sometimes he left home late enough to steal kisses in the Rainbow Academy parking lot. Each time he walked away, there was an awful pang in my stomach.

Sometimes it felt like all I did was watch him leave.

But Sam was a bright spot. It seemed like he was always beside me at work, tugging on my pants, asking questions, hugging me unexpectedly. I wasn't sure how Ty would feel about that, but it had to be okay because I was his day-care teacher. Sam was forming this bond on his own, not because of my relationship with Ty. We'd done a fantastic job of keeping that private and separate, just like he wanted.

Before I knew it, the month was nearly gone. The day before Thanksgiving, Lauren crawled out of bed at half past five and poked me awake, so we could get on the road to Nebraska. Here in Michigan, the weather was spitting snow, but so far, there wasn't any at home yet. With luck, the roads would stay clear long enough for us to get there and back. The Toyota wasn't exactly equipped with four-wheel drive.

A text came in as I grabbed my bag. Ty's picture popped up, along with the message.

Be careful. Come back safe.

I liked imagining that he knew exactly what I was doing and that he could tell when I woke up. Maybe it was crap, but it helped to believe we had a real connection, as he implied a few weeks back. While Lauren was in the bathroom, I crept downstairs in my stocking feet. It was too early to say goodbye in person, so I'd bought this silly thing at the dollar store: orange and russet ribbons, twining around a tiny cornucopia with plastic fruit spilling forth. The kitschy thing looked Thanksgiving-ish and wasn't too heavy to tie around the doorknob.

But as I bent to do that, Ty's door swung open. He was ruffled and barefoot, wearing only a pair of gym shorts, which I guessed he'd slept in. "Sorry, I crashed out on the couch. Wanted to make sure I didn't miss you this morning."

"Huh?" I thought the text was all I'd get. He worked full-time, he had Sam, and there was night school, too. It was a wonder he ever slept at all; I didn't expect him to get up to see me off.

"Give me some credit," he said softly.

I wore a goofy smile as I said, "Okay."

Then he bent to kiss me goodbye. Wrapping my arms around him, I made it count, tasting him until we were both breathing fast. Ty leaned his forehead against mine.

"It's only four days. And then another month until our next

weekend. We can hold out, right?" He sounded like he was living for those two days, as if they were twinkling lights in an ocean of darkness.

"Yep. Since we'll be on break, there's no coursework, no reading, no projects."

"I have something special planned, so you'll need to pack warm clothes, pretty much the best winter gear you have. Bear that in mind."

My eyes widened. "So we're not staying in this time?"

"It's a surprise. Now you should get going before Lauren comes down and catches us making out."

"Would that be such a bad thing?" I asked, surprised. My impression was Sam couldn't know about us, but I didn't realize we were a dirty secret otherwise.

"Not for me. I didn't know if you told her about...us." His hesitation said he wasn't sure how to categorize what we had, the whole FWB situation.

"Yeah. She calls you Hot Ginger, by the way. For the life of me, I cannot get her to use your name."

A sexy, surprised smile curved his mouth, and I suppressed the urge to kiss him. "I can live with that. But since I don't know her, it's more respectful to refer to me as *Mr.* Hot Ginger."

"Noted," Lauren said, standing at the bottom of the stairs with my bag.

"Morning." Ty seemed unfazed, but close-up, a hot flush raced across his cheekbones.

"You got my phone and my purse?" I asked.

"Yep, we're ready to roll. I even brought your shoes."

I grinned. "You know me so well, it's scary."

Quickly, I kissed Ty one last time and then jogged over to cram my boots on. I shrugged into the coat Lauren offered and wrapped up in a scarf while Ty watched. Since I expected him to retreat any minute, I was surprised when he watched us leave. We went out into the predawn gloom on a burst of frosty wind, and only as the door closed behind us did Ty vanish into his apartment. Lauren grabbed on to me, shaking my arm.

"Dear God. *Why* didn't you tell me Mr. Hot Ginger looks like that with no shirt on? I feel like you've violated, like, ten articles of the girl code."

"You're insane," I mumbled, opening the trunk so we could pack it.

"Don't change the subject. He's fucking gorgeous. Some guys look better with their clothes on, you know? And when you finally get them naked, you're like, *Oh, God, he's a bear rug!* And you're pretty sure the night ends with you picking fur out of your teeth."

Shuddering, I said, "I have no words. It's too early for this."

I was shivering by the time I got the key in the door. The Toyota was old enough that it didn't have a remote, and the heater was janky. We had been driving for fifteen minutes before it truly kicked in. Thankfully, Lauren had shut up about Ty.

"Can we eat at a truck stop? My mom says they have the best breakfasts, and you can always tell if the food's good by the number of semis in the parking lot."

Since I'd planned to eat a granola bar and drive for two hours, I sighed inaudibly. "You're too perky for 6:00 a.m., you know that?"

"I'm also hungry. Starving, even. Food might make me sleepy and docile. Otherwise, I might talk about Mr. Hot Ginger. For *hours.*"

"For crap's sake, yes, we'll stop." I pulled off where Lauren told me to, and we devoured a huge breakfast of scrambled eggs, biscuits, hash browns and sausage, priced right at $4.99.

True to her word, Lauren snuggled down in her coat and fell asleep once her stomach was full. I drove for longer than two hours on I-80 West, but she seemed to be napping so well, I didn't have the heart to wake her. But before we switched from interstate to a smaller highway, I pulled off at a rest stop to stretch my legs and use the bathroom.

Nudging Lauren awake, I pointed at the restroom. "Need to go?"

"Huh? Yeah. Is it my turn to take over?"

"More than, actually. Not that I'm complaining."

She poked me. "Saying you're not is the same thing as bitching about it because you're bringing it up."

"Whatever." I took the keys out of the ignition, locked up and hurried through the wintry air toward the brick building.

This was a decent rest stop, clean, and I didn't mind using it. At the vending machine hut, we bought drinks and snacks, so we could keep moving. Lauren took over driving, and I went to sleep. She let me drowse for three hours to make up for the longer shift, and then we switched somewhere along highway 51. Next it was 275, then a string of smaller roads as we headed toward Nebraska. It was an excruciating day, and I was fucking exhausted when we entered the home stretch. It had been dark for a long time, and my back was sore, shoulders stiff, knee hurting.

But it would be worth it to see my family.

When we passed the town limits sign, Lauren bounced in her seat beside me. "Damn, I thought this drive would never end."

"And we have to do it again on Sunday."

She shuddered. "Don't remind me."

"But at least we have Thursday, Friday and Saturday at home."

"I know. It's gonna be awesome. I wonder if anyone else will be back."

"Maybe." It might be cool to hear what our high school friends had been up to.

Thanks to a minuscule downtown area and nothing but fields surrounding it, a stranger would likely describe Sharon, Nebraska, as quaint. With a population just under five thousand and not much in the way of development, it could be kindly described as Podunk, which was part of the reason Mount Albion, Michigan, didn't bother me. Though it was a small town, too, you could drive to civilization much faster from there.

I didn't need my phone anymore for directions, so I turned it off. From memory, I drove to Lauren's old place, a tiny two-bedroom house on the outskirts of town. Her mom already had Christmas lights up, or maybe she just didn't take them down last year. I could picture Mrs. Barrett shrugging and going, *oh well*. Lauren jumped out as soon as I stopped the car.

"I'd ask you in but I'm kind of sick of your face."

"It's mutual." I blew her a kiss and made sure she got inside before taking off.

From there, it was ten minutes to the Conrad household. Getting from one side of town to the other never took longer than fifteen minutes. There was no traffic to speak of, not even a stoplight, though sometimes farmers screamed at each other at our solitary stop sign, which was prestigiously located next to the Stop and Go, a combination gas and convenience store.

Since it was only eight, local time, my parents were up and anxiously watching out the window for me. I had texted my mom twice on the road to reassure her that we were fine. Both she and my dad charged outside to greet me, neither wearing coats or shoes. My dad grabbed my bag out of the back as Mom hugged me.

"Let's get inside." Dad steered me toward the front door, decorated with a turkey, a straw wreath and dried chrysanthemums.

In the house, I noticed a few changes. They'd painted the living room a warm cream, replacing the rose that my dad complained about for two years. New slipcovers on the furniture, a few new bird statues; my mom collected them. My brother, Rob, was sprawled on the couch, more impressive than I remembered, broader through chest and shoulders.

"String bean!" He levered off the couch to hug me, and I elbowed him in the ribs when he tried to turn it into a noogie.

My mom went into the kitchen to make tea. She was the reason I drank it late at night, a small way of holding on to her, I guessed, though I hadn't realized it until now. My dad sank into his recliner with a relieved sigh while Rob turned down the volume on the TV.

"Wow, I outrank sports? When did this happen?"

Rob leveled an inscrutable look on me. "When you started coming home once a year."

"Don't make Nadia feel bad. She's working hard at school," Mom called.

"Speaking of work, how're your grades looking?" Dad raised a brow at me.

When he used a certain tone, I felt fourteen, not twenty-one. "Good. My midterms were excellent, actually."

Once my mom came in with the drinks, I shared my scores and then caught up on the local gossip. By ten, however, I was ready for bed. After such a long drive and losing two hours, it felt much later. *No wonder, it's midnight at home.*

Once I doled out kisses and hugs, plus promises for more

catching up in the morning, I headed up to my old room. Mostly, it was how I'd left it when I moved out with all of my high school treasures still on the shelves, still painted purple and white. My bed here was bigger than the one at school, though. I had a full-size with a good mattress, and it felt luxurious when I snuggled beneath the covers. My mom had washed them fresh; I smelled the fabric softener.

Before I passed out, I plugged my phone in beside the bed. One message from Ty.

Let me know you're okay. Please?

I'd ignored texts from guys before, often because they seemed needy or demanding, but I registered this for what it was. Concern. It was a long-ass trip during uncertain weather. So I sent back,

With my parents, safe and sound. Happy Thanksgiving.

The next morning, I was up before anyone else, a side effect of losing two hours; at home it was almost eight. I was making coffee when my dad came into the kitchen. He stumbled as he spotted me, and I shot him a teasing smile.

"Did you forget I'm here?"

"Just clumsy in my old age."

"Psht. You're what, thirty-six?"

He laughed. Smile lines crinkled his weathered skin. In all honesty, he looked a bit older than his early fifties, though I couldn't recall if he'd looked this way when I was home last summer. I hoped financial worries weren't keeping him up at night.

"Anything you want to tell me?"

220 ANN AGUIRRE

My dad *loved* this game. As a kid, he'd tricked me into confessing all sorts of things, panicked over his alleged omniscience. But I was savvy now, too wise to fall for this again. So as I made breakfast, I told him about the practicum and the kids I wished I could help.

As always, he listened with quiet interest. When I served his scrambled eggs, he put an arm around my waist, his arm trembling a little. It wasn't like him to be so emotional.

"I don't tell you enough, bean, but I'm so proud. Here I barely finished school and you'll be teaching it. You always were so damn smart. Hell, I stopped being able to help with your homework before you hit high school."

Vaguely disquieted, I hugged him. Glancing over my dad's head, I found Rob frozen in the doorway. His eyes were deep and sad, and I knew he'd heard. It couldn't be easy for him, and I wished I could make it better. But our relationship had been strained for years.

*It's your fault.*

A memory surged forward. I was all of fourteen and he was on the verge of graduation. He'd caught me sneaking out and was lecturing the shit out of me. I'd flipped my hair and said snottily, *Like I need life lessons from you, moron. You can't even pass remedial math. Where're you going to school again next year? Oh, right.* I wished an apology could fix it, but seven years later, things were still awkward and broken between us.

I beckoned my brother, wishing we were closer. "Come on in," I said. "Do you want your eggs scrambled or fried?"

"Fried, please. Sunny-side up."

My mom came in a few minutes later, rubbing her eyes, so I cooked for her, too. Afterward, we pitched in as a family on prepping the turkey and baking corn bread for the dressing. Rob chopped celery while I did the onions. As expected,

I didn't hear from Ty, and that was fine; I was too busy gossiping with my mom and helping her with the feast. It had been years since I'd done this, and I was surprised to find I'd missed it. She was a good cook, always managing four things at once, and I tried to keep up.

I was straining broth for the stuffing when she asked, "Are you seeing anyone?"

I couldn't help a blush when Ty sprang to mind, though our relationship didn't fit my mom's criteria. But she was too sharp not to notice. "Tell me about him," she demanded.

"He's hot. Smart. Studying to be an architect, but he also works full-time. He's putting himself through school."

She was smiling as she kneaded the dough for homemade yeast rolls. "I like the sound of that. Is he a junior like you?"

"I'm not sure where he is in the program. He's twenty-four."

"And still in school?" She tilted her head, puzzled. "Money problems?"

I'd rarely lied to my mother, and I wasn't about to start now, especially on Thanksgiving. "Not exactly. He's got a four-year-old. I'm an assistant in Sam's class at Rainbow Academy."

She put down her knife and leveled a serious look on me. "Nadia…"

"What?" Wariness prickled over me.

"Unless this is serious, I won't mention it to your father. It would only agitate him." She said it like that was the last thing either one of us should ever do. "Honey, be careful. This boy has already gotten some girl pregnant and messed up his future. You can do better. Find someone who can start a family with you when the time is right."

Clenching my fists, I had the irresistible impulse to defend

Ty. It wasn't like he was irresponsible or careless. She didn't know him. But since we *weren't* serious, there was no point.

"We just hang out now and then," I said quietly. "I don't really have time for a relationship, and neither does he."

"Oh. Well, that's different. I'm sorry if I sounded unsympathetic. Please don't let it spoil the day. I just want the best for you."

"I know." And I did my best to put her admonition from my mind.

By three, the food was ready, and people started arriving. Rob picked Avery Jacobs up, then Lauren and her mom showed up with a Waldorf salad. Like my mom had requested, sides and salads piled up in the kitchen. Pretty soon the house was full of relatives, friends and neighbors, elderly people who would've been alone otherwise. My mom really was a sweetheart.

Avery took a seat on a folding chair nearby, plate balanced primly on her lap. I hadn't liked her since she ditched me for more popular friends in sixth grade, but if Rob saw something in her, I'd try to be friendly. "So what're you up to lately?"

"Still working at the bank." Not the most promising start.

"How long have you and Rob been going out?"

"Three months or so. Around here, he qualifies as a catch." Though I might be projecting, she seemed to be implying she wouldn't be with him if she could do better.

It took all my self-control not to smack her. Rather than start trouble, I picked up my plate and went into the kitchen, pretending I wanted seconds, when in fact, I only wanted to get away from her. Rob claimed my seat as soon as I vacated it, and I noticed Lauren watching from her perch on the stairs. With a mental shrug, I joined her.

"Hard to fathom, huh?" With a nudge, I nodded at Rob and Avery.

"I have *no* idea what he sees in her." Lauren's answer came out sharp, spoken through her teeth.

"Eh, he's a guy. And she's hot."

"Rob's not like that," Lauren said quietly. "It has to be something else."

"Who knows?"

My mom called from the kitchen, so I hurried to help out. Later, I ran into Mrs. Barrett, chatting with my dad, and I was astounded at the change in her. When Mr. Barrett left, she kind of fell apart, but since Lauren had been gone, she'd apparently gotten a makeover and pulled things back together.

"Looking good," I said to Mrs. B.

She turned with a grin. "You'd be surprised at what L'Oréal can do."

More than that, it was a complete change in bearing and attitude that contributed to the confident package. Lauren had to be ecstatic, seeing proof that even if her dad had broken her mom's heart, it was possible to come back from it.

The Thanksgiving party was decent, as long as I avoided Avery. Rob didn't seem to realize she was settling, and I'd never tell him. But I didn't see this relationship ending anywhere good. She'd always want him to do better, be more, earn more and then bitch at him for being a simple, good guy instead of the overachiever she secretly wanted.

Around seven, I darted into the kitchen, ostensibly to get a drink but really because I just wanted a break from answering the same questions. *No, I don't have a boyfriend. No, I'm still not playing basketball.* With a faint sigh, I sank down at the table and poured some wine. I had no intention of eavesdropping, but when Lauren stopped Rob in the dining room, I was trapped.

"You look tired," she said. "Everything okay?"

It surprised me that she could tell. He didn't seem shocked by her insight, though. "Yeah. I just have some stuff going on."

"Awesome or awful?"

"Good. Or it will be, if it pans out."

Her voice softened. "Keep me posted."

Their conversation intrigued me, but I couldn't grill Rob about his dreams or goals without him getting defensive. We kept in touch through occasional emails, but mostly, I sent him music recs because I didn't know what else to say. Around nine, the party broke up and afterward, I crashed on the couch with my parents in front of the tube. Rob didn't get home from dropping Avery off until long after I went to my room.

The next day, I went shopping with Lauren, Mrs. Barrett and my mom. Getting to the nearest mall took forty-five minutes, something that didn't used to bother me. Fortunately, the others talked enough not to notice that I was tetchy. My mother's comments about Ty still chewed at me, working under my skin.

Yet Lauren shone brighter than I'd seen in weeks, just hanging out with our moms. Mrs. Barrett was hilarious, offering her outfits she'd never wear, and Lauren tried them on, modeling with mock-verve. Shaking the cranky face, I got in the spirit of absurd fashion and accepted my mom's choice of ruffled fuchsia cocktail explosion. The gown looked hideous on me, accentuating my broad shoulders, so I really resembled a dude in drag.

"This is awesome." Lauren held her stomach, laughing. "I miss this."

*You live with me. We could do this anytime.* Maybe for her, it wasn't the same without our mothers snapping embarrassing pictures and threatening to save them for posterity. By the time we headed home, my mood had shifted from melancholy to pensive. *I really wish I could talk to Ty.* He'd been so helpful in regard to Lauren before; possibly I shouldn't get used to talking about important stuff with him, though. I had no idea where I should draw the line between sex and friendship, how long before I stumbled past what he could accept.

"Penny for them," Dad said.

"If I made that deal, I'd feel guilty for overcharging you." Leaning down, I kissed his forehead and went upstairs, simultaneously worn out and wound up.

Shortly after I got in bed, Ty texted. It was almost eleven here, which meant it must be close to one at home.

Can you talk?

Yep. Call me.

My bedroom door was shut, and my phone on vibrate, so it wouldn't bother anyone else. I picked up on the first buzz.

All desire for serious conversation flew out of my head when he greeted me with, "Hope you're up for this. Because I'm ready to let you watch."

*

# CHAPTER NINETEEN

"Hang on," I whispered.

The idea of doing this in my childhood bedroom was even dirtier, but I didn't protest. Instead, I locked the door then tiptoed back to bed. It seemed unlikely that Mom or Dad would come for a midnight chat, but I'd rather not risk it. Once I was settled, I picked the phone up.

"Still there?"

"Count on it." His voice in my ear was delicious. Hard to believe we were a thousand miles apart.

"I've never done anything like this, so—"

"You just need to install an app. I did some checking and this is the safest. Not that I think you'd turn me into online porn."

"If you're nervous, we can just talk." I didn't even mean phone sex.

"It's fine. I want to. I miss you. I'll text you my account info and you can call me once you get set up."

"Okay. Talk to you soon."

I found the app fast, and thankfully, my parents had used the same Wi-Fi password for years. There was essentially no internet on my cell otherwise, and I had only one bar for voice calls. Once I got connected, it didn't take long to get the software downloaded and installed, then I just had to create an account. While I was doing that, Ty sent his username. I added him as a contact and waited for him to validate. Five minutes later, I clicked the video chat button and waited for him to pick up.

*There you are.*

I recognized his bedroom right off, but I was more focused on the bashful half smile he was wearing and the shirt he wasn't. "Hey, you."

"The things I do for you," he murmured.

"I'm not sure how this is supposed to go. It sounds hot, but I've never—"

"Just tell me what you want to see."

My breath stuttered as a hot flush washed through me. Yeah, I liked that idea. My voice came out husky. "Sit down. Take your pants off. Show me how you do it when I'm not around."

"When I'm thinking about you?"

"I hope so."

"Lately, that's always," he said huskily.

This was working for me in a big way, and he hadn't even done anything yet. "I may play, too, but the camera on my phone isn't very good."

"Your face is enough. Just let me see what you're feeling."

*This face, you show me everything.*

"Definitely."

He moved, stripping like I'd asked and for a few seconds, he was out of sight, and then he settled in bed. The lights were dim enough that it was shadowed and sexy, but I could still see him. I wasn't sure how it looked on my end, but he was fully, gorgeously on display. No question at all that he was into this. His cock was long and hard, jutting toward his stomach. Licking my lips, I admired the lean slope of his abs and the taut muscles of his splayed thighs.

"How's that?" he asked, low.

"Mouthwatering."

A little growl escaped him as he squirted some lotion into his palm and went to work with his fist, showing me exactly how he handled things without me. Ty was quick and rough, no finesse, no preliminaries. He was almost completely silent, too, just the jagged gust of his quickening breaths. I wanted to talk, but I was afraid it would distract him, and anything I said might sound scripted.

"Nadia," he whispered. "Is this good?"

I realized he needed encouragement; this was about mutual pleasure, not anonymous voyeurism. "Really hot. I'm… I'm joining you."

He moaned then, increasing his speed. His fist pumped faster, and the camera showed me each arch and flex, the way his thighs tensed. Ty clenched his jaw and his head fell back, as I slipped a hand into my panties. With the other, I held on to the phone, not wanting to miss a glimpse. My breath quickened; I was already wet, aching for an orgasm. Gently, quickly, I tapped against my clit, seeing how my arousal affected him. Ty's hand was moving faster now. So was mine.

"Want you so bad, it's nuts."

"Do you like me watching you?"

"Yeah." The answer was ragged, drawn into a moan.

"I need you to come, so I can. I need to see it."

The words sparked through him like electricity—and there

were slick sounds, like actual fucking, as he pumped harder, growling with each tug. When he let go, spurting on his belly, he was panting and staring directly at me, a thousand times hotter than I could've imagined. I pinched my clit and orgasmed.

With a groan, he fell back onto the bed, so I could see only part of him, but could still hear his voice. "Damn. That's the best sex I ever had with myself."

"Hey, I did my part."

"No joke. God, I miss you."

"Me, too. But we have your December surprise ahead. I'm looking forward to it."

"You're Ms. Brightside, huh? If it's raining, it's good for the grass. If someone steals your wallet, then he was probably starving and needs the money more than you do."

"I wouldn't go that far," I mumbled. But it was true that I was prone to searching for silver linings.

"Whereas my glass is permanently half-empty. But I'm feeling too good to complain about how the world's a cesspool tonight. I think I'll stare at you, instead." He shifted enough so I could see his face, too.

"Seems like a reasonable plan. But Sam will be— *Oh*. This is your weekend off. No early-morning wake-up call. So you can stay up as late as you want."

"Yeah. So I was kind of hoping you'd talk to me for a while."

"What about?"

"I don't care. This is the closest I'm getting to alone time with you for another month, and honestly, I just want to hear your voice."

*Oh, God*. I melted all over my sheets. But I was self-conscious, too. You know how there's always an annoying relative at family reunions and he's like, *I hear you're funny, Nadia, so tell me a joke.* Then you forget all the humor you ever knew. That was how I felt right then.

"And she stops talking immediately. Too much?"

"No, I just blanked, I guess. I could tell you about the kids in my practicum."

"Sure. I don't know that much about what you're studying."

So for a good twenty minutes, I explained what I was doing in the education track, Ms. Parker's warnings regarding burn-out and some of my favorites from the program. "There's this one kid, Riley, he's always smiling, but the weird thing is, it's not because he's happy. It's because it upsets his mom so much if she thinks he's sad. So he never shows any of his anger or frustration, but it can't be good for him. I worry that he'll snap someday."

"You obviously care about them a lot. I think you'll be a great teacher."

"I hope so, if I don't crash and burn before then. It's pretty hard to juggle everything."

"Is that why you're with me instead of an actual boyfriend?" The words hurt like hell.

Belatedly, I realized he didn't mean it in a bad way; it wasn't a denial of us, and I shouldn't have that knee-jerk reaction. *We're not dating. He cares, but he doesn't love you. That's fine. It's exactly according to plan.* But the ache in my chest argued otherwise.

"Nadia?" He came up on his elbows, staring at me in concern.

"I was just thinking. And I guess so. I really don't have time for regular dates." Hesitating, I couldn't decide if I should ask this, but why not? "How long do you see yourself staying single?"

"Ten years, minimum. I might start dating when Sam's in

high school. He'll have his own life by then. I might consider getting married once he leaves home, but I won't want more kids." He sounded so sure, even though he'd be only thirty-eight when Sam left for college. "What about you?"

Taking a deep breath, I decided to be honest. This was probably the closest I'd ever come to telling Ty how I felt. "I'd like to get settled, career-wise, before I start a serious relationship. But sometimes life hands you unexpected opportunities. I wouldn't turn down the right guy, if he came into my life at the wrong moment. I'd just…make room for him. Somehow."

He answered as I feared he would. "Bad idea. Focus on your future. Definitely do *not* screw it up over some asshole."

Suddenly, I remembered our conversation on the Ann Arbor trip, and I wondered if he thought I was talking about someone other than him. I tried to find a way to ask nicely. "Are you worried about…competition, Ty?"

"I shouldn't be. We agreed either one of us could call it at any time…for any reason." But that wasn't a firm denial.

"There's nobody else," I assured him quietly.

"That should not make me so fucking happy. But look at me." His smile was breathtaking, so beautiful, it made me ache.

"I'm just not a player by nature," I said, trying to downplay my fidelity. "I've been with…five guys, total. Including you."

He raised a brow at me. "Not sure I needed to know that."

"Sorry if that was an overshare."

"It's okay. And my number is five, too. Counting you."

"Interesting."

I wondered how many girls there were before Diana and how many after. But if I asked, he'd tell me, and then we'd end the night with me feeling like I couldn't fill the void she left when she went. Sometimes I thought it might help him move on if he knew she was happy—that she'd put the pain behind her. But maybe not. Maybe Ty's scars ran too deep.

"Your face says we're in a bad place."

"That's just my sleepy look. It doesn't play well on video. 'Night, Ty."

"Sleep well, sweetness." He didn't seem to notice the endearment, and I didn't point it out. But it was the first time he'd called me anything but my name.

After we hung up, I basked in it until I fell asleep.

The next morning, my mom rousted me out of bed with the unfair bait of coffee and fresh cinnamon rolls, but I was a sucker for her baked goods. Once I was up, she dragged me to the local flea market, and that kept us out all day. At night, we watched movies with my dad, and Sunday morning at stupid o'clock, she cried as I loaded up the car.

"I just miss you," she said, sniffling. "It was *so* good to have you home."

My dad was more taciturn as always, but he had filled my trunk with emergency supplies: kitty litter, snow chains, flares, blankets, granola bars and bottles of water. He was the one who made sure I wore rain boots and carried an umbrella on stormy days; he also nagged about my grades while Mom offered more emotional bonding. Throat tight, I hugged them both in turn and Dad held on longer than usual.

"I'll come home this summer," I promised.

"Looking forward to it," he murmured. "Drive safely, bean."

Rob stood in the window of his bedroom, gazing down at us. He didn't come down to say goodbye, and I wondered if he felt as alone as he looked. My chest ached as I drove away, musing on the distance between us. I was five miles down the road before I noticed that my mom had put two bags of Thanksgiving leftovers in my backseat. I hoped Max and Angus were up for turkey; otherwise it might go to waste.

Lauren was waiting out front when I got there. She hopped in, staring at her mom's house with a wistful look. "Well, we survived coming home. I wish I didn't have to take off so soon. This was so much fun."

"Wonder what Max and Angus did." I mentioned our roomies, wondering if she'd thought of Max at all over the break.

But she didn't react. "Let's hope the return is painless."

Since it was another sixteen hours, I said, "Doubt it."

"Me, too."

"Do you think Rob hates me?"

"That was random." Classic Lauren, avoiding the question to avoid hurting me.

"Seriously."

"Probably not. But it's hard for him. I don't know if you've noticed, but there's definitely a difference in how your folks treat you two."

I sighed. "Trust me, I'm aware. And it sucks. But I don't know what to do."

"No idea. I'm an only child."

Driving back, we talked more about our families and played the radio to stay awake, switching off as we had before. Eight hours in, the weather got bad, and I had to plug my phone into the cigarette lighter to keep using the GPS app. It sucked a lot of power, but it also reported on traffic, weather and potential problem areas ahead. Doggedly, I drove with both hands locked on the wheel, steering through billowing clouds of white. The night was dark as hell, brightened only by the red taillights of cars crawling ahead of us.

Lauren was chewing her lip. "I know you don't want to miss work or class, but we might have to stop," she said finally.

When the car skidded for the second time in as many miles, I agreed, but first we had to find a place with available rooms. It was almost two in the morning by the time we stopped at a shitty motel that didn't have NO VACANCY gleaming through the snow. I didn't like the look of the place, but I didn't see we had a choice.

"Better than frozen death?" I asked Lauren, pulling into the lot.

"Yay, we get dismembered, instead." But that was her teasing tone, not her terrified one.

In the office, an elderly woman shuffled to the desk in a blue housecoat, her mouth puckered into permanent disapproval. "You girls are lucky, this is my last room. Lots of people are trying to get out of the weather tonight."

*Well, duh. It's a blizzard out there.*

I was pretty sure this shithole didn't ordinarily cost fifty-nine bucks a night, but I had no leverage to haggle, and another car was pulling into the parking lot. "We'll take it."

Between Lauren and me, we scraped up enough to cover the cost, and the proprietor proved what kind of place it was when she didn't ask for a credit card. She gave us a metal key and told us we had room 116, just down from the office. Shivering, I got my backpack out of the car, but left the Tupperware containers. Snow stung my cheeks as I crunched over the unshoveled walk to our room. Inside, it was as horrible as I'd feared with a musty smell and decor that would've been dated back in the '60s.

Lauren shuddered. "So basically, we need to be dry-cleaned when we get home."

The old woman hadn't mentioned that there was only

one bed, but it didn't matter. Since the radiator banged and groaned while providing minimal heat, we'd be huddling together for warmth, anyway. I put on slipper socks, a sweatshirt, sweatpants and my winter hat before turning back the sheets. They were thin and yellowed from frequent washing, but nothing moved. Hopefully, that was a good sign, and I was cold enough to risk it.

"I have never wanted you more," Lauren said, but she put on about as many clothes, and then we got into bed.

It took me forever to fall asleep, despite the ache in my shoulders and calves from a long day of driving. Toward the end, we hadn't come as far as we needed to, so we still had a good five hours to go, provided the roads were clear enough for us to move on. They'd better be since we didn't have enough cash for another night on the road. Plus, I couldn't afford to miss more work or class. Shit, it was stressing me out just thinking about it.

"Oh, my God, go to sleep already," Lauren mumbled, thumping me on the head when I rolled over for the fourth time.

Weirdly, I did.

In the morning, I turned on the crappy, antiquated TV to check the weather report. From a glance out the window, I could see that it had stopped snowing, but I needed to know which roads had been plowed in the night. I punched the air when I heard that I-80 looked pretty clear. After poking Lauren awake, I packed my stuff and carried it to the car.

My breath whooshed out of me. The right back window was broken and all of the leftovers my mom had sent were gone. Speechless, I walked around the car looking for other damage. *Shit, my phone. Did I take it in with us last night?*

I scrambled through my backpack, and it was definitely

gone. *Assholes. You stole Thanksgiving* and *my phone. Happy holidays.* I couldn't think of a single silver lining in this crap-fest, but I strangled my urge to kick things and cuss. *Better to focus on damage control.*

Lauren was brushing her teeth when I ran in. "Need to borrow your cell."

"Why?"

Once I filled her in, she did all the cursing for me. But she turned her phone over with no questions, and I went about changing passwords, canceling accounts and notifying my cell carrier that I was no longer in possession of the phone.

The rep sounded pretty bored as he relayed my options. "So sorry for your trouble, ma'am. I can blacklist the phone for you immediately and send you a SIM card. According to our records, you are not eligible for a replacement, so you'll need to purchase new hardware. We can also supply the serial number for the police and notify anyone who may be trying to reach you."

"Just turn it off. I don't want anyone using my phone."

"Understood. Since you've notified us, you won't be liable for any charges appearing after this time."

"It was stolen at some point in the night," I protested. "I don't know what time."

"You're certainly free to dispute those charges, if they prove to be excessive."

*Shit. The thief probably stole my phone and then called a bunch of overseas numbers.*

But I'd worry about that later. Though it would delay us further, I called the cops and we waited two full hours for a state trooper so I could file a police report. It wouldn't do any good, but at least it was proof for Mrs. Keller that I wasn't a lazy ass who just didn't feel like working.

When the policeman left, it was damn near noon, and I was supposed to be at work soon. I knew the day-care center number by heart, and Lauren's phone had enough juice for me to call in. It was the first time in my life that I ever did, such a horrible feeling, even though I didn't have a choice. I babbled apologies for a full two minutes before she cut in.

"So there was a blizzard, you're four hours away, and some butthead broke into your car. I understand, some days suck." She sounded amused. "Don't worry, we can cover your shift."

"I was hoping I'd be back in time. I didn't plan for the broken window. I have a police report and everything if you need to see it."

"It's fine," she said. "I trust you. Just be careful driving back."

The woman in the motel office "fixed" my window with two plastic trash bags and duct tape, making the Toyota look even classier, and it did wonders for the ventilation. When I said something about damages, she didn't even apologize, just pointed to a sign that said she wasn't liable for items left in cars overnight.

"What a bitch," Lauren snarled as we pulled out of the Motel Hell parking lot.

"It was worth it to see our families," I offered.

*There, that's the bright side. Finally. Time to go home.*

*

# CHAPTER TWENTY

The apartment was gloriously warm; my fingers ached. Max had them between his palms, rubbing briskly. Angus was making hot tea while Lauren filled them in. I let her lead me to the couch, still shivering. If I never drove to Nebraska again, that would be fine by me.

"They seriously stole your mom's Tupperware?" Max repeated.

Lauren confirmed, "Complete with turkey, stuffing, green beans and pie. We were gonna eat those leftovers for a week."

"I'm sorry, but that's hilarious," Angus said.

"Except for the broken window." I wasn't looking forward to the repair bill, but as cold as we'd been for the last four hours of the trip, the glass had to be fixed soon.

Max scowled. "They stole our pie? Now I'm mad. And pie-less. But mostly mad."

"You assume I planned to share it," I said, smirking.

"Oh, you might want to go downstairs and tell the crazy guy in 1B that you're alive." Angus hauled me out of my chair and nudged me toward the door. "He made it pretty clear that he'll pull my head off if he doesn't see you at some point today."

*Oh, shit. Ty.*

I would've called him on Lauren's cell, but I didn't remember his number by heart. Checking the time, I saw it was close to seven and I couldn't recall if he had night classes. Still, even if he wasn't home yet, I'd leave a message on his door. So I grabbed a pen and Post-it, just in case, and said, "I'll be back in a minute."

"Sure you will," Lauren said as Angus murmured, "See you in the morning."

Stifling a sigh, I jogged down the stairs to his apartment and knocked. There were no lights visible under his door, so I figured he must be gone. Quickly I wrote, *Had trouble on the way home. Bad weather, phone stolen. I'm okay. No texting until I replace it.* After sticking it to the door, where he couldn't miss it, I went back upstairs.

Angus made us a sympathy dinner, and we had just finished eating when someone knocked on the door, pounded, really. I stood up.

"It's probably Mr. Hot Ginger," Lauren said.

Fixing an evil stare on her, I crossed to answer, and she was right. Ty stood outside with Sam dozing on his shoulder. *Poor kid. He probably fell asleep in the car on the way home.* The impulse to hug them both nearly overwhelmed me. Ty's shoulders dropped as a sigh seeped out of him, such tangible relief that it shimmered like gold in his brown eyes.

Waving at my roomies, he whispered, "Come down for a few?"

This definitely wasn't protocol, but I nodded. Without bothering to put on shoes, I followed him to his place, and he let us in, juggling keys, backpacks and Sam in a practiced move. He scanned the note as I plucked it off the door and gave me a tired half smile. Since Sam was already in jammies, Ty carried him down the hall and put him in bed. I tensed, waiting for the kid to wake up, but he only curled into his covers and reached for Mr. O'Beary when Ty set the toy beside him.

Once we were back in the living room, he crushed me to him in a bruising hug, and I was astonished to discover that he was shaking. He mumbled into my hair, "You have no idea how worried I've been. First the bad weather, and this morning, you replied to my last text with *suck me loser.* I had no idea where you were and all your roommates could tell me was that you were supposed to be home last night."

Quietly, muffled by his shoulder, I ran through the carnival of crapulence that had been my lot since we left Nebraska. Ty held me and stroked my back, my hair, like he couldn't stand to let go of me. I curled against him, reveling in his tenderness. Finally, I concluded, "And it was freezing on the way home, so much that my hands hurt by the time we got here."

"I saw the broken window on your car when I came in and went straight to your place to make sure you were okay."

"Fine. Just tired, sore and completely pissed off."

"Sit down."

"But Sam…?"

"My mom had him bundled up, throwing snowballs for an hour tonight. Then he had hot soup and a bath. I'll be amazed if he's awake before morning, but…I'm willing to risk it."

This invite was such a huge step; I wondered if he even realized.

"If you're sure." I didn't need further encouragement to curl up on the cozy red couch.

He sat behind me and pressed his thumbs to the base of my neck, rubbing in firm circles. "How's that?"

"Incredible." It was impossible for me to think, let alone speak, while he massaged my neck and shoulders. When he got to my head, I was a warm, sleepy noodle in his arms.

"Why didn't you call me?" Reasonable question. "Lauren had her phone, right?"

Embarrassed, I admitted, "Normally, I use the names in my contact list. I don't remember too many numbers."

"Work and your parents?" he guessed.

"Pretty much. I'm not even sure I know Lauren's number, and we've been friends since second grade. I'm sorry I scared you."

A few moments passed in silence. "You didn't mean to. But I'd rather not live through a day like this one again."

His tone alarmed me enough to shift so I could look at his face. "Ty?"

Tense again, I waited for him to say that we were getting in too deep. Instead, he whispered, "I'm so glad you're home. Sam was crying when I picked him up from school."

"What happened?" There was one biter, a hair puller and two toy stealers in his group. Maybe he had a problem with one of them?

"Nothing, he just missed you. He's used to you being in his classroom."

"I missed you guys, too. I love my parents, but there's a reason I only see them once a year. Next time I'll go during the summer."

"Flying's faster," he pointed out.

"More expensive, too." Though after weighing the cost of fuel, new window and phone, maybe I should've flown. "And it's an hour to fly out of Ann Arbor from here, there are no nonstops, and my parents have to drive two hours to pick me up."

"How small *is* this town?"

"Less than five thousand people. It was a big deal when they put in a stop sign at the Stop and Go."

"Damn. And I thought Mount Albion was bad."

"It's really not." The core population held steady just under ten thousand and the university swelled it by another 6K during the school year. It also made it kind of a challenge to find a decent part-time job, which was why we'd thrown a party for Lauren when she finally switched from food court to fine arts.

"You must be dead tired," he whispered, kissing the back of my neck.

I didn't take it as a prelude to sex, only an observation. But I wished so hard that he was my boyfriend, and we could go to bed together. *Right now. Yes. Please.* I swallowed hard, breath quickening. The yearning sprang partly from physical attraction, but also because I wanted to be close to him— without terms and conditions. *I want you,* I thought. But I couldn't say it. There was no way he'd risk Sam having a bad dream and walking in on us. I went cold just thinking about it; that would tarnish everything. Keeping quiet didn't stop the wanting, though.

I had to hide it. If Ty felt he wasn't meeting my needs, he'd call it off.

*What's the saying? Half a loaf is better than none.* My grandmother used to say something like that in Russian, usually when I was complaining about my dinner. It applied to this situation especially, since my heart might starve without these stolen moments with Ty.

So I nodded, keeping my response simple. "If we're okay, I need to get back upstairs and work on some stuff for tomorrow. I emailed the professors whose classes I missed, but they haven't replied. I swear they're making me sweat on purpose."

"Sounds probable. And yeah, we're fine. I have a design due for Thursday, anyway."

"Would you show me what you're working on before I go?" I stood, hoping the answer was yes. From the pen-and-ink sketches he'd framed, I knew Ty could draw, but I'd never seen anything else.

"Come on." After grabbing his backpack, he led me down the hall to his studio, sparsely furnished with a drafting table and computer desk. Then he got out a thin sheet of paper, tightly rolled to protect against smudging. He unfurled it and set paperweights on each corner, so I could see. "It's supposed to be a restaurant."

It was an external view of a modern, rectangular structure with what looked like an outdoor terrace and rooftop bar. "This would do nicely for a Japanese teppanyaki place."

Surprise flashed in his eyes then a pleased smile. "I haven't gotten that far, but I like it. Maybe I'll finish it with that in mind. The professor likes specificity."

"You're really good. I should hire you to sketch me for my mom's birthday."

"Portraits aren't my thing," he warned.

"I know, I was kidding." Leaning forward, I put a hand on his shoulder and kissed him softly, the sweetest good-night kiss ever. "Thanks for worrying about me."

"Like I could help it." Ty walked me to the door, and I hurried upstairs.

Unsurprisingly, all three of my roomies were in the living room, waiting to scrutinize me when I tapped to be let in. Max did the honors while Angus studied my hair. "So there was talking. Are you and Mr. Hot Ginger in a good place?"

"Lauren! Why'd you tell Angus to call him that? His name is Ty. And yeah, we're fine."

She grinned, ignoring my mock-frown. "He sure is."

Max interjected, "I can take your car to the shop tomorrow. I'm pretty sure we can fix the window. If need be, I'll swing by the junkyard and get a replacement." As I considered the logistics, he suggested, "I'll give you a ride to work on my bike and pick you up in your car on my lunch hour. You can drop me off before you head to campus."

"Okay, deal. How much will this cost me?"

"Depends, but I'll work on it free. So just parts."

Relieved, I hugged him hard around the neck. Until Max came through, I had no idea how I was fixing my car, replacing my phone, buying Christmas presents for my friends and family, plus the usual expenses of rent, food and utilities. My knees actually felt a little weak.

Angus seemed to take it as a personal challenge, though, because he said, "I was thinking about buying you a new phone for Christmas, anyway."

"That's too much." I shook my head. While Angus came from money, I didn't like him buying me expensive things. His boyfriends generally felt otherwise.

"Then I'm using my upgrade and giving you the one I have now."

"I'd let him do it for me," Lauren said. "Provided the SIM fits."

"It should." Angus's current phone was one step up from my old one. "Okay. But I forbid you to buy me anything for Christmas." Beyond touched, I leaned down and hugged them all at once. "You guys are the best friends ever."

"Hey," Max said, tapping the end of my nose. "You're always around when we need you. So it would be pretty shitty if we said 'good luck with life' when you need us back."

When I went to sleep that night, I felt much better.

At Rainbow Academy the next day, Ty pounced as soon as I hopped off Max's bike. He kissed me good morning in the parking lot. I wrapped my arms around his neck and returned it full measure. When he pulled back, he kissed my forehead and each cheek in turn, mouth deliciously hot against the chill in the air. A shiver went through me.

"Keep this up and I'll think you missed me."

"Don't ever doubt it."

The wave of euphoria in the wake of Ty's words carried me all the way to Mrs. Trent's classroom. Sam was ecstatic when I walked in. "Hey, bud."

"My name is Sam! Where *were* you? You were gone forever."

"Was not. It was, like, four days."

Sam pulled on my arm. "My mom's gone forever."

"Yeah?"

"Dad says she's really busy. With science."

I had no idea what to say, but Mrs. Trent started the day's routine, distracting Sam. *Just as well.* I wasn't ready for that conversation. But Sam was clingier than usual; it seemed like he hardly climbed off my lap all day.

At noon, when Max picked me up at work, my car window was fixed. "You are so awesome. I can't even tell you how much I appreciate this. How much?"

"Don't worry about it."

No matter how I argued, Max wouldn't even let me pay for the replacement window, and that afternoon, Angus used his upgrade, passing along his old phone. *My friends are the best.* After such a shitty return from Nebraska, I braced for life to explode further, but my professors didn't bitch about the absence and let me turn in assignments a day late. The next day, my phone carrier came through with a replacement SIM, leaving me in good shape for Wednesday when I had to show Ms. Parker my lesson plan. If she approved it, I'd teach class the following week.

So understandably, I was nervous when I arrived at C-Cool. I waited for a lull, students working quietly at their desks, before offering my work. She flipped through the handouts and markers I'd created; I couldn't tell what she thought from her expression.

Finally, she glanced up. "It's a game show format?"

"I thought I could give out small prizes for correct answers."

Maybe I was wrong, but she didn't seem thrilled. "These students all have focus issues, Nadia. How do you think they'll respond to buzzers and Happy Meal toys?"

"Um. I didn't plan to use buzzers."

But she broke it down for me, all the hundred reasons why this would never work. In my structure, I had focused far too much on the fun aspect, not enough on the learning part. I needed a fresh, creative vehicle to deliver a reading lesson that wouldn't also turn the room into pandemonium. Her criticism was on point, but I still felt horrible. She concluded, "We have to be especially careful in here. A number of our students on the autism spectrum have trouble with too much stimuli— lights, noises, colors. It's our job to manage the environment."

"I'll do it again," I said quietly.

"Have something else ready for Friday, okay? Remember, I'm rooting for you."

"No problem. I'll do better, I promise." If I didn't impress her and finish strong, she'd tell my new mentor for spring semester all about my failures, and when you started with certain strikes, the supervising teacher could make your life hell in so many interesting ways.

"Your idea was creative. In a traditional classroom, it would be a huge success."

That made me feel a little better, enough that I mustered up the will to circulate and help students with their work. An hour later, I left the school, stewing on my mistake, went home for lunch then changed into my work clothes. The rest of the week flew, but I didn't come up with anything that sounded better than what I'd originally produced.

And time was running out.

At four in the morning on Friday, I paced, trying to be quiet, conscious that I might be bothering Ty. Sure, I could structure something on a lesson plan I found online, but I wanted to be better than that. I sank onto the living room floor, surrounded by a sea of balled-up papers. Anyone could copy other people's ideas; that seemed like the mark of a very by-the-book teacher, *exactly* the kind I didn't want to be.

But staring at the crumpled pages gave me an idea. I didn't have any on hand, and it was kind of old-school, but maybe— I got out my tablet and checked a couple of things. *This is better. This can totally work.* I stayed up all night printing up cards and then I stopped at a convenience store on the way to C-Cool to buy a newspaper. We'd need more for Wednesday, of course, provided Ms. Parker agreed.

She was in a good mood, smiling as she taught the lesson and then broke the kids into small groups. Her sets were never random, either; she put students together based on how well they could work together, often with complementary skills. It felt like I had an American eagle flapping around my guts while I waited for her to review my materials.

"This is a great idea," she said finally. "I suspect most of their parents don't even have subscriptions, so they don't look at newspapers very often. This is an interesting twist on vocabulary sentences."

I beamed. "So I'll be teaching on Wednesday?"

"I'm looking forward to it."

Somehow I contained my excitement until I got out to the parking lot. Then I did a little dance beside my car. I still had some stuff to put together, but at least I had a firm direction now. The good mood carried me home, singing, so I was rocking out as I parked the Toyota. Max zoomed up as I got out, but he didn't look happy. In fact, I'd rarely seen him so pissed off.

"Lauren trouble?" I guessed.

"I took your advice," he said flatly. "But she shut me down."

"Oh shit, Max, I'm sorry." Lauren tended to play her cards close to the vest; she was quick with a joke and a hug, but digging beneath the surface took time, effort and a sharp trowel. Maybe I needed to do some gardening.

"It's not like it came as a *complete* surprise, after what happened." That had to be a cryptic reference to their shared secret. "But…it's good to have closure, I guess. She also said there's somebody else."

"Huh?" Max was the last guy she'd mentioned to me, but only to say that sleeping with him had been a mistake. I hated to be the one to break it to him, but… "Sometimes we use that as an excuse when we aren't into the guy asking us out. What exactly did she say?"

"'Let's not make this complicated. We both know this isn't going anywhere.' So I went for it, like you suggested. I said, 'Lauren, there hasn't been anyone else for a while because I've been into you for, like, six months.' She got this sad look, shook her head and goes, 'You only think that. You don't really know me. Nobody does.'"

"That's slightly alarming. I wonder what's going on with her."

"No idea." He sighed, climbing off his bike. "So tell me, Conrad, how do you get over a broken heart?" His tone was facetious, but I could tell he was hurting.

I shrugged. "Nobody's ever broken mine."

Max wore a layered, disquieting expression. "Give him time."

I followed his gaze toward the building, toward apartment 1B, and I couldn't honestly say that he was wrong. But knowing it would probably end badly for Ty and me, it wasn't enough to warn me off. I only needed to think of him for the sweeping warmth to carry me under, drowning me in dreams of him.

"You're probably right. I should quit him, before it's too late. But forewarning won't make me wise."

"It never does," Max said softly.

As he already knew, some mistakes had to be made in glorious color, as the sweetness of irreplaceable memories lasted forever, long after the ache of loss faded.

*

# CHAPTER TWENTY-ONE

The rest of December flew by in a rush. I nailed the teaching aspect of my lesson plan; the kids were engaged when looking for vocabulary words in the newspaper, and nobody melted down. After that, I kept my head down and crammed for finals while also getting ready for the holidays. We got a tiny tree for the apartment and decorated one night while drinking hot mulled wine—courtesy of Angus—and hung up more lights than we really needed.

With little sleep and lots of coffee, I cruised through finals and came out with sanity intact on the other side. Afterward, I did the Christmas shopping; I hesitated over buying anything for Ty, but in the end, I got him a set of quality art pencils. On the way back to the apartment, I mailed presents to my family then wrapped the gifts I bought for my roomies and tucked them beneath the tree.

It was quite a luxury not to have anything on my plate but work for a couple of weeks, almost like a vacation. On Christmas day, we cooked an actual holiday meal, though Angus used us all like sous-chefs, telling us to open this or chop that. At three in the afternoon, we sat down to ham, baked potatoes, carrot-raisin salad and fried Brussels sprouts. For dessert, Lauren and I had made sugar cookies the day before. In lieu of fancy china, we'd bought some festive holiday party plates, mostly so we didn't have to wash them. Some people fought with their roommates or they were indifferent to them, but I loved mine. Maybe it was because we'd all been friends for a while, but they felt like family, and at this time of year, when we couldn't go home, it made all the difference.

"So what're we doing Friday night?" Angus asked, as we settled in the living room to watch *Christmas Vacation*. The best thing about that movie was how much better it always made me feel about my own holiday plans.

"It's Ty's weekend," I answered, before I considered how that sounded.

As expected, Max pounced on that. "You mean we're in a shared-custody situation? Why didn't you tell me? I'd have spent more quality time with you."

"Shut up." Normally, I'd make a crack about his love life sucking, and that was why he was so fascinated by mine, but that seemed insensitive.

"Are you just hanging out at his place again?" Lauren asked.

"He's got something planned. Not sure what, but he told me to pack winter gear."

"Well, that narrows it down," Angus said.

I waved my hands at them, pretending to focus on the movie, like I hadn't been obsessing over this surprise for weeks. *Only two more days.* I was on schedule for a full-day eight-hour shift tomorrow and Friday, so the other teachers could spend more time with their families. Fortunately, working kept me from becoming too impatient.

And then it was Friday. So many kids were out for the holidays that we combined into two classes. Regular lesson plans went out the window, and we mostly showed cartoons while they played. Only five of us were working: me, two other teachers, the assistant director and Louisa, who didn't seem pleased about making kiddie lunches so soon after Christmas. Sam wasn't at school, so Ty must be taking some vacation days and spending them with his family.

*Can't wait to see him.*

I got home at half past six, waved to Lauren and Angus, and went immediately to my room to start packing. Lauren followed me back, perching on the edge of her bed to watch me dig for a down vest. Something in her expression nudged at my memory, and then I knew. This was how she looked when she wasn't sure how I'd react.

"What?" I asked.

"Nothing."

None of my cajoling got her to talk. Eventually, she just said, "Have fun, okay?"

Bemused, I nodded, and she went back to the living room. I had the feeling she wanted to have a heart-to-heart, but maybe now wasn't the time. I set out my best pair of winter boots and packed a spare set, just in case. Jeans, a thick sweater, my coat, hat and scarf. *Gloves…here they are.* Soon, I had all of my overnight stuff in a small rolling suitcase that I rarely used.

Good timing, too. Because Ty texted me soon after, much earlier than I expected.

I'm downstairs. Ready for an adventure?

OMW, I sent back.

Quickly, I shrugged into my coat and hat, grabbed my purse and suitcase, and ran for the door. "Have a great weekend, guys. See you Sunday."

"You sound far too excited," Angus said with mock-disapproval.

He and Lauren hugged me, then I darted off to find out Ty's big secret. He was waiting downstairs by the front door with his own luggage. As I ran toward him, he picked me up and swung me around, then planted a firm *hello* kiss on me. His expression shifted, melted, and it was almost too much for me to bear. I understood what he meant when he talked about my face showing him everything, because now I was getting it back.

"You always look so damn happy to see me," he said, low. "And it's like a fist in my gut, every time. I wait for it not to happen, for you to get used to me, or maybe you're tired or you had a bad day, so you're in no mood to shine, but no. There's always that smile. Yeah," he added, touching my lower lip. "That one. Ready?"

Without waiting for my answer, he grabbed both our suitcases and led the way to his car. The night was cold but clear. He'd left his car running, right by the front doors, so it was deliciously warm when he tucked me into it. Those small gestures stole my heart, again and again, until I was helpless with it.

"I'm so excited. How far are we going?"

"Just a couple of hours. We should be there by nine."

"Oh, my God, tell me already."

"You really want to know?"

I shot him a look that could've steamed paint off a wall. "Yes."

"My boss, Bill, has a friend who runs a ski lodge north of

here. It's a beautiful place, downhill and cross-country trails. I asked him to hook us up with a getaway package as part of my holiday bonus."

"Wow." I was stunned to silence. "You need the money for school, right? I hope it wasn't—"

"If I didn't want this, we wouldn't be in the car."

"Then thank you. I brought warm clothes like you said. But you should know, I'm not a very good skier."

"We'll work on it. But there's also sledding, snowmobiling and an ice-skating pond. Pretty much the whole winter wonderland."

Suddenly, the art pencils I'd gotten him didn't seem like enough, and to cover my sense that our footing had shifted, I asked, "How was your Christmas?"

"I spent the night with my parents, so they could be there when Sam opened all of his presents. He loves their house because my mom goes all out. It's like a holiday store exploded and my dad spends two full days decorating outside."

"The power bill must be insane."

"No shit, he builds it into the budget annually, that leap in wattage."

"It sounds fun. Did your sisters come?"

"Valerie's here, spoiling Sam rotten. Sarah couldn't make it." When he talked about them like this, it made me feel like I knew them, too.

"I was wondering…does Sam ever see Diana's parents?" Her leaving didn't change the fact that they were his grandparents, too.

"Two or three times a year. They live in Arizona, and they don't get here very often. Her dad is in a wheelchair, and it's rough on him to travel."

"Oh."

"But they Skype with him and send presents. They're still looking for her," he added quietly. "Talking about hiring a private detective, last I heard."

*Wow.* Maybe I shouldn't have asked. "Sorry if that was—"

"No, it's okay. The worst thing about it is, they don't blame me for putting her in this situation. They blame her for 'running away.'" With a determined air, he changed the subject. "Hey, how were finals?"

Gratitude rippled through me. By now, I should know better than to ask anything about Diana. The answers always made me sad. "I lived. Pretty sure I scored well enough to hang in for another semester."

"If I know you at all, you did way better than that." Ty glanced at me, smiling, and the softness of his eyes, his mouth, seemed light-years away from the tense, angry guy I'd met back in late August. In fact, even talking about Diana didn't dent his mood as much as it did before.

*Four months. I've known him four months.*

"I aced my teaching practicum." Saying it out loud sounded so much like bragging, but the words sent a happy thrill through me.

"That's fantastic." As we drove, I told him about the first failed idea and the all-nighter that resulted in the second one.

Ty nodded. "I heard you pacing. Some nights it's tough, knowing you're right upstairs."

The darkness and the rhythmic rush of the road beneath the tires made it easier to admit, "For me, too. Sometimes I *do* have a terrible day and you'd make it better. Even being tired, broke, whatever, none of it would seem as bad with you."

His breath caught, and then he wrapped his fingers around mine and carried my hand to his mouth. "You take another little piece of me every time you open your mouth. You know that, right?"

"I'm not trying to."

"Nadia. You don't have to try." Months later, I still got that little flutter at the way his voice deepened around my name, like the syllables tasted different on his tongue.

I turned the music on then, trying to cover the way my hands trembled. It wasn't right that he could move me this much. I had no defense against his honesty. Ty was everything real and raw, a brightness that superimposed upon me long after I looked away, and he had no fucking idea that for me, this was so much more than sex or friendship. It was a need that hammered in my heart, etched into the secret underside of my skin and tapped away at my bones.

For the rest of the drive, we sang along with the radio, and I let my feelings settle to a low simmer. Otherwise, I probably would've cried all over my sleeve. But my first glimpse of the resort stole my breath, shoving other concerns to the back of my mind. As promised, it was a winter wonderland with a chalet-style lodge and glimmering lights along the trails. Wisps of smoke swirled heavenward from cabins farther into the woods, and more lights ringed the ice-skating pond, where graceful figures twirled and spun, lending the place an enchanted air.

Ty drove us past the icy marvels and parked, then he got our bags out of the trunk. "Let's get checked in. I don't know about you but tonight, I just want some room service. We can hit the ground running tomorrow."

"Sounds fantastic."

"Did I mention the suite has a spa tub?" Though his tone sounded innocent, his eyes were not.

"Somehow, no."

Outside, the lodge was impressive. Inside, it offered rustic elegance by way of polished stone and wood beams. A roaring fireplace dominated the lobby, and across the way, five or six people were drinking at the bar. The receptionist was quick and efficient, giving him forms to sign and explaining the amenities succinctly.

Once she processed the reservation and handed Ty the key, she asked, "Do you need help with your bags?"

"No, we've got it. Thanks." Then he turned to me. "We're on the third floor. Elevator's this way. Come on, sweetness." He didn't hug me but he might as well have as he took charge of the luggage again.

The other guests were older, and I wondered how we looked to them. Maybe I just felt weird because I'd never done anything like this before. Nobody paid us any attention as we crossed the lobby and went to check out our room. Which was *gorgeous*. A king-size bed piled high with satiny pillows caught my eye right away. The oatmeal carpet was plush beneath my feet when I kicked off my boots, and the bathroom was bigger than the one Lauren and I shared.

*Yeah, that tub's definitely big enough for two.*

"It's beautiful," I said aloud.

"I've never been here but Bill loves it. Of course, he's fifty-eight. So I'm guessing it'll be mostly his age bracket and maybe a few families."

"I'm not necessarily looking to make new friends," I said.

"That's a relief. Because I feel pretty antisocial."

"Should I leave you alone?"

"Not you. Just the rest of the world." His words hinted that he needed only me, and his gaze confirmed. "Are you hungry?"

I nodded.

"Then let's find the room service menu."

We ordered bowls of stew and salad, and when it came, the waiter pushed a linen-covered cart into the room and set the small table up as if we were in a restaurant. He even lit a candle between us, so my amazement was overflowing when he shut the door. Ty sat down like this was no big deal, but I had the feeling we were getting VIP treatment.

"Getaway package," he explained as he uncovered the food.

As we ate, he told me about his week. "Things have slowed down at work. With the ground frozen, there's a limit on what we can do. No new sites until March or so, which means we're limited to renovations."

"Because the crew can work inside?"

"Yeah, but Bill hates reno jobs, calls it nickel-and-dime bullshit, but those little jobs keep us in the black until we can take bigger projects in the spring."

"Does that mean less work for you? Is it easier to manage?"

"Somewhat. This is the laid-back part of the year."

After we finished, Ty tidied up the table and carried the dishes to the cart, then pushed it back into the hall. A warm flush went through me when he put the DO NOT DISTURB tag on the door and flipped the lock. It seemed like much longer than two months since we'd been naked in the same room.

"You look…determined," I whispered.

"I told myself I'd be cool, but I don't think that's possible between us. I want you so much, and it's been a million years since I touched you. Is it… Are you—"

"Yes," I said.

Ten seconds later, I was in his arms, and he was pulling my shirt over my head. I unbuttoned his with shaky fingers and smoothed my palms up his chest. With a ragged breath, he kissed me, and I tangled my arms around his neck. My whole body ached for him, and he drew me in with delicious heat and the slow delight of his mouth moving on mine, his tongue, mine, rasp of teeth and the demanding press of his hands.

I fell back, bouncing on the mattress, and then he was on me, moving between my legs. My jeans came off and then my socks, until I was in my bra and panties, and the golden heat in his brown eyes swept me from top to bottom, molten as a touch. He pulled my panties off in a rough motion and lowered his head.

"I've dreamed about this," he muttered.

God, Ty was a genius with that mouth. Most guys did this grudgingly, if at all, but he licked and nuzzled, until I came with a tiny scream. My thighs were still quivering when he slid up to kiss me, and I threaded my fingers through his hair. Digging my fingers into his back, I tried to communicate that I wanted more, but his teeth were on my neck, so I could only make *sounds*. I'd never been noisy during sex before, but usually I worried about someone overhearing. These walls were thick, and I didn't care if strangers knew Ty was incredible.

"More," I whispered.

He was trembling, fiercely aroused, when he fumbled for the condom. As he rolled it on, I saw the absolute quality of his desire. "How?" he asked. "How do you do this to me? I've gone longer without sex." My mouth was dry, and I just shook my head, bewildered. "I…I want…"

"Anything."

"All fours." His voice washed me in heat.

He came in from behind, wrapping his arms about me. This position might appear to be about power and subjugation, but I felt only exquisitely taken, and that must be what he craved—the sense of owning me, even if he didn't. Each thrust made me lift my hips and push back until he was frenzied, growling endearments and biting into my shoulder. The friction and pressure were so good, rubbing me just right, and then he added his fingers, stroking me as he fucked. This wasn't lovemaking; it was hard and frantic, like he couldn't take me hard enough, deep enough.

"Nadia, I'm— Are you—"

"Come." I gave him permission to let go, and he did.

He brought me off with his fingers, sensing that I was still thrumming. After, I curled against his chest, breathing hard, while he played with my hair. I turned onto my side, so I could gaze into his face, and I wrapped an arm around him, trailing it down his back in a slow, delicate glide. A perma-smile shaped his mouth, and intermittent shivers underscored how the sex between us just kept getting better.

*It's because he trusts you.*

Before, there had been a wall, some portion of Ty kept in reserve, but the door was open now, and the full, unreserved beauty of him staggered me. He was impish, silly even, and adorable in his demands. The night I cuddled him, he'd given some hint, but I could see Sam in him when he plopped his head in my lap and said, "Pet me."

I did.

The rest of the weekend, we'd eat and make love, play winter sports and get cold, then warm each other up. There would be hot cocoa in our future and more kissing. Plus, I wanted to make use of that tub. But with him smiling up at me, just so, his eyes on fire and full of my reflection, it was fucking impossible that I would ever be happier than this.

# CHAPTER TWENTY-TWO

As predicted, the rest of the weekend was phenomenal, but all too soon, normal life recalled us. Classes resumed, along with my regular work hours, and Ty became a few words on my phone or a tired voice for a few minutes a night. The Wednesday after we got back, I was supposed to have my first meeting with my new practicum mentor, and I was obsessing over what to wear when someone knocked, such a light tap that I wondered if I'd imagined it.

Until I threw the front door open and found Sam in his pajamas, bright flags of color in his cheeks. "Daddy is sick. And I don't feel good, either."

All thoughts of school and work flew out of my head. "Let me get my stuff, then we'll go. Don't worry, bud. You did a good job finding me." Though I was scared shitless at the idea of him leaving his apartment since the door locked behind him. What if I wasn't home? How sick must Ty be, if he couldn't get to his phone?

Sam proved how cruddy he felt by not responding to my

*bud* overture. Nor did he ask for any dinosaur jokes. Worried, I followed him downstairs and saw that he'd wedged Mr. O'Beary into the door. So he wouldn't have been locked out if I didn't answer. *Smart kid.* I put my hand on his cheek, and yeah, he was definitely flushed with fever.

"Get in bed. I'll bring you some juice and medicine, okay?"

When he nodded, a coughing fit swept over him. *Flu, maybe, or bronchitis.* I found OJ in the fridge, so I poured a glass of that and then I turned up a bottle of general-symptom children's Tylenol, so I checked his age and poured the right amount into the plastic cup. Sam was curled up with Mr. O'Beary when I came in, covers pulled up to his chin.

I put the juice down and gave him the medicine, which he drank obediently, though he made a horrendous face. "Tastes like evil."

"Worse than broccoli?"

Soberly, he nodded. "Can I have soup later? My throat hurts."

"No problem. You have to stay in bed, though, or you won't get better. I bet you'll be sleepy soon. Do you want a story?"

"Will you?" His eyes were irresistible.

So I read to him in a soft voice, and before I was half done, he winked out. I tiptoed out and went to check on Ty, who was still in bed. I doubted he'd ever failed to wake when Sam came to poke him, so no wonder the kid came upstairs. He'd kicked his covers off, and he was sweating profusely, his cheeks hot with the same fever as Sam. I remembered how he'd thrown himself into tobogganing, staying out long after I gave up and retired to the lodge.

First I sponged him off and fixed his covers. Then I got some Nyquil from the cabinet and pestered him until he roused enough to swallow it. But he didn't seem to register who I was, just moaned, rolled over and went back to sleep. To take care of them, I had to clear my day, though. I had a twinge in calling in to work so soon after my first missed day. Hopefully, Mrs. Keller didn't take it for an imminent disciplinary problem. I faked being sick and she said it was better for me to stay home. *Hurdle one, overcome.* The next problem was my practicum.

I didn't have the woman's phone number, so I sent an email.

Dear Ms. Roberts: I woke up this morning with a fever. Sorry I can't make our meeting this afternoon. I'll see you Friday.

While this might impact her impression, I'd never leave Sam and Ty when they needed me. One last thing to do. While Ty's work number was in his cell phone, I couldn't really call in for him. So I went to his studio and swirled the mouse to wake up the computer. No password. I opened his mail account, searched for "Bill" and was relieved when a few emails popped up with the company info in the man's signature. I read a few emails between them to get an idea of Ty's tone with his boss. Then I typed,

Bill, sorry I can't make it to work today. Sam's sick and my throat's on fire. I figure you'd rather I contain the germs. Back as soon as I can. Ty.

A few minutes later, a reply popped up.

No problem, kid. Feel better.

*Whew.* I felt like I'd just completed an undercover mission. Relieved, I went into the kitchen to see about the soup Sam wanted. There was chicken in the freezer and I found noodles in the cupboard. Carrots, celery and onion completed the recipe, and I quietly set the chicken to boiling. I didn't have much else to do, so I took a nap on the sofa while waiting for the chicken to fall off the bone and for the water to turn into stock.

At eleven, I checked on them, but they were both still asleep. I'd wake them when the soup was ready. I strained the broth, then added the vegetables. Half an hour later, the noodles went in, and I had homemade soup. I made a tray for Sam and carried it to his room with some herbal tea and toast. He was awake, but in bed, like I'd asked.

"I went to the bathroom," he told me. "But I got back in. I have to rest."

"Good job. Hungry?"

"A little. Throat still hurts."

"Maybe the soup will help. Eat it and I'll get you a scoop of ice cream, okay?"

Sam brightened. "Deal."

Hopefully, they had some. If not, I'd get my stash from the freezer. I chatted with him as he ate, pretending to tickle Mr. O'Beary. They did, in fact, have some vanilla ice cream, so Sam ate that with a gleeful expression. He seemed to be feeling somewhat better, but to make sure he rested more, I read to him until he fell asleep. *Finally.* I was worried about Ty, too, but I knew he'd prefer me to look after Sam while he couldn't. Yet he hadn't eaten anything since I'd been here, and I had no idea what fluids he had the night before. *He might be getting dehydrated.*

So I made a tray for him next, same menu as Sam, and I carried it into his room. He didn't seem quite as feverish, and when I sat down on the bed, his eyes opened. Ty almost spilled his lunch trying to shove me aside in panic. "Sam!"

"He's fine. He's asleep. He had tea and juice and soup and medicine. Don't worry, okay? I've taken care of everything."

He looked more than a little loopy from the flu meds. "Work?"

"Handled. Eat some soup or Nurse Nadia will get cranky."

With a bleary smile, he let me prop him against his pillows. Exhaustion was likely making this bug hit Ty harder than Sam. Kids were usually resilient, and neither of their fevers seemed high enough to warrant a doctor visit. With my help, he downed most of his soup and half of his tea, then he stumbled to the bathroom.

"What day is it?" He seemed to be fumbling to remember my schedule.

"A sick day," I said firmly. "Back to bed."

By evening, they were both feeling a lot better. Sam and Ty were curled up watching TV when I brought the last round of soup, tea and medicine. Sam glanced up at me with a sleepy smile, then he said to his dad, "I knew she'd fix us."

Ty froze. Before, he was relaxed, groggy, obviously feeling like shit, but enjoying the rare chance to watch cartoons with his son. But I saw it dawn on him that I shouldn't be here—that we had separate lives—and this wasn't one of our weekends. My presence didn't speak to friendship or sex, but something else entirely. I knew what it said; that I loved them enough to put my life on hold, if they needed me.

And it was true.

"Why are you even here?" It was the first time he'd thought to ask.

"I went upstairs to get her," Sam answered.

*Shit. That won't help, buddy.* Instinctively, I understood that

Ty wouldn't like learning how much Sam trusted me. It wasn't like I was using the little guy to get closer to his dad. Hell, I'd never do that. But Ty wore a sharp, terrified look, like all of him was recoiling.

"You should've called Grandma," Ty said gently.

"That's stupid. Nadia is right upstairs, and she loves us."

Ty's throat worked. His eyes met mine, darkness swirling. "But Grandma's feelings might be hurt. You know she enjoys taking care of you."

"Oh." Sam was crestfallen, mouth trembling. "I didn't think of that. I was scared cuz you didn't get up."

Seeing that Sam was about to cry, Ty hugged him around the shoulders. "Don't worry about it. You did a good job."

*Maybe if I leave now, it'll be okay.*

"I have to get going," I said.

Ty didn't get up, didn't let go of Sam, and his voice was too quiet. "Okay. Thanks. We'll be fine from here."

*Without you,* his look added.

All that night, I waited for a text but it didn't come. The next day, I went to work with a knot in my stomach that only swelled with Ty's silence. Sam was back in school, completely recovered. Mrs. Keller didn't seem to realize I'd lied and that made me feel worse.

She even patted me on the arm. "So glad you're feeling better. A number of kids were out yesterday, too. I think something's going around."

Her assistant made a sour face. "This time of year, there always is."

In my classes, I was a zombie, staring at the professors droning on. After failing twice to take notes, I gave up and recorded the lectures. Once I squared things with Ty, I'd feel better. Right? The ache in my chest didn't abate as I drove home. If anything, the feeling intensified as I parked out-side our building. *He's probably not even home yet.* I didn't see his car, so I went upstairs and tried to read some assigned chapters, but the words danced before my eyes. My stomach churned until it hurt. Around six, my phone finally pinged. With trepidation, I flicked open the message.

Come down. You can let yourself in.

Completely without context, the grave tone sent me run-ning down the stairs. When I stepped into the apartment, Ty had his back to me, hands braced on the counter, head bowed. My first thought was—

"Sam, is Sam okay?" He was fine when I left Rainbow Academy this morning.

"Yeah. I dropped him off with my mom." When he turned, he wore such a somber expression that it scared me.

"Don't you have night class?" My knees felt weak as I col-lapsed on the sofa.

"You skipped everything for me yesterday. So I'm return-ing the favor." But from his tone, this wasn't sweet or good. He was so pale that he was shaking. Not from sickness, at least not like yesterday. This was something else, pain chewing at him from the inside. Ty took a deep breath. "I am completely, hopelessly in love with you."

The smile formed instinctively; I didn't think I'd ever hear those words from him. Happiness sparked briefly, guttered like a candle in the wind. From the bleak look in his eyes, this wasn't a joyous moment. There wouldn't be a kiss to cele-brate the occasion.

"Ty—"

"I was fooling myself that we were just friends, no strings. It'll never be that way with us. And that's why this has to stop."

The emotional blow knocked the breath out of me. "But—"

He shook his head and backed around the table, keeping it between us when I stood up. "Let me finish, or I'll never get this said."

"Okay. Sorry." I hovered before the couch, torn between the desire to run and to demand he listen to me, instead. Silence won out.

"I can't go on like this. One weekend just isn't enough. The past two months, I've started resenting Sam. I can't—I can't have that, Nadia. God, I'm jealous of your fucking roommates because they're there when you wake up and when you go to bed at night. But that's not even the worst part. Yesterday you proved that you'd throw away your future for me. You ditched work, the practicum, without a second thought. That was never part of the deal."

"I didn't ruin anything. I still have my job, and I'm sure I can smooth things over—"

"This can't continue," he said flatly.

"We can figure something out." My tone was soft, thick with threatening tears. Losing Ty and Sam would break my world open like a tremor on a fault line.

"No, sweetness. We can't."

If he was angry, I could stand it. But he was just so tired and sad that my tears spilled over. I clenched my fists, wanting to argue, but I'd promised when we first started this that if and when it stopped working, it would end. But the ground was opening up beneath my feet, and when he stopped talking, it would swallow me up.

"You're sure?"

He nodded, an ocean of longing and anguish in his brown

eyes. "I've been thinking, and our upstairs/downstairs thing? It's a metaphor. How many times have I hung out at your place, Nadia?" When I made a zero with thumb and fore-finger, he said, "Exactly. You can come into my world, but I can't live in yours. So it's always you, coming to me. Me, holding you back."

"You're not," I whispered. "I'm happy."

*The pieces fit. I love you so much, Ty.*

Tears could strangle you and steal your voice. I hadn't known that until this moment. My heart was made of broken glass, slicing upward until my throat was cut. I couldn't speak.

"I don't see how that's true. You do all the giving, make all the compromises, and everything's on *my* schedule, because it has to be, or there's nothing at all. But that's not fair." Sucking in a deep breath, Ty went on shakily, "We…we're just not in the same place, and I won't let you regret me."

"You're only three years older," I said, incredulous. "We're both in school—"

"And those years were life-changing. I have Sam. *You* need to meet other guys, and you'll never do that with me on the scene. At this point, if I saw you with someone else, I'd prob-ably kill him, even though I can't call you mine."

*I* am *yours. I always have been.* Pain was an ice pick, chip-ping at my insides, until there was only blood and shards of bone. Before, I thought people who threw around the word *heartbroken* were full of shit. But I couldn't breathe for the vise tightening around my rib cage. It was like drowning, losing all the light beneath night-drenched waves.

"This isn't right, Nadia. I have to let you go."

"I don't want you to," was all I could manage.

"That face." He finally came around the table, closing the distance between us, and I knew, I just *knew* he was going to frame my face in his hands, as he always had. "How can I live without this face?"

*You're killing me. Don't turn the knife.*

"So don't." It wasn't quite begging. Any minute, I would quake apart at his feet and he could sweep up the dust. Maybe he could keep me in a jar on the shelf.

Ty shook his head, all certainty and sorrow. "We met too soon. This *can't* work now, much as I wish it could. You deserve a guy who can be there for you all the time, someone without so much baggage."

"Sam is *not* baggage," I snapped.

"He's also not your son." Such a gentle tone for such awful words.

"And you're not my boyfriend. I get it." I bowed my head for a few seconds, fighting the tears. Then I broke away from his hold. "Does it matter at all that I love you?"

"Love isn't a panacea," Ty said wearily. "Or a magic pill. Diana loved me, too. But she didn't stay, and I won't put Sam through it again."

"I'm not her," I answered. "You won't even give me a chance!"

"Can you honestly say you're ready to move in and be with me, be Sam's mom and live happily ever after? You've spent enough time with him to know exactly what that means."

*I'm twenty-one years old. I can't, I'm not.* That was my first, instinctive thought. And Ty read it in my face, in the slump of my shoulders. A light in him guttered and died.

I stopped fighting then because he was right after all, damn him. I would probably never forgive him for it. "So this is it. How does it end?"

"Like this." Stepping close, he swiped his thumbs across my eyes, dusting away the tears, then he pressed his lips to my

eyelids, one at a time. I raised my face, showing him everything one last time. Ty kissed me softly, honey and salt, hello
and goodbye, and all the words we would never whisper again,
holed up in bed on a snowy afternoon. He ran fingers through
my hair with an awful finality. My breath came out so loud
it was almost a sob.

"No regrets. You are a hundred times more wonderful
than I deserve."

This hurt so much; it made me angry. I had no experience
having my heart torn from my chest, and he was being so very
kind about it. His kindness made me cruel. "My mom said I
could do better."

Ty held my look steadily. "You can. Goodbye, Nadia."

"Bye, Daniel." I was even colder than I'd dreamed I could
be. That was never what I called him, only what she did. And
then I left, like her, because he made me.

# AFTER THE AFTER

# CHAPTER TWENTY-THREE

Completely numb, I stumbled into the apartment. Max took one look at me and leaped off the couch. He was at my side in an instant, arm around my shoulders. I couldn't breathe for choking back the tears. My breath came in sharp bursts, bordering on hyperventilation.

He sat me down, rubbing my back. "Okay. Okay."

Squeezing my eyes shut, I collapsed on him, and Max didn't say anything else for a long time. Finally, he offered, "This might sound stupid, but I've been writing down the things I like about Lauren. I'm not sure it's helping me get over her exactly, but…it *is* helping. Maybe you can try something like that."

"Maybe."

I loved that he wasn't asking me to explain. For over an hour, we just sat together, holding hands. I didn't cry; I couldn't. When I heard Angus coming up the stairs, his tread too heavy to be Lauren, I retreated to my bedroom and closed the door. Always, I had plans and goals; I focused on what had to be done and worked through it. This situation was no different.

So I got out a clean notebook and started writing. I set down how I felt in this moment, and then I wrote about meeting Ty. Maybe I'd save the journal and read it later, once the memories weren't so fresh. *This way, I can keep them with me.* Or hell, maybe I'd burn it. For now, the important thing was to finish.

I wrote until 3:00 a.m. and only stopped because Lauren came to bed then. I pretended to be asleep, and she didn't bother me. There was a new distance between us, not because I didn't care to share my pain, but because she'd chosen not to talk about hers. I fell asleep with the knife of losing Sam and Ty still in my chest, and it hurt to breathe.

Friday morning, I went to my practicum meeting, where I apologized profusely. Ms. Roberts was about ten years older than Ms. Parker had been, and she seemed more maternal, peering at me in concern. "People often get sick around the holidays," she said, dismissing my worries with an easy wave. "And I can definitely see that you've been ill. Mind that you don't let yourself get too rundown."

"I won't," I promised.

The rules and expectations were more or less the same, and I left feeling like she'd give me a fair trial. *See, Ty. I didn't wreck anything.* Outside the school, I sat in my car for at least five minutes, resting my head on the steering wheel. I skipped lunch and went home to change into my work uniform. I got to Rainbow Academy, knowing each day I spent with Sam would open the wound all over again, and I couldn't let him see even a shadow of my pain.

In class I must've done a good job because he never gave me that big-eyed, worried look. He chattered and hugged me like always while I fought to keep the damage in check. *It'll get easier,* I told myself. *It has to.*

That weekend, I holed up in my room and wrote more, until I came to the stopping point, our breaking point, and it was like a key turned in the lock, setting me free. I could breathe again because I had all the things I loved about Ty committed to ink and paper. The hurt dulled from dreadful-unbearable to the low throb of a broken bone, properly set. In my demented rush to finish the draft, I'd only thought of getting it out, like I was lancing a wound, and I'd pictured myself possibly burning it all, like an effigy, a symbolic cleansing.

But now, as I touched the pages, I couldn't bear to imagine seeing everything I adored about Ty going up in sparks and ashes, only embers against the night sky. No, I'd keep it, instead. Someday, I'd want these words, needing to remember how these moments felt, before life went flat and quiet, and I learned to live without my heart. As I got back to my normal life—life without Ty—occasionally the pain flared.

Like two weeks later when Sam announced, "Daddy's sad."

"Oh?" It took every ounce of self-control to ask the question casually.

"Yeah. He draws your face a lot."

My insides squeezed, and mumbling to the lead teacher, I excused myself. In the bathroom, I crouched inside a stall and cried until I saw stars. The wound widened, but I breathed through it. I put cold water on my eyes, and when I went back to Mrs. Trent's room, I was an iceberg.

Though I tried not to let on, Sam picked up on my mood. He tried to climb on my lap, and I couldn't let him. I told myself it was because I had work to do, but he must've sensed my reservations. His face crumpled when I set him down, big brown eyes swimming in tears.

He clenched two small fists, and he kicked me in the shins. "You're mean! And I hate you!"

"What's wrong?" Mrs. Trent came over, kneeling down to study him in concern because this behavior wasn't like Sam. *Shit.* This was exactly what Ty wanted to avoid.

"He wanted to look at a book together, but I have to clean up first." It sounded plausible, and Mrs. Trent glanced at Sam, brows raised. Guilt stung me.

"That's not why. You don't like me anymore. You haven't told me a dinosaur joke in forever and you *never* smile."

*Get it together. You can't let the breakup affect how you treat Sam. He deserves better.*

"That's not true. I'm sorry if it seems like I've been cranky lately. Give me five minutes and I'll read to you, okay?"

Sniffling, he nodded, watching with worried eyes while I picked up toys. Once I finished, Sam climbed into my lap, and I did the voices for his favorite story. When I finished, he hugged me around the neck; I resolved not to let my misery impact him ever again. In the days that followed, I worked. I studied. I did everything I was supposed to, tiptoeing around the hole inside me. Some nights, I dreamed of Ty. It was never profound, just those little things, like him opening the car door or framing my face in his hands, and I always woke with my face wet with tears. *I don't know how to be brokenhearted. I wish you hadn't taught me.* A few times a month, I saw them coming and going, father and son, twin copper heads shining in the sun. Their circle was complete without me. I turned away from the window; I never went out on the balcony anymore, and *not* because it was too cold. Probably it was a good thing Ty had never hung out here in the apartment with me. I'd have to move.

Toward the end of January, my roommates threw a small party. Courtney and Emily came, and a new guy Angus was dating, Del Webber. He was cuter than the ex-boyfriend, J-Rod, African American instead of Puerto Rican, plus sweeter and kinder, too. Luckily, it wasn't the kind of bash we hosted for Lauren, just a few close friends, plus beer and pizza in honor of my birthday. There was cake, one Lauren and Angus baked. They lit candles and sang to me, and I could only wonder, *Does Ty know? Is he listening for my steps? Or has he stopped?*

Objectively, the night was a success. I had fun. I opened presents. Afterward, I thought, *So I'm twenty-two.* Lauren was oddly quiet after everyone left, and I decided I'd had enough. Leaving cleanup to the guys, I said, "You and me. Now."

A small sigh slipped out, but she nodded and said inexplicably, "This is what I was waiting for, anyway."

In our room, I shut the door, sat down on my bed and folded my arms expectantly. There was most definitely something on her mind, but I couldn't imagine what. "Well?"

She curled up on the floor beside my bed and rested her chin on the edge of the mattress, a pose familiar since high school. "We talked a little before about how I'm not sure PoliSci is right for me."

"I remember. Did you decide to change your major?"

Lauren shook her head. "It's not that. There's no easy way to say this, so I'll just come out with it. I'm going home."

"What?" That didn't even make sense.

"You wanted so bad for us to go to college together, and when we were eighteen, I wanted it, too. But I hate Michigan. I miss Sharon—never thought I'd say that—and I miss my mom." From her expression, this wasn't homesickness talking, something most people got over freshman year. "I tried so hard to make this work, but...this is your dream, not mine, Nadia. I didn't want to let you down, but I just can't pretend anymore."

"So what're you going to do?" Somehow I didn't yell at her or make this about breaking a childhood pact. I had to be better, stronger, than that. Somehow. Even though most of me was screaming that I couldn't give up Lauren so soon after Ty.

*It's too much. This can't be happening.*

"I already lost my scholarship," she said softly, not looking at me. "I tried to prepare you when I said I didn't do well at midterms. I did not, in fact, make it up at finals. So…Mom can't afford tuition now, and I'll be withdrawing before the cutoff date. I'm going home in four days." She didn't sound sad, though. It was more like there was a smile hidden like a sunrise at the back of her throat, and she was just waiting for me to say it was okay, so she could let herself feel the happiness and relief.

I managed to say, "Shit. When I said *one day, I'll wake up sad as hell because you're not here,* I didn't realize it would be so soon."

She let out a choky laugh, the smile finally cracking the solemnity of her face, but tears sparkled in her eyes, too. "Yeah, that caught me off guard. It's why I cried that night. I knew this day was coming."

"Why didn't you tell me?"

"Because you'd have tried to talk me out of it by suggesting another major or making some other change that didn't involve leaving Michigan."

"You're probably right," I admitted. "Is this why you shot Max down?"

Lauren shook her head. "He's just not for me. I like him as a friend, but I want even more to go home."

"I can understand that." *Okay, not really.* Sure, I missed my parents and Rob, but as for Sharon, Nebraska? No. I didn't want to live there again.

"Maybe you should come with me. You need to stop thinking about Mr. Hot Ginger, anyway. If he's not smart enough to see what he has in you, then he needs a kick in the nuts." That was 100 percent friend loyalty talking.

"Nothing he said was wrong. That's part of why it's so painful."

"If you say so. I talked to Courtney, and she wants to move out of the dorms. Her roommate is constantly smoking in the room and hiding her stash in Courtney's stuff. She's to the point that she's afraid of getting arrested. Unless you object, I plan to sublet my half of the room to her for spring semester. I won't leave you guys hanging on the rent."

"Courtney's fine. I mean, she's not *you*, but we can manage."

"I'm so glad you don't hate me. I thought you'd freak and remind me how we promised to be in caps and gowns at the end of college, facing the future together."

Since I'd considered doing exactly that, she was proving how well she knew me. Fresh tears stung my eyes, and my voice was thick when I pretended how much I'd changed. "That was a really long time ago, LB. We were, what, fourteen? People change."

They did, and I didn't want them to. Sometimes, when things were perfect, I wanted them to remain exactly the same. But life wasn't static. It went on.

*I'm losing my best friend.*

It was hard not to feel that way, even though Lauren was talking about how we'd Skype, email and see each other when I came home in the summer. Six months, when we hadn't been apart for more than a couple of days since we were eighteen and hopelessly lost on campus, that first week. I nodded in the right places, but she was clouding over, probably because I had the worst poker face in the world. Thanks to Ty, I knew that, but I couldn't fix it.

"Nadia, don't cry, or you'll get me going."

I dug the heels of my hands into my eyes, but it didn't help. With a choky sob, Lauren climbed onto my bed, cursing quietly. "See, this is exactly how I didn't want it to go."

We held on to each other and cried, and for me, it was a farewell to childhood, admitting that sometimes, no matter how much you wanted something, it would never, ever come true. She petted my hair and we stayed up superlate, talking about old friends, people we hadn't seen in years and in some cases, would never see again. When the light cracked in through our windows, I heard the closing of a door. It was probably Max leaving for work, but for me, it was symbolic, and Lauren felt it, too.

She got up then and retreated to her own bed. "I don't have anything to do, except pack, so I'm going to sleep."

"Okay," I said. "Do you want a going-away party?"

"Nah. That's why I waited for your birthday, two birds, one stone." There was a calm about her that had been missing for months; I'd been too wrapped up in my own shit to notice.

"How are you getting home?"

"Angus bought me a plane ticket. I said I'll pay him back when I get my last check, but you know how he is. Courtney's buying my furniture, so I just have my clothes. I was wondering if I could borrow your big suitcase."

"Help yourself. I won't need it." Quietly, I processed the implications of that; Angus knew before I did.

In the abstract, that probably meant I mattered more, or that she didn't want to ruin my birthday, but I could focus only on the fact that she'd waited until four days before she left. Basically until she had no choice at all. There was an invisible lump in my chest as I got in the shower. Since it was the weekend, I didn't have to work, but I couldn't be at home.

Normally, at a time like this, I'd text Ty or call him, so I could hear his voice when he said my name, and that gorgeous, syrupy warmth would spill through me, smoothing over the bad patches. That wasn't an option anymore. So I dried my hair and dressed, like I had somewhere to be. Lauren was asleep or pretending. I didn't feel like talking to Angus, either, so I got my keys and went downstairs.

Of course, since this was the worst I'd looked since the breakup that wasn't really one at all, technically, I met Sam and Ty going out at the same time. They were dressed for the weather, Sam's eyes bright above his scarf. Ty was back to looking pale and miserable, pretty much exactly how I felt. For Sam's sake, I mumbled a greeting and rushed past to my car, pretending I was in a hurry, except there was nowhere in the world for me. Ty lifted a hand and then dropped it, probably knowing there was nothing he could say.

*Yes, there's something wrong. No, it's none of your business. You want it that way.*

The sidewalk was slick with icy patches, graying snow melting atop dead grass. I fumbled my keys then dropped them. With a sigh, I knelt and scrabbled for them in the cold, starting when someone touched my shoulder. Not Ty. It would *never* be Ty. Pain flowered fresh and sharp, exploding in my chest like a scream.

Max stood behind me, one hand in his pocket, and I could see his fingers clenching into a fist and then relaxing, a helpless, pained gesture that told me everything. "Angus told me about Lauren."

I nodded as he pulled me up.

"Come on, Conrad. Let's get some breakfast."

Though I'd rarely been on the back of his bike, I followed him over and put on the helmet. Sam was waving at me from the backseat of Ty's Focus, and I raised my hand, showing him everything was fine. *You're a good kid.* Max swung on and glanced at me expectantly. With a spurt of defiance, I swung onto the back and wrapped my arms around his waist. I wasn't trying to make Ty jealous because it wasn't like that with Max and me, and it never would be.

Max zoomed out of the parking lot, leaving the complex behind. Breakfast didn't sound very good at the moment, and as if he sensed how I felt, he headed for the highway. It was incredibly cold, but the rushing wind drove out the pain, leaving only numbness, and it was a welcome relief. For an hour, there was only Max's back and the hiss of the road, roar of the tires and rumble of the engine.

By the time he stopped, my fingers were locked into icicles at his waist. Gently he pried me loose, and we stumbled into a truck stop. We had to be close to Ann Arbor, though I'd lost track of the direction. Shivering, I slid into a booth across from him and he ordered us both coffee to start. I studied the menu, knowing I had to eat, not wanting to. But I wouldn't be a damsel who pined, so I got waffles.

"I never understood the bike until now."

"It's freedom," he said simply. "I've had it since I was fifteen, and whenever shit got unbearable at home, I'd take off."

Cupping my hands around my mug, I observed, "Running doesn't solve anything."

"No, but it leaves you in a better place to deal when you get back. And sometimes whatever was bothering you isn't there anymore."

"So you'll be riding around until Lauren leaves?"

He gave a wry half smile. "Maybe. I think maybe she was right, though, about me not knowing her. I had no idea she was so unhappy here."

"She's not easy," I said. "We've been friends for a long time, and I don't know her like she does me. I feel bad saying that. And I'll miss her. I'll miss her sense of humor. I'll miss her big brain and her loyalty. I'll miss knowing she's around if I need to talk."

"You can talk to me," Max said.

"I'm not sure that'll work. Sometimes if I'm freaking out about something, I climb in her bed and poke her awake. She always talks me down, even at four in the morning."

His look was surprisingly somber. "If you get in my bed, Conrad, I promise I won't take it the wrong way."

Somehow I managed a shaky smile. "The way this semester is going, I might do that."

"There's no shame in leaning. Seems to me, we've been taking turns."

"Okay," I said. Our breakfast came, and to my surprise, the perpetual knot in my stomach unraveled enough for me to eat. "How do you feel about Courtney moving in?"

"I'm fine with it. She's in a shitty situation, and I'm glad we can help her out."

I agreed. *See, there's the bright side. Lauren leaving means we can save Courtney from her crazy roommate.* At this stage, I couldn't come up with a silver lining to losing Sam and Ty, but maybe one day. Hope was a tiny bubble, light as air and rising in my chest.

"Top you two off?" the waitress asked.

At Max's nod, she refilled our cups and I lifted mine. He

clinked his against it. "To Lauren," he toasted with a bittersweet smile.

"And to survival," I said, because giving up was never, ever a choice I could make.

*

# CHAPTER TWENTY-FOUR

Courtney moved in the following weekend.

Though we'd gone to a bunch of the same parties over the years, she was more Max's friend than mine, and it was bizarre to have her carrying boxes into our room, putting stuff away where Lauren's clothes used to be. What I knew about her boiled down to this: her last name was Kaufman, she was Jewish, she was studying business, and she hated her current roommate in the dorms—from what I'd heard, with good reason. She was a short brunette, just over five feet, with strong features and a flair for the dramatic. Oh, and she also liked to mess with high people and make out with Max.

*It's only until the lease runs out in August.* I could put up with anything for six months.

To be sociable, I said, "Do you need help unpacking?"

"No, thanks. I'm a little OCD about organization." Her gaze swept my jumbled bookshelves. "Will it bother you if I alphabetize?"

"No, I guess not." I pulled books down at random and put

them back exactly the same way. But if she had to impose order, it wouldn't ruin my day.

Lucky for her, I wasn't a slob. I kept my dirty clothes in the hamper and I washed them on a regular basis; my half of the closet was decent.

With a faint sigh, I left her to settle in and joined the guys in the living room. "This feels so weird."

Angus nodded. "I cried at the airport, after dropping Lauren off."

"Just give her a chance," Max said, surprising me.

An hour later, Courtney joined us. She was quiet when Lauren would've been cracking jokes and throwing popcorn at the TV, but I got the impression she was sussing us out, trying to figure out where she fit in the apartment hierarchy. Not that we had one.

Eventually, she asked, "Are there any house rules?"

"There's a work schedule," I said.

So far, there hadn't been much trouble. Nobody made any huge messes, we took turns doing various chores, and the worst problem we had was bickering over who ate the last yogurt. Then I explained how we were splitting the food bill and hoped she wouldn't be one of those food labelers who would stare suspiciously to make sure we hadn't touched her ramen.

"Works for me. If you were wondering, I don't keep kosher, so you don't have to worry when you're shopping."

"That's a relief," Angus joked. "Max would die without ham."

Max muttered back, "Would not. I'd just be very sad."

Courtney smiled at us tentatively. "You have no idea what a relief it is to be here. Everything I own reeks of weed." *That explains her pleasure in hustling high people.* "Toward the end, the

RA was obsessed with busting Madison, and she was constantly finding reasons to knock on our door."

I teased, "Will you bend spoons with your mind for us?"

"Oh, God. I can't believe you remember that."

We stayed up late talking, all four of us. Things didn't seem quite so dire in the morning. Courtney was here, nothing exploded, and she paid her rent on time. I didn't poke her awake in the middle of the night, of course. And I didn't go to Max's room, either.

The first week of February trundled by in a wave of work, school and applying strategies I'd learned in the first practicum. Now I led a lesson every week, and Ms. Roberts was less proactive than Ms. Parker. It wasn't that she was a bad teacher, but…she was tired. To her, my presence offered a break, and she was more interested in resting than teaching me. I tried not to let it bother me.

It had been a while since I went to the exercise room, so I changed into sweats after work and headed over. When I walked in, Ty was on the treadmill, running as if zombies were chasing him. His face was ruddy with exertion, his gray T-shirt damp with sweat. He glanced up, stumbling when he realized it was me. I nodded in greeting and climbed on the elliptical. The silence was awkward, but what could I say?

*I miss you,* I thought. *I hate this.*

He finished his workout in silence and switched off the machine, turning away to blot his face with the towel. "I have to go. Night class."

"See you." I held my breath until he left and then crumpled over the console, closing my eyes against an intense wave of longing.

On Valentine's Day, I stayed home with Max and Courtney while Angus took Del out for a romantic evening. Unsurprisingly, we watched *I Hate Valentine's Day*. Courtney and I ate half a pound of chocolate while Max sighed at us. He hadn't talked about Lauren in a while.

She emailed me often, chirpy notes about people back home, my parents and hanging out with my brother, Rob, working on his new house. There was stuff about a pregnant classmate, her mom's new boyfriend, how she planned to transfer her credits and take computer classes online. I didn't share her news with Max; it wouldn't help him to hear how happy she was.

"I know why I'm depressed," Courtney said, glancing over at me. "What about you?"

I didn't know her well enough to tell the whole story, so I just said, "Recent breakup."

"Me, too. Well, sort of. The fallout is fresh, anyway."

"You want to talk about it?"

"Are you easily agitated?" That was such a strange question that I arched a brow.

Max snickered. "She's trying to figure out if you'll be weird after you hear her deal."

"I'm already weird," I said.

"Point. She's cool, Courtney, you can trust her."

Now I was curious. I paused the movie and shifted on the couch, giving her my full attention. She repaid that focus by putting down her bucket of Hershey's Kisses. "It's not that I mind people knowing, but sometimes girls are strange about this, especially if we share a room. I'm bi, but I'm not remotely into you."

I laughed, pretending to protest, "But...my dreams."

"Anyway, I was with this chick, Amy, for a while. Before me, she'd never been with a girl. I'm not sure if it was a phase or she was college-curious. Whatever. It lasted a couple of months, but she was so high-maintenance—and I say that as a Jewish woman." When she flashed me a grin, I knew it was okay to chuckle. "So I broke up with her, and she told everyone, all over campus, that I got her drunk and seduced her. Which is such bullshit. She's the one who said she'd always been interested. Now people act like I'm a predatory lesbian, scheming to snatch away people's straight cards with my irresistible girl sex."

"Is that why you were kissing Max at the party?"

She shook her head. "I like kissing Max. He's good at it. You should try it."

He shot us a horrified look. "Can you *not* pimp me out, Kaufman? Just for the sake of my fragile self-esteem."

"I did kiss Max," I said. "Freshman year, first time I met him. Then he said—"

"Oh, God, not again." He dropped his face in his hands.

Courtney ordered, "Shut up, you. I want to hear this."

I cracked up. As bad lines went, it was my favorite. "'Do you know karate? 'Cause, girl, your body is kickin'.'"

"I was in my gangster phase," he mumbled.

Courtney almost fell on the floor laughing. "That's the best thing I've ever heard. Do you mind if I steal that? I'm pretty sure I have the street cred to pull it off." She threw up some random gestures that were meant to pass as gang signs, but I suspected they were ASL. "Don't leave me hanging. Did that work for him?"

"I laughed. But he did, too. Then we got drunk and made out."

"As you do," she said wisely.

"Why must you dredge up our sordid past?" Max wondered aloud.

"Because it's hilarious. So then, I heard a bunch of guys

talking about how many girls Max had banged, and betting I'd be next. I made a point never to let him feel me up again."

He pulled a face that was pure dejection. "And I've been so lonely."

"I can understand your scruples," Courtney said to me. "I'm glad I didn't know you when you were a freshman, dude."

"That's a popular opinion," he muttered.

Angus came home an hour after the movie ended. We'd hooked up a laptop, like Ty had downstairs, and were watching Netflix instead of cable. I was ready to suggest canceling the service to save money, but Angus watched certain shows when they came on, and he'd probably be crushed if I pointed out he could watch them anytime online. In some respects, he was a traditionalist.

"So how was the date?" Max asked.

Angus sank onto the sofa between Courtney and me. "He's fantastic, but I'm not sleeping with him yet."

"Don't tell me somebody got you a copy of *The Rules* for Christmas." That was Courtney. She glanced around. "It wasn't me."

"No, I just want to take it slow, after Josh. That was… It was years. I was starting to think maybe he was the one. I don't want to get hurt again."

"You'll always get hurt." The words popped out before I could stop them but I didn't mean them to sound so bitter. "You just have to make sure the person's worth the pain."

"Deep," Courtney said.

"Happy Valentine's Day, motherfuckers." Max stood and arched his back, and I grabbed his cynical ass in a tight hug.

Angus and Courtney got in on the action, and for a few seconds, I felt a little lighter, like the hollow in my chest might one day fill up with other things. I went to bed in a better mood.

The rest of February sped by, occupied with work, classes, homework, practicum and the occasional social event with my roomies. They made a point of dragging me out of the house whether I wanted to go or not. Sometimes they went drinking, though I never got wasted over Ty like Angus had Josh. I just kept pushing forward.

In March, I realized it had been two months since we broke up, though I couldn't claim that word. *He was never my boyfriend.* But he *was* the guy I loved. And still did, in all honesty. The feeling hadn't faded. Sometimes, sometimes, I had weak moments.

Like tonight.

I was sitting on the floor of my closet, hiding, because I was afraid of what the sound of his voice might do to me. There were four saved messages in my voice mail. I hadn't played them since the day I walked out of his apartment, but tonight, need rose up until it might strangle me. If I didn't listen to these, then I might call him. That would be a worse way to torture myself.

So I plugged in my earbuds, put them in and played the first one.

*Hey, Nadia. I just want you to know I'm thinking about you. Call me.*

That one, I played four or five times. I thought about erasing it, but I couldn't bring myself to do it, not yet. Maybe I'd store these on a USB drive and keep them in a box, along with the notebook that contained my memories of him. Maybe, if I gave all of those feelings a new home, my chest would stop aching. A sound principle, if you believed in transference.

Message two: *It's me. Sam said you showed him how to tie his shoes today. He was so excited, you have no idea. And it means so much to me that you're good to him.*

Ridiculously, I touched a fingertip to my phone, as if Ty lived in there because some evil wizard had cast a spell and locked him away from me like a genie in a lamp. But nothing happened apart from the solitary tear trickling down my cheek. I didn't like feeling this way, but I had no idea how to stop.

Message three: *I miss you. God, this has been a shit day. Call me back?*

I played it twice before moving on to the last, the most recent one. He'd left it the day after we got back from the ski trip. Message four: *Hey, sweetness. I had an amazing time. There's just something about you…. Anyway, thanks for being with me. Talk to you soon.*

The closet door banged open.

For a supremely awkward moment, I stared up at Courtney and she gazed down at me. The silence was horrendous. "So…I'm not exactly inexperienced at coaxing people out of closets, but I didn't expect to need that skill set with you."

I burst out laughing. In that moment I felt sure we'd end up close, not social friendly or *I don't hate you when I'm drunk,* but full-on friends. "I was afraid you'd accuse me of doing weird shit to your clothes."

"I can see you were having a moment with your phone. Listening to ex messages?"

"How did you know?"

"It's a classic wallowing strategy. You might also put on a shirt he wore or do bizarre things with his pictures. Been there, done that."

"How long did it take to…stop?"

"With some people, it doesn't. They never leave you. The

guy I dated in high school...to this day, I still talk to him in my head. We have these long, involved conversations, and I imagine him advising me on my love life."

"That's weird, Courtney. Why don't you just call him?"

Her breath hitched. "Because he died when we were seventeen."

"Jesus. Now I want Angus to take us out and get us drunk."

"I heard that!" Suddenly, he was standing outside our room like an alcoholic fairy godfather, dangling his car keys.

It ran through my head that I shouldn't go out tonight. Responsibilities like bills, work, classes, practicum careened through my head until I shook it, denying all the reasons I wasn't allowed to have fun. One night wouldn't ruin my life. And I needed a break from trying to prove to my parents that I was worth the way they'd scrimped and saved to get me here.

"I'm in," I said. "Courtney?"

"Fuck it, why not?"

Laughing, I put away my phone and threw on a sparkly, backless halter and my sexiest pair of jeans. Angus nodded his approval when I came out ten minutes later. Courtney wasn't far behind. She was wearing more makeup than usual, giving her a sultry look.

"All right, ladies. Let's do this thing."

Angus took us to Heat, the closest bar to campus. Since it was within walking distance, it was pretty much always packed with freshmen and sophomores keeping the place loud every night. I appreciated his flawless sense of setting because this was definitely the right venue for us to make asses of ourselves. Considering the people around us, we'd probably be the least obnoxious idiots in the place, even if we got mad drunk.

Courtney and I started strong with tequila shooters. I knocked back four, serious about a liquid cure for what ailed me. She shrugged and kept up, then we went out on the floor to dance with Angus. He already had a crowd around him but he made room, nudging people away so we could form a tri-fecta of booty-shaking. Courtney was a terrible dancer, worse than Max, but it didn't seem to trouble her. Me, either. Two more shots, and I wouldn't care if I took my top off.

Someone came up behind me and moved with me. I couldn't see his face, but it didn't matter. Dancing wasn't the same as taking him home. Arms over my head, I swayed side to side, trying to pretend I felt sexy instead of so incredibly alone. The guy put his hands on my hips. I worked in a slow circle, spinning to face him. The strobing lights made his face look weird and demonic; his eyes flashed red. *You're so drunk.* This was fun, right? Exactly the kind of excitement I was supposed to have in college and then reminisce about after I settled down.

I moved away from Gropey and got closer to Angus. He took the cue to glare, driving the other guy off. Courtney was laughing at something, and as I twirled, I spotted a face in the crowd, and shock went through me like a lance. It was dark, smoky and loud. I was wrong; I had to be. But for a few seconds, I thought I'd spotted Ty, and it knocked the buzz right out of me. Tracking through the crowd, I stopped danc-ing and took a second look. No, this kid was much younger, shorter, too. Only the red hair was similar, and he had a mess of freckles. He noticed me looking and signaled, like we were connecting across a crowded room.

*Nope. Sorry. You're not Mr. Hot Ginger.*

To cover my near meltdown, I danced, but I didn't drink more. *You're fooling yourself if you think booze can wash this away.* I remembered how Courtney had said, *With some people it doesn't. They never leave you.* Maybe, ten years from now, I would still be having conversations with Ty in my head, remembering everything about him with this awful, aching clarity.

*Jesus.*

I tried it now in the silence of my head. *So work is going well. Grades are up. Everything's on track, except for how much I miss you. Do you think about me?* Courtney had said she got answers from her ghost, but my subconscious was silent, possibly because the guy haunting me was alive and well, living in 1B.

As planned, Courtney got shit-faced, and when Angus was helping her to the car at 2:00 a.m., he realized I was stone sober. She tipped over in the back, giggling, and he shrugged. I circled around the front to the passenger side.

Angus slammed into the car, frowning at me. "I'm pissed off at you. The whole point of this was for you to participate in the age-old letting-go ritual."

"I'm not ready," I whispered.

*I might never be.*

In the backseat, Courtney was singing superloud about how this shit was bananas. I didn't disagree.

*

# CHAPTER TWENTY-FIVE

March blended into April, and April to May. Study, work, skim chapters, memorize material, go to the practicum, joke around with the roomies: that was my life. And time marched on. One low night, I crept into Max's bed, and he held me. We didn't talk, and the next morning, he said nothing about it. I didn't feel much better about Ty and me, but he still didn't answer when I talked to him in my head. At this point, I had no idea if that was good or bad.

I had just finished the last of my finals when my mom called. I'd tried to keep up with them better, sending regular emails—not that she nagged me about it. Today when I answered the phone, her tone was off, echoing with forced brightness.

"Hey, how did exams go?"

"Pretty well, I think. I worked hard this semester." There had been no reason not to. No weekends away, no sex, no dates. If not for my roomies, people might've thought I'd joined a cult structured around abstinence and lack of fun.

"If you have time, your dad and I need to talk to you. Can you call us on Skype?"

"Sure," I said as a cold hand twined around my intestines. In the years I'd been away at school, my parents had never shown any interest in video chat. "Just let me get my laptop."

"Okay, honey. We'll be here."

*Something's really, really wrong.*

On the way to my bedroom, I almost threw up. Somehow I choked it down and called them, as requested. It took a few tries for them to answer, and I could imagine Mom and Dad arguing about how to do it, just like the stupid pine tree. The mental image put a smile on my face, so I didn't look scared or sick when they finally picked up.

"There you are," my dad said.

He'd aged visibly since Thanksgiving, even more lines, more gray in his hair. That was enough to worry me, but the look in his eyes? I'd never seen anything like it—a reeling combination of fear and despair, reinforced in the slump of his shoulders. I couldn't stand it. The only time I ever saw my dad cry was when he buried my grandmother, but that was a grief I could understand. As a kid, you think your father is invincible. You tell other kids that he can beat up their dad, and he will, if they don't leave you alone.

This man was frightened. He resembled my father, but there was none of his quiet strength, none of the certainty, only hesitation and confusion. That was *not* my dad. Never in my life had he ever shown any sign that he didn't know everything. *He's dying,* I thought, and then I wanted to jam a metal spike into the brain that could consider such a thing.

*I take it back. I take it back, okay?*

The silence went on too long, and my mom took Dad's hand, as if to give him courage.

"Here I am," I answered eventually. "What did you want to talk about?"

*Cancer, it's cancer.*

Stark terror flooded me, sparking behind my eyes. Apart from me, the apartment was empty, so there would be nobody to catch me after I hung up with them, after I pretended to be strong and sure, all the things they'd need from me. I schooled my face, trying—for once—not to show everything.

"I don't know how to break this to you," my mom started.

My whole body locked.

Dad touched her lightly on the cheek, such a tender gesture for so many years together. "No, I should tell her."

She breathed in. Out. "Okay."

"Last year, I was diagnosed with Parkinson's. I've tried to manage it so I could keep working, but I'm not steady enough anymore. At the end of the month, I'll be unemployed."

For a few seconds, I was beyond breathing as thoughts whirled in my head. *What the hell is Parkinson's?* I'd heard of it, something to do with Michael J. Fox, but I couldn't remember anything. *Is it terminal?*

"Give me a sec, okay?"

Quickly I brought up the browser and Googled. *Disorder of the brain that leads to shaking (tremors) and difficulty with walking, movement and coordination. Can be genetic or caused by environmental factors like exposure to pesticides.* Then I read a quick article about how Michael J. Fox had been battling it for over twenty years. Relief crackled through me when I realized it was a degenerative condition, but not an automatically fatal one. *It doesn't mean I'm losing him in a month or even a year. It's treatable.* I flipped back to the chat window and found my dad hugging my mom.

"Sorry, I just wanted to know more. I figured it would be faster to read it."

"You're taking this pretty well," Mom said.

A deep breath trickled out. "I thought it was worse. Do you want me to come home? I can quit my job to help out, whatever you need, Dad."

*At least the school year's over.* At first, I wasn't thinking about leaving Mount Albion, but I could. My credits would transfer and—

"Only if that's what *you* want," he said. "Don't do it for me."

"Or us," Mom added. "We'll be okay. Rob's here, and your father and I, we can weather anything, as long as we're together."

*I want that,* I thought. And then, *I had that.*

Mom smiled as he squeezed her around the shoulders. "The reason we're telling you this, honey, is because it impacts your future. Your dad tried so hard to hang on until after your senior year, but it's not going to happen. On my salary, we can't afford our bills and your tuition, too. I'm sorry, but this last year, you're on your own."

My dad picked up, continuing as couples who had been together a long time often did. "You needed to know what's going on, so you can make plans. Tuition will be cheaper in state, but you won't have a scholarship. You could transfer like Lauren's doing, and you'll save money by living at home. But don't come back expecting to take care of *me*. I'm not that sick yet."

Mom nodded. "Your dad will look for work, but the economy's rough right now."

"At my age and with my health problems, it's unlikely I'll find anything." The admission came out coated in shame, as if he hadn't already done *so* much. "In time, I might get disability, but it won't be enough to help you. I'm sorry, bean."

I said in exasperation, "Would you stop apologizing? Dad, I only care about you. I couldn't give two shits about tuition right now."

My mom frowned. "You should. All you've talked about since you were sixteen is getting your degree."

*Because I want to make you proud.* I wanted to teach, too, but for as long as I could remember, my parents praised me for being smart. They talked about how I'd get out of Sharon and make something of myself. No retail job for me, no minimum wage. I'd never wash dishes or mop floors. I was too clever for that, bound for better things. So I had been trying to live up to their expectations: never miss work, study hard and don't fuck up my chances.

*Maybe it's time I said it out loud.* But I couldn't look at them while I did, so I stared at my hands. "That's because I don't want to disappoint you. I thought you'd be upset if I took longer than four years or I didn't get summa cum laude or—"

"Only if you're unhappy." My mom sounded shocked, shaken even.

Timidly I glanced at the screen. My dad whispered something to my mom and she nodded. "If it's okay with you, he's going to lie down. This seems like a talk we need to have alone first. I'll fill him in later."

I nodded. "Bye, Dad. I love you."

"Love you, too." At home, he would've mussed my hair or poked me in the side.

It was harder to share certain things in front of him. Since he was the strong, silent type, I always felt like he thought I should be, too. Rob took after him in that respect; my brother never admitted to a feeling that I could recall. So my mom was kind of the bridge between all of us, trying to make us understand each other—with varying degrees of success.

"Okay, let's back up. You mean you're doing all of this for us?"

"Well, no. But…" I struggled to find the words. "I do feel some pressure to perform. My grades have to stay above a certain level for my scholarship, and if I don't do well here, then it's like you wasted all of that money on me, when you should've kept it for yourselves. Now that Dad's sick, you might need it more than ever. So I never miss work because I don't want you to think you made a mistake, believing in me, trusting me."

"Nadia, honey, it sounds like you spend an awful lot of time fretting about us, what we think and how we'll feel. But it's *your* life."

"And there's a right way to live it, huh, Mom?" I didn't realize her warning from Thanksgiving was still eating at me, but I could quote it by heart. "'This boy has already gotten some girl pregnant and messed up his future. You can do better. Find someone who can start a family with you when the time is right.'"

"I sound incredibly judgmental." She rubbed a hand over her face, but her weariness wasn't enough to shut me up.

"Not just you. Everyone. According to the world, there's a *right* way to do things. I should get my degree in four years— if it takes more, I'm a failure. Next, find an awesome job, and then, only then, look for someone to share my life. We should be married 2.5 years before we reproduce. Then if I'm infertile or he is, people will look down on us if we adopt, if we consider in vitro. One of us will be a failure again, faulty genetic stock, and if I don't want kids at all, there's something wrong, because normal women love babies, don't they, all of them?"

My heart broke for Diana, who had loved Ty and dreamed of a life with him, and then she ran from domestic bliss, to a future without diapers, where she could work with lab equipment, instead. And too many people would say there was something *wrong* with her. Because what kind of monster could desert her own child? At this moment, I hated everyone in the world, myself included.

Now that I'd started venting, I couldn't shut up. My mom listened, wide-eyed, as I babbled on, "God forbid if I fall in love with a girl. My roommate Angus, he's *completely* wrong, according to some assholes. In some states, it's not even legal for him to get married. Doesn't matter that he's the sweetest guy. Society says he's not even allowed to have a family."

"Nadia, are you telling me you're gay?" Mom managed to ask.

"What? No. I'm…" *Falling apart.*

The months without Ty finally caught up to me. I couldn't hold it in anymore, and the misery came out in endless word vomit. My mom would never want to Skype with me again, because I told her *everything*—about Ty and Sam—and this love that wouldn't go away, no matter what I did or how I did it. By the time I finished unloading, my face was smeared with tears and Courtney had tiptoed in and out of our room, clearly not wanting to intrude.

"You love him," my mom said quietly.

"God, yes. But I'm twenty-two. I'm too young to be tied down, right? And with Sam, it just can't be anything less."

"I was twenty-one when I had Rob. Twenty-five when you came along. And your dad was twenty-six when we got married. I was nineteen. My mother told me he was too old—that it would never work out. She didn't like his family, either, or the fact that one of his brothers went to prison.

But…he was the right person for me. So I didn't listen. I married him, anyway."

That was news to me. My grandmother, who made winter soup and black bread, she'd disapproved of my dad?

"She never gave any sign that she didn't support you two."

"Not after I proved to her that it could work…and that he was good to me. Telling her wouldn't have been enough. She threatened to disown me, but once she saw, she understood."

From the strength of their relationship, my mother made the right call back then. With my parents together and happy, I'd always been an oddity at school. So many relationships ended in divorce, maybe because some people were terminally stupid at nineteen and shouldn't be in charge of a kitten's well-being, let alone a baby. But others, like my mom, could start young and build a beautiful life with someone.

*With my dad.*

That was when I suspected what she was getting at. I froze, staring at the screen. "What are you saying?"

"I want you to be happy, that's all. I don't care about college, except that it's your dream to teach. Obviously, I want better for you than I had, but I can tell you've thought about Ty a lot and that you understand how it will be with him. If this boy will put the smile back on your face, you have my blessing."

"He's not a boy. He hasn't been since Sam came along."

My mom smiled. "Fair enough. But I'm forty-seven years old, and anyone under thirty seems like a baby to me. What are you going to do?"

"About college, tuition or Ty?" The tension eased out of me. Until this moment, I didn't realize how much worry I was hauling around.

"All of the above."

Pausing, I pondered my options then shook my head. "I'm

not sure. I need to think. Right now I'm too emotional to work it out and be sure I'm making the right choice."

"Keep me posted," she said, smile widening. "You know, I like this Skype business. It's harder for you to lie to me."

"Impossible. Take care of Dad, okay?"

Her eyes were beautiful and serene. "I've been doing that for twenty-eight years. I'm not likely to stop, just because he needs me a little more."

"Hug Rob and Dad for me."

"Of course. Bye, honey."

Stunned by the honesty I'd unleashed between us, I staggered to the bathroom to blow my nose. My eyes were so red, it looked like I was having an allergic reaction to my face. A few minutes later, Courtney brought some ice in, wrapped in a towel. I took it gratefully and balanced it on my nose, sighing as the coolness soothed the sting.

"Heavy family drama?" she asked.

"You have no idea."

"I got a few pieces, here and there. Dad's sick, you're challenging the current world order and ready to march for gay rights?"

"Well, yes and yes, but there's more." Quietly, I filled her in.

"Wow," she said. "I understand the conflict. It's not like you can date Ty in the traditional sense. You have to accept both of them."

"I am. I do." Until that moment, I didn't realize how complete the internal shift was, but as I spoke the words, I recognized their truth. "I've tried the bar scene. I tried meeting other guys, but when someone else touches me, it just makes me sad. I don't want to drink until I barf. I don't want the type of fun I'm supposed to be having. I just… I want Ty, that's all."

"It sounds like he was pretty adamant when you split, though."

"He was." The weight shifted from my chest for the first time in months. "But I think it's because he's trying to put me first. He talked about me ruining my life over him. But… Lauren? To the rest of the world, she's a failure. She flunked out of college. Lost her scholarship. Now she's back in Nebraska, living with her mom. How's that not crashing and burning?"

Courtney nodded, like she wasn't sure where I was going with that.

I went on, "But…she's happy. For her, getting out of Michigan was a huge relief. And that's how I feel right now. I don't have to live on other people's timetable anymore. I can do what I want, whatever makes me happy. That's…freedom."

She cocked a worried brow. "You're not planning to ditch classes and stash pot in my underwear drawer, are you? Because that's what drove me out of my last housing situation."

I laughed. "Not even remotely. I still plan to graduate. I don't know yet if I'll take out loans to finish or drop to part-time. I have the summer to decide, though my instinct is to slow down. The idea of going into debt freaks me out."

Courtney patted me on the back with a commiserating look. "I'm right there with you, but unfortunately, I'm already in hock to the man. Well. To my parents, which is worse than the government. What are you going to do about Ty?"

"What I've done almost since the first time I saw the guy," I said softly.

"And that is?"

I offered a mysterious smile. In my head, I was Boadicea and no man could stand against me. "Love him so much, it hurts."

*

# CHAPTER TWENTY-SIX

For two days, I pondered my next move.

Then I went to see Mrs. Keller at Rainbow Academy. She glanced up from her paperwork, surprised to see me in early. We hadn't changed my schedule to summer hours yet, so I was still working part-time. I'd discussed this decision with my mom and dad and they supported me. So I took a deep breath as she invited me to sit.

"What's on your mind?" she asked.

"My circumstances have changed, due to some family issues. I was hoping you might be able to keep me on full-time in the fall since I'll be enrolling in night class, instead, probably just one per semester for a while."

She didn't ask for more personal details, a fact for which I was grateful. "Do you have a preference as to classroom assignment? And are you interested in being a lead teacher?"

"Am I qualified?"

"Not to teach kindergarten, but for any of the other rooms, yes, between your experience here and your college credits."

"Then yeah, I'd love for you to consider me as a lead."

"I haven't told anyone yet, but Mrs. Kimball is going on maternity leave in August, and I suspect she won't be back. I've heard whispers that she's planning to open an in-home day care when her baby's a few months old."

"She teaches three-year-olds, right?" Better than the twos, anyway.

The director nodded. "Are you interested in taking over for her in August?"

"Yes. I can also handle forty hours a week, as soon as you can increase my hours."

"People are already asking for vacation time. I'll need you to work more, probably starting in June. But you'll be in Mrs. Trent's room or floating until August."

"Okay, I really appreciate it."

Buoyed by that success, I went home in a good mood and Skyped with my parents to inform them. Loans would get me into a teaching position faster, but I'd rather go slow and pay my way bit by bit, as I could afford it. I still planned to reimburse them, someday, but like theirs, my situation had changed. Maybe I'd hopped off the fast track, but that wasn't a bad thing.

*It's just life.*

"Any change on the Ty front?" my mom asked.

"Not yet. I had to figure things out at work first."

"I get it. You want to devote full attention to him when you go for it." She sounded disturbingly invested in my relationship issues.

"I don't know how I feel about your enthusiasm," I said.

Wisely, my mom changed the subject. "Oh, by the way, Rob broke up with Avery. It happened a while ago, but I forgot to tell you—with everything else going on."

"That's good news," I blurted.

"I'm with you there."

"How's Dad doing?"

"Coping. He doesn't like his new limitations, but I'll help him adapt. He's definitely not cutting down the pine tree. Are you still coming home this summer?"

"Yeah, but I plan to fly, not drive."

"Okay, honey. Just let us know when."

Soon after, we disconnected the call. Angus was in Europe, and this time, he'd taken his boyfriend with him on his father's dime. I had high hopes for him and Del. Max was still working at the garage, and Courtney had gone home for a few weeks, though she was still paying rent. With only Max and me around, the apartment felt really empty, but since I didn't want witnesses for what came next, it was for the best.

Unless Ty's schedule had changed, he'd be on his own this weekend. *Two days left.* So I hauled out my notebook and wrote the rest, everything that had happened since the breakup. Now the account was complete. Drained, I took a shower and then went to bed without dinner. Angus would've badgered me; Max came in too late to notice.

Friday evening, I came home from work and collected the Ty journal I'd created. Sucking in a sharp breath, I marched downstairs and left it outside his door in a bright red box with a bow on it. I wondered if he'd realize I was showing him my soul. Maybe he'd burn it for me or return it unread. But I didn't think so.

At one in the morning, I heard his patio door open and for the first time, I went out. Like that first night, I saw him standing below, and my heart opened like a flower. In the moonlight, he was everything beautiful and broken; I loved him to madness. There were no brakes for me anymore, just an endless rush toward him. And I'd fall if he didn't catch me.

"That was a terrible thing to read," he said quietly, not looking up. "I'd just started getting over you."

"Liar." I said it with complete confidence.

He glanced up then, and I could tell it shocked him to find me smiling. Leaning forward, I lowered the basket down to him. In it, I'd placed a red heart cut out of construction paper. Childish, yes, but I enjoyed writing *Nadia + Ty 4-ever,* like I was twelve, and the world was never so complicated as trying to figure out whether he *like* liked me.

Ty plucked the heart out and cupped it in his hands, as if it was a butterfly that might soar away on the night wind. "Why this? Why now?"

"Can I come down? Will you let me in?"

He made a muffled sound, but his answer was clear. "You know I will."

Steps light and sure, I dashed out of my apartment and down to his patio gate. I tapped lightly, waiting for him to open the door. In a few moments he did, and I was struck by how thin he was, not just lean, as if losing me had leeched the life from him.

"I thought I saw you in a bar," I said. "But it wasn't you. It was some other ginger devil."

"Did you take him home?" There were five paces between us, fireflies and the golden gleam of his solar lamps. His garden smelled of flowers and green things, delicately come to blossom in the warmth of the afternoon.

"No," I said. "But you knew that already, somewhere in your bones."

"Why are you here, Nadia? There's nothing left to talk about."

I took a step toward him. "That's where you're wrong. You think you can plan love. Pencil it in for later. But really, you're just scared of being hurt again. But here's the thing, Ty. What I feel for you, it isn't going away. Neither am I. You could call me in five years, ask me to come, and I'd get in the car and start driving."

He smiled softly and shook his head. "Then you're crazy."

"In ten years, that will still be true. I've had a lot of time to think, and none of it's changed. I love you, and I love Sam, too. I understand what it means to be with you. It won't be a storybook life, with everything happening on some perfect schedule. I don't care about that."

"You'll change your mind." But he sounded dazed, gazing across the four short steps that separated us like I might storm the battlements and cast down all his archers.

I planned to.

"Bullshit. My dad's sick, Ty. My parents can't afford tuition, and I can't keep my scholarship when I drop to part-time. But you won't hear me saying, *Damn, I'll never be a teacher now.* I'll get there. It'll just take longer. I won't give up on that, and I won't give up on you, either."

"Nadia…" There was a world of loneliness and longing in that tone.

I knew it intimately; I wore it like a charm about my neck. "If you send me away today, I'll knock tomorrow. I'll say this again. And again. Until you're ready to believe me, and I don't care how long it takes. I do *not* fucking give up on the things that matter, and nobody's ever mattered more to me than you. When you asked before, I wasn't ready…and neither were you. That was just a challenge you threw down to get me to back away."

"Was it?"

"If not, then it was the crappiest proposal ever." There, I made him smile. He was still holding the red heart, stroking it between his fingers.

"I want to believe you," he whispered.

The unspoken "but" hung in the air between us. I only smiled and let myself out of the garden gate. Upstairs, I expected some surge of disappointment, but it didn't come. I had time. Besides work, what did I have to do besides convince Ty to take a chance on me?

Saturday morning, I went downstairs with French toast and scrambled eggs. I was kind enough to let him sleep in, so I didn't bang on the door before ten. He'd clearly been up late the night before, I hoped thinking about me. He was gorgeous and rumpled and so very kissable. Smiling, I offered him breakfast.

"This is day one," I said. "I still love you, even if you're stubborn."

As he gaped, I went back upstairs. A muffled curse drifted up to my ears as he shut his door. *I am an irresistible force.* Sunday morning, I went shopping and bought a present for Sam, a big box of crayons, along with a dinosaur coloring book. I wrapped them up and knocked on Ty's door just before noon. Despite the weekend off, he didn't look any more rested than he had on Friday.

"What?" he demanded, running a hand through his hair.

"This is for Sam. I know you'll be picking him up later."

His expression softened slightly. "Thanks. He misses you. I mean, I know you see him in school, but I still hear about your soup and your stories and—"

"I love you," I cut in. "And I love him. There's no reason for us to live like this. You've cut yourself off from life, not to protect Sam, but because you don't think you deserve to be happy. You punish yourself because you misunderstood Diana, and you hurt her."

"Stop," he said roughly.

"I won't. I never will. Every day I will be at your door, reminding you that I'm here, and I'm not leaving."

With that, I turned, but he grabbed my arm and spun me around. A thunderous frown built between his brows, but it broke against my smile. With a sigh that was almost a moan, he put his forehead against mine, his breath soft on my cheeks.

"Don't let me wreck you," he whispered. "I've tried so hard to stay away and yet here you are. What do I have to do, flee the country?"

"I'd come after you. The timing might not be ideal, but you are. *We* are. And deep down, you feel it, too."

"God, yes." His sigh of surrender tingled against my mouth.

Then we were kissing, hard and delving, with his hands roving my body like he'd die if he didn't touch me. Ty backed me into his apartment and kicked the door shut behind us. *Thank God for his parents and for weekends off.* He cupped my face in his hands and kissed every inch of it, heated, wild with need.

"Tell me," I ordered.

He knew. "I love you. Oh, God, I love you so much. And I hate how I am without you."

The beauty of this moment? His admission didn't mean he'd lost, but rather, that we both won. "Me, too. I wasn't lying when I said I'm happiest with you."

"Your parents will hate me," he predicted. But he didn't seem overly concerned as he kissed my collarbone, sending a hot shiver through me.

"That's not true. I've already told them all about you. My

mother advised me to pester you every single day—she's a fan of winning by attrition."

"Seriously? She... They know about Sam, too?" Apparently, I'd managed to surprise him.

I nodded. "They're looking forward to meeting both of you."

"Mmm. I can't think about that right now. I will later, I promise. But right now—"

"You have a little while before you need to pick Sam up, and before then, you want to fuck me until I can't walk straight."

*"We,"* he corrected softly. "We're picking up Sam later. No more lines, Nadia. If you're ready, then so am I. Otherwise, though, you're spot-on."

He took my smile for assent and carried me to his bedroom. We got naked in record time, and to Ty's credit, he tried so hard to be slow and tender. But neither of us could wait. I rubbed against him like a cat, reveling in the heat of his skin. Then I ran my hands lower.

His breath hissed through parted lips. "Yes, like that. God, you'll kill me."

Ty moved with my hands, giving up on more extensive foreplay, but for me, this had the same effect. I was desperate to touch him, taste everywhere. My teeth grazed his neck as I skated my fingers down his hip. He pushed against me, and I rocked back.

"Mmm. Please," I whispered.

In five minutes, he was in me, gasping and shivering, and I couldn't stop stroking him. His mouth took mine, again, again, matching the tempo of his thrusts. It was messy and delicious when we came, a fierce and wrenching pleasure that had me digging my hands into his back. I bit him on the ear and he almost pounded me through the mattress, groaning with the force of the orgasm. Afterward, once he disposed of the condom and came back to bed, I curled onto my side and reached for him. Ty put his arms around me as if I might disappear.

But I wouldn't, not ever.

"That was incredible," he mumbled.

"Agreed."

"There hasn't been anyone else. One day, this winter, I saw you across the parking lot. You were with your roommate."

"I remember."

"I just *saw* you, and I was hard as a rock. You waved to Sam and got on that asshole's bike, and I wanted you so bad I couldn't breathe." This was his version of a Nadia journal, and he was offering a glimpse of his soul, just as I had with mine.

"At my lowest, I listened to your phone messages, again and again. I saved every one you ever left me."

"I listened to your footsteps overhead, and just about every night, I pretended you were coming down, that you'd be in my bed when I turned over."

After that, we had no choice but to make love again. This time, it was dreamy and sweet, sitting up, arms around each other's backs. It was almost two when we took quick showers, and then I went upstairs to put on a decent outfit. To meet Ty's parents, I didn't want to look as if I'd been rolling around in bed with their son all afternoon. Even if it was true. Once I tamed my hair and put on some makeup, I ran downstairs to meet him.

His smile when he saw me melted my heart; it likely always would. "Ready? I called my parents to let them know you're coming. Are you okay staying for lunch?"

"Sure. We can take Sam out next Sunday." I dared him to argue.

"When the weather's this nice, he likes the park."

"Then I'll pack a picnic lunch."

Ty's eyes went liquid; there was no other way to describe it. In fact, the naked love and longing was almost too much for me to bear, a sweetness that would strangle me. But I breathed through it and followed him out to his car. I was nervous on the ride to his parents' place, mostly because we were fledgling-new, and this was akin to throwing down the gauntlet.

I shouldn't have worried.

When Sam saw me, he ran over to give me a hug, just like he did in school, but this time, I knelt to return it, closing my eyes against the rush of love. *It's not just Ty. Sam's mine, too.* I might not have any legal claim on him, but I adored this kid.

I whispered in his ear, "Which dinosaur could jump higher than a house?"

Sam thought about it, then said, "I dunno."

"All of them, silly. Houses can't jump."

His giggle washed through me like sunlight as Sam squeezed me around the neck. "I missed you, Nadia."

Ty's folks were great, five to ten years older than mine, and absolutely doting grandparents. Pleasure just about unraveled me when he introduced me as his girlfriend. His mom and dad seemed delighted to meet me.

After lunch, she pulled me aside to whisper, "I'm so glad he's smiling again. I've been so worried about him since—"

"Diana."

"He *told* you about her?"

I nodded. Then she just hugged me so hard. I took that to mean I had her support. It also should be noted that Mrs. Tyler did not have hobbit feet.

As for Sam, after lunch he asked why I was there on a Sunday. We were in the backyard, where his grandparents had set up a play set, and Ty was pushing him on the swings. Each time Sam soared up, he kicked his feet like he could touch the sky. I knew that feeling; I got it every time his dad glanced in my direction. Other people might not understand this move, but happiness mattered more to me than coloring between the lines.

"Nadia's going to be around a lot more," Ty said to Sam.

"How come?"

He seemed to weigh his answer and then said, "Because I love her."

That, apparently, was not a revelation to Sam. "Oh. Me, too."

"How would you feel if she came to live with us someday?" That was a huge leap, but maybe it was better to put it on the table, so Sam wasn't surprised down the line.

"Would she stay in your room or mine?"

"Mine," Ty said.

"Okay, then. But she has to make hot dog casserole." As far as Sam was concerned, the conversation was over. "Push me higher!"

We stayed until past dark. And when we left, we went home together.

*

# CHAPTER TWENTY-SEVEN

"I can't believe you talked me into this," Ty muttered.

The three of us took up a whole row on the plane, and Sam was beyond excited. We were heading to Sharon to spend the Fourth of July with my family, where they'd meet Ty and Sam for the first time. Ty had driven us to Ann Arbor, and until now, he was mostly silent, listening to Sam chatter about the plane.

"They'll love you," I said.

"So you claim. I'm expecting your dad to threaten me."

"He might. Pretend to be terrified." Amusement colored my tone as I smiled at him over the top of Sam's head. "Oh, I have a brother, too. He's more likely to pound you."

"He has to catch me first."

The flight was only a couple of hours, not long enough for Sam to sleep. But he was tired and grouchy when we disembarked. I cheered him up with dinosaur jokes as we waited for our luggage, then we headed outside, where my parents were parked and waiting. Mom bounded out of the car and ran toward the doors. Dad came slower, and I saw evidence of the Parkinson's in the excessively careful way he moved. I also noticed that Mom was driving, something that never would've happened before.

"Is that your mom and dad?" Sam asked.

I nodded, hugging them both, then I said, "This is my boyfriend, Ty. And Sam, of course. He's our pet leprechaun."

"Nadia!" Sam yelped, but he was grinning up at my parents. Then he offered a small hand for my dad to shake, and I registered the exact moment he imprinted on their hearts, just as he had mine.

"We should get going," Mom said. "It's two hours to Sharon. Has Nadia told you anything about the place?"

Ty appeared to ponder, climbing into the car. "Only that it's small."

"That's about the size of it," my dad said.

On the drive, we made casual conversation, avoiding the topic of Dad's illness. He grilled Ty politely, but he stood up to it well, I thought. Every now and then, my mom caught my gaze in the rearview mirror, and she smiled with her eyes. A couple of hours later, we reached the Sharon city limits, and I was actually glad to be back.

"The Fourth is a big deal around here. They put on a huge fireworks show at the county fairgrounds. People drive an hour or more to see it," I informed them.

"Wow," Sam said, obviously impressed.

Part of me couldn't believe Ty was here with me, meeting my parents, pulling into the driveway of the house where I grew up. But he was looking around the neighborhood with interest. "That's a craftsman bungalow," he noted. "Those are usually fantastic in terms of both design efficiency and elegance."

"I can probably get Jay Oliver to let you see the place," my dad offered. "He and I aren't real close, but when he finds out you're studying architecture, he'll want to show the place off."

That was definitely an olive branch; Ty grabbed it with both hands. "That'd be great."

At the house, Rob was waiting in the living room. Lauren was there, too, and I hugged her until her spine popped. She looked so much brighter, no shadows in her eyes and an easy smile that told me she'd made the right choice, no matter what the world thought.

"You're in summer school?" I asked.

"Yep. Most of my credits transferred. I'm basically a sophomore, but I'm happier in computers. I can do something useful, something concrete. There are still problems, of course. I'm the only girl in a lot of my online classes and you wouldn't believe how much crap I get."

"And you dish it right back."

She grinned. "Hells yeah, I do. So tell me, is Courtney your new best friend?"

"Friend," I said. "Not best. That'll always be you."

Lauren hugged me, and Rob watched us from across the room. The attention was surprising; I'd never seen him so focused, and there was something about his eyes—but when Ty came up behind me, I lost interest in my brother, who was way less compelling than the guy kissing my neck. He wrapped his arms around me from behind, resting his chin on my shoulder. I recognized this tactic; though he didn't realize it, he was using me as a shield while he figured out the family dynamics.

Sam climbed up on my dad's knee. "Tell me a story."

"What kind?"

"Something awesome."

That could be interpreted a lot of different ways, but for my dad, the answer was obvious. He used to tell this one to Rob and me, but it was brand-new for Sam, and since it involved a runaway backhoe, I suspected the kid wouldn't budge until the end. By the time he left Nebraska, Sam might be obsessed with heavy machinery.

My mom called from the kitchen, "Are you guys hungry?"

I glanced at Ty, who nodded. "Yeah, we could eat."

She fixed a quick meal of soup and sandwiches while Rob added the leaf to the table, since he and Lauren were staying to eat. At Thanksgiving, there had been definite tension between my brother and me, but tonight, he was easy, smiling, as the rest of us talked. That was a relief, even as I wondered about the shift.

Though I was afraid it might be awkward, my parents made it easy for Ty and Sam. Ty's major fascinated my mom, and my dad took him to see the craftsman bungalow, as promised. When they came back, Ty was glowing with enthusiasm; he and Rob had a good talk about the merits of various building methods. By the end of the first night, it was like Ty and Sam had always been part of the family. But then, my mom was good at that; it was one of the things I loved most about her. She had a gift for making people feel at home. When she used that talent for Ty and Sam, I had to hug her. She squeezed me back, seeming surprised.

Then she whispered, "I'm sorry for what I said before. It's crystal clear to me that you're happy with Ty. And Sam is adorable."

Lauren went home around nine, and Rob left soon after; apparently, he'd moved out a few months back. I took Sam into the backyard to count fireflies. He was really wound up, and I imagined it might take some work to get him settled down. Focusing on the fireflies helped, though; they flickered against the night in golden sparks. Ty stood on the back porch, watching us, but he didn't come out into the yard.

"No, like this," I said quietly. "Be really slow and gentle." I showed Sam how to cup his hands. "Because they're beautiful and we don't want to smash them."

It took almost twenty tries before Sam got a firefly between his palms, and then he stared down in wonder. "Can we keep him?"

"No. If we put him in a jar, he'll die."

"I don't want to hurt him." Then he opened his hands and wriggled his fingers until the insect took off. Five feet over Sam's head, the firefly lit up.

As if it was a signal, others glowed all over the backyard like tiny Chinese lanterns. Sam spun in a slow circle. "It's really dark out here."

"That means you can see the stars better. Look up." Kneeling beside him, I anticipated his gasp of wonder.

*Maybe Sharon's not so bad after all.*

"Wow," Sam said.

"Let's get you inside. I think you need a bath and a bedtime story. It's almost ten."

"But I'm not sleepy."

Smiling, I ruffled his hair, and he slipped his hand into mine. I led him back to the porch, where his dad was waiting. Ty took over, and I listened to the welcome sound of them laughing, splashing around in the bathroom, while my dad whispered to my mother in the kitchen. Their voices sounded conspiratorial, but it didn't raise my hackles. They were definitely talking about Ty and Sam, but not in a bad way.

Then my dad came out into the living room and sat down beside me. He switched off the TV without asking if I was watching it. "He's not who I'd have chosen for you, but I want you to be happy, bean. Your mom's been talking at me for a couple of months, reminding me that I wasn't her mother's first choice, either. So...I just want you to know, you have my approval, too, if that matters at all."

A startled sound escaped me. I leaned over to hug him. "Of *course* it does."

He patted me on the back, and I felt the faint tremor that ran through his arm. "If he hurts you, I can still kick his ass."

"I know."

"And...your mother says you two can share your old room. Sam can sleep in Rob's." He spoke that offer grudgingly.

"I'll let Ty know. Thanks, Dad." Standing up, I kissed his forehead, then climbed the stairs to find out where Ty was with tucking Sam in.

They'd just finished the bath, and Ty was drying him off while explaining why fireflies glowed. He was much more scientific about it than I'd have been, but it didn't appear to diminish Sam's delight. I beckoned them both into Rob's room, which still smelled faintly of body spray. Sam didn't mind; my brother's sports trophies transfixed him.

"He's really good at football, huh?"

"Yeah, he was." It was a little sad, truthfully, because Rob might be one of those guys who peaked in high school and would spend the rest of his life looking back.

"Will he mind if I have his room?" Sam asked.

Ty glanced at me; I shook my head. "He's got his own place now."

"Okay, then." Sam snuggled into the clean sheets, glancing up at us expectantly.

Ty produced *Goodnight Moon,* and Sam made it almost to the end before falling asleep. Tiptoeing out, I left the hall light on, as my parents had done for us when we were kids. With the door cracked, Sam shouldn't be scared if he woke up in a strange bed; there would be enough light streaming in for him to figure out where he was. And Mr. O'Beary was beside him, too.

"Am I sleeping on the couch?" Ty asked.

"Nope. You have permission to share with me."

"Really?"

"Don't look so surprised. My parents aren't that old or particularly religious." Taking his hand, I led him down the hall to my room.

When I shut the door behind us, Ty bent his head and kissed me. Tension seeped out of him, as if he'd expected this visit to be more of a trial. I wrapped my arms around him and ran my fingers down his back. He shivered, gazing down at me with smoky eyes.

"You shouldn't get me worked up. I'm not having sex. Your parents are right downstairs. It seems—"

"Dirty?" I teased.

"Disrespectful. Don't laugh."

"I'm not. Your desire to be decent is adorable."

We took turns using the bathroom to brush teeth and whatever else. Then he settled beside me in the full-size bed I'd slept in since I was eleven years old. That was a bit startling, like my two worlds had finally converged, but it was a good feeling. Ty settled me against him, and I sighed in pleasure. He made the same noise when I trailed my fingers up and down his back, the way some other girl had done to drive him crazy. But she wasn't the one who still had a hold on him. Diana might as well be in the bed with us because she was still a shadow at the corner of his mind.

"You have to let go," I said softly.

"Of you? Never."

I curved my palm against his cheek. "Of the guilt. You made a mistake by not listening to Diana, yet you can't regret it because of Sam. But then you look at him and remember how much you hurt her. It's an endless cycle, and you have to break it."

He put his face against my shoulder, his mouth moving against my skin, so each word felt like kisses. "I don't know how."

"I do." And then I told him.

The next day, my mom packed a picnic, and we drove to the fairgrounds. It was a gorgeous day, bright and sunny, and we found a great spot near the swimming area. Compared to Lake Michigan, it wasn't much, just a man-made pond with an artificial beach, but Sam seemed to be having a blast. He wriggled the whole time Ty applied the sunblock, then he was off and running. He zoomed up and down the shore and yelled incomprehensible stuff at us that I pretended to understand.

"He loves it here," Ty said.

"I'm glad. My parents adore him already, so they'll definitely want us to come back." Watching Sam, I remembered what Ty had said about no more kids. "Are you still sold on him being an only?"

He slanted me an inscrutable look. "It's negotiable."

"I'll keep that in mind."

My dad sat with Sam, patiently constructing a sand castle. Since he had been building things his whole adult life, he was insanely good at it. Ty and I both fell asleep in the shade, and when I woke up, the structure was so big, so elaborate, that it had a moat and a working drawbridge. People were gathered around, watching my dad show Sam how the pulley worked.

Beside me, Ty stirred and slipped his hand into mine. I

squeezed gently. When he tugged, I rolled over to face him. His eyes shone, and his face was tight. Wordless, I traced a fingertip down his chin, silently asking him to talk to me. But it took him a few seconds to find his voice.

"I would've robbed Sam of this," he whispered. "Of having more people to love him. I was so angry at Diana, so sure I could be enough for him, it never occurred to me that he deserved more. We would've been so fucking lonely without you, and I never would've known. I wouldn't have noticed when I changed from a tired, grumpy asshole into a bitter old man."

"That won't happen," I said gently. "Sam and I know how to make you laugh."

"Thank you." By the fervor of his tone, he meant for more than just those words.

Around three, Lauren and Rob showed up in time for the picnic lunch. My mom had packed fried chicken, potato salad, carrot and celery sticks, orange Jell-O wigglers, which made Sam clap his hands in delight, and Rice Krispies treats. I ate until my stomach hurt. Afterward, I leaned back into Ty's arms. When the sun dipped below the horizon, the fairgrounds got more crowded and we packed up, then took the picnic supplies to the car.

Keeping only quilts for watching the fireworks, my dad picked a careful path across the gravel, my mom's hand on his arm. A stranger might think he was supporting her instead of the other way around. Ty wrapped an arm around my shoulders as we settled onto the blanket, and Sam climbed into my lap. I kissed the top of his head, breathing in the scent of warm boy, sunshine and orange Jell-O. His mouth was stained from all of the wigglers he'd eaten, and he chattered excitedly, telling us about his day, as if we hadn't been there with him. As ever, Ty's replies were slow and patient.

"Nadia's dad can build *anything,*" Sam told him. "He said I can call him Grandpa Ned. Is that okay?"

Ty glanced at me over the top of Sam's head. I nodded. If my dad had said that, it meant he was already one of the kid's biggest fans. Apart from Diana, Sam affected pretty much everyone like that. I wondered how she'd feel about my stepping into her shoes, and then I realized it didn't matter. It wasn't as if I was taking possession of her life; she'd never been part of this. Not really. Wherever she was, I hoped she was happy.

As it got dark fully, Ty pushed to his feet. Sam started to follow him, but I shook my head, whispering, "Your dad needs to do this on his own."

"What?"

"Say goodbye."

Sam tilted his head, puzzled, but he stayed on my lap, tracking Ty's movements through the crowd. When he came back to our blanket, he had a bottle rocket in his hand, and as I'd suggested the night before, there was a piece of paper taped around it. I didn't ask to read his final words to Diana; those were for him alone, but I knew there would be the apology he couldn't speak in person, because she didn't want to be found, and a wish for her to find joy in her work and peace in the decision to leave everything behind.

Without looking at us, Ty took a deep breath and lit the fuse, then he planted the bottle rocket in the ground. When it shot upward in an arc of spitting orange light, Sam's eyes widened. It exploded overhead in a crackle of light, and bits of charred paper fluttered down like Christmas in July. Deep in my heart, I hoped that maybe Diana felt it, somehow, and she knew she was truly free.

*No regrets.*

Watching the scraps of paper drift to earth, I thought about Max. Connections were everywhere, binding people together. If not for him writing about Lauren, I never would've written down how I felt about Ty, never would've shown him my soul, scribbled out in ink. And Ty would never have purged Diana from his conscience. Someday, he might even think of her without ugliness being the first thing on his mind.

I glanced over at Lauren and started because she was resting, ever so slightly, against my brother. He reached for her instinctively when she leaned in, his arm possessive around her shoulders. I had a hundred questions, and as if she sensed me staring, she glanced over. Her eyes widened, but I just smiled. Whatever that was, she'd tell me when she felt ready.

Lauren smiled back and mouthed, *Thank you.*

On the other side, my parents were curled up together, waiting for the fireworks. It was impossible for me to imagine anything more wonderful, but then, Ty came back. He wrapped an arm about me; and in that instant, the heavens cracked open in cascades of wonder, brightness blazing in kaleidoscopic shapes that made Sam bounce with excitement. Beneath the booms and pops of each new formation, I rested my head against Ty's shoulder.

"I love you."

I didn't realize I'd said it out loud until Ty whispered the words back to me. He kissed my cheek and then Sam's head, touching us as if we were all he needed in the world, his sun and stars sharing a quilt with him. Contentment radiated from him in a way I'd never known—and my heart burst with fireworks, spilling colors like the sky.

# THE EVER AFTER

I guess you've figured it out by now; I tricked you. There is, in fact, a happy ending. But if you'd known that my story became *our* story because I made a choice, would you have read until the end? People are fascinated by dark things, broken things, damaged things. You wanted to learn the exact moment it splintered apart, but would you have been as interested in watching me put the pieces back together, if you'd known? I wonder.

Because what I said before about the telling of stories, his and hers, and the unspoken question about staying together? That's the real choice. And it's a battle, every single day, to make the center hold. When I chose this, I didn't expect it to be easy. It's a battle I'm determined to win, and the prize is Ty's love.

A year after meeting him, I moved into the apartment downstairs.

If anyone had told me, before, that I'd weigh my options and decide to become a mom at twenty-two, I wouldn't have believed them. Occasionally it sucks, especially when Sam wakes us early, but then he's rolling around and I'm tickling him, and he's smiling so damn bright. The other day he called me Momiya, and it made me so happy, I almost cried. Ty doesn't look so tired anymore; he doesn't even call himself a grumpy asshole these days. Because I'm here, shouldering half the weight.

It's worth it because I'm part of their lives, every morning and every night, every Sunday afternoon in the park, pushing Sam on the swings. I make hot dog casserole, read *Goodnight Moon* and play trucks before bed, even when I have projects of my own. Because I'm one of two people in the world who makes Sam's face light up like a sunbeam, and I cherish that, even when I'm exhausted. Even then.

Like Ty, I work full-time, taking classes at night. I'll achieve my dreams. In time. My dad's still out there, trying to beat the odds. So am I. Life is messy and unpredictable; sometimes it's a punch in the gut, and sometimes it's so beautiful, it brings tears to my eyes. Life isn't a fairy tale. It's work, sand in your shoes and a sick kid at five in the morning. Sometimes you meet your partner too soon, but love persuades you to leap, trusting that he'll catch you. Life is real and it's *right now*. Life is fireflies in your palm, gleaming gold, and then setting them free. In the best moments, life is fireworks. Sometimes life is having the rug pulled out from under you and the one you love helping you up. But most of all, life is what happens when you open the door and let beauty in, even if it doesn't fit according to your plans.

And *my* life? Is the one I've built with Ty and Sam. Us, together? Yep. I want it that way.

# BONUS SCENE: SHEER LONGING (TY)

I stood just inside my patio doors, head resting against the glass. Sam had been more wound up than usual tonight, excited about starting school, and it took six stories to get him to sleep. If I had any common sense, I'd haul my ass to the drafting table instead of going outside to torture myself with a gorgeous girl I couldn't have.

Ignoring the voice of reason, I stepped outside and stared up at her balcony. Before, she'd said she was avoiding me, which explained all the nights I'd spent waiting that she never showed. Nadia had me so tangled up, it was nuts. I was thinking about going back inside when she joined me. From this angle, she reminded me of Juliet, forever out of Romeo's reach, and I shut down the urge to quote Shakespeare. Her smile was so fucking bright that my breath hitched. While I struggled to be casual, she lowered a basket to me.

"What's this?" I asked, catching it instinctively.

"My mom sent treats. I'm sharing them, so we'll both have delicious things."

Surprise and pleasure warred for the upper hand, and the latter won by KO. I smiled as I unloaded the basket, taking stock. "Let me heat some water. I could use a cup of tea."

"Sure."

Quickly I went inside and popped a mug in the microwave. I almost spilled it coming back out, like she'd disappear if left unattended for two minutes. Nadia made me feel so unsure of…everything. Until she crashed into my life, the routine never deviated. Now instinct had a hold of me, pushing me out of my comfort zone. I opened the sliding glass doors and carried my drink over to the wicker sofa, where I'd set the treats.

"Back." I flopped down, angling my head so I could see her. The darkness made it impossible to discern her features, but it was enough to know she wanted to sit out here with me. *God only knows why.* This was such a bad idea, a conclusion she'd come to herself, if she knew how much of an asshole I really was.

"Cookie first," she ordered.

Gingersnaps didn't usually do it for me, but their sharp sweetness and the heat on my tongue made me wonder if this was how Nadia tasted. *She does now.* I licked the crumbs from my fingers, aching. Her legs were fucking incredible, and one long look from those sea-blue eyes, and I had a hard time remembering what the hell I meant to say. For a few seconds, I pictured kissing her hard, shoving her up against my bedroom door— *Right. Cookies.*

"Phenomenal," I managed.

She didn't seem to glean anything from my tone, thank God. *The last thing I need is for her to decide I'm a perv.*

"Gingersnaps are my favorite, though at Christmas she does

a peppermint-and-white-chocolate cookie that's a serious contender."

"Sounds like you miss your family."

That was a harmless observation, part of the *getting to know you* crap that used to come naturally. It had been so long since I cared about anything or anyone but Sam. Tunnel vision kept me going, eyes on the horizon, but sometimes it was so fucking lonely that I went to sleep wrapped around a pillow.

"Yeah."

*You used to be good at this. Be a normal person.* Talk *to her.*

"Where are you from?" I asked.

She seemed pleased, happy about my interest. *You have no clue, beautiful.* It had been a while since I'd felt this snap of pure attraction.

"Nebraska, toward the South Dakota and Wyoming side, if that helps."

"I've never met anyone from there."

Mount Albion wasn't a prestigious college, though its reputation wasn't awful, either. There were a hundred other college towns like it in the Midwest. I never pictured myself being here this long. I'd always wanted to live in California, and I had a sister there who was always bugging me to visit. But traveling with Sam always sounded like too much trouble.

"I usually get 'not in Nebraska anymore' jokes, and then I have to decide if I'm going to remind them that's Kansas or play along."

"What do you usually do?" Her answer would reveal a glimpse of her personality, and I was more fascinated than I should be.

"Play along."

*So she's on the sweet side, huh?* That dovetailed with what I knew about her, particularly how good she was with Sam.

Earlier, when she took his hand and led him away, my stomach knotted up. It was so fucking hard to watch him walk away, but she made it easier. Everything about Nadia promised, *Don't worry, you can trust me.* Too bad I hadn't just been burned by love; Diana had set me on fire and stomped on my ashes, and only now did it feel like life might be returning. When I could least afford such a beautiful distraction.

I realized she was waiting for me to answer. *Duh, dumbfuck. That's how conversation works.* "You don't like conflict, huh?"

"Not if it can be avoided. I'm not what you'd call pugnacious, no. But I like to think I don't back off important issues. What about you?"

The question knocked me back a few figurative steps. Diana was always in the back of my head, reminding me how bad I'd screwed up. My shoulders locked, guilt and regret tightening around my neck like a noose. "No. I don't. Even when I should."

Nadia went quiet. She didn't answer for so long that I thought for sure she'd picked up on my mood. Most people didn't pay attention to the nuances. If I told them I was a grumpy asshole, they accepted it, and left me to wallow in my bad attitude.

But she didn't ask what I meant; instead, her voice flowed over me like auditory expiation. "We all have things we'd do differently in hindsight."

The tension flowed out with my next breath, leaving calm in its wake. I marveled at the sweetness of the feeling. "What is it about you?"

"Huh?"

For some reason, I blurted out the truth. "You make me... better. Calmer."

*Smooth.*

"Like a sedative?" Amusement colored her reply.

God, her voice was sexy, low and husky, as if she hovered on the verge of confiding a dirty secret. That was part of why I couldn't get enough of these stolen conversations, however unwise they might be.

I rushed to explain. "I didn't mean it like that. Just...I'm worried pretty much all the time that I'm dropping the ball somewhere, about to face-plant, but when I come out here and hear your voice, everything backs off, like, ten steps. I can breathe again."

*Wow.* Nadia went to my bloodstream like sodium pentothal, making me tell the unqualified truth. I hadn't talked like this since...Diana. The comparison chilled my blood, even as I told myself, *No big deal.* It wasn't normal for me to have no relationships whatsoever, and it was past time I made some new friends.

Equilibrium lasted only until Nadia murmured, "I'm glad you look forward to this as much as I do." Sharp, searing desire flared to life, and I tried to smother it as she went on, "I wasn't trying to intrude that first night."

"I know. But the unit had been vacant for a while. So I guess I forgot I wasn't alone anymore." That came out *way* more intimate than I intended, and I ran in mental circles, trying to figure out how to retreat without sounding like a dipshit.

*I'm dying here. I swear I had more game in high school.*

But she answered lightly. Somehow, no matter what crazy shit I said, she made it okay. "Nope. You're stuck with me now. By the way, we're having a party tomorrow night, at least thirty people, and the way word gets around, it may be more like fifty. I hope it won't be too loud for Sam to sleep."

The conversational gambit put us back on platonic, neighborly territory. "Thanks for the heads-up."

Talking to Nadia was like ice-skating on a frozen pond. I could be racing along with the wind in my face and then, through my own idiocy, hit a hidden bump and dive headlong before I realized I was in danger of falling. *What the hell were we talking about?* I rubbed my head.

"Are you mad?"

"No, I'm problem-solving." Plausible excuse. Better for her to think I was focused on Sam instead of reflecting on how bad she made me ache. "I'll put him to bed with headphones on. Don't worry, you're not the only people with social lives around here, and most of them don't check in with me."

Her response was hesitant. "I'd invite you to come, but—"

"Another time," I cut in. "My folks watch him the last weekend of the month. They tell me to get out, have fun, but I usually just sleep as much as I can."

"And that's the *only* time," she muttered.

"I heard that." Smirking, I shifted so I could see her better. Maybe that was a mistake. She'd sat forward, as well, elbows on the balcony railing, and the moonlight found hollows at the base of her throat and between her breasts. Her shoulders were bare and smooth, gleaming until I couldn't think of anything but touching her skin. Dark hair spilled down her back in tousled curls, and I imagined sinking my hands into them, kissing her until— *Fuck.* I shifted, hoping like hell that she couldn't tell how hard I was. She licked her lips, which didn't help.

"I wasn't trying to slip it past you," she said.

*Slip—what? Oh. Yeah.*

"That doesn't seem like your style."

"I only meant that you *look* tired. Not that you aren't

also—" Too bad she stopped talking. It seemed like the rest might be intriguing.

Against my better judgment, I prompted, "What?"

"Nothing."

There was no way I could go to bed without finding out what she almost said; we had a definite moth-to-flame vibe going. If I kept circling, sooner or later, I'd catch fire. But she might be worth the pain.

Curious, I tried a coaxing tone. "Finish that sentence. Please, Nadia?"

She hesitated. "On one condition."

*Of course.* There was no way she'd just answer without tying me up in codicils. I didn't *want* to be disappointed; I hated that I was.

"What's that?"

"Answer one question for me."

"That depends on what it is." I was already losing interest in this game. She probably wanted to hear why I was a single dad and what went wrong. Women often painted me as a tragic hero, and that pissed me off. I didn't deserve bonus points for taking care of my own kid. That was why I preferred hooking up with girls who knew nothing about me, another reason I should stop talking to Nadia.

But she veered toward the unexpected. "Tell me what you dream of designing, once you're a big-deal architect."

"Oh." I silently apologized for my cynical, shitty mental accusations, eating a peanut butter cup as I tried to decide if I should reply honestly. "It's good to hear you say it so implicitly, like my success is assured. The road feels really long sometimes."

"I can imagine."

"I've been in school since I was eighteen, but after Sam

was born, I cut down to part-time. Anyway, you didn't ask to hear me whine." I paused, doubt bashing me in the head. "Damn. I don't know if I can answer this after all. I've never told anyone."

"It's okay, but…in that case, I won't be completing my sentence."

I swore. Hell if I'd punk out before she did, even if this made me look incredibly lame. "You drive a hard bargain. Okay. I want to design churches." To cover my awkwardness, I took a sip of the cooling tea. "I doubt I'll be able to right away. I'll probably end up doing offices or condos to start, but eventually? I would desperately love to design a church someday, see it built from each individual stone to stained glass panels so I can stand inside it and marvel."

"Why?"

"So I can thank God personally for Sam." The truth slipped out before I could stop it.

*This girl is straight-up dangerous.*

I waited for her to say something, anything, but the silence just stretched on and on. *Damn. I should've known she wouldn't get it. Right now her biggest commitment is midterms.*

So I pretended it didn't matter and paved it over. "That probably sounds dumb. Or pretentious. I can't believe I—"

"No. Not at all. It's the most amazing thing I've ever heard. Sam is *so* lucky to have you, Ty." Her voice sounded soft, unsteady.

"I'm the lucky one. I just wish I could remember it for more than five minutes at a time." I hesitated, tilting my head, and she tried to hide her face in the shadows, but as she shifted, I caught the glint of tears on her cheek.

"Are you crying?" One heartbeat, two, I had no idea how to react, how I should feel.

She sniffed audibly. "Maybe a little. Shut up. It's just…so very sweet."

Confusion resolved into a fierce ache. I had the sense that she got me. Most of the time, I lived in a dark fucking hole with Sam as the torch guttering against the endless tide of exhaustion. My life was one night after another, treading water until that was all I remembered how to do. Maybe it was crazy, but her dangling that basket tonight seemed symbolic, like the lowering of a lifeline.

It was hard to speak past the sudden tightness in my throat. "I'm glad I told you."

"Me, too."

Somehow I shoved back from the visceral impulses flooding me. In that moment, I wanted to charge up the stairs and bust down her door. *Fuck my plans, fuck the rules.* She was gorgeous in the moonlight, haunting even. But then I remembered Sam, always Sam. So I kept my ass in the chair.

"But we had a deal, remember? No backing out." The stakes hadn't changed, and I'd survived confessing a sentimental secret.

"I wouldn't." She paused, heightening the suspense. "Not that you aren't also…hot as hell, completely irresistible in every conceivable way."

The satisfaction of hearing that from Nadia stole my breath. But before I could respond, she bolted, leaving me with a lukewarm cup of tea and a savage erection.

*Christ. I want her so much it hurts.*

★ ★ ★ ★ ★

# PLAYLIST FOR
## *I WANT IT THAT WAY*

F★★kin' Perfect—P!nk

Afraid of Everyone—The National

Out of Mind—Tove Lo

No Below—Speedy Ortiz

Let Her Go—Passenger

I Need My Girl—The National

Story of My Life—One Direction

Ways to Go—Grouplove

Burn—Ellie Goulding

Try—P!nk

Impossible—James Arthur

Some Nights—Fun

Just Give Me a Reason—P!nk featuring Nate Ruess

Just Say Yes—Snow Patrol

Thank you!

I'm so glad you read *I Want It That Way*. I hope you enjoyed it.

Would you like to know when my next book will be available or keep up with my news? Visit my website at *annaguirre.com/contact* and sign up for my newsletter. You can also follow me on Twitter at *twitter.com/msannaguirre,* or "like" my Facebook fan page at *facebook.com/ann.aguirre* for excerpts and contests.

Reviews help other readers, so please consider writing one. I appreciate your time and your support.

*I Want It That Way* is the first book in a new adult romance series. The other books are *As Long as You Love Me* and *The Shape of My Heart*.

Again, thanks for your readership; it means the world to me.

# ACKNOWLEDGMENTS

Thanks first to Laura Bradford, who still shines after all these years.

Much appreciation to Margo Lipschultz for loving this book as much as I do. Really, that gratitude extends to the whole team at Harlequin for moving mountains so readers could enjoy this story as fast as possible. They've done a phenomenal job under incredible pressure, so I tip my hat to all departments that contributed to the project's success.

Thanks to Michael G., for patiently answering my questions about teaching special education. Any mistakes or liberties are my own.

No list is complete without the wonderful friends and colleagues who help me in so many ways. Thanks to Lauren Dane, Megan Hart, Bree Bridges, Donna J. Herren, Helen-Kay Dimon, Vivian Arend, Tessa Dare, Rae Carson, Amie Kaufman, Robin LaFevers, Yasmine Galenorn, Myke Cole and Jenn Bennett. So many hugs to Courtney Milan, Karen Alderman and Majda Čolak, who believed in this book and encouraged me before I started typing. If not for your certainty and support, it's possible I never would've written this. Thank you all so much.

Big love to the loops that must not be named. You cheer; you listen. You keep me sane. Your achievements make me proud and push me to work harder. Before I joined your number, I never truly understood the importance of sisterhood. Thank you for teaching me.

Thanks to my family. I couldn't do this without you. Your patience, generosity and understanding make it possible for me to soar ever higher. Love you all.

Finally, thanks to my readers for following where I lead. I hope you all travel as I have, stumbling over rocks, falling into sunlight with a few scratches, but none the worse for an unexpected tumble. May the world always surprise you with its hidden beauty, and may there always be new books on your shelves.

★ ★ ★ ★ ★